CHASING OTHELLO

BOOK 2 of The CHASING CLEOPATRA Chronicles

TINA SLOAN

Chasing Othello: Book 2 of The Cleopatra Chronicles

Copyright © 2022 by TATI KHAN Publishing. All Rights Reserved.

For information about this title or to order other books and/or electronic media, contact the publisher:
TATI KHAN Publishing
tinasloan@gmail.com

ISBN: 978-1-7330577-6-9 (softcover)
       978-1-7330577-7-6 (eBook)
       978-1-7330577-8-3 (audiobook)

Printed in the United States of America

Cover and Interior design: 1106 Design

To Steve, Renny, Helen, Hazel, Mather, and Field for all the fun you bring to my world

And To Serena Turner, Jeffie Durham, and Meg Pearson for all your wonderful help

To my friends who kept me going as I wrote and stopped and wrote again Suzie Moore, Siri Mortimer, Anne Ford, Christabel Vartanian, Lia Reed, Suzie Kovner, Maureen Chilton, Cindy Scott, Stephanie Flynn, Mary Morse, Alicia Wolfington, Eaddo Kiernan, Ann Calder

Prologue

FIONA

Several years ago, three years, five months, two days ago, to be exact, I was sitting on this very bench in this very dress in this very garden when I met Jimbo Isom. My dress, the palest of green, blended in perfectly with the exquisite lawns of the garden. I was reading a book about Kim Philby, the famous English spy and traitor.

Jimbo was an Ironman. Everyone in Honolulu knew him and almost everyone worshipped him. He was so handsome with his piercing blue eyes, blonde hair, and perfect physique that tingles radiated down my spine when he biked up to my bench.

Jimbo gazed at the garden with a bewildered look. "What is this magical place?"

For so many reasons, I was scared to speak. But finally, after what felt like an eternity, I answered him.

"A garden belonging to a very wealthy man."

He nodded and smiled. "And are you the wife of that very wealthy man?"

"No, but I do work for him," I murmured.

PROLOGUE - FIONA

The god got off his bike and he sat next to me. I was overcome by such a wave of gratitude that this person existed in the same world I did—and that of all places, he was choosing to sit on this bench, next to me. He looked over at my dog-eared hardcover book and started to read the page I'd marked aloud. "The English love their secrets, the knowledge that they know a little more than the man standing next to them; when that man is also a secret keeper, it redoubles the exquisite relish of ruthless, treacherous, private power," he paused, letting the passage sink in. Then he'd closed the book and looked at me in a way that I'll never forget. "Why would someone like you be reading something like this?"

I just stared at him and didn't answer.

He kept looking back at me, curiously. "What's your name?"

Again, I didn't answer and he knew I was a dissembler. And I knew he was one. But I am not sure he ever knew how good I was at it and how addicted I was to the drug of deception.

Christmas Day 2011

CLEO, 1

Last night, Christmas Eve, I led Tripp Regan to my sanctuary, a hidden cliff dwelling on my property where the ceiling and the floor and the walls are painted white and scattered with colorfully patterned rugs and huge orange, red, and white pillows.

While he stood at the opening, astonished by its existence, I lit candles throughout the cave so Tripp could see its wall hangings, reminiscent of cave dwellings in Cappadocia, Turkey. This cave was not unlike the caves he and I slept in when we climbed Mount Kilimanjaro in Africa so long ago. That event is what later prompted me to create this cave retreat. I had made it to remember the man I loved, who died.

I spent the night and most of Christmas morning in the arms of a man I had loved long ago, though back then he had a different name and different background—the identity I knew him by had been a cover for his CIA job. And I'd fallen in love with this cover: Danny Mortimer, who later "died" in a plane crash, leaving me inconsolable.

Yesterday I discovered that this fancy New York lawyer, Tripp Regan, with dark hair and blue eyes, a brusque manner, and a boisterous family, had, indeed, once been the blond long-haired hippie with a lazy Southern accent, Danny Mortimer. It turns out that Danny had not died. After realizing his cover had been blown, he'd faked his death in a fiery plane crash. I'd never truly gotten over it.

In his CIA mode, Tripp Regan—who in his real life was Danny's polar opposite—had shown up in Hawaii and asked for my help. And then somehow, on Christmas Eve, fueled by champagne and even more reminiscing about past times together in Africa, we ended up making love.

I was loving Danny, not Tripp, but I still gave into it. He and I are extremely strong-willed, but last night we were powerless to stop the inevitable. There's that tug one feels when near a certain person, a tug I tried mightily to ignore but which slowly pulled me its way.

Last night, when Tripp touched my hand getting the champagne bottle, I felt the tug. I didn't look at him, pretending that I felt no shock of electricity and had no desire to be lying next to him on one of the soft carpets, no desire to be held in his arms. When the silence came between us like a fog, I pretended that it was because we both had nothing to say. But really, it was just that we had to say it with our bodies—not with words.

Each time we passed the champagne bottle back and forth, we used it as an excuse to move closer. I looked down at my jeans and T-shirt and wanted nothing more than for him to rip them off, but again I pretended nothing was happening. I wondered if he was pretending, too, as we both kept drinking, so our inhibitions would float away.

He finally said, "Except for you, I have never been disloyal in my life…" meaning to his wife and children "…but I can't stop this." He took my face in his hands and turned it to him, kissing me with such overwhelming passion that it was as though he was drowning in me. We held hands, then laid down on the rugs and pillows, kissing all the while. Yearning for what could have been and never would be, we knew this was our only time together.

Making love with him felt very much like fate. Being together felt wonderful. He had taken the initiative, though I felt his fear and helped him along the way. What we were going to do, and there was no way to pretend anymore that we were not going to make love, provided me with closure. I won't ever see him again.

Tripp Regan is happily married with three sons, which he failed to mention in Africa—and for that, he will never be forgiven. But last night in my sanctuary, we laughed as we got caught in our clothes, and then were both shy about looking at one another naked. But the ferocity of longing over many years soon took over, and it thrilled me to touch him and be touched. We kissed hungrily, in part for the yesterdays we never had, for the tomorrows we would never see together.

We loved one another for the people we were years ago under the vast African sky, not who we were today. It was an entirely joyous but bittersweet reunion.

TRIPP FINALLY CLIMBED down the next day from my private hideaway to catch his plane with his family back to New York while I retreated to *Sweet Dreams,* my rambling Tuscan house with its pale green shutters and a courtyard of white roses and a bubbling fountain—surrounded by decorated Christmas trees. In my living room, I turned on the television to see the news. There was wall-to-wall coverage of my neighbor Jimbo's death.

None of the news stations had any idea that yesterday's shocking events had been my doing.

My phone had been ringing off the hook with calls from people who'd known Jimbo. Everyone was in shock that this man, who for the last four years had fooled everyone on the Hawaiian island into believing that he was a gorgeous Ironman in training, was, in truth, a deadly terrorist by the name of Mohammed Abdul Rahman, intent on blowing up Pearl Harbor.

And of all days, to plan the deadly explosion for today, Christmas Day—which is also my birthday! But in the end, I had prevented that nightmare from happening.

I didn't phone anyone back. After listening to their messages and watching the news, I felt numb. I had killed someone whom I knew well—or thought I knew well. Jimbo had been my best friend. He had duped me into living on my property. He had tried to kill me. While media reports made a big deal of revealing Jimbo's identity as Mohammed Abdul Rahman, they were also reporting that he'd died in a biking accident. But it had been no accident. I'll never forget when he grabbed my arm as we paused at the top of the steep Koolah Cliff on our bike ride. I had figured out who Jimbo really was, and he knew it.

"I really hate to do this, Cleo," he'd said—I think sincerely—as he was about to toss me down to my death on the rocks far below.

"Do what?" I asked with superficial naivete, about to put into use training that had long been preparing me for such a moment. Since I was twelve years old, I'd been working secretly with a Navy Seal who trained me in the Israeli defense program's practice of Krav Maga. It was my secret obsession. I had been raped when I was very young and didn't recover for decades. To know I could protect myself gave me a sense of power.

CLEO, 1

Yesterday that training had allowed me to send Jimbo over the cliff. I will never forget the stunned look on his face as he was falling to his death. He had underestimated his opponent, something I learned to never do. Later, Tripp and I got together in my secret hideaway. It was a Christmas Eve to remember.

Now I gazed around my house at the huge gleaming Christmas tree with decorations my mother collected over the years, as well as garlands and wreaths. This year's holiday has been so strange and eventful. Even with a blight on it, I smiled at my favorite season. I turned off the TV news. As I always do on this day, I put on Christmas carols and went toward the kitchen to heat up some fudge sauce for my breakfast. And in a basket in the kitchen was a black kitten with a huge purple bow and a card, "Happy Birthday, Cleopatra." Tripp must have gotten someone from the CIA to put it there last night. The cat was so tiny and so precious and so reminiscent of our last day together in Africa when Danny and I had seen a black cat whom he said was like the Egyptian Queen Cleopatra. I picked her up and she nestled into my arms. I named her Endy for the perfume of mine that Tripp and I both love called Endgame.

I devoured the hot fudge sauce hugging Endy as I did. After all, it is my birthday. Tripp Regan and I had celebrated it early last night.

JAKE, 1

Twenty seconds ago, my dad Tripp Regan, who, for my entire existence, has told me he's a corporate lawyer for Weinstein, Forbes, Regan, and Lowe—informed me that he actually works for the CIA.

The CIA. Surprise! Roll the tape...

As Dad gingerly made his way down the aisle of the Delta plane, he walked past my brother Matt, who was dutifully studying yet another book on plants, past my ex Julia, busily batting her long lashes at my younger brother, Ricky.

Dad was about to turn into his row where my mother was sitting waiting for him, when I frantically motioned him over to me. He gave me a look, I can tell he's tired, and he trudged down the aisle toward me.

I grabbed his wrist and pulled him close to me. "I was right the whole time, wasn't I?" Here I was, trying to be as quiet as possible for the sake of the other passengers. Little did I know, it was also a matter of national security.

My father shook his head. "We'll talk about it later," he hissed.

"But Dad—"

"Jake, not now," he said sternly. He wasn't messing around.

I've heard that blunt tone many times before. But then he leaned closer and whispered something in my ear that I'll never forget: "Cleo had to..." He paused. "Jimbo was—as they said on the news, a terrorist."

I could feel the color draining from my face as an avalanche of shocking new information rushed over me. So, Cleo did kill Jimbo totally on purpose. Holy shit. Why did he say she had to?

Even though I saw her push him over that cliff with my own two eyes, I had convinced myself that there was a plausible explanation, that it had been an accident like the news reports said. Why would Cleo kill her best friend? It made zero sense.

"Wait. But—"

"Jake, we'll talk about it later," he hissed again.

But I couldn't let it go. I had to know what was happening, and I had to know right goddamn now. "Dad, c'mon!" I pleaded. "Please! Just tell me what the hell's going on—"

His face got real close to mine just before he confessed through gritted teeth: "I work for the CIA."

LOL. Good one, Pops. There's no way he wasn't pulling my leg, I thought....

I looked up at my father's forever imposing figure. Our eyes met as he hovered over me like he's done a gazillion times before: standing over my desk to help me study for a test or preparing me for an important job interview, or when he helped me with my golf swing or hitting the perfect slapshot to get me ready for a big hockey game. The dude was dead serious.

If what Dad's telling me is true, when he missed a game of mine as a kid because he was "in court" or "on a business trip," in reality he was probably undercover and killing terrorists. Is my dad kind of like James Bond? That'd be cool.... All

JAKE, 1

I know about the CIA is what I've seen in movies or read in books, so he might as well be telling me that he's Santa Claus or Count Dracula. When I look up at the old guy standing in the aisle, his cold hard stare sends shivers down my spine. It sinks in that my father is a trained killer who's now telling me to shut me up.

Say no more.

I sit up straighter, take a deep breath, and give him a nod. Man to man. Don't be fooled by my boyish good looks. There ain't nothing this twenty-eight-year-old can't handle, even something as totally mind-blowing as this.

Then, stoic as usual, Dad turned back around and up the aisle to sit a few rows in front of me with my mom.

Okay, a totally new question. Does Mom know? No way. Homegirl can't even watch the Bourne movies because they're "too scary." Although, at this point, who the hell knows who's telling the truth. Anything is possible. Old people have hidden depths, I guess. They'd need to, I suppose, in order to get through The Depression without a cell phone.

"Good afternoon, folks, and on behalf of the entire flight crew, we'd like to wish you a very Merry Christmas," says the captain over the cabin's speakers. If I had my way, this plane would be grounded in Hawaii and I'd be forced to stay here and process all this craziness on the beach with, like, a million rum punches.

"Count yourselves lucky," says the captain. "Due to the storm, this is the first flight out of Honolulu in twenty-four hours."

Some loser passengers cheer the news. I hate these people. Act like you've been on a plane before, nerds.

"We're number three for takeoff and hoping for a smooth ride to Los Angeles," El Capitan concludes.

The same losers cheer again, but there are more of them this time. They're multiplying.

As the plane climbs to ten thousand feet, I unpack Dad's confession. I'd always thought the old man was pretty legit, what with him being a partner at his law firm, but this CIA newsflash raises his cool factor off the charts. Does this mean the whole lawyer business is a scam? Did he ever even go to law school? Is his whole life a lie? Is *my* whole life a lie?

The most screwed up part is that even though she's a confirmed killer, I'm still nuts about Cleo. In my defense, Jimbo was an international terrorist and my girl saved us all from nuclear destruction with her insane Krav Maga skills. Now that's hot.... I can see her gorgeous face as she turned away after killing Jimbo. She's the most beautiful woman I've ever seen and now that I know she killed a terrorist, I might never recover from her charm.

Suddenly the plane rocks from turbulence. *Hell, yeah.* Take me back to Cleopatra, Pele! "Pele doesn't want me to leave!" I say, a half-serious plea to the Hawaiian goddess to keep us there.

Mom spins around in her seat and looks at me as if I've just gobbled down a batch of crazy pills. Whoops.

The captain comes over the loudspeaker again. "Hi, folks. Apologies for the turbulence. We're putting the seat belt sign back on as we've just received word that we're approaching some weather up ahead. There's a chance that we may have to return back to Daniel Inouye, but we'll be sure to keep you updated."

What up now, cheering losers? Come on, turbulence. Help out your boy and take me back to Cleo. I pondered the thought of moving to Honolulu. My buddy Ren just relocated from New York to Aspen and another friend is talking about moving to Atlanta, so Hawaii isn't totally bonkers. One thing I've realized after this incredibly bizarre trip is that change is good. I'm sick of the Wall Street finance grind. The thought of being chained to a desk during the week and coming home to a white picket fence hits differently once you find out your dad has been hunting terrorists for God knows how long.

The captain's calm authoritative voice returns. "Good news, folks..."

God dammit.

"We've been rerouted and we're climbing to thirty-nine thousand feet, continuing to LAX, and then onto JFK. So sit back, relax, and have a good flight."

The loser convention goes berserk.

MIRANDA, 1

Our bright red Ford SUV pulls up to the curb outside Baggage Claim.

"Tripp, you were so right to insist on buying that red car," I say to my husband—who's not just handsome but smart and considerate. Lucky me. "There are hundreds of black SUVs circling. We'd never find ours."

"But Jimmy J would always find us," he says, waving, then greeting our driver, who insists on being called by his first name and the first initial of his last. Tripp opens the door for me to sit in the front seat as Jimmy J gets out to help Jake and Ricky with our mountain of stuff. The golf clubs, suitcases, and tennis rackets clank and rattle together as they're loaded into the crammed trunk. Matt, my middle child who is low on the scale of Asperger's, stands off to the side, watching his brothers as usual.

"You guys have a nice vacation?" asks Jimmy J once he's back behind the wheel and we're all belted in.

"Yeah, it was awesome," says Ricky, my youngest, now twenty-four, and by far my nicest child. He and Jake, my oldest, look very much alike. Devastatingly handsome, just like their father.

Once we're all packed in and are off, Jake stays uncharacteristically quiet as he gazes longingly out the window.

"I saw a lot of cool birds and plants," Matt chimes in.

"Glad to hear it," says Jimmy J as he waits to merge with the stream of black SUVs.

No one talks for a few moments as we all remember our chaotic family vacation to Honolulu. Jake has fallen out of love with his girlfriend Julia, and in love with a much older woman whom everyone says is the most beautiful woman they have ever seen, though I'm not sure I agree. It seems that Ricky's unrequited love for Julia might no longer be unrequited. Matt came across more new species of plants than he knows what to do with. And something that I can't quite put my finger on has happened to my husband. Oh, and let's not forget about the near fatal helicopter accident. All five of us are, understandably, still processing the last ten days.

Jimmy J has always been allergic to silence. "Been pretty cold here.... Lows in the twenties, but actually, we got into the fifties one day last week and tomorrow should be above freezing. The heat's on as high as it goes right now. Figured you'd all be used to that warm Hawaiian sunshine!" Jimmy J's world revolves around the weather.

"Goodness, I hope it warms up soon!" I laugh. "The hard part about taking a tropical vacation in the dead of winter is the shock of returning to the cold. I can hardly feel my fingers and toes."

"How's Clemie?" asks sweet Ricky.

Jimmy J's daughter Clemie works as a receptionist in Tripp's office, and his wife Jeannie is my housekeeper and she also helps serve at my parties.

"She's great! Just got herself a boyfriend ... finally." We all laugh.

"Boys, look there's Julia waving goodbye," I say.

"Where?" Ricky perks up.

"She's jumping into that taxi." I point to the left.

Julia is beaming—either because she's finally gotten away from us or because she's found a new friend in Ricky. Jake abandoned her almost instantly after meeting Cleo. And Julia is so lovely, she didn't deserve that. I had thought that one day she'd be my daughter-in-law, but now she doesn't even look at Jake. Nor does he notice or care. In his mind, he can only see Cleopatra Gallier.

"Julia!" Ricky yells out the window, but her taxi has already pulled away. He's hooked on her and I think he always was in love with his brother's girlfriend. Now *he* can marry her!

To my left, Tripp smiles over at me. He looks mussed up, having slept in his clothes for the past few nights. Even his hair looks wild. He seems tired and exhilarated at the same time. The fact that he missed Christmas Day and barely made the plane will fade away—not to mention that when he finally arrived, he smelled mightily of Cleo's perfume. This seems impossible as I had met the two Chinese men who picked him up at the hotel last night to work with him on the China Project so how was Cleo involved? I am not stupid and know she has great power over my son Jake, but Tripp? We have been married for nearly thirty-two years and he has never given me reason to doubt his fidelity. He is right here with me and he just gave me our signal. As he leans over to kiss my cheek, he squeezes my knee. And that makes everything alright. Well, maybe not completely alright, but I am not going to question him as he is with me and we have three children and a lovely life which I want to keep and most of all I want to keep him as I love him so very much. So for now I will say nothing. I learned early to be like a chess player and give nothing away till checkmate and it has worked for me. Stanley Kubrick found the game of chess so entrancing, because he said, "It trains you to think before grabbing." I agree and so I smile and squeeze Tripp's knee back. I am playing chess.

We squeeze one another's knees to indicate: "I love you." This started when we were first married and living in a tiny apartment near Tripp's law school. Across the hallway from us was a young married couple from Russia named Sergei and Hilde Kominitz. Sergei was in Tripp's class and Sophie and I became great friends. Sergei and Sophie had a young son, Dimitri. Those two were always smooching, and I remember feeling grateful Tripp and I weren't outwardly demonstrative like that. Happily, my husband felt the same way, so he and I made a pact to squeeze one another's knee if we wanted to signal "I love you" while in front of other people. And over the years we have done it just about everywhere, from parties and funerals to kids' sports events. His squeeze makes everything all right.

Jimmy J merges into traffic but after twenty yards of driving, he hits the brakes. We're stuck in traffic even before we exit the airport to get onto the expressway. It doesn't bother Tripp. Little does.

I turn around and watch as he opens his briefcase. "Tripp, do you appreciate I know where each thing goes: your watch, phone, Kindle, two white handkerchiefs, breath freshener, spare toothbrush, iPad? They are all in perfect symmetry with your wallet and sleep mask and those pills for your high blood pressure, which worries me constantly."

He laughs and shuffles it all into a different pattern. I love when he goes along with my teasing.

I whisper to him: "What were you and Jake talking about when you got on the plane? You two looked so intense."

Tripp smiles and glances at our oldest son sitting beside him. "Shockingly, he wanted to know how my China deal went." Turning, he pats Jake on the shoulder. "Thoughtful of you, Jake, asking about my work like your mother always does," he says through a huge yawn.

I sense Tripp doesn't want to keep talking and would prefer to sleep again. He slept on the plane, but still looks exhausted.

Jake smiles. "Yeah, Dad. People are full of surprises ..."

"I thought Mr. Wu and Mr. Chen were very pleasant, Tripp." These were the Chinese investors he was working with in Hawaii who came to our hotel to pick him up. "Were they just as nice when you worked all Christmas Eve, or did they get grumpy as the negotiations dragged on?"

He smiles, then glances at Jake. These two look like they know something the rest of us don't. But I am not the curious type. Tripp has told me on multiple occasions throughout our marriage how refreshing it is to be married to someone who takes things at face value and doesn't question every little glance. A person who believes that the apple on her tray is just that, an apple. What else would it be? He loves that I'm traditional and that I'd be unimpressed owning a Range Rover or Prada dresses—which I'd look ridiculous in. I'm probably thirty pounds overweight anyway, and with my age factored in, I'd look like a joke in those clothes. Who is this Prada, and why does he only make clothes that look good on young rail-thin girls?

"Sorry, Miranda, it's been a long few days." Tripp's eyes start to close again and though I want to wake him, I don't. The boys are sleeping as well. Matt lets out a snore. My dear sweet Matt has my red hair and freckled skin and is much shorter than his two brothers that age-wise, he's sandwiched between—and usually, like me, he wears a few extra pounds.

I get out my needlepoint to work on the belt I'm making for Tripp's birthday. It will feature a helicopter to remind him of the adventure we just had. And I pull out an old Agatha Christie paperback to make a cozy nest for myself for the ride back into Manhattan, already a racket of honking, jostling cars and trucks.

CLEO, 2

After all the crazy events in Honolulu, my father insisted I go see a doctor in Dubai for a stress test. All I wanted to do was sleep, and he was worried about me. I was worried about me too.

Part French aristocrat, part Algerian, my father Didier currently lives in a luxurious compound in the Dubai desert. He also has a house in Paris, a chateau in France, and a lovely villa on the beach in Algeria near his vineyards. He's in his seventies and still just as handsome as a movie star—an aging French movie star. He's tall and lean with a full head of graying dark hair and a cigarette almost always dangling from his lip. Women cannot seem to stay away from him. He is charming and attentive and his quick mind finds amusement everywhere.

Along with some of the most important men in the world, he works for The Business. Everyone who does so remains anonymous. Many of them were, like Daddy, at Oxford when they were tapped to join. The Business is a group of wealthy and powerful men who do whatever they can to keep us safe. They have no rules to abide by. They are a top secret undercover operation that goes where no one else dares.

I was sitting in the doctor's office in Dubai, wondering just how stressed I really was, when the physician my father sent me to took my hand and calmly informed me: "Cleopatra, you are going to have a baby."

Looking around his office, I instantly became dizzy. The upholstered red chair I was in seemed to move, and the rug on the floor looked like it had shining stars in its blue background.

I couldn't speak or sort out any of my many reactions. I was shocked and exhilarated and maybe even a bit daunted at the prospect of being a mother. I was completely unprepared and completely overjoyed all at the same time. I certainly didn't want my friends or my TV audience in Hawaii speculating on who the father was.

An abaya, which is a long robe worn by women in Dubai, seemed a perfect way to hide my pregnancy—at least until I figured out my next moves. Draped in a comfy abaya, I planned to stay in Dubai with my father to have the baby.

I emailed Pudge and Pudding, the producers of my TV show *Close Encounters* as well as my great friends, to tell them that I was unable to return to Honolulu and host the show, how sorry I was, how I knew I put them in a tough spot, but circumstances made it impossible. They have been so good to me, and I hated to leave them like this but I saw no other choice. I was devastated to be giving up a job I loved where I was interviewing writers and celebrities and politicians visiting Hawaii as well as local chefs and athletes. It made my life so full as I was always studying the interests of the people I interviewed and those interests ranged all over the place.

I scrambled and tried to arrange for Walter, the Navy Seal and my Krav Maga trainer, to join me in Dubai. Since he understandably would not, I asked him to send me lessons for a pregnant woman that I could use once I hired a trainer here in the Dubai desert.

I was working out for two now. I asked Walter not to mention the pregnancy to anyone and was grateful for his lessons and started looking for a trainer. The one I found came to the house five days a week so I had my Krav Maga.

Once I was settled in my father's Dubai home, I felt safe even though I was still alone with my wonderful secret. All that stress Daddy was so worried about evaporates in a tidal wave of life growing within me—given to me by a man who is happily married and the father of three boys.

I slept with Tripp for just one miraculous night. Since he's in his fifties and I'm in my forties, I worried that our child might not be healthy. I did prenatal tests to detect genetic conditions, as well as DNA testing, early ultrasound, CVS in my first trimester, and in my second trimester the Quadruple test for birth defects and another ultrasound.

Once I knew my baby was a girl and that she was just fine, I danced in the desert sand barefoot under the moon, praying she'd be blessed. As the pregnancy progressed, I became awed by the transformation taking place within me. My baby's father might feel it in his sleep, dream it, but I doubt very much that he'll find his way to knowing he has another child coming into the world on the other side of the globe—in a desert not a city, in an oasis not a townhouse, under a star-strewn night sky, not a smoggy urban sky with stars out-shown by city lights.

With the renewed energy of having a daughter on the way, I decided to use this period to help girls who like me had been sexually abused. My father's close friend who had violated me when I was only nine years old caused me such pain and fear for decades that I embraced the girls in a local underfunded shelter. My father offered resources since he had seen the toll the rape had taken on me. The girls were not from Dubai, but from Europe and America. I hired my Krav Maga teacher to instruct the girls in self-defense, and a psychiatrist to help them work through their traumas. This focus kept me busy and, with the help of my abayas, no one noticed that I was quite pregnant. My height helped too. One little girl who was about the age I was when I had been raped was named Delia. She cried all the time and I took her little hand every day when I arrived and she walked with me as we did the rounds. About three months later, I decided to tell all the girls as we sat in a circle about what had happened to me. How the man I trusted came to my bedroom while I was asleep and put his hand over my mouth as he pulled my nightgown off. The girls all were shuddering as I was and Delia climbed into my lap and patted me. We all cried together and then one by one several girls spoke and the psychiatrist nodded at me that it was alright. We had ice cream and cake that day and we all brushed each other's hair and I brought them a special present, a necklace made of nothing valuable that would be stolen, but that held a special meaning for us who had been victims of abuse. It was a lotus flower. The main significant meaning of the lotus flower is that since it grows in the mud, it represents the rise over hardship and struggle. It also represents the transformation to beauty and strength. It was a tiny talisman they could hide if they couldn't wear it on the thin necklace I gave them. Delia smiled for the first time as I put it on her and explained what it meant.

The next week it was gone and she was so bruised and upset that I took her home that day with two of my father's bodyguards. We brought her back to our house after seeing what she was being used for. The bodyguard said he would find her a home with his wife's very large family. She never returned home and Delia stayed near me every day at the clinic. She was terrified they would come and take her back. I went again with the bodyguards to see her family which consisted of five men—her three brothers and two uncles. My father joined us and there was no question of their interfering in her life again.

TIME FOR THE DISCLOSURE, so I knock on Daddy's study door. He looks up from his laptop screen and waves me in. "Thank you for protecting Delia, Daddy and there is something wonderful I want to tell you."

He is sitting at his regal mahogany desk, as usual in a dapper navy blazer, school tie, and cigarette dangling out of his mouth. He closes the laptop, which may well hold some of the world's deepest darkest secrets.

Didier gives me an inquisitive look as I take a seat across from him. He glances at the photos of me as a child on his desk. His favorite is the one of me standing in a green dress with my dark hair in braids looking over my shoulder at him. And he has a large one of me as a two-year-old at the beach in Algeria, covered in sand and beaming.

I nod at the pictures. "Not too long from now, you will be able to add another photo to your collection." I smile.

Didier cocks his head and crinkles his brow. When he says nothing, I pat my stomach. "Daddy, you are about to be promoted to Grandfather."

"Cleopatra!" He jumps to his feet and rushes to my side, taking me in his arms.

"Can you believe it?" I say. "A little girl due in September!"

CLEO, 2

While Didier is as ecstatic as I am, he holds it in his careful way. His incredible restraint is much appreciated. He doesn't ask the identity of the man who has given us this joyous moment, though I suspect he has a pretty good idea.

He also knows I will tell him when I am ready.

April 2012

TRIPP, 1

I sit idle in my Wall Street office just off Pine, and it isn't like I don't have a lot to do. There's always important work to be done, but today, I'm distracted. I can't focus on either one of my careers: my cover as an attorney at Weinstein, Forbes, Regan, and Lowe, the firm where I've been a partner for the last twenty-six years, or even on my second career, my real career and life's work, as an undercover operative with the Central Intelligence Agency.

Frustrated by my lack of focus, I stand up from my big oak desk, shove my cell phone into my suit pocket and trudge outside onto bustling Wall Street. It's not yet eight in the morning, but the city has been pulsing with life for hours. Busy New Yorkers hurry by clutching big cups of coffee, phones to their ears, or to their children's small hands. After a relentless never-ending winter, spring has finally sprung. An air of relief hangs in the atmosphere as New Yorkers are at long last able to dash out of their apartments without that heavy winter coat. We have all shed a layer and feel a collective sense of liberation.

I enter Zuccotti Park at the Broadway and Liberty entrance to make a phone call on my second cell as I have so many times before. Annoyingly, my favorite bench is occupied by a babbling homeless man who is enjoying the benefits of today's warmer climate as he has stripped off his shirt entirely. I move away from him and settle under a tree where there's no one else around.

I pick up my cell and call a DC colleague. "Castillo, who does our recruiting these days? Is it still Ruiz and, uh, Owen?"

"Joshua Owens is in the Manhattan office, sir."

"Owens. Right."

Silence on his end.

Castillo wants to know why I'm asking. In the sixteen years that he and I have worked together, I have not once asked about recruiting. I never gave it much thought after my own recruitment years ago at The University of Michigan through my undergrad drama teacher, Mrs. Huneke. As far as I'm concerned, fresh recruits always just magically appear at the start of each quarter.

I kill the suspense. "Think my son Jake might be a good fit."

A pause. "Jake's the—"

"My oldest."

"No kidding. I remember him from a Fourth of July party years ago. He was just a little squirt back then, pissing in the kiddie pool."

"I hope he doesn't do that anymore. He's twenty-eight now."

A FEW DAYS LATER, I'm in a small, cramped office on the sixth floor of an anonymous building in Midtown. The stale, stagnant room lacks any personality or warmth. Nothing hangs on its walls and the desk that separates the odd-looking man across from me is made of rigid steel. Joshua Owens has been plying me with questions for almost thirty minutes, as if I'm the new recruit. He's an old school guy who moved out of active duty and into recruitment five years ago after undergoing triple bypass surgery. He scribbles my responses on a yellow legal pad.

"Any languages?"

There it is. The question I've been waiting for. My ace in the hole. "He can get by in Russian."

Josh briefly looks up at me from his yellow pad. Now we're talking. Russian isn't traditionally taught in the American school system, not like Spanish or French anyway, so this gives Jake the edge that he so desperately needs.

"He studied Russian at Middlebury?" Owens asks, having suddenly perked up.

Not exactly. "He played hockey for their team, the Panthers, and every February there was a big college tournament just outside St. Petersburg. Middlebury brought in a Russian tutor because they didn't have one on staff to teach the players the basics—so they could at the very least, you know, ask for directions or order a cheeseburger when they were out on the town."

"Oh. Okay. So, he just speaks the basics then? 'Please,' 'thank you,' that sort of thing?" says Owens.

"Well, Jake's been obsessed with hockey ever since he was about six years old and even today, once he takes an active interest in something, he goes full throttle. Jake got so consumed with the famous "Miracle on Ice" that he can probably still name not just the entire Team USA roster, but all the Russians players as well—including each of their positions and stats. Vladimir Kutov this and Vladimir Petrov that—if memory serves, there were about ten Vladimirs on Team Russia. Anyway, those hockey trips with Middlebury might have been the first time Jake went to Russia, but his cultural knowledge extended well beyond the average college kid. Miranda and I were actually surprised when he chose to major in economics and not Russian. We used to joke that he might one day join the Bolsheviks and turn into a communist."

I thought that might get a chuckle out of Agent Owens, but no such luck. A CIA recruit is probably not the best audience for some Commie humor.

"Anyway, he went back to Russia—on his own a few times after Middlebury."

"Really?"

"Alone or with a friend?"

"His girlfriend. Well, ex. Jake met her in New York one, maybe two years out of college. Natalia was from a big family out in Volgograd, formerly Stalingrad, and she'd take him there every summer with the rest of her family to visit the Russian side.

"Natalia?"

I think for a second until it comes to me. "Nabatov. Natalia Nabatov." Owens scribbles her name down on his yellow pad. I'm sure he'll look into Natalia and everyone she's ever met as soon as we wrap up this meeting. Jake cared a lot for Natalia but sometimes I thought he might've stuck around a little longer because of her father. "Her father, Leo Nabotov, was in the NHL and played for the Rangers, Islanders, and the Devils."

"Convenient," Owens cracks a smile for the first time.

"I'll say. He and his wife Elena moved to Rye after he was drafted to the Rangers, and they raised their four girls there. Luckily, they never had to move even after he was traded twice. Anyway, the Nabotovs mostly spoke Russian in their home because Elena and Leo didn't want their girls to grow up without learning their native tongue. I don't know about the other three, but Natalia spoke beautiful English. At the time, I remember that the Russian thing could drive Jake nuts because he'd just be sitting at the dinner table not knowing what the hell was going on. Speaking the language just a bit during an annual trip to Russia is one thing. Trying to chime in among a family of six very spirited Russians is something else entirely. But after about a year or so of dating Natalia, Jake picked up on a lot and was able to build tremendously on the Russian that he learned in St. Petersburg."

"How long did the relationship last?" Owens asks, flipping over the page of his pad.

"Two years. Maybe two and a half."

"Has Jake kept up with the Russian?"

I can't lie to Josh Owens but Goddammit, I'm tempted. Why couldn't Jake have at least stayed friends with Natalia? Surely he'd be fluent by now. Jake was never all that forthright about their break up, or any of his girlfriends for that matter, but something tells me he was the one who screwed it up. He was pretty young when they met, only twenty-two or so, and so it can probably be chalked up to bad timing. Jake just wasn't ready. "Um, not as much as he could have but he can certainly still get by," I tell Owens.

Owens nods and jots a few more things down. "So, beyond the passable Russian and helicopter incident a few months ago, what makes you think Jake would make a valuable contribution to the Agency?"

"Well, I'd hardly call it a typical 'helicopter incident,' Josh."

I wait for him to respond, but he says nothing.

"We were shot at multiple times by one of the deadliest terrorists on the FBI Watch List. Death seemed pretty damn inevitable, but Jake remained completely calm. Nine out of ten guys would've just panicked or shut down entirely. Not Jake."

"Okay, so, cool heads run in the family."

Owens is trying to downplay.

"Yeah, but not just that. He was incredibly proactive. Jake jumped into action in a way that, quite frankly, stunned me. Had I not been there, Jake would've found another way to save all our lives."

Owens nods.

"Look, Josh, I know we have a high bar here. The absolute highest, as we should. So, let me save you some time before you ask if he served in the military or law enforcement. He hasn't. And he doesn't code and he sure as hell isn't a techie. When you do a background check, you're gonna find out that sometimes he comes home late and sometimes he comes home drunk. But let me tell you, I have climbed the ranks in this agency for one reason and one reason only: instinct. And that same instinct tells me that Jake will not only make the cut, but also he'll thrive. Gun to my head, I'd guess he's like his old man. You can drop him into any situation, and he'll get whatever we need—especially from women. He's a very good-looking kid. I've seen it happen a hundred times with my own eyes."

Owens chews on that for a minute. "Alright, we'll take a look."

"That's all I'm recommending. If you guys like what you see and he makes it into training, let them figure out what he's best at. And if not, no hard feelings."

Another pause. "Will do." Owens caps his pen.

"Great," I stick out my right hand as I start to stand. "You can get all his info from my office."

Owens and I shake. "Thank you, sir."

Minutes later, I'm out the door and dodging pedestrians on the crowded sidewalk. It's true I am using nepotism to our advantage. But after our near-death experience in the air, I would've made the same recommendation had Jake been my son or some random cocktail waiter.

My time in the field, where most of the action takes place, is winding down. Even before the Abdul Rahman op turned so complicated and deeply personal, something that I'd been dreading most of my adult life began to take shape. First, it was the achy knees, then the occasionally stiff fingers, and then the morning soreness in my lower back lingered on well past lunchtime. My brain used to work like Google, capable of instantly conjuring up the names of anyone from a past case: suspect, asset, witness, informant, family member, milkman, anyone. But over the past few years, really ever since I turned the big five-oh if I'm being honest, the limits of this gift have started to rear their ugly head. One of the kids in comms, a big Schwarzenegger fan and whose name I'm blanking on at the moment (see what I mean?) used to call me "Total Recall." Don't let anyone fool you, we're real jokesters over at The Central Intelligence Agency.

Someone who was undoubtedly much further over the hill than me once said, "All good things must come to an end." As far as most men of a certain age go, I'm in excellent shape and of a relatively sound mind. But in the CIA, your personal best isn't necessarily good enough. I refuse to be one of those old codgers who wears out his welcome, staying too long at the party. I've still got what it takes, but it might be time for me to step into the office, to stop jumping out of airplanes and pass the baton onto some other young buck.

And all the better if it's Jake.

May 2012

JAKE, 2

I have never been this nervous. Today's the day. My first interview with the CIA. It's still hard for me to comprehend. *My interview with the CIA,* who woulda thunk it? I had my best suit pressed, a navy Paul Smith that's special for a few reasons. It's the first suit I ever picked out and paid for myself and I bought it for no special occasion—I saw it, I wanted it, I could afford it, and damn, it looks great on me.

Sitting alone in a room with less personality than school detention, I yank on the blue and silver Middlebury cufflinks my buddies and I all bought together at our five-year reunion. The unsmiling woman who escorted me from the elevators to this barren room confiscated my phone at the door, so there's nothing to do except wait in here like a chump. In past job interviews, I'm usually waiting in some sort of bustling, glass-walled lobby with ringing phones, opening and closing doors, and other people. But that's civilian stuff; the CIA is different. They can't exactly have a room full of undercover hopefuls lining the room and sizing each other up, with or without their iPhones.

JAKE, 2

The modest, nondescript office is downtown—sorry, normally I'd provide more detail, but in this case, then I'd have to kill you. Or however the saying goes. What I can say is that it's a small shell office that operates out of the U.S. Department of State Building. The CIA's field offices in New York City and everywhere else for that matter, are by design, pretty top secret. I did some googling and found that prior to 9/11, the Agency kept an office in The World Trade Center (whoops) and that the attacks severely cramped their work for the next several months. Several other offices are scattered throughout Midtown, Lower Manhattan, and even Brooklyn. But where? Your guess is as good as mine.

It's against Agency protocol for my father to help me prep for my interview. All he advised was that I should try and steer the conversation toward topics that appear attractive to The Agency—my solid grades at Middlebury, travel abroad, knowledge of Russia, career at the bank, and the now infamous helicopter fiasco in Honolulu last year. *Duh, Dad.* He wasn't exactly telling me anything I didn't know already, but I suppose that's really all he could say without getting into trouble.

Ah, Natalia Nabatov. I didn't think much about her after Julia entered the picture. But lately, ever since my father and I have been discussing the CIA, memories of Natalia have come flooding back like a powerful tsunami. A hot, sexy, firecracker of a tsunami with a great ass. I'll never forget the way her big baby doll eyes sparkled under the glow of the Tao dance floor.

I was out at the club with two clients of the bank—Jeff something and I have no idea what the other bro's name was. They were in town from Cleveland and desperately wanted a night out on The Big Apple town. Tao, or really nightclubs in general, have never really been my scene, but what the client wants, the client gets and as low man on the totem pole, it was my job to show them a good time. Which I did.

I wanted to go to bed. It was a Thursday and it had been a long week of pulling nineteen-hour days on my relatively new trading desk. After wining and dining Jeff and good ol' what's–his–name at L'Artusi in Greenwich Village, I was hoping that they would want to call it a night and mosey back to their five-star hotel. It was already past midnight. But they were just getting started, and I was to be their tour guide. Lucky me. One thing that was absolutely nonnegotiable for them both was a table. Two fat cats from one of the biggest investment firms in the Midwest were not about to stand around a night-club like some schmos from the Jersey Shore. They wanted bottle service and they wanted the women to come to them. The thing was, it was already late, it was Thursday, and it was springtime in New York. The city was electric. Tables at all of the best clubs—at the time, 1OAK, Bungalow 8, and Cielo were already gone. Then I remembered Tao. I promptly called the number I found online and we headed over.

It happened like it does in the movies. Jeff and what's-his-name were yukking it up with a group of women more enamored by our table than our sparkling personalities when I took another lackluster sip of my vodka soda and looked across the dance floor.

Everyone parted like some drunken Red Sea, and there was Natalia. Blue eyes, red gold hair, and a perfect body squeezed into a skintight silver dress—every single hot girl and then some owned one of these dresses at the time: Harvey or Henry Ledger. Natalia was in her own world, dancing by herself to Nelly Furtado's "Maneater." For a few minutes, I just watched her. It felt as if I was glued to the leather banquette as

I drank in this mystery woman with so much more fury than my watered-down vodka soda. She was perfect.

The song ended and I had to talk to her. I downed the rest of my drink for a few ounces of liquid courage.

"I like your moves," I blabbered. *I like your moves? Jesus.* I might as well have asked her if she comes here often or if she was wearing space pants.

Natalia just laughed. She could tell I was anxious. Back then I wasn't the smooth, suave ladies' man that I am today. Back then, a woman like Natalia scared the shit out of me.

She smiled, stuck out her tiny hand, and grabbed mine. I'm almost positive it was shaking, and I prayed she didn't notice. "I'm Natalia," she told me.

Of course her name is Natalia, I remember thinking. A girl like this is no Nancy or Kathy. A girl like this has the name of a Bond girl.

"Nice to meet you, Natalia," I smiled back. "That's a beautiful name. I'm—"

"Jake Regan?"

I jump as a man's raspy voice jolts me out of my Natalia Nabatov fantasy and back into this nondescript office. I wipe the corners of my mouth in fear that the mere thought of Natalia might have caused me to drool. I turn and look up at a small unsmiling man.

"They're ready for you, Jake."

Here goes nothing.

JULIA, 1

Today, I'm so happy I could die.

After six months of pure bliss with Ricky, we're moving in together. I know, I know, it might be a little quick. But we have known each other for quite a while.

We found the cutest little apartment in the West Village on Bank Street just off Hudson. Emphasis on "little," but I guess that's just the price you pay for living in the best neighborhood that New York City has to offer. Miranda and Tripp were thrilled when Ricky and I told them we have decided to take our relationship to the next level. At this point, I don't think Jake really cares. He was probably more surprised than anything. I don't believe he ever thought that his baby brother and I would get so serious so quickly.

Luckily, Jake's job has relocated him to Washington DC so he won't be around much for the next year or two. I pray that he finds a nice gal down there who makes him just as happy as Ricky makes me. I long for the day when it will no longer be awkward between the three of us.

Someday...

DIDIER, 1

I was just taken with a passage in a book I am reading about Vera Nabokov, the wife of the Russian writer Vladimir Nabokov, most famously known for his book, *Lolita*. To paraphrase the passage, 'a curriculum vitae, crude as can be, has a style peculiar to the undersigner. I doubt whether you can even give your telephone number without giving something of yourself.' Taking that idea to its logical conclusion—no one can hide. There is a trail we all leave no matter how subtle. This trail fascinates me as I believe I leave nothing behind when I do my work for The Business. I imagine someone giving their phone number in a clipped way leads to an impatient person. This might give me hours of amusement seeing trails of my associates. Cleo's perfume Endgame would give her away instantly. I know who the father of her child is as his trail is most visible but Cleo does not see it.

July 2012

JAKE, 3

I made it into training. Passing the background check was a breeze. Despite having a pretty rollicking time during my late teens and into my twenties, surprisingly I never actually got into much trouble. No DUIs, no arrests, and no drugs—except the occasional hit off my friend, David's, bong. But everyone knows pot doesn't count. I'm almost embarrassed to admit that I don't even have a speeding ticket. A big part of this, I suppose, is because I was always terrified of disappointing my parents—but really, my father.

I only needed to see that sad look of utter failure on his face once for me to realize that I'd prefer never to see it again. When I was fifteen years old, I snuck out to some lame party with my dumb friends and having no idea how to handle my booze, I got absolutely wasted. I must've only had like five beers, but when I stumbled home at God-knows-what time—I'd love to say it was like two o'clock in the morning, but I have a feeling it was closer to the eleven o'clock hour—I couldn't see straight. The memory is a blur, but apparently I was making all sorts of racket while whipping myself up a tasty premidnight snack.

Believing that all three of his sons were upstairs tucked in bed all safe and sound, Dad figured we were getting burgled by a crazed Upper East Side prowler. He quietly snuck downstairs with my Little League bat in hand, ready to knock one out of the park.

I'll never forget that look and how it felt directed toward me. He was so disappointed.

He didn't even have to say why. I already knew. It wasn't that his bonehead fifteen-year-old son had snuck out with his bonehead friends and had a few beers, it was that the decision I'd made was the first sign of squandering my infinite potential.

From a very young age, Dad made it clear that the sky was the limit for me, that I was capable of anything. He treated Matt and Ricky the same way, but as the oldest son that notion seemed to resonate even more profoundly with me. And so that was all it took. Did I ever get bombed after that night? Duh. I'm not a narc. But I was smart about it, never getting too out of control or letting my hangovers paralyze me in bed the next day, rendering me incapable of any productivity whatsoever. And that has made all the difference.

Unlike the background check, the polygraph was nerve-wracking. I wasn't worried about lying, but I was worried that it might *seem* like I was lying or like I was trying not to lie. It's that whole idea where you're trying so hard not to do the one thing that you're not supposed to, that you end up looking guilty or suspicious in the process. If it looks like you're actively trying *not* to lie, you might look like you have something to hide.

At first, the questions were pretty simple. Lucinda, the polygraph examiner, a heavyset woman whose dark hair was tied in a tight bun, scared the shit out of me—and not just because she had just hooked me up to a lie detector. She looked like she could've been a linebacker for the New York Giants. Lucinda affixed six different sensors to my body: two small metal plates to my finger to record sweat gland activity and something called a plethysmograph, which monitors blood volume. The corrugated rubber tubes on my chest and rock-hard abs record respiratory activity, and then a fancy blood pressure cuff monitors my cardiovascular activity. Broken down in the simplest of terms, "polygraph" literally means "many writings" and refers to the way in which selected physiological activities are simultaneously recorded. The questions are mostly yes or no and meant to be very simple.

"Is your name Jake Regan?" Lucinda asked.

"Yes," I answered definitively.

The black needle barely moved against the white paper. That meant I was telling the truth.

"Were you born in New York City?"

"Yes," I answered definitely again.

The needle hardly moved.

"Is your father Tripp Regan?"

"Yes."

The black needle did its thing.

"Have you ever used illegal drugs?"

Oh, boy. Here we go. I took a deep breath and answered truthfully. "Yes."

I could feel the beginnings of sweat seeping out the glands on my forehead. I took another deep breath, willing myself to remain chill just like my forever calm, cool, and collected father. The needle moved against the paper, making longer black markings. I wasn't lying, but this question made me a little tense.

"Marijuana?"

Another deep breath. "Yes."

"Anything else?" Lucinda asks, looking at me.

"No." And that was the truth. I have been in the same room as cocaine many-a-time but never tried the stuff. The needle didn't move much, indicating that this really wasn't a lie.

"Have you ever lied on your resume or a job application?"

Yikes. I had to think about this one. Nothing specific comes to mind, but doesn't everybody? "No?" But it came out as more of a question and my lack of authority manifested on the page. The needle moved like crazy.

"Are you positive?" Lucinda looked over at me.

Calm, cool, collected, I told myself. *Calm, cool, collected.*

"No." Shit! A bead of sweat dripped down my forehead toward my brow. The needle went crazy again and long, black lines appeared on the paper before me. "I mean, yes. Yes, I'm positive that I have never lied on my resume or on a job application. Final answer."

The lines were less sweeping this time. I was anxious, but I wasn't lying.

Lucinda nodded. "How many times have you been to Russia?"

I knew this was coming. "Six."

"Is a Russian woman named Natalia Nabatov your ex-girlfriend?"

Saw this one coming too. "Yes."

"You dated Natalia for two years, correct?"

"Yes. Well, it was more like two and a half."

"Did you ever sell U.S. government secrets to her or anyone in the Nabatov family?"

Hello. Part of me is flattered that Lucinda could even think I was capable of such a thing. I took another deep breath and answered in a controlled tone. "No."

"Did Natalia or her family ever ask you to gather American intelligence on their behalf?"

"No."

"Are you telling the truth?" Lucinda looked over at me.

I looked her dead in the eye. Two can play this game. "Yes. Yes, I am."

And the black needle indicated that I was.

Lucinda switched gears. "Do you know who was responsible for the helicopter incident you and your family were involved with last year?"

You bet your ass I do. "Yes."

"Was it the Russians?"

"No."

"Was it Mohammed Abdul Rahman?"

"Yes."

"Have you ever met Mohammed Abdul Rahman?"

"Yes." I wanted to elaborate. I wanted to tell Lucinda that the only reason I met this asshole is that he happened to be living on the property of the very beautiful woman that I was sleeping with and that he was using an alias and posing as any normal, patriotic American. But I don't. Keep it simple, stupid.

"Did you have any prior knowledge of the foiled Honolulu terrorist attacks that were to be carried out on Christmas Day, 2011?"

"No."

"Do you know anyone who did have prior knowledge?"

"No."

No big, sweeping movements from the needle.

AND THAT'S THE GIST of it. No one ever shared exactly how well or how poorly I did that day with Lucinda, but I must have done alright because now I'm in Virginia, at Langley, undergoing rigorous training for the CIA. Get this, there's actually something called The CIA University. That still makes me laugh because it sounds like something so fake and so false that it'd appear in a children's spy movie featuring Bugs Bunny and the rest of the Looney Tunes gang. But it's real. Oh, it's very real.

The next eighteen months will be one big test—physical, sure, but even more mental. Training will cover all the intricacies of spotting, developing, recruiting, and handling foreign assets and stealing the most closely-guarded secrets of America's enemies—and in some cases, our friends. Translation: hardcore physical training and in-depth mental preparation. I'm told that as trainees, we learn all about role playing—though I already have some experience in that department, if you know what I mean ... and that traps will constantly be set for us to reinforce Murphy's Law—whatever can go wrong, will go wrong.

Besides my dad, my family thinks that I'm working for a DC-based financial consulting firm. I'd been moaning about being over my job at the bank for a while now, so the career change makes sense. The move to DC is a little less believable, but almost anyone will believe that someone will relocate for the right number, and so I assured them that my new paycheck was worth it. I was hired to help fledgling companies increase shareholder value and improve efficiency, or at least that's what my friends and family think.

The next year and a half will not be easy. There will be many, many times that I'll want to throw in the towel. Once a trainee becomes an operative, they are tasked with completing complex, challenging, and highly classified tasks usually working completely solo. The purpose of training is to see who buckles under the pressure and who can take the heat. The dropout rate is extremely high.

Wish me luck.

A SMALL GROUP OF classmates and I run around DC at all hours of the day and night. We recognize the license plates of cars that are tailing us, differentiating the training surveillants from the real ones, and marking drop sites with pieces of white chalk. It's wild to me that all of the nearby civilians are completely unaware as to what's happening all around them.

Our first operational assessment is called a bump, which basically means that we have to find a target of interest in a public place and come up with a reason to get him or her talking. The goal of the first meeting: scoring a second meeting, an opportunity to continue the conversation at a different location at a later date. A second meeting, and third and fourth and on and on, gives the operative a chance to build the relationship with the target and more important, access to whatever information they might have. Information is key. Knowledge is power.

The targets that we're assigned to are all characters played by actual case officers a.k.a. the real-life spies we lowly trainees dream of becoming one day. Some are here because they want to pass their knowledge on to the next generation, others are here because they're simply worn out and would rather do a less stressful tour back home, and others are here because they've been sent to the penalty box—they messed up in the field and now they have to make amends.

Our instructor drops manila folders onto the tables in front of each of us. Mine opens with a photo of a middle-aged woman walking down a crowded city street. She reminds me a bit of a young Judi Dench with a bad haircut. The write-up is scant. She's a civil servant and knows about an imminent attack to be carried out at an American Embassy. She's objected, but has been ignored and the local station believes she might be a viable target.

Beyond that, there are only a few words about her. She went to the University of Milan and is a huge fan of IL SENTIERI, whatever that is.

Tacked onto the end is a surveillance report. In the mornings, she likes to buy her coffee at Cafe Milano in Chevy Chase near her apartment. Sounds like I'm going to Cafe Milano. She sits on the left side and likes to start her day with a chocolate croissant and an espresso.

The next day, I pull into a spot near Cafe Milano. I'm driving a rented Honda Accord, designed to safeguard my cover from any real-world surveillants sent by the Russians or the Chinese or the Middle East to get a jump on identifying the CIA's next crop of spies. I glance at myself in the rearview mirror. My reflection doesn't exactly inspire the type of confidence that it normally does. Sweat pours down my forehead, my skin is flushed, and my hair is matted to my skull.

Inside, there are gobs of early risers desperate for their caffeine fix. I get in line and scan the room as casually as I can. I'm feeling considerably less James Bond and considerably more ridiculous. No sign anywhere of a surly case officer posing as an informant, pretending not to know I'm here. Is it possible that I'm just a crazy person who dreamed up this whole CIA thing? Am I Leonardo DiCaprio in *Shutter Island*? Oh, God.

But then I see her. Sitting in the back corner, she's reading a Soap Opera magazine. After researching IL SENTIERI, I bought every soap mag there is. IL SENTIERI is the CBS soap opera GUIDING LIGHT which is dubbed in Italian and is rated as the top TV show in Italy. It is shown during siesta there which probably helps its ratings greatly.

This is it. Holy shit, this is it. Either I'll ace the assignment like I have most things in my charmed life or I'll screw it up so royally that they kick me out of the program altogether.

I step up to the unsmiling barista with blue-and-pink hair and order a cappuccino. Thirty seconds later, I have a tiny white cup and saucer in hand to balance with my stack of photos as I head over to her.

I sit in the empty chair near her. My heart is pounding. I set my coffee, pen, and the stack of headshots of me on the table next to her. Methinks she's waiting for me to make the first move. I let her wait. Mostly, because I'm terrified. And it probably feels more natural that way. I open my pen and start to sign the note attached to each photo. My hands are shaking as they move across the card. I stiffen my fingers, hoping that'll help. It doesn't.

I can feel her stealing a glance at my stack of photos. I want to catch her eye, but I force myself not to.

"Are you an actor?" she smiles

It's now or never. I turn to her and return her smile. "Me?"

She nods.

"Well, I recently had a walk-on part in a soap opera in NYC so I am sending my photos and resumes to agents and managers hoping for an audition. Not much on my resume yet though."

"No KIDDING. Which soap opera?"

I hope she isn't going easy on me.

"Oh, do you watch them.? I have a friend who stars on the *GUIDING LIGHT* and she got me a walk-on part so I can get my union card."

"What part does she play on the soap opera?" She looks really thrilled.

"She plays a doctor. She is visiting me now as she has a gig here. We used to date when I was in NYC."

"Well, I love that show. I know just who she is. There's only one female doctor on that show. I would really love to meet her."

I give her a smile. "Oh. Well I know she adores her fans. Happy to set up a date for you to meet. How can I reach you?"

She begins to give me her phone number, then stops and stares at me.

"Helluva first meeting, kid. But I really do want to meet her. Can you do that?" "Well, no." Her face falls.

"I can get you in to visit the set in NY if you want and you can meet the whole cast." I must know someone who knows someone in NY who can do that. She laughs and leaves.

September 2012

CLEO, 3

Curled up in a cozy chair in my father's study, I gaze out the large French window at the patio fountain made of tiles in differing shades of blue. From this vantage point, I call my very lovely and very organized baby sister in England. "Beebe, can you please come to Dubai? I rather need you." Since I am now nine months pregnant, this is quite an understatement.

She knows I'm not one for making idle requests, and I expect she senses the urgency in my voice. The only other time that I asked Beebe to get on a plane for me was after "Danny" died. I leaned on her then in Algeria, just like I'm hoping to lean on her now in Dubai.

As always, Beebe responds with simplicity and calm, "Of course. I need to look into travel, but hopefully I can arrive tomorrow or the next day. How does that sound?"

"It sounds perfect." Perfect, like Beebe. I imagine her taking my call in her castle with all the weaponry of her husband's forebears on the walls alongside once magnificent tapestries that are looking a bit forlorn these days. Or more than likely, Beebe was arranging flowers in one of the drawing rooms when I called. I can picture her carefully arranging her roses in elegant vases on marble tables amid silver frames of weddings from decades before.

"I'll send along my flight info once I have it booked," she says. I hear Beebe tapping her long, manicured nails on a marble table, as she adds, "I've no doubt there's a good reason for your request, Cleo."

What a polite way to ask a question. And there was no reason for me to delay sharing the news.

"I imagine you'll find this hard to believe, but ... well, I'm going to have a baby!!"

Beebe says nothing, but I can hear her tapping her nails as she processes what I've just told her. I imagine a big smile, or I hope that is the case. "Do I know the father, Cleo?" she quietly asks.

"No, you don't, Beebe." I'm not ready just now to answer that particular question, even when posed by my sister. I've yet to figure out exactly how I will handle the matter of my baby's paternity. "I hope my request doesn't interrupt anything too pressing in your schedule, Beebe," I say, being polite too.

Beebe's husband, Lancaster, is most certainly away on his autumn schedule of shooting and fishing all over the world and her two boys are away at school. But to be honest, I was quite sure Beebe would come, even if she had many things that are pressing.

She lives in an ancient, somewhat drafty castle, and there's always work to be done in its enclosed rose garden. Beebe is the president of the Dorset Garden Club and helps out at the centuries-old church nearby. She's also on the boards of several charities and she and Lancaster are philanthropists, so I am guessing that coming to see me will necessitate her excusing herself from numerous meetings. Of course, Beebe would never tell me if my request throws a wrench into her schedule. Calm, collected, and looking fabulous, she will just arrive in Dubai as though nothing could be more convenient than to be beckoned to my father's desert conclave.

AFTER SHE DISEMBARKS FROM her United Air Emirates flight, Beebe is met by friends of my father's, members of the Abadi family. My father is very close to an important sheik in the United Arab Emirates, so great efforts are made by the sheik to honor and protect Didier's family.

Beebe is ushered by these gentlemanly escorts through a back door to get her passport stamped in a private room, then she's escorted to a fleet of black SUV Escalades.

I wait for Beebe in my favorite place, reading on the stone balcony overlooking the long winding driveway. Nestled among sand dunes, my father's house is built like a fort with green courtyards and lush gardens surrounding it. As with most things in his charmed life, my father has typically been ahead of the curve. He was given the oasis many years ago, way before the rest of the world had heard of a place called Dubai.

Since then, Didier has used it as a retreat and as a meeting site with his friends, many of whom are in The Business with him. To borrow his phrase, "The Business protects the world. Our connections all over the world, quite simply, fight evil." All of the men in The Business attended Oxford and belonged to the same club over the years, including the UAE Sheik, hence this home in Dubai.

After the motorcade of six black cars finally pulls up in front of the house, Beebe emerges from the third car, dressed in a bright green suit and carrying quite a large green purse brimming with who-knows-what. She smiles her thanks to the Abadis as they drop her onto our doorstep looking like she's just stepped off a Milan runway. Being her sister, I do notice, however, that she's gained a few pounds. Actually, maybe more than a few. Sadly, she was not blessed with the same fast metabolism from her father as I was from mine. But she got our mother's platinum blond hair while I got my father's dark wavy hair.

But as I am thinking this, I fall apart. Seeing my sister I can finally let go of all the fears and worries that I've been suppressing. Wearing an abaya while practicing Krav Maga every day helped me believe that despite being pregnant at forty-four, and not having a father for my child, everything is normal.

"Ah, those hormones are working for you, Cleo," Beebe grins as I run into her open arms. "Look at you," she says, "you're twinkling!"

Ever since she was a girl, Beebe has sworn by Guerlain's Shalimar. She carries a travel-size bottle with her at all times, and I can tell she spritzed herself on the ride from the airport. I inhale the scent with pleasure. Our mother wore Shalimar, so, of course, Beebe, her shadow, wore it too.

She raises her perfect eyebrows at my very large belly, "I wish you'd called me earlier."

"I know. I just—well, honestly it took quite a while for everything to sink in. When was the last time you heard of a forty-four-year-old having a baby?"

"Oh, please!" Beebe puts her arm in mine as we take a stroll around the gardens. "I am so happy for you, Cleo and so glad to be here with you for this event." "Thank you, Beebe, there is no one I would rather have with me, " I say as I crush her into a hug.

"Have you been thinking of our mother lately, Cleo? Amazing how much I missed her both times I was pregnant, but she was always jaunting around the world."

"Yes! Honestly, I laugh when I think of her carrying us for all those months. I can't imagine her pregnant, can you? I really can't."

"Well, I'm sure she had the most elegant maternity clothes. Undoubtedly, Chanel made her yellow chiffon maternity dresses," Beebe says with a smile.

"Oh, how she loved yellow. It made her platinum blond hair look even blonder."

Beebe laughs. "She certainly preferred dressing up more than she liked being around us."

"Staying at home with an extra thirty pounds must have been pure torture for her! I wonder if she went out during those months. We should ask Didier tonight. My father loves talking about Sandrine."

"Oh, I'd love to hear what he has to say. My own father smiles with a faraway look at the mention of her name but will say not a word."

Our mother, Sandrine, had married Beebe's father several years after leaving my middle sister Tree's (she had been conceived beneath a tree in Woodstock) father whom she married after leaving my father. She had a history of marrying, decorating her new house, leaving and marrying another man to repeat the process. During her time with each of her three husbands, she gave them each a daughter.

"Well, Beebe, Lancaster is so very British upper class, isn't he?"

We both grin, and Beebe tightens her grip on my arm. I am feeling so grateful that I bowed to fate and asked my sister to come, rather than stiff-upper-lipping my way through my baby's birth.

Beebe seems to hear my thoughts and says, "I'm so glad you realized you needed me. Did you call Tree as well?"

"No ... I adore our sister but I knew if she came, it would mean that Crystal and all the dogs and probably the boys would come too. They never seem to leave each other's side."

"Yes, good decision. It would be a bit of a madhouse."

"I love when they visit me in Honolulu but find myself hiding in my room quite a bit! And breathing a giant sigh of relief when they leave, even though I can't wait for them to hurry back. I will call her soon though."

We laugh again as, with maximum attitude, my black cat comes swishing over to meet Beebe.

"Oh, and this must be Endy!" Beebe coos as she picks up Endgame, Endy for short.

As does everyone, Endy instantly loves Beebe. The cat was given to me last year in Honolulu by Tripp as a goodbye gift. He has no idea about the other little gift he gave me. When my baby arrives, I wonder how Endy will like being upstaged by the new ruler of my life.

I show Beebe into one of the guest rooms, and she starts to unpack. All her clothes are neatly and precisely organized. She has gray shoes with a gray dress and blue sweater and a plastic bag of blue earrings and then white slacks with white flats and a blue shirt with tiny pearl button earrings in their plastic bag.

"If you agree, I am going to send for my sons' beloved Nannie—her real name, no less—to join us. She retired, but I know she is bored."

"Oh, Beebe! That would be wonderful!"

Beebe smiles and continues unpacking other sets of matching clothes. Looking up at me, she says, "I'm sure you must already have a crib, a bassinet, a changing table, and diapers."

I nod.

"That's a good start, but we need lots of other things."

"I knew I did the right thing in calling you."

"What about a carriage and a car seat?" She loves to organize and feel useful.

"Not yet." I admit that I'm rather behind. "I don't know other women here, Beebe, so there've been no baby showers, and certainly the Arab men I know would hardly give me fluffy pink baby dresses."

I can see this mention of my baby's gender pleases Beebe immensely.

"Oh, I can't believe I haven't asked! Fluffy pink baby dresses certainly gives me a clue."

"Yes, a girl." I smile, resting my head on Beebe's shoulder. A girl.

Nine months ago, my world unraveled when I met the Regans and now I am reraveled by this baby. It seems impossible to me that, in twelve days, I will be a mother. Even that word: *Mother*. "I hate to think our mother won't meet my daughter," I say to Beebe. "You're so lucky that Sandrine met your boys—Tree's boys, too—but I'm too late to the party."

Beebe refuses to be negative. "On the bright side, she'll have four cousins and two sensational aunts who will worship her and treat her like the princess that I'm sure she will be." She always knows just the right thing to say.

"Let's plan for you to come to us for Christmas every year!" says Beebe, her eyes lighting up with excitement. "Having a baby—and a baby girl at that!—will make the holiday even more special." Beebe removes her toiletry bag from her suitcase and arranges all of her makeup and face cream in a neat little row as if they were soldiers at Buckingham Palace.

"Beebe, I do believe you put those out in the order you use them? Eyes first, then foundation, then blush, then lipsticks. Goodness, look at all the different color lipsticks!"

"Oh, yes. A different color for each different outfit! You know me, I always come prepared." She laughs and her eyes crinkle. I had forgotten how much I love her crinkling eyes when she smiles. And wonderfully, my baby sister is always smiling.

"But I bet you didn't bring your abaya?" I say.

"My a-what-a?"

I laugh. "I'm only joking. You can borrow some of mine." I walk over to the spare closet, which is full of my abayas, some with gorgeous and intricate designs. I pull one of the long black robes out for Beebe. "These are abayas, and because the Abadi family is joining us for dinner tonight, we will wear them."

"The nice people who met me at the airport?"

"Yes, we wear abayas out of respect for their culture. And as I've found out, these outfits are ideal if you're expecting! I've worn one ever since I found out I was pregnant, but some of these are small enough for you."

"Oh, they're fabulous. And certainly more comfortable than anything I brought!" She yawns.

"I hope you aren't too tired. The Abadis will be great company."

"Oh, I'm fine, though I may have a bit of a lie-down before they arrive." She sits down on the bed.

I plop down and snuggle next to her. It's getting harder and harder for me to stand for more than five minutes.

"Perfect, I need a lie down too. And then later we can chat and chat and chat." This is a phrase we always said to one another while growing up: *Let's chat and chat and chat!*

My sister and I agree to meet in the library in an hour to do just that.

SPENCER, 1

A little less than a year ago, I was interviewed about my recent film *The Last Touch* on Cleopatra Gallier's show in Honolulu, *Close Encounters*. After the segment, I intentionally waited for her in the parking lot. She was so breathtaking that I wanted to see if she was really the sorceress that she appeared to be.

When I spotted her leaving the studio, she had changed from the pale green slacks and sweater she wore on the show and was now in a blue-and-yellow sundress with yellow sandals. As a movie director, costumes are very important to express a character, so I always notice people's clothing. She gave me a wonderful smile as she sauntered over to me, which made what happened next absolutely astonishing.

"Cleopatra, thanks for having me on the show. You gave my film a nice box office boost I am sure."

"Thank you for saving the show, and your new film sounds terrific. I am sorry I didn't have a chance to meet you before we went on air."

"That's—Well, I waited because I just wanted to tell you that our parents were once friends."

"Oh really? Who are your parents?" She was smiling broadly.

"Richard and Genevieve Rensellear."

She froze. The smile disappeared and she mumbled, "Oh, yes, yes..." and walked away fast with no apology. I'd mostly forgotten that incident until I was visiting my mother today at her house in London's Pimlico.

Mother loves blue. Her clothes and her house are decorated in different shades of blue. Best of all are the big blue glasses she always wears. She rides her bike all over our part of town and everyone knows her. We both have blond hair, though hers has become quite gray. We both have long lashes, though hers cover blue eyes. My eyes, like my brother's, are green. And both of our teeth are very, very white.

I was asked to do a toothpaste commercial when I was young by a friend's father who worked in advertising. My mother was adamant when she said no, but I begged for days. When she relented and I spent a whole day in a film studio, I knew what my profession would be. Now I direct films and have never stopped loving it. I have been extremely successful and am quite prominent in my field. My films gross over thirty million dollars and I have won a few Oscars. I love my work and really enjoy making my spy films. I'm also a family man. My wife and I eloped at age eighteen—way too early but how well it has worked.

Today, September 24, is the thirty-fifth anniversary of my father's death, which is why I am in London visiting my mother's home. As that scene in the parking lot with Cleo Gallier weirdly flashed through my mind, I brought up the forbidden taboo subject: the suicide of Richard Rensellear, my father.

"Do you know why Dad killed himself?" I asked her as I sat where I always do, in her parlor's blue chair with tiny white checks. She had once told my brother Giles and me that Dad had left a note, but all it said was that he was very sorry, and it laid out her financials and instructed her which lawyers she should see.

I was only eight years old, and Giles was ten when Dad shot himself at his club in London. Giles was so stunned that he never fully recovered. My brother is very sensitive and adored my father, but then again, so had everyone who knew him. Or so I thought.

By the look on her face, I could tell my mother was surprised at this question after thirty-five years. "Why do you want to know now? After all this time?"

"I suppose I haven't been ready to ask until now."

"Well," she paused, "the few weeks prior, he was drinking much more than usual."

"You never told me that."

"You never asked."

"WELL, MOTHER, THE SUBJECT was taboo and so painful to you, I never wanted to bring it up. Which of his friends spoke at the funeral?" I asked. "I was a child and really have very little memory of his funeral. It was all rather a blur."

I took note of their names as she told me, though I didn't know any of them. They were his business friends and university friends. Twelve years after my father's death, my mother remarried. She waited until Giles and I were through school, out of the nest, and on our own. Rupert, her husband of the past twenty-some years, is a fine man who loves her, his dogs, and his collection of stamps. Whenever I'm filming in some interesting place, I always send him the stamps from that country.

"Did you see much of the Galliers afterward?"

My mother seemed stunned by that question. "The Galliers, no, why?"

"No reason." I debated whether or not to tell her about Cleo's odd reaction when I mentioned Dad's name. I decided against it. "Remember, I did Cleopatra Gallier's talk show a little while ago? I guess that made me think of them."

"Didier was your father's friend, not mine and they were divorced by then I recall," she said, looking lost in thought.

"Mom, what is it?"

"Oh, nothing. I just think there were secrets between all those men."

"What sort of secrets?"

"I don't know. Your father never spoke to me about them. But they were a tight-knit group, secretive and I suppose very powerful. They still are, I am sure, very powerful."

Hmm. I began to see a film idea forming. All of a sudden, I need to find out why my father chose to die. Why has it taken me until now to seek the answers—to actually want and need the answers?

Dad's finances were excellent, and he was a good friend, father, and husband. He was happy his last night on Earth. My mother said all the men at the club had emphasized that he'd been smoking his cigars, drinking brandy, and regaling everyone when he suddenly stood up and excused himself. He went upstairs.

Hours later, the shot came.

What he was doing was writing to my mother and making sure that we'd all be in good hands. *What happened to make him get up and leave for his death?* You don't just have a few brandies with friends, then go to your room and shoot yourself. If he'd planned it, he would have done all this ahead of time.

Mother retrieves and shows me the letters she received after Dad died. She kept these for us for when we grew up, if we ever wanted to know how beloved he was.

"Mom, how were you able to go on without any answers? Or do you have them?"

She lit a cigarette. She rarely smokes, and so I knew I had triggered something important. I repeated the question and asked if she knew something more.

She was wavering but finally stood, pulled her shoulders back and walked out of the room. She returned with a letter on my father's club stationery. "After he wrote this letter upstairs, he walked out of the club to mail it himself. The doorman said Sir Richard had told him he needed a breath of fresh air and wandered down the street, but he returned soon after, chatted about the weather, wished the doorman a good night, then went to his room and the shot was heard."

In this letter I held, he wrote, "*No one should see this but you. I need you to understand I have done something terribly dishonorable, and the only answer is to take my life or I will be disgraced, as will you and our sons. This is the only way. Now no one will ever know. I have given my word to take my life in return for the deed I have done. I'm so terribly sorry, Genevieve. Only one person knows, but my sin is sealed. Forgive me. You were all the world to me, and I committed a horrible act once and it is costing me you, and our sons, and my life. As my favorite writer, George Bernard Shaw, said, "The truth is, hardly any one of us has ethical energy for more than one really inflexible point of honor." And this is my one inflexible point of honor so I will do it immediately and with great love to you and great sorrow not to be able to grow old with you. Yours in life and now in death, Richard.*"

I sat there reading and rereading over and over this thirty-five-year-old letter.

Mother lit another cigarette watching me with such sadness. "Spencer, what could he have done that was so awful? And who is the one person who knows who made him take his life? Richard was a good man, loved by everyone, so what dishonor had he committed that was so awful that he died for it? I know he was involved in helping England, but was he a spy gone wrong? I have asked certain of his friends, and they said he would never have done anything to hurt anyone and never his country. What could have happened on that night?" Another cigarette was lit before she went on. "As I said, he was drinking a lot the last months before his death and traveling all over the world. I did notice he had a gun in his briefcase but when I asked him why, he just shrugged. I really thought nothing of it. But it was like he was hiding from someone. I'm still haunted that I didn't realize something was wrong when he was drinking and traveling so much—that I didn't ask him what was troubling him. No one saw him talking with anyone they didn't know that night. Since I married Rupert, I no longer dwell on it. You and your brother kept me busy for years while you grew up, as I wanted to help you get over this. I thought you were too young to understand—not that I ever understood, not totally. Your brother asked me all the time about it but I never showed him Richard's letter. It would have hurt him. You are strong and can perhaps discover this dishonorable act he refers to, but never tell your brother. Promise me, Spencer. Richard was in a desperate place and did what he felt was the honorable thing. But the pain he caused us all these years.... I guess I want to know what happened." Tears filled her blue eyes fogging her glasses. "Perhaps I'm brave enough now."

I realize she's giving me her permission to find out what dishonorable act caused her husband's death. I suffered without the answers of why my father killed himself, without having him in my life. Incredibly, this has made me a better husband and father.

September, 2012

CLEO, 4

At six fifteen, Beebe and I are in the library, sipping iced teas. Beebe looks appalled and ill at ease while I tell her all about the vast security system here at Daddy's compound. I realize that, of course, she hasn't a glimmer of an idea of what Didier Gallier really does. She knows of his vineyards outside Paris and in Algeria, places she's visited, but not about The Business.

Beebe is more like her conservative, reserved, proper British father than she realizes. No doubt she was horrified at the ostentatious display by the Abadi family at the airport earlier—the escort and the fleet of black cars would have stunned her. But as usual, Beebe says nothing, taking all of it in while remaining ever cool and collected.

My father knocks on the library door. "I'd be delighted to greet you on the terrace."

When we wander out, or rather when I plod out with my enormous stomach, Daddy beams at my half-sister, greeting her with open arms. "So glad you're here, Beebe. And how lovely you look. You look more and more like Sandrine each time I see you!"

Beebe is an exact duplicate of our mother: elegant and blond and small. I, on the other hand, resemble my tall dark-haired father, though I, too, was blessed with my mother's violet eyes and dimples. Our sister Tree is like Mother in her coloring, but she has a different build; she's very athletic like her father.

Beebe smiles. "Sandrine was so beautiful. Of course I take that as the highest compliment. "

"As you should!"

"Cleo tells me you'll tell us some stories about our mother while we wait for your granddaughter," Beebe says.

He smiles, thrilled to be back in Sandrine's orbit, as well as to be having a grandchild. "My pleasure. The way you are standing so regally right now, for example. Sandrine appeared exactly like you when we first met. Five feet two inches, am I right?"

"That's right."

"Sandrine always wore the highest heels—to be closer to the stars, she'd insist. I enjoyed that image of her being those few inches closer to the heavens."

"She really was quite vain," Beebe said, as if she hadn't just recently unpacked a suitcase full of makeup. "All those shoes she had were so lovely. I remember we would ransack her closets and try them on. Well, Tree was never terribly interested, but Cleo and I were in heaven wearing gold stilettos and green strappy sandals. We'd parade in front of the mirror, pretending we were just like glamorous Mommy."

Didier smiles at these images. "I'll be delighted to tell you some Sandrine stories," he says, "but right now, I think you two should get dressed as the Abadi cavalcade is arriving shortly."

In my room, Beebe puts on a black abaya and, upon my advice, adds lots of gold bracelets. I tell her, "The women in the

UAE love jewelry and wear the most beautiful anklets, earrings, and gold bracelets. When this was more of a Bedouin culture, women here used to carry their inheritance in their jewelry."

"REALLY, CLEO? I SUPPOSE we still do that in a way. My rings and pearls would be what I'd grab first if I needed money. A worldwide sisterhood, based upon our jewelry."

Beebe giggles. "I love these Arab men. They are so handsome in those long white cloaks. So handsome, just like that movie star in *Lawrence of Arabia*. What's his name?"

"Omar Sharif, though Peter O'Toole looked pretty good in whatever he wore too ... Let's rewatch that movie while you're here. It's one of my favorites. Ralph Fiennes in *The English Patient* also looks quite good in all of those drapey garments. Good grief, we are sounding like high school girls with movie star crushes."

"Oh, Cleo, you are more beautiful than any movie star. I think our mother was jealous of you. I was, for sure, but let's talk more about those white cloaks the Abadis wear."

"Kanduras. They originated in the Bedouin culture to reflect the sun's rays. I am sure the Abadis must each own hundreds of them. They always look so fresh and uncreased, I bet they change them all the time. And I love their white head scarves—held on with that black rope—which, since I am giving you a lesson, is called an agal. In the Bedouin days, agals were used to tie up camels. Now these dandies perfume them! I've had plenty of time to learn about this culture these past months. I've also been doing some work in a local shelter for abused girls."

Beebe looks at me, surprised. She doesn't know I was raped when I was nine by my father's friend, and how long it took for me to get over it.

"When I found out I was having a baby girl," I told her, "I decided I needed to help young girls, Beebe. If you like, we can go to the shelter this week to see the girls. They will fall head over heels in love with you. Believe me—they need love. My favorite is a little girl named Delia. I am so glad you will meet her."

Minutes later, I look at my sister in the mirror as we stand side by side, putting on makeup. "If it comes up, one of the men you'll meet tonight, Raj Abadi, went to college in Boston and married his American college sweetheart and she now lives in purdah—according to him, by her choice."

"Purdah?" By the look on Beebe's face, I can tell she has no idea what I'm talking about ... and why should she?

"She lives with her mother-in-law and never goes out. Fascinating life choices we all make, aren't they?"

"Well," Beebe says with a chuckle, "it's not so very different in my castle with Lady Maureen." Lady Maureen is Beebe's glorious mother-in-law, and when Lancaster is off shooting or fishing for months, and her sons James and Mark are at Eton, Beebe does live in a fabulous version of purdah. And she loves it.

Before we go down to greet the Abadi brothers, I put kohl around Beebe's eyes and mine, just like the women in Dubai do. I wonder whether we should wear headscarves. Normally I don't, but with Beebe's platinum blond hair, it crosses my mind. But I drop the thought as we hear the cars approaching on the front drive.

"As-salaam alaikum," I greet the Abadis at the front door. The five brothers are all here and I have explained to Beebe the wives never come. It is a different culture than ours and the women don't go out. I realize how lucky we are to be able to do whatever we want. But I know the Abadi's wives, except for Raj's American wife, grew up in this culture as did their mothers and I imagine they are very happy to be married to such wonderful men.

"Cleo! As-salaam alaikum!"

The Abadis would no doubt be quite surprised if they knew I killed an Al Qaeda leader with my bare hands just nine months ago. Important representatives of Dubai, these men are so gracious. They own hotels and malls and car dealerships and have real estate in the islands off Dubai too. They have their fingers in all the industry in Dubai.

We go right into dinner and they start to laugh as they outdo one another offering ways to keep us occupied before the baby comes—boats to explore the islands, drivers for shopping trips to insider places, a visit to the top of the Burj Khalifa Hotel, the only seven-star hotel in the world, to see its Royal Suite. Only occupied a few times a year, I saw it when I was visiting Didier a few years ago, and I know Beebe will love it. The faucets in the bathrooms have huge rubies for hot water and huge emeralds for cold water and solid gold bidets and toilets. The rooms are insanely ornate. Beebe and I are also offered desert demonstrations of falconry and invited to watch the young men who have ridden since birth perform for us on their steeds.

"Beebe?" my voice trembles. My abaya is turning red before my eyes. I stand up and the blood is suddenly pouring down my legs. "Beebe!"

"It's alright, Cleo." Beebe comes right over to me and takes my hand. The Abadis stand and leave talking into their phones to the hospital and to organize a group of cars to move us quickly through any traffic.

Less than five minutes later, Daddy and Beebe are helping me into a black SUV. I start babbling about anything but what is happening to me.

"We really need to cut down that palm tree ... It's sending roots out and they're pulling up the pavement. Did you notice the flower centerpiece is wilting? Oh, please tell the cook I am sorry not to have finished dinner ... although maybe we will as this is nothing." If I keep talking, maybe I can ward off the growing fear. I'm drenched in blood.

I am examined in mere minutes after our arrival at the hospital. After taking a look, Dr. Khalifa assures me I am fine. "Sayeda, Cleo, you're experiencing placenta previa, quite common in older mothers. The baby is fine. And now, we will go in and bring her to us."

"Yes, Doctor, God willing." I hold the nurse's hand tight and won't let it go as they wheel me into the operating room. *Trust* is all I keep saying to myself and then, *There is nothing to fear but fear itself,* which I think FDR said. The meds must be kicking in ... and then I am out cold.

I WAKE UP IN A HOSPITAL room to find my father holding my daughter. And standing next to Daddy is Beebe, and she is beaming.

A few minutes later, I fall back to sleep, smiling, knowing all is right with the world. I have a child, a baby girl, who looks perfect. For days, I have fevers which can happen with Cesareans. And my baby is jaundiced, so she has been living in intensive care.

After a long week, I finally hold my daughter in my arms. I've heard stories of holding your child for the first time, but I had no idea how intense that love could really be. I wept when the nurse put her in my arms. My daughter, Zelli Sandrine Gallier. I want the world to be good to her. I want fiercely to protect this baby of mine from any pain. She has my dimples and dark hair but her eyes are very blue. She is sleeping and I bless her with what every mother sends her newborn. I bless her with love and joy and peace.

The nanny that worked for Beebe for years, Nannie, arrived a day ago and now gently smiles at Zelli and at me as I start to fall back asleep again. Three days later, we are finally allowed to go home.

Beebe tells me she has subsequently learned so many things about Sandrine from Didier, and I expect I will be the recipient of her new knowledge soon. In the meantime, I'm so grateful that Nannie is here. The house and room for Zelli are all organized. And I am also grateful for the money I inherited from my mother's brilliant art purchases when she lived in Paris with my father. They will allow me to do everything for this baby.

Beebe has visited Raj's wife, the Boston girl who chose to live in purdah, and she has been to see the Burj with my father. He also took her to the local center for abused women and she met Delia. Beebe looks at me strangely as she speaks of Delia and the women and I think someone must have mentioned how I was part of this group of women.

Everything is perfect, though with my scar, it hurts to laugh, and Beebe's funny stories make me laugh and wince.

Zelli and her blue eyes fill our days and nights. I couldn't imagine greater happiness. I start making plans for her, what I will teach her and how we will travel together and where we will live.

And in the shorter term, there's the question of what I will do when I need to fill out the form naming who her father is. I worry that raising Zelli with no father will be hard on her. But then I know she will have such love from my sisters and her grandfather that she will be more than fine.

"Oh please, let her be alright."

CLEO, 4

I realize I will be praying for her night and day for the rest of my life as does every mother the world over.

FIONA, 1

Jimbo was desperate to know who owned the magical garden where we'd met. It was the principle, he said. But had I revealed the secret identity of the owner too early, I worried that Jimbo would no longer have any use for me. I needed to keep him captivated because despite myself, I'd begun to live for our little rendezvous. Gradually, our encounters became more regular and more intentioned and I couldn't have been happier.

One day, about six weeks after we'd first met, Jimbo did not show up at the garden on Monday as he usually had. We hadn't yet agreed on a proper meeting time but it was unspoken—or it felt that way to me. For hours, I waited on our bench, hoping, wishing, praying that at any moment I'd look up and there'd he'd be, riding up on his bicycle as if he were my prince on his stallion, coming to take me away, to rescue me from this cruel world. I know that sounds silly, crazy even, but that was the effect that this mysterious man had on me.

But minutes turned to hours and eventually I gave up on him. We'd had a perfectly pleasant time, exchanging stories about living in Hawaii last week when, once again, Jimbo had asked if who owned the garden was still a secret. I insisted it still was. Why did he want to know so desperately? Cat and Mouse. But who was the cat and who was the mouse?

The following week, I was sitting on my bench as I always did on Mondays, hoping for the best. I tried to trick myself, pretending that I no longer truly cared if the Ironman showed up and convincing myself into believing that I was enjoying my alone time in the garden as I had before Jimbo strode into my life. After all, this garden was my sanctuary, my haven. I was here for me. But then, as I was flipping the pages of my current book of choice, Miranda Carter's biography on Anthony Blunt, *His Lives*, all of that thinking crumbled. I looked up and there he was.

"You're here." Jimbo smiled as he got off his bicycle.

I tried not to seem too eager. "I am."

He grabbed his water bottle and took a thirsty sip. "I came last week but couldn't get in."

I'd completely forgotten about the gate code. "Oh, you don't have the code?"

"No, I came in behind the workers' cars the other times," Jimbo said as he sat beside me on the bench.

And then for hours, we talked about nothing, and about everything. About our unusual childhoods, about religion, about our mutual love for spy novels, and the general state of the world. All the while, we were both dissembling and it wasn't yet clear who was the more formidable opponent.

Then, finally, Jimbo got up off the bench and hopped on his loyal steed, his sleek black bicycle.

"Next time, you'll tell me your secret."

I glanced up at him. "And what secret is that?"

"The secret of who owns this garden."

"Ah, that secret ..." I smiled.

"See you here tomorrow?"

FIONA, 1

I knew I couldn't see him then. "Next Monday," I told Jimbo and gave him the gate code so that he'd never have any trouble accessing the garden again.

I couldn't wait until next Monday. My life thrilled me. I was living in a paradise and I had met a man, a man whom no one but me knew was a dissembler. I longed to discover his secret.

JULIA, 2

I can't even remember the last time I listened to my "I'm Nearly Engaged!" playlist. Cringe. I think it must've been all the way back on that godawful flight from JFK to Honolulu with that nice red-headed flight attendant: Jessica with her Jimmy Choo's.

Even though 2011 is only a year plus in the rearview, it feels like a lifetime ago. Looking back, I can't help but laugh (and squirm) at how utterly embarrassing I was back then. Following Jake all around Honolulu like a sorry little lap dog while he screwed that older woman behind my back. Pathetic!

Cleo. I guess part of me should be down on my knees thanking her for prying Jake out of my arms and pushing Ricky into them. Tonight I'm especially grateful.

It's the night before Thanksgiving, one of my very favorite nights of the whole year. Sometimes I think I enjoy the night before a holiday—the night before the Fourth of July, the night before Christmas, or the night before New Year's Eve—even more than the actual holiday itself. The anticipation of joy and merriment and romance never lets you down. You can always get rained out, or not be gifted that hot little leather jacket number you had your eye on, or worst of all, miss out on that perfect New Year's kiss when the clock strikes midnight. But on the night before, life is still rife with endless possibilities.

Jake will be at the Regans' house for Thanksgiving dinner, and I can't say I'm exactly looking forward to the reunion. Ever since Ricky and I got together in Honolulu, it's been weird all around—with Jake and me, with Jake and Ricky, and the whole Regan family. It took a little while for everyone to adjust to the whole brother swaperoo, myself included. For months, Jake couldn't even look me or Ricky in the eye. When we'd all be out in public, Miranda would introduce me as Ricky's "friend" and Tripp kept calling Ricky by Jake's name. Don't even get me started on Matt. Tomorrow is sure to be interesting.

But enough about tomorrow. Tonight I'm going to forget all about the worries of the future and focus on spicy rigatoni because Ricky has made a reservation at one of the all-time great New York City Italian restaurants, Carbone.

A piece of advice for those who've never been: if you can, exercise as much restraint as possible at lunchtime in order to save enough room for all the impossibly delicious antipasti, macaroni, secondi, and contoroni. And the bread. Oh, happy day, the bread. Take my word for it. Molto bene!

"Are you kidding?" Ricky asks, an incredulous look on his handsome face as I step out of our ensuite bathroom and into the bedroom that I recently finished decorating.

"What do you mean?" I ask back, though I already know the answer.

"Just when I think you can't get any more beautiful..."

"I'm wearing the most loose-fitting outfit I own." I laugh. "I might as well be wearing a muumuu!"

"I love it," Ricky flirts as he moves across our bedroom. He puts both strong, muscular hands around my waist before bringing me in for a sweet kiss.

JULIA, 2

I look down at the gold vintage Cartier watch left to me by my late mother, Constance. "Shoot, babe, we should go."

"We can be just a little late, can't we?" Ricky winks as he goes to town kissing my Jo Malone-spritzed neck.

"Carbone waits for no one!" I say with a giggle.

"Alright, alright." He presses a few buttons on his iPhone. "The Uber should be here in... yikes, one minute."

"WE'LL HAVE A BOTTLE of Dom Perignon, please," Ricky tells our portly waiter.

My almost jaw drops two flights of stairs. "What? No, babe. That's way too expensive. I'm totally fine with a bottle of Cab."

Ricky cracks a knowing smile and looks back at our waiter. "The Dom, please."

The waiter smiles, nods, and goes off on his merry way.

"Is there a special occasion I'm unaware of, Daddy Warbucks? When he only smiles in response, I say, "Wait. Did you get the promotion?"

"Not yet. Do I need a special occasion to celebrate with my number one gal?" Ricky says as he helps himself to some more of the best bread in the Western hemisphere. If I was still with Jake, I'd probably go a little easier on the carbs. But that's just one of the many, *many* perks about dating his younger yet somehow light years more mature brother. And so I dig in with glee.

Ricky doesn't totally have money to burn with his salary from *Slate* magazine, but the man does like to spoil me. Expensive champagne here, a weekend getaway there. Jake was like that in the beginning, but that came to a screeching halt like four months in. And even though Ricky and I have been going out for more than a year, the treats just keep on coming.

JULIA, 2

They say, when you know, you know. I used to think that was such a ridiculous statement. On one hand, well, of course you know. You know that the person who you're with is "the one," the person who you want to spend the rest of your life with, the person who you want to laugh with, cry with, and sleep with until your dying day. The person who you know you want by your side during the best of times and the worst of times. Of course you "know" these things. Why be with this person in the first place if you don't? But then again, how can you ever really know? Most relationships fall apart. Half of marriages end in divorce. Even in relationships destined not to last, something tells me both parties "knew" all of the above as well. Or, at least I hope so or then what else is the point? Riddle me that. But with Ricky, *I know.* He knows too, I can tell.

Suddenly the house speakers stop playing their classic Italian instrumental music—probably something like Vivaldi or Puccini—actually, it could be Yo-Yo Ma, for all I know. I've never been an ace with classical composers.

"Are you sure your mum doesn't need help with anything tomorrow?" I ask, debating another piece of bread.

"Miranda always makes holidays look so easy, but—"

No way. I hear the restaurant's music. It's track sixteen of my "I'm Nearly Engaged! Playlist:" "Marry You" by Bruno Mars starts blaring from Carbone's speakers. This song always reminds me of my favorite episode from *The Office,* the one where Jim and Pam finally get married and all of their co-workers surprise them when they dance down the aisle. I tear up every time. Jim and Pam. Now that's a love story. Sometimes Carbone plays the occasional Sinatra or Dean Martin ditty, but I can't remember the last time a classy joint like Carbone played anything in the Top 40.

I turn to Ricky and laugh. "I can't believe they're playing this song."

But there's a knowing smile plastered across his face. Last month, Ricky borrowed my iPod to go to the gym because his was out of power. It slipped my mind that I still hadn't deleted the world's most mortifying playlist and lo and behold, when Ricky returned to the apartment an hour later all hot and sweaty, he was blasting my boy Bruno—and that's hardly the most embarrassing song on the playlist. Ever since then, the playlist has been an inside joke between the two of us, but in my defense, the songs are pretty darn catchy.

Bruno is getting louder and louder and Ricky won't stop looking at me with this goofy smile as if he somehow knew that Carbone was going to—Oh my god. This is it. This is how it happens. Ricky slides off his chair and kneels at my feet. Even though I've admittedly imagined this moment thousands of times, I still can't fully comprehend that it's actually happening to me right now. My hands start shaking, and I can feel my chest flush with heat. Ricky's eyes stay focused on mine and his smile never disappears as he reaches into his blue blazer. Ohmygod, ohmygod, ohmygod. He pulls out a little black box and opens it to reveal an emerald cut diamond—ooh, it's big!—bracketed by two sapphires. This is really happening.

"Julia Turner..."

Breathe. Okay, you're not breathing, Julia. Don't forget to breathe!

"Yes?" I stammer.

"Will you marry me?"

I realize that besides the sounds of Bruno's pipes, the entire restaurant has gone silent. All eyes are on Ricky and moi.

"Yes!" I swallow. "Yes, of course, I'll marry you!"

JULIA, 2

Ricky half-stands as he crumbles into my quaking arms and gives me the best kiss of my entire life. The kiss is perfectly choreographed to the arrival at our table of our lovely, portly little waiter with the bottle of Dom. Everyone at Carbone—fellow diners, waiters, busboys, and even the snooty hostess—are smiling and applauding.

I'm not wearing the perfect outfit at the perfect beach before the perfect sunset. Instead, I'm in a muumuu, it's barely sixty degrees outside and our breaths smell like garlic.

I have never been happier.

TRIPP, 2

Miranda, Jake, Matt, and I have just gotten home from the Carol Sing at St. James Church on Seventy–First Street. On the walk back, while the snow started to fall, making the city feel like one of those little snow globes, Miranda informed me that Julia and Ricky are going to be late for dinner because they're stopping by a Christmas party for Julia's office first. I'm always the last to know everything.

The four of us are heading up to the living room on the "green carpeted stairs with the banisters covered in lovely holly and Christmas greens when Miranda stops short and gasps. My heart drops. When I get to the top of the staircase, I see what the rest of my family is staring at.

The entire living room is filled with white roses. They're everywhere. I mean, everywhere.

Could it be… ? No, I doubt Cleo would.

"Who sent these?" I ask.

"I don't know," says Miranda breathlessly. "Ask Jeannie."

Jeannie, our housekeeper and Jimmy J's wife, has worked for us for over thirty years. Jake excitedly sprints out of the room and into the kitchen. I can tell my firstborn is thinking the same thing I am. Moments later, he returns, crestfallen.

He reads from a small white card. "Thank you for having me at your festive celebration this evening. Looking forward to it. Sincerely, Ambassador Fayazid."

I'll admit that a small part of me is disappointed. Say what you want about Cleopatra, she never fails to fascinate. Miranda looks like the weight of the world has been lifted off her shoulders. I met Ambassador Fayazid just a few months earlier at my New York office. His family is thousands of miles away, at home in the UAE, so I figured it'd be a nice gesture to invite him over for Christmas dinner.

The ambassador arrives shortly thereafter with not one, but two excellent bottles of Pinot Noir. I knew he'd be a good addition.

"Thank you so much for the beautiful flowers, Ambassador!"

Upon his arrival, Miranda is beaming. She's still ecstatic that the sumptuous flowers didn't come from Cleo.

"What flowers?" he says back, poker-faced.

The smile vanishes from Miranda's face and reappears on Jake's. "The roses? There was a card—I thought it said they were from you?"

A sly expression slowly works its way across Ambassador Fayazid's tanned face.

"I'm only joking," he says jovially as he eyes the table full of flowers. "You know, I sent the white roses because I met an amazing woman on horseback in the desert a few weeks after you offered me this lovely invitation. Riding alongside her was her father, Didier, a friend of mine, and he introduced us. I told them I was living in New York and returning there in a week's time. She asked if I had friends in New York and when I told her I'd been invited to a Christmas Eve dinner by my lawyer, Tripp Regan, she advised that a thoughtful present for his family would be white roses. And then she said something so poetic, 'Did you know the Earth laughs in flowers?'"

Jake looks like he's seen a ghost. I'm sure I do, too, but I usher everyone over to the dining room table, mostly as a distraction maneuver. The table is full of silver trays that come out every year to be polished, and huge silver candelabras and silver bowls of holly and bright red napkins on a white tablecloth.

Miranda loves to decorate for the holidays and the carols have been playing since December first. The boys tease her, but they, too, love the ritual.

I DISTRACT MYSELF BY carving the turkey, for my sake as much as Miranda's. She may play innocent, but my wife is no dummy. If she sensed that anything went on with Cleo two years ago, I want to reassure Miranda now by my nonreaction at the mention of Cleo's name that she means nothing.

Matt mercifully chimes in: "I love these white iceberg roses, especially with the snow and ice tonight. I like the saying, 'The Earth laughs in flowers.' That sounds so Cleo. She was probably thinking of me since she knows how much I love flowers."

At every opportunity he gets, Matt can and does tell you all about foliage and bird life. Similarly, Miranda's parents would tell you at every chance they got about geological formations, her father, and the Roman gods and goddesses, her mother.

"Did I hear the name Cleo?" Julia asks as she and Ricky arrive in the dining room.

More distractions. Thank God. Miranda looks euphoric at their arrival.

Julia says sweetly to Ricky: "I have to admit, I love Cleo now. She's the one who brought us together!"

Looking up from the turkey, I catch Jake rolling his eyes. "Does Cleo live in the UAE, Ambassador?" he asks.

"Yes, I assume so. If I didn't know her father, I would've thought she might be a Saudi princess. She had a stallion horse, and her abaya was diamond-studded of the sort only royalty can afford. When she and Didier rode off into the desert, the abaya billowed behind her. It was a sight I will long remember."

My phone rings from inside my gray flannels, but my ringtone sounds different. I know that Miranda's gentle nudge is coming. That's her way. A gentle nudge here, a friendly pat there. After more than thirty years of marriage, we know the subtext behind every one of each other's gestures.

"Work," I inform Miranda with a bit more edge than I intended.

I answer my phone, but instead of a voice, the username ENDGAME appears, and a photo pops up. It's of a baby girl who looks to be about a year old, hugging a black cat with a huge purple bow. She has blue eyes and dimples. And there's a caption: *Zelli—your eyes, my dimples.*

Then the photo evaporates. It's onscreen for no more than eight seconds before it's forever lost in cyberspace. The entire table is staring at me. I hate when all eyes are on me—reminds me of drama class with good ol' Mrs. Huneke.

"Wrong number," I shrug and return to carving the turkey. Cleo would've been sure I couldn't trace the photo so why even bother?

Coincidentally, the baby picture arrives two years to the day after I gave her the kitten … and apparently a child too. My hands are shaking so hard I can hardly carve the damn turkey. A baby girl named Zelli with my blue eyes. Unable to speak, I am grateful Jake takes over the carving.

"What else did Cleo say to you?" Jake continues to probe the ambassador as he slices the turkey. Apparently his CIA training has yet to teach him how to hide his emotions, though Cleo Gallier has that effect on nearly all men.

"We spoke of horses," said Ambassador Fayazid. "Dubai is a mecca for incredible steeds."

Jake falls silent and looks confused. The ambassador is pretending—I'm sure this is a setup—that he doesn't know anything more.

He came to my law firm for advice. I expect Cleo was behind that too. Well, she's got style, I can't deny her that. And Ambassador Fayazid likely just sent her a text instructing her that now was a good time to message me. Long ago at a breakfast with Cleo at the Honolulu Marathon I told her that if I ever had a daughter, I wanted the baby to look like her, and I would have called her Zelli. My wish came true.

I must find them. Looks like I'm heading to Dubai.

December, 2013

SPENCER, 2

I have finally started writing a screenplay for my new film, which I expect to be a rather creative way to find out who killed my father, Richard Rensellear. I kept putting it off with other projects as it is likely to be quite painful. Yes, he pulled the trigger, but someone gave him no way out. And maybe that's what he deserved, but either way, I need to understand why. Driving another person to suicide is a form of murder and will make an interesting premise for a film or documentary, and perhaps a cathartic journey for me. I have just wrapped up my last picture, which is doing very well, so I have some time before I start the new one, which at this point is titled *Oracle*. It deals with a man and a woman (what doesn't) who meet while working in Rwanda. She has come over as a nurse and he as a doctor. During the genocide in Rwanda, many doctors and hospital workers were killed so medical professionals in the U.S. and other countries offered their services to teach in hospitals. Of course the nurse and doctor might not be what they seem to be, which is true in most of my movies.

I expect my father's so-called "dishonorable" act took place right before he started drinking and traveling the world.

I decided to track down his secretary from back then, who would have organized his trips. I remember Miss Bracken well. Back in the day, she was young with brown bangs and was invariably kind to my brother and me. At the funeral, she came over to us and gave us both a photo of our family that my father had on his office desk. He was so young in that picture, which I have in my bedroom in Hawaii.

Thirty-five years later, Miss Bracken must be married. Tracking her down might add suspense to the film. I wonder if it was the spy game that he was involved in.

I cannot forget Cleopatra Gallier turning white at the mention of my father's name. Perhaps she knew what he did. If it was spying, it would make sense she was so upset. But how would she have known? She was a young child at the time like I was.

I'm back at my mother's home in London. I haven't spent a Christmas with her in several decades and she asked if I might come this year as she will be celebrating her seventieth birthday. My wife and girls chose to stay in sunny Hawaii for the few days I am over here with my older brother and stepfather. Her birthday is December 23 and she is looking a bit like her age recently. She has been able to look youthful for a long while. But time does catch us all.

Sitting at the desk in my mother's study, I'm looking up Cleopatra's show, *Close Encounters*. According to Wikipedia, it's been "Off the air since December 2011," and then, it says nothing else. Weird, so production shut down shortly after my appearance ... These days, talk shows don't always last long, but hers seemed popular. I know this because I remember having my assistant look up their numbers before agreeing to go on. Morning talk shows tend to get the most eyeballs as legions of career men, and especially women, have them on as background noise before heading off on their commutes. I google the name "Cleo Gallier," and hardly anything shows up. Maybe she died, but then there would be an obituary, wouldn't there?

My tech gal loves this stuff, so I text her: "Q. I gotta job for you." Her name isn't actually Q but that's basically what Becky Polaski does for me; she's the gadgets-and-gizmos guru to my slick James Bond. *Ha.* I've never actually even met Becky in person. My DIT, digital imaging technician, on one of my first film's hooked me up with her. That was over eight years ago and ever since, Becky has been solving all of my tech-related issues and crises. In an increasingly technologically focused world, everyone should have their own Becky.

"Shoot," she answers.

"See what you can find out about Cleopatra Gallier. Cleopatra, spelled like the Liz Taylor character." I spell out her last name.

"That's it?"

"Yes, and by that I mean anything and everything." I smile, having a feeling that it won't be as easy as Becky thinks.

"Call you back in five."

Forty minutes later, my phone rings.

"Who is this chick?" Q asks.

"I'm assuming that means you couldn't find anything."

"Very little. And I went deep, man. Even my guy with an entry into the CIA was blocked. It is as though she doesn't exist and never has."

"Jesus."

"Sorry. I swear, I tried. You sure she's a real person?"

"Positive. We've met. She's very real."

"And very secretive."

"Alright, see ya. Onto your next check, Kay Bracken."

Becky, as usual, hangs up before I can even tell her good-bye. Back to her gadgets and gizmos, I suppose.

I lean back in the leather desk chair and get lost in thought. This is the problem with working in Hollywood. My mind is so easily manipulated, jumping to the wildest and most outlandish conclusions that I learned from movies.

A few minutes later, I get a text from Becky: *Easy one. Unfortunately, Kay Bracken died thirty years ago from a brain aneurysm.*

Thirty years ago. Damn. All her notes about my father's travel itineraries must be gone too.

I need to track down Cleo Gallier. Even if she was a child when my father died, she knows something about him or his death—of that I'm sure. I'm curious why her show ended so abruptly, and how her identity has been so thoroughly scrubbed from the internet that even a master techie can't find anything about her.

I'm heading back home to Honolulu in a few days to be with my family. I'm also eager to get back in the waves. I surf at the Banzai Pipeline, which is actually the main reason we moved to Hawaii. My wife, Melinda, and I are huge surf nuts. Riding those massive waves clears my head and soothes me in a way that no amount of meditation, or any other form of exercise even comes close to—and trust me, I've tried. I go to LA to shoot my movies, but mostly I prefer to be in Honolulu with the easy "vibe" and my family, though teenage daughters don't always give off an easy vibe.

The people who own the TV station Cleo's show was on might know something. I remember they had silly names. I am determined to unravel the strands of this spider web. It is getting more interesting with each answer I don't get.

New Year's Eve, 2013

JAKE, 4

Ricky popped the question to Julia only six weeks ago. They were graciously planning to skip an engagement party, just one step on an endless worldwide wedding tour. But when Mom gets an idea in her head, it's pretty near impossible to convince her otherwise. She's never aggressive but has her own wily way of getting whatever she wants.

So ... guess what I'm doing this New Year's Eve? Attending an engagement party for my younger brother and my ex-girlfriend. I'm a single, virile, good-looking guy in CIA training, and yet here I am: the dutiful brother.

Doubles, my parents favorite night club, handles everything, and since everyone will already be in the City over the Christmas holidays....

"It's perfect!" Mom insisted.

At the time, Julia countered, "Miranda, that's really kind of you but we don't need an engagement party. People are so busy this time of year anyway."

"Yeah, I doubt anyone needs to add yet another party to their dance card. Especially on New Year's," Ricky added.

"Your father will be in town, won't he?" said Mom. "Tripp hasn't had a chance to really celebrate you two yet. A New Year's Eve engagement party would be the perfect opportunity!"

Mom went back and forth with the happy couple for a few rounds, but somehow eventually got them to see her side.

If it was any other year, I'd be pissed. Pre-CIA, New Year's Eve was my thang. It was one of my favorite holidays and one that I looked forward to every year. Don't get the wrong idea. It's not like I'd head down to Times Square and voluntarily freeze my ass off with a crowd of tourists from Sheboygan, Wisconsin. No way, they're freaks. Instead, a group of Middlebury friends and I would determine the most exclusive party at some downtown hot spot and post up there for the night. But those days are over. Six months ago my life took a drastic left turn, and I'm not about to screw it up now.

Straightening my tie, I step out of the Uber onto the corner of Fifty-Ninth and Fifth. *Brrr.* I rub my hands together and blow hot air into them. It's about as cold as you'd think the last day of December in New York would be.

"Got it, bud?" I turn back to brother Matt as he takes his time getting out of the black Suburban.

"Yes, Jake. I'm okay," says Matt, a sliver of frustration in his voice.

"Let's wait for Mom and Dad," I shiver.

"You can. I'm freezing," Matt proclaims as he breezes past me toward the entrance of the Sherry-Netherland Hotel.

I agree with my brother and follow him inside. I'm pretty sure I have not set foot in this place since Suzie Rae's fabulous debutante afterparty. God, she was gorgeous, but this studly guy from Tennessee moved in fast, and since she seemed pretty engrossed with him, I moved on. I do wonder where she is now from time to time.

Standing behind a podium at the entrance, a man dressed in a nicely pressed tux greets us with a smile. "Happy New Year's Eve, gentlemen. Name?"

"Hey, yeah, Jake Regan. We're here for the engagement party."

"Splendid! Go right down, Mr. Regan." After he checks off our names, he gestures to the hidden door on our right. This leads to a red-and-pink mirrored flight of stairs.

I smile our thanks as Matt and I make our way down. Christmas decorations are still in place, which gives the place a festive vibe even though it's been a full week since everyone found their presents under the tree. I check myself out in the mirrored walls as we descend further into the hotel. Lately, I look as if I've physically stepped up my game a notch (if that's even possible). My arms are stronger, my stomach is firmer, and my thighs are wider. I wonder if anyone can tell just by looking at me that I'm training to be a CIA Agent. Let's hope not.

"Are you nervous, Jake?" Matt asks.

"Me? *Nah*, you know me. I don't get nervous. Why?"

"Well, Julia used to be your girlfriend ..."

At that, I have to laugh. "I appreciate you checking in, little bro, but that was a long time ago. Trust me."

"Yeah. Ricky and Julia are a much better couple anyway."

Count on Matty to give it to me straight. "Wow, thanks!" I laugh, putting one arm around Matt's neck and giving him a noogie with the other. With his Asperger's, he hates being touched by anyone, so it's a little game we play.

"*Ow! Ja-ake!*" Matt whines as we make our way into the party.

The roar of that party—probably a pretty lame party—grows louder as we approach. Old friends laughing, new friends shaking, glasses clinking, and music playing. I'm surprised to hear Drake's banger, "Started From The Bottom," at some place so goddamn stuffy as *Doubles*.

About twenty or so guests have already arrived, most of whom are crowding the happy couple or crowding the bar. Clearly, people want to put in an appearance early so they can slip out sooner rather than later and get on with the rest of their New Year's.

Matt trails me as we navigate our way toward every party's holy land: the bar.

"Well, look who it is: the brothers Regan!" And so it begins.

Any function of this nature is like an intense game of avoiding-relatives. No matter how many times you kill them with kindness or how many excuses you make to refresh your drink, there will always be more popping up from out of nowhere.

On the way to the bar, we're greeted with handshakes, hugs, and pats on the back. Matt and I finally cross the threshold where I am able to order a Corona for Matt and a tequila soda for myself from a bartender who looks like there's someplace he'd rather be.

I have to keep my cal count low as we're starting a particularly intense training schedule down in Langley in the New Year. I need to be in top shape if I'm going to make it out in one piece.

As Matt and I wait for our drinks, I scan the party. Damn, there's actually some talent here. I don't know why I'm surprised. Everyone knows the number one hot girl rule: hot girls are not loners. Where there's one, there are usually others. They flock together like birds. It must be embedded in their DNA.

Having dated the bride for over two years, I recognize a lot of her friends. There's Kathy, one of Julia's friends from the city. I'm pretty sure she hates me. Oh, and get a load of who she's gabbing with: Brenda. She is a famous ballet dancer. We went to see her in some ballet at the Joffrey. Too bad she hates me as she is just gorgeous. And over there you have … I wanna say it's Sandra? No, Stephanie! She's either an old friend from Julia's home in Gibraltar or from The Sorbonne. I remember she was a terrific artist. Because of my past with Julia, even flirting with me is breaking "girl code," which is a real bummer because let's just say it's been a while.

Stephanie is breaking girl code and smiling at me. And I am smiling back. She looks really great. Tempted to head over to her when the bartender hands Matt and me our drinks, I squeeze the lime into my cocktail, then turn to my brother.

"Cheers, bro."

"To Ricky and our new sister, Julia." Matt raises his glass. He has always been the most thoughtful of the Regan brothers. *Our new sister.* I have been so busy with training that I hadn't even thought of that.

Speaking of the brothers Regan, I catch Ricky's eye from across the party for the first time. He gives me a big smile, then rolls his eyes, embarrassed by the big fuss that all of these people are making over him and Julia. I know he's only making this gesture for my sake.

If Matt is the thoughtful one, Ricky, among his many other gifts, is the kindest. And lately, he's the happiest too. He can roll his eyes all he wants, but he ain't fooling me. Right here in this room with all these people and most notably, with Julia on his arm is exactly where that dude wants to be. Unless you were living under a rock, it was obvious that Ricky had a thing for Julia since Day One. Part of me thinks I should have stepped aside earlier, but the Lord works in mysterious ways.

"Ready for your toast, Jakey?"

JAKE, 4

I almost spit my tequila soda into my mother's eye after she pops out of nowhere. "Exsqueeze me?"

She's looking at me like I'm speaking Swahili. "*Exsquee*—Jake, what are you talking about?"

"What are *you* talking about?"

"I—your toast."

"What toast?" I ask her, losing patience.

Matt's watching us as if he were front row at Wimbledon, his head ricocheting back and forth between Mom and I like we were Venus and Serena. Dibs on Serena.

"The one you're giving." She smiles, careful not to look out of sorts. Mom knows the spotlight is on her tonight.

Taking a step closer and lowering my voice, I match her imperturbability. Let's be real, just as many eyes are on *moi*—especially when you factor in all the babes who, despite the Julia factor, are definitely still checking out your boy ... Yes, tonight belongs to Ricky but that doesn't mean I still can't be looking fly in my Loro Piana. I take a deep breath and keep my voice down. "Mom, you only mentioned a toast once. Honestly, I thought you were joking."

And now, as she looks me in the eye, I can tell she thinks that *I'm* joking. "Why would I joke about that?"

"I don't know, Mom. Don't you think it'd be weird if I said something? Lest, I remind you—"

"Yes, Jakey. Everyone already knows all about you and Julia."

As I look around the room in exasperation, my eyes again meet Ricky's. He gives me another smile. I hate to sound corny, in fact I avoid sap in all forms, but until this very second, I don't think I ever realized how much I love my youngest brother. I clear my throat as if to purge all the mush and gush that has temporarily seized control of my (strapping, ripped) body.

"I mean, does Ricky want me to say something?"

"You know your brother. He'd never say, but—"

Sigh. "Alright. I'll do it. But it's gonna be short."

"The best toasts usually are, Jakey." Mom smiles.

I've just made her the happiest woman on earth like only a favorite son can.

"Matty?" I nudge. "Stand up there with me, bud? You know I can't do it without you."

A beat. "OK."

My father, who has always possessed an uncanny sixth sense when it comes to avoiding family conflict, finally joins us after dodging a gaggle of Mom's tennis gal pals.

"How's everyone doing? We having fun yet?" Dad puts one arm around Mom and the other around me. He always honors Matt's need not to be touched.

"Oh, yeah. A real hoot." Sometimes I just can't help myself.

About thirty minutes and half a tequila soda later, the chiming of metal on glass quiets the party, which has swelled to about fifty or sixty guests. I gotta hand it to Ricky and Julia for corralling a group this size on New Year's at such short notice. Maybe they're more popular than I give them credit for. Julia's rollicking book club must have finally gotten off the ground.

The seas part, and I can see that the man holding a knife to his glass is none other than my number one fan (not) and Julia's father, Mather Turner. If Mather had his way, yours truly would be swimming with the fishies at the bottom of a lake somewhere. Not that I blame him.

"Good evening everyone and thank you so much for spending your New Year's Eve with us on this very special occasion."

A woman in a catering uniform hurries up and hands Mather a mic.

He thanks her, takes a breath, and starts pacing the red, pink, and white carpet. I glance over at the lovebirds. Ricky has one arm around Julia's waist, and she already looks to be on the brink of waterworks.

"As many of you know, it was just Julia and me back in Gibraltar for the longest time. Constance, Julia's mother, died when Julia was only seven years old." Mather turns to his daughter. "I can't imagine what it must have been like for you, Julia, growing up without a mother. Instead you were stuck with an old fuddy duddy who didn't know the difference between trainer shoes and a training bra!" *Hardee-har har.* "Julia, the day you were born was truly the *ne plus ultra* of my entire life. When your mother and I decided to have a baby, I surely didn't think that I'd end up doing the majority of the childrearing on my own. But I think we did alright, kid ..."

I'll spare you the rest of Mather's toast but by the time he wraps it up, there's hardly a dry eye in the house. He charmed them all with his rugged English accent and obscure European references and dopey dad jokes.

So how am I supposed to follow that? Satan, a.k.a. Mom, nudges me from behind. I'm too annoyed to acknowledge her. I know what her little prod means: *You're on, Jakey boy.*

I steel myself, take a breath, and bring the butter knife I'm holding—and want to gouge my eyes out with—up to my glass. *Ding, ding, ding.*

At once, sixty heads turn in my direction. One hundred and twenty eyes are on me, including Julia's, whose look like they're about to bulge out of their sockets. I throw her a reassuring look with a single flick of the eye and, in return, she smiles coyly and I can tell that she's understood. It's funny, the secret language of a couple never totally fades even long after a break-up. And even after one party gets engaged to the other's little brother …

The woman with the microphone scurries up to me and I thank her before I bring the mic up to my lips. Here goes nothing …

"Get it, Regan!" shouts Glazer, a fratty mutual friend of Ricky's and mine, from the back of the room. Glazer went to Middlebury with me and now works at the magazine with Ricky.

"Thanks, man." I start with an awkward laugh. "And good evening! To echo Math—*uh*, Mr. Turner's—opening sentiments, thank you to everyone for being here with my family tonight on New Year's Eve to celebrate my little brother and his stunning bride-to-be. You guys make a beautiful couple. Really," I try to toe the line between earnest and detached. "And big thanks to my parents, especially my mom—sorry, Dad—for putting this little shindig together," a smattering of polite applause. "For those of you who don't know me, which is hopefully very few, I'm Ricky's older, wiser, cooler, and all around much more interesting brother, Jake."

I pause for laughter, for which there is some. "Ricky, God knows why, has always looked up to me. If I was playing Mario Kart, Ricky had to play too. If I tried out for peewee hockey, Ricky was right behind me. They say, 'imitation is the sincerest form of flattery.' And I think that's true … except when you're a brooding sixteen-year-old with a rep to protect. I just couldn't shake the little pipsqueak! My mom thought I was nuts for refusing to wear matching Adidas tracksuits as my twelve-year old brother!"

A bit more laughter.

"But you know, sometimes it was nice having the little twerp around. He had no problem standing in any-sized net while I practiced line drives at his head. Even when we played tennis, he didn't even mind picking up all the balls between games while I sat and fanned myself in the shade. For the longest time, I kicked his ass in *everything*." I pause again. "But then, during Ricky's sophomore year in high school, much to my chagrin, we switched places and Ricky was suddenly better at every single sport. And that wasn't even the most infuriating part ... No, what really chapped my ass, was that Ricky wasn't only a suddenly incredible athlete, he was seemingly incredible without even trying! It was just, like, one day, *wham*! I'd like to think that he was secretly toiling away, perfecting his slapshot at all hours of the night just so that he could keep up, but who knows. Around this time, Ricky also sprouted a few inches, and so I quite literally had to start looking up to him too."

Up until this point, I've mostly been playing to the crowd but now I turn to Ricky, looking him directly in the eye and my tone becomes more serious. "Little brother, at some point over the past few years, I not only started looking up to you because you're literally one inch and three quarters taller, but I also started to look up to you, metaphorically. Besides being an all-star athlete, you're kinder than Mother Teresa, secretly funnier than any cast member on *SNL*, you have more charm than a prince, more patience than a saint, and you're smart as a whip—though, honestly, I have no clue what the hell it is you do at Slate." The audience chuckles along with me.

Ricky, laughing now, too, looks relieved. He casually wipes away a tear.

"Ricky was all of these things—well, mostly—before Julia, but I do seriously credit her with bringing out the best in him." As I turn toward Julia, I notice that she looks like she wants to crawl out of her porcelain skin.

"Julia, I have absolutely no idea why a nice gal like you wants to spend so much time with our wacky family, but we're eternally grateful. And after a lifetime of loud, sweaty, messy boys, my mother is especially so. You're also giving my father the daughter he never had and Matt the sister we all know he secretly wanted. Jules, I'm so lucky because I get your friendship for the rest of my life. Well, or at least for as long as you decide to put up with this guy." I point to Ricky and smile. I raise my glass and toast Ricky and Julia.

Everyone follows my lead.

"To the happy couple." The room repeats it after me. "Alright, now let's eat, shall we?"

I made them laugh, I made them cry, I made them contemplate their life choices. If I were a film, I'd be part of the Marvel franchise, baby: a certified hit!

Ricky and Julia hurry over and give me a joint bear hug.

MIRANDA, 2

As the mother of the groom, and a very handsome groom at that, I'm to wear beige and essentially disappear into the walls. Having been blessed with such an attractive family of boys, I've become quite used to blending into the background.

I already have my beige dress and matching shoes, having bought them both at the two corner shops I love on Lexington Avenue. The mother of the bride does all the work and she deserves all the attention with a more colorful dress. However, in this case, I have been asked to step in. Mather, Julia's father, who might have been flirting with me at the engagement party, asked if I'd be a surrogate for his wife who died when Julia was seven. I was delighted to jump in and promised I would.

I reserved the date and time that Julia and Ricky had requested at St. James Church and offered a reception at the Colony Club near our apartment. Most touchingly, Julia has asked that I get ready for the big day with her and all her gorgeous bridesmaids. Drinking champagne, getting our hair and makeup done, taking photos. I can hardly wait.

Julia, God bless her, is quite used to doing things in her own way as she's understandably been doing all her life.

I think Julia is perfect, but she certainly does things differently than I do. She is sending out invitations from a place called The Printery, not Tiffany. She's getting a four-layer chocolate cake, not a white one, though I admit that's something that I'm looking forward to. The flowers are lovely, white and red roses, as red is Julia's favorite color but I would have preferred what Tripp and I had: an all-white motif of orchids from my friend the fabulous florist, M. Barlow. However, it's not my wedding, I keep reminding myself, and so I go along with it all and smile.

On New Year's Day, the day after the engagement party, Julia and I are having a cozy time inside our Sixty-Second Street townhouse while the boys are out cross-country skiing in the park. Ricky wanted Julia to join them, but she said she was feeling a little "tired" from last night's festivities at *Doubles*.

She opts to stay home and read with me by the fire. Julia has her nose buried in a novel by Jessica Knoll called *Luckiest Girl Alive* while I'm reading one of my beloved Agatha Christie's.

"Mrs. Regan?" Julia looks up from her book.

"Julia, I think it's high time you start calling me Miranda."

"Okay, *Miranda*." She smiles. "Why do you think your marriage to Mr. Regan has been so happy? Any tricks I should know about?" Julia pulls a tartan plaid throw over herself.

I can hardly believe my ears. I can't remember the last time anyone has asked me for marriage advice, let alone a millennial. I'm taken aback. "How nice of you to ask, Julia. I'm flattered! "

"Well, I mean, you've been married for over thirty years. You must be doing something right!"

She does have a point. "Oh, I don't know… I'm sure I must seem like a boring Hannah Homemaker compared to a career woman like you."

That gets a laugh out of Julia, as I suspected it would. "Not everyone wants a career, Miranda. Live and let live, right?"

I agree.

"There's nothing wrong with living for your family," Julia adds. "I just hope you have some self-care and me time is all."

Self-care is one of those concepts that makes the women of my generation roll our eyes. It's as if the young gals of today feel it's their God-given right to get monthly facials and massages, weekly manicures, and have their own personal trainers. How any girl on a budget in New York City can afford all of that self-care nonsense is beyond me.

"Oh, don't worry about me ... What do you think I'm doing right now? Curling up in front of the fire with a good book and popcorn is my definition of Me Time! I couldn't be happier sitting here with you," I tell Julia as I start in on the popcorn.

"It's the little things ..." she grabs a handful of her own.

"Anyway, to answer your question, I think I have a knack for keeping everyone happy. To me, that's part of a long marriage. I smile and put up with things that aren't always the way I'd necessarily want them to be."

"Such as?"

"Well, once you realize that nothing's ever perfect, you're way ahead of the curve. Tripp's not perfect and neither am I, neither is Ricky, and please don't take offense but even you, Julia, are not perfect!"

"Oh, God. None taken."

"I've always thought it's best not to argue over unimportant things like who walks the dog or who chooses what we watch on television. Over the years, I've taken up many of Tripp's hobbies—even though deep down, I didn't love them all. I can't tell you how many marathons I've run with him all over God's green earth. And you'd be amazed by the number of tennis tournaments I play at our club every summer! I learned backgammon and chess when, trust me, I would've much preferred sitting right here in our house reading my mystery books."

"Well, if you don't mind me asking, why do you do it?"

"Making my family happy makes me exceptionally happy."

A pause. "I get that."

But does she?

"Yes, I mean, even though I can't stand the smell of brussels sprouts, oh I hate it, it's one of Tripp's favorite dishes and so I promised myself a long time ago that I'd make them for him once a week. Holding my breath for twenty minutes is well worth the expression on his face when he sees what's for dinner."

Julia takes this in as she grabs another handful of popcorn. I get up to fetch some M&Ms from my secret stash in the kitchen, which I love to mix in with the popcorn. It's probably the reason I weigh more than I should, but I love to eat, and I've become an expert at wearing the perfect clothes to hide my extra pounds.

Sitting back down on the couch, I pour the entire huge bag of M&Ms into the bowl of popcorn. Thank goodness Julia is here or I'd probably eat the whole thing.

"Wow, Miranda. Rock and roll," Julia laughs at the big bowl of chocolaty, buttery goodness.

I laugh along. "Have I ever told you about my mother, Julia?"

"Um," she looks back down at the bowl. "I don't think so, but Ricky's definitely mentioned her a few times."

"Oh, the boys hardly knew her. My parents weren't the most involved."

"Yeah, that's the gist of what Ricky said."

With the fire crackling, the huge flowering poinsettia plants around us, and comfy sofas to hide in, the scene is perfect for this talk. Our library has British racing green sofas and dark wood paneling. I spent years making our home warm and cozy. "I grew up without a mother, like you. Mine was alive, yes, but she preferred to live with the Roman Gods of Mount Olympus seven days a week. She was never there for me, nor was my father. He was a geologist who was too busy teaching, traveling, and writing about rock formations. They married quite late in life and were both stunned when I arrived on the scene. They never expected a child at age forty-three and forty-six, but they were very kind to me, even as their true loves were their studies. I think they often forgot about me," I say with a laugh. "I mean, they had food and clothes for me, but benign neglect may be a proper way to describe how I was raised."

"God, Miranda. I had no idea. I'm sorry."

"No, no. I only tell you this to help you understand why my family's everything to me."

"Yeah, it makes total sense."

"I envied all the other girls with parents who asked about their day and bought them bicycles and new clothes at the start of every school year," I say, trying to make light. "When I made the cheerleading team in college—"

"A cheerleader, Miranda? No way!"

I smile and nod. "I asked my parents what they thought, and they just patted my hand and told me how proud they were. During our conversations, I'd see them sneaking looks back at the stacks of papers on their desks, always wanting to disappear back into their work."

"I'm sure you made a fantastic cheerleader."

She really is a sweet girl. "Actually, I was!"

We're laughing again. As wonderful as it's been to raise three sons, I'm ecstatic that, after all these years, I finally have a daughter. "Well, I wasn't much to look at, but I had such fun being on the team with those girls. I was as plain then as I am now. I had no role models, and even less of a clue about love until a teacher gave me a book." I take one last handful of popcorn. "Don't move, I'll be right back."

I put down my Diet Coke, hurrying into my bedroom to get the book. *The* book. As I walk back in silently over the thick carpet, I wonder at Julia asking me about marriage. I have my red hair pulled back, and I'm dressed in a red blouse for Christmas and gray slacks.

What makes someone look good in one color and not another, I ponder as I sit back down near the popcorn medley. I have a close friend, Lia, on Sixty-Second Street who recently did Color Me Pretty, and I might just give that a try next week. She told me that they put different sheets of color palettes up to your cheeks and based on your skin tone, eye color, and hair, decide if you're spring, summer, winter, or autumn. Then, like my favorite scene in *Pretty Woman*, I imagine they bring you piles and piles of clothes in those tones for you to try on. I hand Julia my treasured tattered book.

Her eyes bulge as she reads the title. "*Advice to a Young Wife from an Old Mistress*. You're kidding?" As a happily engaged woman, I doubt Julia wants to be thinking about mistresses and I can't blame her.

"A teacher at my college gave this to me. Dr. Penni Cutler was very pretty, very happy, and not married. As a fellow professor, she knew my parents but unlike them, she was also a golfer. One day, while I was studying in the library, Dr. Cutler came to my cubicle, sat on my desk, and asked if I'd like to play golf with her.

'*Golf, Dr. Cutler? That's nice of you, but I don't know the first thing about golf,*' I told her.

'*Alright then, come out and walk the course with me Saturday and see what you think,*' she said. So at nine in the morning on Saturday I put on my sneakers and met her."

"Okay ..." Julia isn't exactly sure where I'm going with this.

"As you know, sports aren't exactly my thing, but cheerleading and walking with Dr. Cutler were. I'd join her every Saturday as she played. And it was during one of these walks that she told me the story of this book, a true story, about a thirty-year love affair between an eminent man and the divorced woman who was his mistress. Penny, as I was now calling her, was laughing when she told me that they caused a great scandal. They met for the first time in his office for a work assignment she had. On his wall, he had five museum quality paintings. Studying the paintings, she turned to him as the door closed when he walked in, '*How can you stand it?*' she asked. Meaning their beauty. And he replied, '*How could I stand it without them?*' I love that. I always imagine they fell in love right there."

"Penny had just hit a great long drive up to the green when she turned to me and pulled a small book out of her golf bag. '*The mistress told their story to the writer of this tattered book on the promise she'd never divulge their names,*' Penny told me. Now whenever I reread it, I want to know who they were because they seem so wonderful. I did some sleuthing, but I still can't figure it out. Michael Drury is the official author, but she recently died so I'm afraid we'll never know."

"And what happened to Penny?" Julia asks.

"Oh." I laugh. "She married a famous golfer amid a great scandal. I was her witness at their wedding. I gather she'd been *his* mistress for a long time!"

"Well, I definitely don't approve of a guy cheating on his wife, but I do love a good mystery," says Julia. "I can read it and maybe try to figure out who the offending parties are?"

"Yes, well, and when you read it, you might not think of them as offending parties. There were circumstances alluded to that made it impossible for him to leave his wife. I'm guessing she had Alzheimer's or some horrid disease, so he wouldn't leave her."

"Alright, I'll give it a read as soon as I'm done with this." She gestures toward *Luckiest Girl Alive*.

"There are some dates and hints all throughout the book. If it helps, here's what I have worked out so far. One, he was famous. Two, she was seventy-four when she told their story to Drury. Three, the book was published in 1965 which means she was born around 1890. Four, she'd been married, had a son, and was divorced before she met Matthew. That's not his real name but how she refers to him in the book, so I'm guessing she was approximately thirty-five when they met around 1925. Five, a scandal for over thirty years must be in the papers of that time. And six, we know they had thirty years together until he died. So the years of the scandal would be somewhere between 1920 to 1960." I pause, a bit winded after that long ramble. "How's that for deduction?"

Julia is smiling. "Jeez, Miranda, how many times have you read this?!"

"Again and again and I'll continue to read it."

"Well, you certainly do love your mysteries."

"Yes, Nancy Drew and I spent hours together when I was a child. But I'm losing the thread. We have this snowy day to discuss a marriage between yourself and Ricky." I open the book to one of the pages I have dog-eared. "Here is a quote from the book: "*Men must be bold or die inside and nobody was ever bold without being sometimes wrong. Marriage produces its own downfall when it tries to prevent boldness and sew up the future, and hope, and daring, in a bag.*""

"You see, I sent Tripp off on his China or Greek or Hungarian work trips without complaining or moaning about how difficult it was to take care of three young boys on my own for long stretches of time. Instead, I allowed him to have his 'boldness' free of guilt. And after all, I was happy then, too, as it was a time I could have the boys all to myself. And now when Tripp goes away, I have my Me Time to read and watch my PBS mysteries and spend a whole day in my bathrobe if I want to."

"I mean, whatever works for you," says Julia, "though I have a feeling Ricky leaving me alone with our future children to gallivant around the world for months on end isn't gonna fly with me, but again live and let live."

"I'm the person my parents never dreamed of being. And I hope my sons are good parents as well."

"Oh, I'm sure they will be. I can't wait for Ricky to be a father."

"Me too! I don't imagine Matt will marry. I'm afraid my middle son only has eyes for his plants!"

"Yes, I hope every girl can find themselves a man who looks at them the way Matt looks at a rhododendron!"

"I hope you and Ricky will always check up on him after Tripp and I are gone. I know Jake will help, but probably not with the consistency Matt might need."

"Oh, Miranda, of course we will. I adore Matt and he adores Ricky, so that'll be a piece of cake."

"You know, I wrote a short story called 'The Rose Tree' about all of this."

"Really? Miranda, I didn't know you wrote!"

"Well, it's a secret hobby. I love to—*oh dear*, here are the boys tromping back, and I don't have the chili ready." I rush off into the kitchen.

Julia comes to help and tells me she wants to read my short stories. Maybe I'll let her.

Two Years Earlier

FIONA, 2

From then on, Jimbo and I met regularly every Monday. This was far and away the highlight of my every week. I never mentioned that I lived in a very charming little house on the garden property, but I expected he'd find out about it one day and invade it to secret out my life. He'd want to know what mysteries I was hiding because I, too, was doing my best to find out his mysteries. Cat and Mouse.

When he finally got into my house, I wasn't there. He nearly fooled me.

"I knew you'd find out …" I said to him the next time we met on the bench. I'd been counting: this was our tenth meeting.

"Find out about what?"

"My house."

"Your house? I have no idea what you're talking about," Jimbo shrugged. He shifted, but didn't look over at me.

I played along. "Are you sure?"

"Quite." He paused. "What about your house? What's going on with it?"

"Someone broke into it, or at least I think they did. But whoever was behind it was fairly devious."

"Oh?"

"Yes, I almost didn't notice."

He paused again. "Then how do you even know someone was there?"

We still had not looked at each other. We were both committed to winning the game, the dissembling game.

"Well, whoever it was, found the key I kept hidden inside my canary cage."

Jimbo laughed. "You have a canary, Fiona? Aren't you just full of surprises."

Oh, he had no idea what surprises I was full of ...

Jimbo shook his head. "Well, out with it. What did this hidden key of yours unlock?"

"Oh, you know, all of the usual stuff," I said as I looked straight ahead at the big blue, cockatoo statue. Except it wasn't all of the usual stuff. It wasn't all of the usual stuff at all.

"Jewelry? Cash? That sort of thing, I assume?" Jimbo asked, his eyes glued to the big blue cockatoo too.

"Wouldn't you like to know ..." I smiled.

"Hey, everyone has their secrets. I understand."

Both of us were determined to keep up this charade, this cat and mouse—and neither Jimbo nor I had ever been a mouse a day in our lives.

"Yes, everyone does ..." I turned to him and wondered if he knew my deepest darkest one—not the fact that I loved him, the other secret.

But Jimbo's face was perfectly stoic. Oh, he was such a good dissembler. But he had not found out what the key unlocked, of that I was positive. He glanced over at me. "And what interesting things are you doing this week, Fiona?"

I had to stay interesting. It felt like my duty, and that was in part what kept him here. What intrigued him was what I knew and did.

"I'm looking for someone to use as a cover for some work in Manila."

His interest was piqued. Well done, me. "What do you mean by 'someone?'"

"Someone who can plausibly travel in and out of Manila a few times every year."

His eyes glazed over as he gazed out at the toucan sculpture to our right. I have learned that this is a part of Jimbo's process. Whenever he was digesting something, turning it over and examining it from every angle, his eyes would focus on whatever object was in front of him and he'd be quiet for a long while.

"What about a professor?" he finally asked me.

"A professor?"

"Yes, I know of a Shakespeare professor at the University of Miami. Dr. Marcus Pearson." He put his hand to his throat. That was his 'tell.' I'd seen it a few times when something was important to him—not good in a dissembler. I have no 'tell.' Why was Marcus Pearson so important to him, I wondered?

So I looked into it. Dr. Pearson was, indeed, a Shakespeare professor, and I spent a long time figuring out how to use him as a cover identity without leaving my fingerprints all over the place. Dr. Pearson looked quite heavy in his photos so I had to wonder how Jimbo knew him and why he selected him to be used. Not that skinny people don't know bigger people, but I was surprised at Pearson's photo. I went to the University of Manila online via my personal computer in my garden house that Rustikoff keeps clean. I researched their Shakespeare conferences to see which universities they hire their professors from. I discovered that professors from the University of Georgia and the University of Maryland were usually there for the conferences because of their strong Shakespeare departments.

I sent a gift anonymously of a pretty hefty sum—money, I now had a great deal of, thanks to my work with Rustikoff—to the University of Manila and asked the academics who hire visiting professors to look into a professor Dr. Marcus Pearson at the University of Miami who might be a good lecturer at their Shakespeare symposiums. Money talks and lo and behold, Dr. Marcus Pearson was invited to attend the very next conference. It was all put in place thanks to the bribery, subtly sent with no return address, an anonymous donation via a Bahamian bank saying Pearson would be a good candidate. Fear left me completely. Love is a powerful drug, and the heart wants what the heart wants.

When I told Jimbo I had made Dr. Pearson the cover, he looked at me with such amazement and happiness that right away, I craved more of that look. It was the air I breathed. I became single-minded to achieve that acknowledgement once again. That year, 2009, Jimbo gave me his Ironman medal. He had placed ninth. I still wear it under my clothes by day and at night.

"Fiona, you are amazing," he said.

"Thank you. But you're surrounded by amazing women, aren't you? You live on the property of one of Honolulu's local celebrities. Cleopatra Gallier must certainly be amazing too."

"Yes, she is," he said. "But the difference is she's amazing for the world. You are amazing just for me."

TRIPP, 3

My whole life changed when I got the phone call from Chris Castillo.

"You're not gonna believe this," Castillo warns.

Well, that's never good. "Should I be sitting down?" I ask, my teeth clenching and chest tightening.

"Probably. Are you alone?"

I take a seat on the cream-colored, monogrammed, uphol-stered bench that's been at the end of our king-sized bed for as long as we've lived on Sixty-Second Street. It's normally just there for decoration so I'm glad to put some much-needed mileage on it as I brace for Castillo's impact. "Yes. Alright. Go ahead."

"Okay, so a few hours ago, I was waiting for my flight back to New York at Austin International. I told you about my daughter's swim meet, right?"

"Right."

Castillo is a man devoted to the CIA, his wife, and to his daughter's swim meets. There's a chance Ana will qualify for the Olympics so he never misses one of her meets if he can help it. He's as knowledgeable and detailed about Ana's race times as he is about his work for the CIA, the most trustworthy and reliable man who is perpetually dressed in a blue blazer, turtleneck, and dark slacks with slicked back dark hair and high cheekbones. And yet his posture is appalling, so a lot of the time he looks older than he is.

"Anyway, I was studying stats for Ana's meet when I noticed this guy who looks kind of familiar walking down the concourse." Castillo pauses for dramatic effect. In another lifetime, he was Marlon Brando with a Brooklyn accent. This drives me nuts, which, I'm sure, is Castillo's biggest motivator. "I'm tryin' to place him when finally, *wham*! It hits me. I realize this guy looks a helluva lot like a slimmed down Dr. Marcus Pearson."

My heart stops. And then, almost instantly, it starts beating so hard and so fast that I think my whole chest might burst into tiny pieces. The day of Dr. Marcus Pearson's death remains one of the darkest moments in my professional career as a CIA agent. The professor died on our watch—*my* watch, really—after we assured him that he could trust us, that his precious life was safe in our hands. We instructed Pearson that he was not to vacate his tiny apartment without one of our men guarding him. But one afternoon he disobeyed orders and went out to buy sandwiches for a few other professors who were coming over to watch a football game on his new flatscreen TV.

"Keep in mind, I did Pearson's surveillance all those years," says Castillo.

"Yeah, I remember," I take a breath. "Get to the chase, man."

"I'm getting there. I'd memorized Pearson's walk, you know, and his hand gestures. Even how he sneezed. Everything. And I'm telling you, this guy in the Austin airport was Dr. Marcus Pearson, risen from the dead. Only in this version, he's clean shaven, about ninety-five pounds thinner, and dresses like Colonel Sanders."

I'm about to lose it. "Are you seriously telling me you think Pearson is alive?"

"Well … hold on. As he's walking to his gate, he gets one of those charley horse things. Back when I was keeping tabs on Pearson, he got them all the damn time. He had this routine where he'd walk around in a million circles to get rid of them. It was wacky. He'd bring his fists up to his shoulders, then open and close his fingers over and over. Guy looked kinda psychotic doin' it, but it must've done the trick." Another dramatic pause. "Well, guess what, this guy did the same exact thing—kept walking around in goofy circles, opening and closing his fists."

"You're tellin' me you think Pearson's back from the grave because some guy in an airport got a fucking charley horse? Castillo, c'mon, I don't have time for this."

But he keeps going. "So, I went over to him while he's doing his thing. I never met Pearson and he doesn't have the first clue that I even exist. So he'd have no way of recognizing me in case it turned out to be him. Anyway, I'm my usual smiling, charming self and I say, 'Hey there. You know my wife gets charley horses all the time. She's convinced it's all the chocolate she eats.'

"He laughs politely but sure as hell isn't as chatty as the professor. But I stay on him. I tell him I was in Austin for a few days and ask if he lives here. He just keeps doin' his thing, walking those circles. Which was fine. It gave me a chance to study him up close. And that's when I saw it." He's doing it again.

"Spit it out, Castillo."

"His ticket to Houston in his shirt pocket. I waved adios, then went straight to the gate and got a ticket on his flight."

"Okay…"

"Wanna guess where this guy was flying to from Houston?"

Call it a hunch. I don't miss a beat. "Honolulu."

"*Bingo.* He hopped on an Hawaiian Air flight. Wu and Durita are waiting for him at Inouye. I'm boarding a different flight there as we speak. Didn't want to take the same plane, in case I spooked him."

"Wait. You're on a flight to—"

He cuts me off again. "I just sent you some footage of him I took. What do you think?"

My phone vibrates. "One second."

I put Castillo on speaker before pulling up the video. He might have missed his calling as an Oscar-winning actor but Castillo's jittery camerawork sure leaves something to be desired.

"My hands were a little shaky."

No kidding. Castillo's camera follows a slender man in khakis and a bow tie. It's hard to get a good look at his face while he trudges through the airport. There are a few shots of his profile but it's one of the most crowded airports in America and so whatever images Castillo manages to get are brief and blurry.

But I recognize that walk. I studied that walk and mimicked that walk. Castillo is right and now, finally, I understand why he completely diverted his plans. Then again, walks aren't exactly snowflakes or fingerprints—it's not beyond the realm of possibility for two people to have identical walks.

"Okay, I'll bite. Let's say this is Pearson. What's his game? He faked his own death to what end? Don't get me wrong, the professor was smart as a whip but in more of a bookish, spent—Saturday-nights-in-High-School-reading-Shakespeare-all weekend, kinda way. I'm not sure I can picture him building a car bomb."

"What if he had help?"

"From?"

The other line is silent. The only thing I hear is the tick tock of the grandfather clock across Miranda and my bedroom. *Tick-tock. Tick-tock. Tick-tock.* I expect that what's now running through Chris Castillo's mind is the same thing that's running through mine.

"No. You don't actually think? No, it's not possible ..."

"Security team's doing a deeper dive into Pearson."

"For what, Chris? To see if Pearson has ties to Al Qaeda? He was a fucking Shakespeare professor."

Castillo takes a moment before giving me an answer. "AQ knows how to get around a background check, blow up a car, and hide someone away."

I need to be careful not to raise my voice too much because Miranda is downstairs. She knows better than to interrupt me when I'm on a work call and the last thing she'd ever do is eavesdrop, God bless her, but still. If I was at headquarters, I'd be screaming my bloody head off. "Are you honestly telling me that there's even a whisper of a chance that one of our assets was actually an undercover terrorist?!"

"I don't know yet. I'm just keeping you in the loop."

"Call me back the second you know anything. And have someone book me a flight to Honolulu, just in case."

"It's already done. Stand by."

I hung up. I've always been pretty realistic. I'm no spring chicken. But old habits die hard, and the alpha male in me hasn't croaked yet. This phone call was all the proof I needed that I'm still in the game. I really did believe that my undercover days were in the rearview and that the Mohammed Abdul Rahman op was my last mission in the field.

But then, that goddamn video. That guy in the bow tie looks an awful lot like Dr. Marcus Pearson. That video has lured me back. What pisses me off is that I went to great lengths to get Dr. Marcus Pearson's book, *I Am Iago*, posthumously published by Raines Cassell Books. Since he died on my watch, or so I thought, it was my tribute to him. Raines Cassell is a boutique publisher where the sister of an agent over here happens to work. Raines Cassell is no Random House, but I'm a CIA agent, not a literary expert. After I got back from Honolulu in 2011, Castillo and I poked around the agency to see if anyone had connections to the publishing world. Lo and behold, Johnny Mellon in Cyber Ops spoke up, introduced me to his sister Louise, and we made the whole thing happen. The book was a modest success for Raines Cassell with all the proceeds going to the Shakespeare department at The University of Miami.

If the professor really did fake his own death, the joke's on me if Miami names a brand new wing after him. Now I'm even questioning whether or not "Professor Pearson" even wrote the damn book in the first place.

My phone rings again. I take a breath, then pick up.

"Confirmed. It's him."

Son of Sam was busted because of a parking ticket. The Yorkshire Ripper was hauled in for having false license plates. And now, Dr. Marcus Pearson gets nabbed because of a goddamn charley horse.

It's the little things that get you caught.

PEARSON, 1

What blankets me is the identity of disguise. The past year has allowed my cloak as a slender, rather obvious caricature of a holiday maker to come into being. I had thought my portly, happy-go-lucky persona Dr. Marcus Pearson was who I was but finding out my brother was alive and that I could help him ripped the veil off. My brother whom I had idolized and who had become one of the most wanted terrorists in the world needed my assistance. Finally, I had found a life that I was actually living, not just reading or teaching. I came alive and shed my professorial life. I haven't had time to miss it, though I still read my beloved Shakespeare all the time at home, the only place where I am allowed to read it. We had lived during our childhood in the Philippines where our parents were friends with Imelda and Ferdinand Marcos and where my brother was converted to the beliefs of Al Qaeda. He had taken his trust fund money and joined AQ proving over the years he was a powerful warrior for them. His passion for jihad was like my passion for Shakespeare but mine was on paper. His was real. And now I am going to become a warrior and do what he has left for me to fulfill in a letter I received right after his death.

Othello told me my brother Mohammed Abdul Rahman was killed by a woman, though the world thinks he was in a biking accident. Cleopatra Gallier, I know that name. My brother lived on her property, but now Othello can't find her. She left Honolulu after she murdered my brother and has been hiding ever since.

Finally, I am on my way to Honolulu to fulfill my mission. Othello has fastidiously coordinated every detail under my new name, Odin James. This is not the first time that I have changed identities. I was born Peter Olson, son of Jim and Jessica Olson, and younger, adoring brother to Patrick. When my parents' friends Imelda and Ferdinand Marcos fell out of favor with the Filipino people, we all went to Honolulu with them. My brother stayed in the Philippines and never left even when our family returned to our home in America. We had become a family of three when Patrick stayed behind. Patrick converted to Islam and eventually turned to violent extremism blowing up a Bali nightclub killing hundreds and turning on Americans. When people realized he was my brother my parents and I went into witness protection as rage turned against us. That's when I became Marcus Pearson, ultimately Dr. Marcus Pearson, and changed my identity for the first time. I'd fallen in love with the works of William Shakespeare in a High School English class in our new home in Oregon, so putting on a disguise of a new identity made me feel like Feste who became a priest or Malvolio who dressed as a woman in *The Twelfth Night*. Or even like Bassanio who hid his true identity, pretending that he was a man of wealth and privilege from one of my favorite Shakespeare plays, *The Merchant of Venice*.

Othello, a code name for a friend of my terrorist brother, that I clearly chose as an homage to my past life, has been a master puppeteer waiting in the wings, pulling the many strings of my secret life for over two years now. It was he who orchestrated my fiery, violent "death" on that hot Miami day—a day that now feels like a lifetime ago. To the world, I died in an instant, in a blazing glory, my body burnt to a bloody crisp from the bomb that was planted in my car when the CIA had foolishly turned their backs. But that's not what really happened. Instead, as Othello and I meticulously planned, I hurried down to the basement of my apartment building as quickly as my hulking legs would take me. I had rehearsed the downward voyage several times, but still, my heart was pounding and my hands were shaking far worse than I'd anticipated. The thing that I remember the most from the moment when I had at long last arrived in the basement was the sound of a leaky faucet in the laundry room. *Drip, drip, drip.* In the haze of that chaotic moment, it sounded like footsteps, footsteps of the men who I worried would be chasing me for the rest of my life, into my next life as Odin James. Even now, I shudder everytime I hear a dribbling, drizzling faucet. But in those moments, I remind myself that no one is chasing me, no one is looking for me. Instead, they are only mourning the memory of the big, jolly professor. I could hear the car exploding, people screaming, and men running down the steps from my third-floor apartment, realizing in horror that I had left the apartment I was ordered to stay inside and as a result, "died" on their watch. I hated to cause them problems, they'd been so kind, but their pain was worth it if it meant I would be reunited with my long lost brother again. My brother the international terrorist Mohammed Abdul Rahman.

I hustled across the laundry room, over to the washing machine on the far left and tried to push it away from the concrete wall. My hands, wet with sweat, slid right off the white porcelain-coated steel.

"Shit!" I cursed at myself.

I wiped both hands off on my blue jeans, and pushed the machine again. The steel dragged loudly against the concrete floor, making a screeching sound that I worried the building's janitor or one of the maintenance men would hear. But I didn't have the luxury of worry. I crept into the hidden crawl space, grabbed the flashlight that I planted just yesterday, turned it on and turned back to the washing machine. I grabbed the plastic handle that I'd ashered onto the back of it during my first trial run of this very escape. The Whirlpool drags across the floor again, but it was worth it. I had to cover my tracks. I can't leave any traces of my escape route or raise any suspicion whatsoever.

My flashlight lights the way. Othello had discovered that this building had been built over an old, abandoned train station so I'd broken my lease and moved six blocks from my old apartment. It was all so that I could have access to this very tunnel, the dark, spooky, rat-infested tunnel that would lead me to my brand new life, my third life. I took several sharp breaths, keeping the claustrophobia at bay as best I could. The tunnel spit me out at a garage, a block away where I was picked up in a run-down black Fiat by the man I'd spend the next two years of my life with. His name was Joe Blow or at least that was what he told me to call him.

Emerging into the daylight was by far the most dangerous moment. Someone could recognize me. Someone could easily recognize me as I climbed into the Fiat parked at the curb. I had stashed a bike helmet, sunglasses, and a bright red jacket and, fortunately, it was only ten steps to the car. I was bundled into the back and off we went, blazing into my new life as Odin James where I would lose over one hundred pounds and learn combat training and how to use weapons. The journey was difficult leaving my life which was comfortable as portly Dr. Pearson to become a warrior. But blood counts and my brother wanted me to join him. Only his death prevented our meeting after my transformation took place.

SPENCER, 3

After I left London and my mother a few weeks ago, I happily returned to my family and our house in Honolulu. Now holed up in my home office, I searched through the digitized notes I'd prepared before my appearance on Cleopatra Gallier's show. The interview took place right after *The Last Touch* had wrapped before Christmas. There it is: December 23rd, 2011. And I see on the document the studio's address. It was out near Diamond Head. I remember she was an excellent interviewer and had certainly prepared before the show. She had watched trailers of my film and certainly studied my bio.

I had written on my agenda the names "Pudge and Pudding," and it started to come back. The couple owned the studio.

Picking up my cell, I phoned for an appointment telling the woman, Pudding, I think, that I was looking for Cleopatra Gallier. She bellowed out "So are we. Come right on over." So I did just that.

PUDGE AND PUDDING WERE ridiculously charming, as they'd been the first day I met them. I was brought into their huge offices and offered coffee, which was delicious. No surprise that with names like Pudge and Pudding, their proffered donuts and coffee cake were also terrific. They seemed to be caricatures, and I was suddenly envisioning them in my upcoming film as comic relief. Pudge was short and sturdy wearing an Austrian jacket which nearly closed over his huge stomach and Pudding was a bit taller than he was with big brown eyes and an even bigger girth. She was wearing a bright orange tunic and big dangling orange earrings.

"I'm looking for Cleo and wondered if you could help. Do you have any idea where she is?"

Tears ran down Pudding's heavy face as she looked at me with big brown doe eyes. "All we know is she was in Dubai but she stopped responding to us almost a year ago, so she could be anywhere by now."

Dubai. Interesting. I nod.

Pudding wiped away her sudden tears. "We got a letter from her in early March of last year, which was around when she was supposed to come back to Hawaii."

Her husband Pudge nods his enormous head. "We sure miss that girl."

"She wrote to us, telling us she couldn't come back but didn't say why," says Pudding.

"And that we should find a new host for her show," Pudge chimes in.

"Right." Pudding looks down at her feet. Her black Birkenstock sandals reveal bright pink toenails.

"Cleo emphasized how much we meant to her and how much the show meant to her," says Pudge, "but again, she gave absolutely no explanation about why she was leaving so suddenly."

It strikes me that Pudge was put off by Cleopatra's leaving. Despite sending a letter, suddenly walking out of your friends' lives without any reason is a pretty insensitive thing to do.

"She must have had a good reason," I said, looking at Pudding first, then Pudge. "Did anything happen to Cleo before she left?"

Husband and wife share a look. They both nod. "Her best friend on the island was killed," Pudge tells me. "You probably heard about it on the news. Jimbo Isom, a.k.a. Mohammed Abdul Rahman? Not only was he Cleo's best friend, he was actually planning a terrorist attack on Pearl Harbor while he was living on her property!"

"Oh, wow. Yeah, I obviously heard about that, but I didn't realize Cleo knew him."

"Yup," Pudge nods his gigantic head. "Those two were thick as thieves. And then to have him betray her—well, all of us really—in such a shocking fashion."

"He was never my favorite," Pudge chimes in.

"I had lived here in Honolulu when this went down, but I don't remember the exact circumstances. Remind me how this Jimbo died again," I probe.

"A biking accident," Pudge said flatly.

"Yeah, it had rained some earlier that day, so the roads were slick," Pudding adds. "He just skidded clear off the Koolah Cliff at this one gnarly turn."

"Cleo was with him. I think it messed her up pretty badly."

"Watching your friend fall off a cliff might do that to you," says Pudding.

Oh, wow. Now I knew my movie idea had legs. I needed to find the people who recovered the would-be terrorist's body.

"Her life was happy before Jimbo's betrayal?" I ask.

"Oh yes, she was very happy," Pudding says.

So why did she change her whole life and go into hiding? And in Dubai? I have to get Q on it.

Pudge adds, "I expect she's coming back. She hasn't sold her house—"

Pudding interrupts. "Yeah, and she said we could use it whenever we wanted, but we haven't taken her up on that. It would make me too sad to be there without her."

Pudge puts one of his gargantuan hands on his wife's shoulder. "I went back once. Just to see Jimbo's house or whatever the hell his terrorist name was. Anyway, it was all boarded up by the CIA or FBI or some such. It is way past Cleo's house and actually overlooks the Naval base. Pretty convenient for him."

So a terrorist lived on Cleo's property. There are many spider webs and, boy, will I enjoy pulling the threads to get the answers.

"Do you remember when you were on the show how one of the other guests was paralyzed with stage fright?" Pudding laughed. "'Cause that was Jake Regan. Cleo was crazy about him."

Pudge cuts in. "We all thought she had eyes for Jimbo, they were always together, but she flatly denied that."

Interesting. "You don't by chance know where Jake lives, do you?"

"I should have it in our old show records," says Pudge and went in to look into it. A minute later she returns with a slip of paper she'd written on. "Jake Regan, 80 North Moore Street in New York City."

Pudge hands me the address.

Pudding smiles as she eats her custardy donut. "I remember Cleo saying that Jake was staying at the Halekulani Hotel with his family over Christmas. He and Cleo only met when they got into a car accident ... and the rest of their love affair is history."

I couldn't wait to leave and look up Jake Regan and learn more about Mohammed Abdul Rahman and how he could have died like that. With such a daunting task before me, I needed to get to the Banzai Pipeline to surf. It's how I work things out. Not in dreams, the way my wife works out her problems but in deadly combat with some of the biggest waves in the world. Surfing heals whatever ails you.

Before I head to the beach, I contact Q, sending her on a search for info on the circumstances surrounding Mohammed Abdul Rahman's death.

I am pretty sure it was no accident. You don't make spy movies like I do without being a very suspicious person.

TRIPP, 4

"Welcome aboard, Mr. Regan. And thank you for your loyalty," the perky male flight attendant greets me as I hurry onto the plane.

Sweat glistens on my brow and forehead as I'm among the last passengers to board Delta Flight 303 with nonstop service from JFK to Inouye Airport. My cab driver was none too pleased, having to put up with me barking instructions about the quickest route to the airport. I want to get to Honolulu pronto.

I slide into the plane's second row and all but melt into my window seat. When I sprinted out the door with my carry-on and not much of an explanation, Miranda must have been surprised by my last-minute farewell. I wasn't scheduled to leave for my "work trip" to Dubai, to see Cleo and my daughter, until tomorrow so I had to recycle an old excuse that I've used a thousand times when anything unexpected comes up—the ol' a client needs me sooner than expected.

She was already cooking dinner, and one of my favorites at that, lemon pepper chicken with creamed spinach, when I broke the news.

Like clockwork, Miranda took it like a champ. "Oh. Okay, well, have a safe flight! Call when you land!"

Miranda rarely asks even the most innocuous of questions so she's either the most indifferent woman on the planet or she already knows the answers. I've fantasized about her being a secret agent, too, and what it'd be like for two spies to be married to each other without ever knowing. Then again, maybe I've seen *Mr. & Mrs. Smith* too many times. With Miranda's alleged fear of heights, seeming inability to stomach even the mildest of violence on TV, or tell even the whitest of lies, she might just be the best spy that the world has ever known. I chuckle to myself as I recline the seat back. Fantasizing about the secret identity of my wife beats obsessing over an old asset who has turned out to be something far more sinister ...

I reach into my briefcase and pull out Marcus Pearson's book, *Iago*. It's a long shot, but the professor's weapon was his pen. I'm praying for a miracle, hoping that a tiny clue is buried beneath Pearson's ramblings about his favorite trio: Othello, Iago, and Desdemona. I'm hoping there might be the slightest hint about how or why Pearson brilliantly deceived the CIA and me so deeply and for so long. The homely, amiable Professor Pearson I knew was a far cry from the sinful, conniving man that he apparently has become. Double identities.

In school, poetry and love stories were hardly big passions of mine, but thanks to the University of Miami professor I realized that Shakespeare was a huge fan of double identities. In fact, the whole plot of *Othello*, Pearson's favorite play, is about the hero's struggle with identity. Initially, Othello presents himself as this Venetian hero whose strong character is proof of his perfect soul. But then, as his "friend" Iago's vengeful spirit grows, Othello falls deeper and deeper under his dark spell, allowing his character, and ultimately his identity, to distort under Iago's will.

"*Speak of me as I am,*" the guilt ravaged Othello begs in the final scene after Iago has convinced him to stab his young, innocent bride to death. But Othello had already fallen victim to Iago's "*I am not what I am*" motiveless malevolence. And as with most Shakespeare tragedies, none of the characters in *Othello* lives to see another day.

I can't imagine that, deep down, the good Dr. Pearson is as evil as Iago. I have to believe that he's inherently Othello, but that somewhere along the way he got mixed up with his own version of a nasty Iago and fell under his dark spell.

My eyelids flutter up and down as I open the book. It's been a long day. Carelessly, I thumb through it, and read Pearson's thesis that Iago was protecting Othello, who seemed to have given up being a warrior for Desdemona. When the city needs him back as their fighter, Iago sets out to redeem him.

Marcus Pearson has transformed Iago into a hero. That's a new idea, I imagine, but I have not the foggiest idea as to what I'm even looking for. And then right before I fall asleep, the pages tumble to the dedication page. *To my brother, whose light was put out too young.*

ELEVEN-AND-A-HALF hours later, we touched down in Honolulu. I unbuckle my seatbelt and gather my blazer and briefcase from under the seat in front of me so that I can dart off the 747 the moment the door opens. After we taxi for what seems like three hours, finally I hear the *ding* I've been waiting for. That fantastic *ding* that signals the door has been opened and all us sardines are at long last allowed to vacate this tin can. I explode out of my seat, remove my carry-on from the overhead bin in one fell swoop, and am off like a rocket.

My phone rings as the perky male flight attendant, looking somewhat less perky from the eleven-hour ride, bids me adieu.

"Welcome to Honolulu, Mr. Regan. Enjoy your stay."

I nod thanks as I hurry off the plane and answer Castillo's call. "Hey, I just deplaned."

"I'm in Arrivals." He sounds on edge.

"Everything alright?"

One of Castillo's famous dramatic pauses, but this time it feels unintentional, as if he really doesn't know how to answer. "Not exactly."

Chris Castillo's cryptic words propel me through Inouye airport with even more gusto. Crisscrossing and zigzagging through young kids who have strayed from their parents, teenagers with their noses in cell phones and dilly-dallying old folks who stop to marvel at the wonders of the modern airport every few paces.

"Good flight?" Castillo asks after I eventually negotiate my way into Arrivals.

"Yeah, yeah. Fine. What's up?" I ask, breathlessly. "And please, spare me the long-winded bullshit."

"In the car." Castillo motions for the exit, grabs the handle of my black roller bag, and leads me out to the parking lot.

Two minutes later, we're in the backseat of a black Ford Explorer.

"Alright, cut the suspense. What the hell's going on?"

Castillo hands me Pearson's file. For the first time in his life, he gets straight to the point: "Agents found this in his storage facility."

I flip it open, dreading what's inside. The top document is a photo. A close-up of monogrammed, silver cufflinks. The letters in the monogram are hard to make out. I squint. Then I see it. *JSO* James Samuel Olson. That is on one side, but on the next page is a photo of PSO. James Samuel Olson is the father of Patrick Samuel Olson a.k.a. Mohammed Abdul Rahman, the Al Qaeda terrorist I hunted for years and who has haunted my dreams for even longer. He was an Ironman in Honolulu preparing to blow up Pearl Harbor when Cleopatra Gallier killed him. They had been best friends till she realized who she was harboring at her guest house and when he figured she knew who he was he went to throw her off the Koolah Cliffs. But Cleo had trained since age twelve in secret the art of Krav Maga and she turned the tables and killed him. No one knows this but my son Jake who saw her throw him over and told me. No one else knows.

"What the hell is Dr. Marcus Pearson doing with Jim Olson's cufflinks?" It's a stupid question with an answer that I'm not sure I even want to know.

"We think ..." Castillo clears his throat. "We believe that Marcus Pearson is Paul Samuel Olson, Abdul Rahman's brother."

My headache is instant. Mohammed Abdul Rahman is our Iago, after all. An endless stream of questions scrolls through my brain like a stock ticker at the bottom of a television screen. Was Pearson corrupt from the beginning? Or was he radicalized by his brother after he had already started working with us? The fact Pearson faked his own death and is now in Honolulu has to mean something. What's he up to?

"We think or know that Pearson is his brother?"

"We're about 90 percent. Now he goes by the name Odin James."

"Dare I ask the obvious question?"

Castillo sighs. "Of course Ops and Security did a thorough background check on Pearson, as they do on any potential asset. The fact that he changed his name when his family entered a government program at the age of nine blocked a lot of our intel. We think Al Qaeda must have helped him create a new identity." He pauses. "Boss, there's no way we would've missed this unless Pearson had their help." Castillo can hardly look at me, nervous for my reaction.

But the truth is, this is my screw up just as much as anyone else's. I was inside the professor's apartment more than any other agent, talked to him more than any other agent, knew him better than any other agent. Never once did I suspect anything was awry which proves to me I am no longer on top of my game.

"So, what's the plan?" I ask. "We need agents at Cleopatra Gallier's house. He might be in Honolulu to go to his brother's old cottage."

"Yeah. Well, your instincts are right, as usual."

Here we go again. "Spit it out," I ordered.

"Wu and Durita followed Pearson from the airport. He went straight to Ms. Gallier's. And you guessed it. He's hunkered down in Rahman's old cottage."

"Jesus. Okay." At the risk of sounding trite, I can't believe this is real. "Have them hang back. We want to catch this asshole in the act."

"In the act of doing what?"

"I don't know. Think he suspects we're on to him?"

"We don't think so, but he got a call when he got off the plane which was untraceable which puts up a red flag. We're taking nothing for granted this time. I hope I didn't spook him in Austin."

I nod as the Explorer pulls up to the CIA field office.

Castillo and I thank our driver and head into the brick building for a briefing. Inside, I shake the hands of some agents that I've met before and others that I haven't.

"Good to have you back," says Chester Wu.

"Good to see you, Wu," I nod. "You too, Durita."

Back in 2011, Agents Wu and Durita posed as Misters Chen and Huang as part of my "China deal" cover story for Miranda's benefit on Christmas Eve. Since then, Wu and Durita have moved up the ranks. Three years ago, they were both counterterrorism analysts, agents who assess the intentions and motivations of foreign terrorist groups like Al Qaeda. From understanding the plans and capabilities of these groups to identifying specific threats to the U.S. and our interests, counterterrorism analysts are the ones who are supposed to preempt attacks and disrupt terrorist networks. Even though Abdul Rahman wasn't either of their cases anymore, this one was personal to us all.

I look from Durita to Wu. "You tailed Pearson to the Gallier residence?"

Chester Wu nods. "Yeah. He looks completely different from his photos."

"It's amazing what Jenny Craig and some push-ups can do." Durita smirks. Durita seems to have need of Jenny Craig. He has put on a good thirty pounds since I last saw him when we brought up Jimbo's body from the bottom of the cliff a few years ago. He used to be very slight and looked like he never needed to shave, but now he has sure bulked up. He turns to me. "I'm sorry if this is difficult for you. I know how closely you worked with Dr. Pearson. A few years back, I had an asset turn on me too. It stings."

"Yeah. More than anything I'm just pissed at myself for not seeing it earlier. What happened to your guy?"

"Dead."

I nod. "Has Pearson moved from Abdul Rahman's guesthouse?"

"Nope," said Wu. "If this former fatso so much as takes a piss, we'll know about it."

That's what I like to hear. "Alright, good. How's Ops, Wu?"

"Eh, still getting my feet wet." Wu smiles. He has a very warm, congenial smile. I'm sure it served him well in the field.

"And what about you, Dorito?" A lot of the guys call him that. I've even heard someone call him Cool Ranch. "I hear they promoted your ass all the way up to Chief Info."

"Crazy, right? What about you? What's your next move?"

I smile and shrug.

After I disclose the dedication in Pearson's book "to my brother whose light was put out too soon" my fellow agents agree that it has to be a reference to Mohammed Abdul Rahman. I stand up so fast that I bump my chair over as I realize this is not possible. "This dedication is all wrong. The timing is way off. Pearson was 'dead' before his brother died, so he couldn't have written that dedication. So who wrote it, and why and how did it get into the book? I am guessing whoever called to warn him as he landed that we were on to him was also involved in that dedication. Durita and Wu find out who handled the book and see if they have any info on the dedication." They both open their computers as we continue the briefing.

I learned that three officers knocked on Pearson's old apartment in Coral Gables yesterday afternoon at around the same time I was boarding my flight.

To the surprise of absolutely nobody, the new tenants, a nice young couple in their mid-thirties, did not hold onto any of Pearson's old stuff. All his belongings were sent to a local CIA facility as his next of kin—surprise, surprise—could not be reached at the time of Pearson's death. He was unmarried, and we thought he was an only child. His parents had both died. Even still, to fulfill their due diligence, the three officers did a thorough search of Pearson's old digs and came up with a grand total of squat.

Across town, two other officers accessed Pearson's locker at the Agency's Miami storage facility. In the unfortunate event that an asset dies while he or she is working with us and no next of kin can be located, their belongings are transported to a special facility. Your government tax dollars are being put to good use, I can assure you … If no one claims said belongings after twenty-five years, they are disposed of. The reason we keep them for so long is in case incidents like this arise.

When Officers Keough and Ventura unlocked Dr. Pearson's locker yesterday afternoon, they didn't find much of anything. There were hardly any photos of Pearson as a child, which, given this latest wrinkle, makes a lot of sense. It didn't bother me back when I used to go to his apartment. Lots of people don't hold onto photos from their childhood. In fact, it always struck me as slightly weird when a grown adult has piles and piles of old photos of themselves receiving their first communion or dressed as the Wicked Witch of The West in their seventh-grade play.

Needless to say, there weren't any photos that linked Pearson to his homicidal brother. No paperwork either. They hoped to find phone records connecting him to Mohammed Abdul Rahman or some sort of money trail with an unknown foreign entity, or even newspaper clippings where Rahman's name was mentioned. There was nothing.

They almost didn't even bother going through his clothing. Clothing rarely leads to any real, concrete clues. But every once and a while, we get lucky. I don't know Agent Keough personally, but Castillo does and he tells me he's a meticulous agent, sometimes infuriatingly so. These types can be exhausting to work with, but their fastidious ethic can be invaluable.

Ventura had been ready to scram for over an hour. Given the odds of finding anything worth a damn, Ventura wanted to blow off the wardrobe. But Keough insisted that they stay and leave no stone unturned.

The blazer was one of the last items Keough happened to look through. And thankfully, like a good little upwardly mobile agent, Keough was familiar with the Rahman case. When we cracked it—or, rather, when Cleo threw her terrorist tenant off the cliff—a lot of the up-and-coming agents hoping to work on future high-profile cases such as this one diligently studied the Rahman case.

Keough had seen these cufflinks he found before, but in another file: Mohammed Abdul Rahman's.

THE BRIEFING LASTED for hours. By hour three, I was starting to feel intensely claustrophobic. I needed to get out of that beige conference room and practically sprinted to the car that the agency is loaning me. Castillo ditched the Explorer, and I drove us both to our hotel.

"I mean, really. What are the odds?"

"That we'd unknowingly pick the brother of the international terrorist as our asset?"

"It can't just be a coincidence. We have someone in the Agency who set this up. It has to be that. We have a traitor in our midst. Someone called Pearson when he got off the plane. It has to be one of us letting him know we are on to him."

I met Pearson five years ago. When I recruited him, he must've gotten in touch with his brother and warned him. Mohammed, not believing his good fortune, jumped at the opportunity and told his brother to let us use him.

The professor was the connective tissue of the whole plan. This explains how Rahman and Al Qaeda knew every movement I made in Manila. How I felt someone was following me, and how my game was constantly thwarted. They knew when I was coming and what I'd be doing and when I would return. Pearson fed Rahman everything.

But how did they get me to use Pearson in particular? This, I don't get. We interviewed several Shakespeare professors for our purposes before choosing Pearson. Again, the awful thought comes that someone in the Agency was in contact with Rahman and set this up. I almost shake at the thought. But it is more than possible. It is most likely.

FIONA, 3

Jimbo had to know that I loved him. I never married and now I think that I finally understood why. I was looking in all the wrong places and—inexplicably!—I found the love of my life at age forty-five in an incredible athlete who was a passionate believer in Al-Qaeda. That he was an Al Qaeda leader stunned me. That was his dark, dangerous secret that he finally revealed to me. He was dissembling to the world, pretending that he was here in Honolulu to compete in the Ironman. By the time I met Jimbo, he'd been competing—and doing quite well—in the Ironman competitions for two years. Other people I had engaged with were so dry and so limited. No imaginations and no desire to play cat and mouse. I needed that game. I lived for that game.

I already knew a great deal about AQ ideology from studying it, well, really since 9/11. In layman's terms, a follower of Al-Qaeda supports the removal of all foreign and secular influences in Muslim countries, perceiving them all to be corrupt departures from the true Islam faith. Fundamentalist followers of Islam are incredibly devout, many of them believing that a Christian–Jewish alliance led by the United States is conspiring to destroy Islam. They see Westerners as the enemy, and nothing more. And we are.

As I came to understand that this was Jimbo's belief, he skillfully drew me into it. So many have converted for love. We'd wander through the vast acreage of the garden where to the east we could vaguely make out the landing strips for planes. I kept imagining the various gardeners observing us, assuming we were lovers out for our weekly romantic stroll.

"Are you ever going to tell me?"

"You mean the secret of the garden?"

He laughed as we turned a corner toward the huge, hulking peacock sculptures. The peacocks are his favorite sculptures in the garden and I suppose that is fitting. Jimbo's high cheekbones, piercing blue eyes, blond hair, and perfectly fit physique are his colorful plumage of feathers. Everyone in Jimbo's vast and varied orbit is attracted and charmed by his breathtaking feathers. His feathers are what get me to finally reveal my secret of the garden.

I take a deep breath. "Anatoly Rustikoff, a Russian oligarch, owns it."

"You're kidding," he almost laughs.

I shake my head. "He has more money than God but he is dying of a mysterious illness."

"How mysterious?"

"Well, as I said, no one knows. But a few years ago, after a trip to the Amazon with his wife, Rustikoff returned to Russia a changed man. He became convinced that a certain tree bark found in the Amazon held great healing properties and realized that the trees might be the one thing that could actually keep him alive. And what do you need to keep trees alive?" It was a rhetorical question, but I instinctively turned to Jimbo for an answer.

"Birds." Clever man.

"Correct. So, what does the Russian oligarch who has everything except time do?" This time, I answered my own question. "Why, he builds a secret sanctuary where he can grow his own bark, of course with a multitude of exquisite birds."

"But why here, why not in Russia?"Jimbo asked.

"Because of the temperatures. Russia was too cold. Hawaii was perfect and Rustikoff has tentacles everywhere. No one loves a bribe more than the Brazilian government, so he had no problem getting the bark out of South America. In order to retain the bark's pureness, Rustikoff opted to build his own private sanctuary but seeing as he lives thousands of miles away, he needed somebody local to look after it. Someone he could trust."

"So, that's where you enter the picture," Jimbo nods as we come back to our bench and sit in our respective places.

"Everywhere, the underworld knows one another and I've been doing 'favors' for people for a long time." I pause and look over at Jimbo. I had never seen him this riveted. "I have access to a lot of people."

"What kind of people?"

I knew Jimbo was going to ask me that. What I'm about to reveal is a big risk but one worth taking. "Police, lawmakers, local criminals. Everyone."

"Everyone?"

"I have a good reputation," I nod. "That carries a lot of favor. And people know me, including Rustikoff's employees. They asked around about me and eventually, I was approached. I agreed to keep his sanctuary off the radar for a fee."

"A very large one, I'm sure," Jimbo smiled.

"You noticed the landing strip for the cargo planes?"

Jimbo nods. "But barely. It's very well hidden."

"Rustikoff flies in everything he needs. The birds, the trees, everything. And from time to time, he flies in, too—with his artillery of bodyguards, his wife who never leaves his side, and friends. It's quite the entourage."

I looked out at the garden, then back at Jimbo. I could see his wheels turning from across the bench. "Well, this is by far the most interesting conversation I've had since I got to Honolulu," he smiled.

At that moment, I felt pure joy. I was like a schoolgirl receiving an A+ on the exam she had studied day and night for. I think that was also the moment Jimbo knew where he'd get the financing he needed for his next jihad.

Nothing in this world corrupts like love, and I became Jimbo's willing helper. Back in those days, I was often reminded of the words of Aretha Franklin in her song, "What I Did For Love." It became my anthem, and it still is. I knew Jimbo was using me, but I wanted him to. I craved his praise and his attention and when I was not with him, he was all I could think and dream about. I hummed my song and he loved my voice so I sang it to him in my falsetto that resembles the Vatican choir boys as we wandered through the garden. We decided to name the garden Jannah, which means "paradise" in Islam and Jannah is the final abode of the righteous Islamic believer. I have often wondered, were we tempting fate with that name?

"Kiss today goodbye, And point me toward tomorrow, We did what we had to do, Won't forget, can't regret, What I did for love."

And so it began. I did unimaginable things for love.

January 2014

PEARSON, 2

The wheels of the massive 747 skid onto the runway and my whole top half lurches forward as the pilot jams on the brakes.

I turn to the woman next to me, whom I've avoided for the past eight hours, and she offers me a friendly look. Her brown eyes bulge as if to say, "yikes."

I was hoping that I'd manage to get some rest on my long sojourn, but I couldn't sleep a wink. I couldn't even read my book or watch one of Delta's in-flight movies for $6.99. I'm too wired, too excited. I am on my way to fulfilling the mission that I have been in training for the past twenty-four months. I look out the window at the sun shining and tropical palm trees, instantly feeling closer to my older brother whom I haven't seen since we were teenagers. He'd be proud.

But just as my excitement is growing, I receive a devastating text from Othello. The text is only two words. *They know.* I know in an instant who he means by "they." There's no one else that it could be except for The CIA. The CIA knows I'm here. But how can this be? My fingers, quaking in fear, move across my phone's keyboard, as I type that very question to Othello.

Moments later, I receive another text. *Charley horse.* I can always tell when Othello isn't alone. His texts are brief, curt even. At first, I'm baffled. The CIA knows I'm in Honolulu because of a charley horse? And then it hits me. The Austin airport. That irritating Hispanic-looking man who came up to me and kept droning on about his wife's charley horses while I was walking off one of my own. I thought it was a strange encounter, but I just chalked up the man's affable, if not overly familiar, attitude to him being yet another friendly southerner. But he knew who I was. A stranger in the airport knew exactly who I was. I had never even laid eyes on the man before, but he knew me.

My fingers type furiously. *Who is he?* Thirty seconds go by without a response from Othello. I wipe my sweaty brow as the plane pulls into the gate. Another thirty seconds tick by, then another. Finally, after two-and-a-half minutes, my phone buzzes. This time, it's a longer text. Othello must be alone now.

Othello tells me that the man's name from the Austin airport is Chris Castillo and that he had worked with Tripp Regan on my case for years. The reason I had never met him was because this Castillo person worked behind the scenes, on my surveillance. He had been studying me for years and that's why he decided to approach me, not out of concern for a stupid charley horse. Having lost one hundred pounds, I look like a shell of the man that I once was as Dr. Marcus Pearson. I have essentially shed one whole person, but still, this Chris Castillo recognized me. What are the bloody odds? Othello booked all of my travel. This is on him.

Stay calm, Othello tells me. But that's a hell of a lot easier said than done.

I'm in full panic mode now. I text him back as the flight attendant opens the cabin door. *Stay calm?* The game has completely changed. Instead of making my way to my brother's house under the cloak of anonymity, now I have a target on my back. Daniel Inouye International will be crawling with the CIA. *How can I possibly stay calm?* I look out the window and contemplate my options, but I don't have any. It's not like I can stay on the plane, avoiding the CIA, until it takes off for its next destination. I have no other choice. I have to get off this plane and face the CIA.

Even though I'm sitting toward the front of the plane in the fifth row, I take my time getting off the plane. Not only do I need several more minutes to calm myself down, but also I need to blend in with the crowd. The woman sitting next to me offers me a small smile as she exits the row. But I don't follow her, not just yet, until more people pass.

As I finally slide out of the fifth row, I remember something that I learned from Tripp Regan. Tripp naturally walked at a much quicker clip than my usual lumber, but he was so good at fully embodying me because he was able to nail the way I walked. It was actually quite remarkable. And so I decided that I'd make my grand entrance into the airport with a limp, hoping that I'd somehow be just a little bit less recognizable to the CIA.

Stepping off the jet bridge, my eyes dart around terminal three. I'm relieved to find that the place is a mob scene. It's the Wednesday before the long Martin Luther King weekend, so perhaps these travelers are getting a jump on the holiday. I'm grateful for them all, but any one of these people could be undercover agents working for the CIA. Glancing around nervously, none of these strangers' eyes meet mine, as I nervously look around for the restroom that Othello instructed I duck into. Ah, there it is.

I step inside the restroom across from Hudson News where Othello has stashed another set of clothes for me. I hurry into the first stall, which has an "Out Of Order" sign hanging on the doorknob, and change into a dark T-shirt, shorts, sneakers, a wide-brimmed Panama hat, and glasses. The CIA will most likely still recognize me but it might at least give me a few minutes head start.

I hobble outside to the arrivals curb, open my phone, and order an Uber to take me straight to my brother's cabin. I try not to keep looking over my shoulder as I wait for Kamir in a white Toyota Corolla.

Less than four minutes later, I'm in the backseat of Kamir's car pulling out of the airport on my way to Cleopatra Gallier's property. I go straight to my brother's house, a mile down the driveway from the main house.

My heart is pounding as I get out of Kamir's Corolla. He gets my bag out of the trunk, my eyes are glued to my brother's little house.

"Enjoy your trip," Kamir smiles as he hands me my bag.

"I will," I smile back. Oh, I certainly will enjoy my trip.

There is still police tape on the front door. I push open the wooden door, holding my breath at what I'll find inside. If only my brother would be waiting here for me with open arms, but instead, I am surrounded by nothing. The CIA removed all his items. I put my bag down and walk across the small living room, toward the kitchen and open the refrigerator. As promised, Othello left food and drinks inside. Thank goodness, I'm famished. The food on the plane looked inedible, and at the time, I was too excited to eat. There's water, Diet Cokes, and premade turkey sandwiches that he picked up at the deli.

I'm to wait until darkness falls before I make my way to my brother's cave. Othello hid a map underneath the floorboards in the bedroom that will show me the way. Finally, at 8:15 pm, I open the front door and begin my trek to the cave. All I can hear is the ocean's waves crashing on the beach below me and the soothing chirps from the crickets. Less than twelve minutes later, I have reached the base of my brother's cave. I'm looking up at the rock face, figuring out the best plan of attack, when I hear a noise. My head whips around, and my eyes dart every which way trying to find where it was coming from. It sounded like a branch snapping in two. Othello told me that the CIA was instructed not to follow, but maybe he got it wrong. Maybe he just told me that only to mitigate my fears, ensuring that I would stick to the plan and carry out my brother's final wishes. I wait, frozen in this little patch of dirt, for someone or something to emerge out of the shadows. But after what must have been five minutes, I am still alone. The only sound I hear is my own beating heart.

I turn back to the cave, take a deep breath, and begin to scale the jagged rocks. When I step inside, I have to laugh at the cave's luxury, though judging by Cleopatra's house and property, surprised is the last thing I should be. There are several empty bottles of champagne in the corner covered in dust. Did Jimbo come here often, I wonder. My eyes settle into the darkness and I spot the large orange hanging rug on my right and hurry over to it. I recognize it by the sunset embroidery that my brother talked about. I pull aside the rug and look behind it.

The sinking feeling that someone is following me, watching my every move, stalking me like prey persists. I want the barretta. I need the barretta. Jimbo had left specific instructions: the twelfth stone up from the bottom and the second one into the left. That's where he hid the treasure trove of goodies that I traveled almost four thousand miles for in order to fulfill the most important of missions. The stones, all different sizes and shapes, have been painted a bright, pearly white. I'm sure Cleopatra hired a decorator who took care of every little detail. My fingers trace each of the painted stones until I reach the twelfth one up. I smile, my labored breath full of anticipation, as my fingers slide over two more stones to the left. Apart from its larger size, it looks like all of the other stones. I tap it, but it doesn't quite sound like it's hollow. A bead of sweat drips from my upper lip and falls onto the cold, hard floor. What if I can't find the rock? What if I fail at the mission that I have dedicated the last two years of my life to before I have really even gotten started?

Then I hear it again. But this time, it isn't the sound of a branch snapping or my heart pounding, it's a whisper. The sound of someone outside whispering. At least I think that's what it is. Then again, maybe it's my nervous mind merely playing tricks on me. I crawl toward the cave's entrance, as quiet as I can and peer outside. I peek down at the ground twenty feet below me, half expecting to see half of the CIA's Honolulu branch with their guns cocked. But there's nothing. I take my phone out of my pants pocket and text Othello. I haven't heard from him in hours. The thought had crossed my mind that perhaps this was a giant set-up. What if Othello was playing me while he worked both sides? It would take years of planning and patience, but that's not completely out of the question.

Am I alone? I text Othello. Then I look back out the cave, waiting to see if someone really is there or if it's only my imagination. I don't want to hear back from Othello. I can't let my brother down, even from the grave, and so I turn back inside the cave and get back to work.

My fingers run along each of the stones again until I'm twelve up and two over. At first, the big stone doesn't budge. I grit my teeth, get on my knees, and pull at the stone with both hands. Slowly, it starts to loosen from the wall but it's making a scraping sound that I worry is too loud so I stop what I'm doing and look back down at my phone. Othello still hasn't responded to me. What could he possibly be doing? I look out the cave again, but still, I don't see anybody or anything. God dammit, Othello. I wish he'd give me an update, any update at all, but it seems as if I'm on my own.

I move back to the rock. I have a job to do. I pull on the rock again, and finally, it lands on the rug with a thud. I'm too distracted by the vault to care about the thud. I move closer to the wall and almost let out a giddy, gleeful shriek at what I see inside. The vault is filled with cash, two guns, ammunition, photos of some garden and planes on the tarmac with trees being unloaded. There are passports with my brother's face on each one, and lists of AQ leaders, lots of lists, leaders all over the world. There is also a photo of my brother with his wife who looks pregnant. Now that I am thin, I look much more like him with our similar features and the same thick hair. Neither of us lost our hair, I'm happy to report. A smile washes across my whole face as I stare down at my brother—the brother I'd give anything for if it meant getting to spend one more day with him. If only I got to see him just once before Cleopatra Gallier killed him.

My job is to take this money to my brother's wife and fellow AQ jihadists in the Philippines. The CIA would love to get their fingers on the very list that I'm holding in my hands, these names of AQ leaders and the plans that my brother has made for jihads around the world. I pick up the revolver, and then the Beretta to see which one I like best. The Beretta, definitely the Beretta. I slide it open and fill it with all fifteen bullets.

The last thing that my brother has hidden in the vault is the small pipe bomb. He wisely left this there for me in case I had any unwanted visitors upon my retrieval—I'm still not convinced that I do not. I need to think, so I lay down on the soft carpet, and place some of the colorful cushions beneath my head. Othello has not returned my texts in hours, there's no way that's a good sign. Ever since I got to my brother's house, the sinking feeling inside my chest has only grown and grown. I have to face the sad music that I'm completely on my own. If the CIA knows that I'm in Honolulu, I don't see a way off of this island for me. Chris Castillo ruined everything. Two years of ultimate sacrifice, focus, and commitment down the tubes in an instant all because of a stupid charley horse.

If I'm on a suicide mission, I'll be damned if I don't go down swinging. Hopefully I'll be able to make it out of this cave alive. But there is no guarantee of that, so I close my eyes and visualize shooting my way out of here if I need to. The CIA cannot get anywhere near my brother's AQ list, even if he did cleverly write it in code. And that's why there's a bomb. If I have to, if worse comes to absolute worse, I will burn down this cave if it's the last thing I do. Still in my visualization, I see myself calmly climbing back down the rock face until I am safe on the ground once again. Othello will be waiting there, finally reemerging, and will take me to the safe house that we had discussed. But that sort of happy ending is getting harder and harder to believe and visualize.

Another sound snaps me out of my visualization. My eyes jolt open and I'm on my feet in an instant. I grab the Beretta and creep over to the cave's entrance for a third time. It takes me several seconds until I see it. Off in the distance, about four hundred yards to the left, there's a Prius parked on the dirt road. That car wasn't there before, that I know. That I know for certain. My eyes sweep the ground beneath me, searching for whoever was driving that car. Whoever drove that car here is also here to kill me.

If it wasn't for the moon reappearing from behind a cluster of clouds, I probably would have never seen him. But at least Mother Nature is on my side. The man is coming straight toward the rocks and for a second, I think there's something about him that looks familiar. But there's no time for me to dwell on him as soon I spot several more people on the periphery. God damn you, Othello. What have you done? The chances of me making my great escape vanish all at once as I realize that I am vastly outnumbered. I have no other choice but to trigger the bomb. Even if I fail at bringing back the money to my brother's family, I will not make things worse for his mission. I will not let these names get into the wrong hands if it's the last thing I do. And it seems like it will be.

Someone is climbing up the rocks. There isn't much time left now. I hurry back over to the vault, no longer worrying about how much noise I'm making, grab the bomb and use the lighter to ignite it. Immediately smoke is all around me, but still, I'm able to find my way back to the cave's entrance. I count to ten, aim the gun, and pray.

January 2014

TRIPP, 5

After getting settled into my room at the Waikiki Beach Marriott, I hop into my rented Prius to clear my head. I need the evening air. The Marriott's no Halekulani, but I have little choice: it's not a good look for government agents to be yukking it up at five-star hotels unless they're on vacation and paying their own way.

I'm still struggling to believe that Dr. Marcus Pearson—formerly Paul Olson and currently Odin James—was the second son of Patricia and Jim Olson, close friends of Ferdinand and Imelda Marcos, the corrupt dictators in the Philippines. He was born three years after his older brother, Mohammed Abdul Rahman.

Why was he in Honolulu? Perhaps to find his brother's grave. I know Jimbo was cremated but I have no idea where his ashes are. Could he know that Cleopatra was responsible for his brother's death? Impossible. No one but Jake who witnessed it knows she killed Abdul Raham, and Jake's not talking.

It's not until I pulled into the familiar driveway that I realized I was even driving to Cleo's. Security cameras are still affixed to each of the trees that dot the long, shaded driveway that takes me up to her house. Though we removed the feed into Jimbo's old cottage half a mile from the main house, the cameras should still be functioning. I wonder if Cleo, halfway around the world in Dubai, has just gotten an alert that an intruder has entered the premises.

I pick up my cell phone and dial. "Hey, Marquez?" I say to Joe Marquez, one of the agents keeping tabs on Pearson.

"Yes, sir."

"Just a heads up that I'm approaching Ms. Gallier's house. I'm not going anywhere near the cottage but FYI, I'm in a black Prius with Hawaiian plates." I read him the number.

"Oh. Okay. Copy that." Something in Marquez's voice sounds off.

"I know the property, no need to worry, I'll be fine," I tell the young agent before hanging up.

To be cautious, I kill the lights on the Prius. Castillo couldn't believe his ears when I told him I wanted to rent a Hybrid.

"You going full bleeding-heart on me?" he joked.

Normally I'm more of an SUV kind of guy, but this time I wanted something quiet.

I can't believe that fate has brought me back to Cleo's—or, that once again, I'm on the hunt for an international terrorist who has decided to hide out in Honolulu. Jake would lose it if he knew where I was. Come to think of it, Miranda would too.

A shiver runs down my spine as Cleo's rambling white house with green shutters comes into view. The house has that vacant look since she is no longer living here. Intel says her maid comes to clean a few times a week, but she has been warned to stay home. I park in the same spot that I did on another night like this one two years prior. By instinct, I look over at the empty passenger seat next to me and suddenly crave Cleo's company.

You smell like you.

Poking around the house crosses my mind, but in case Pearson is lurking somewhere nearby, I play it safe and decide against it.

Come on, I want to show you something.

And suddenly, it's Christmas two years ago.

The car doesn't make a sound when I restart it. Using the stars as my guides, I hope that I can remember the way to Cleo's cliffside hideaway. All I know is that I'm on the lookout for a sheltered road which leads to a large rock face.

Aha, there it is. The road is craggy and jagged, making for quite the treacherous ride in my puny Prius. But the car is as quiet as a mouse, and that's key. As the rock croppings come into view, I'm transported back to my time with Cleo years ago on Kilimanjaro. I shake off the memories and concentrate on the task at hand.

I click off the engine and get out of the car in search of the cave. The cave where my daughter was conceived on Cleo's Christmas birthday. But where the hell is it? I'm reminded of Alain Fournier's classic, *The Lost Estate,* in which the character Meaulnes is lost before coming upon a house in the mist. Meaulnes stumbles into a wedding party, and there he finds his true love. But he makes a mistake: leaving to go home. Returning a week later, Meaulnes tries to find the house and his love but cannot.

I, too, cannot find the cave again.

I scale the rock face, searching for the cave's entrance. When I climb too high, I retreat back down and start again, trying a different route. But it's no use. It seems absurd that

I cannot locate the cave that is so luxuriously outfitted with white walls, thick cushions, rugs, and candles. Cleo's creation was so different from the caves full of bats that she and I had slept in on Kilimanjaro …

Okay, I'll try just one more time. Goddammit, I know I didn't imagine being in that cave with Cleo—we have a sixteen-month-old daughter to prove it.

Perhaps I should have taken this failure to find that cave as a warning.

My instinct to retreat back to my king-sized bed in my air-conditioned hotel room at The Waikiki Beach Marriott should have kicked in. But as I'd feared, my instincts really had started to flatten and dull. Or maybe I was just stubborn, the old pro who refuses to recognize when it's quittin' time.

About halfway up the rock formation, I glance down at the ground below me, about a fifteen-foot drop. Agent Marquez is below me on the rocks waving his hands.

"Marquez?" I shout down at him as quietly as I can.

He nods. He's out of breath. "Pearson left the cottage about an hour ago."

"Jesus! Well, where the hell did he go?"

"He walked in this direction. Agent Quinn and I didn't want him to make us and so we stayed back about a hundred yards and we lost him."

"Where's Quinn now?"

"On the eastern side of the perimeter."

I need to think. "Okay, I'm coming down—"

I felt the bullet before I spotted Pearson. At first, I couldn't tell which direction the gunshot came from and, in my haze, I assumed that one of the officers assigned to Cleo's property had accidentally discharged his weapon.

TRIPP, 5

After the bullet tore through my chest, I realized it came from a slightly elevated angle.

I lose my grip on the rocks. As I'm falling down, down, down, I see the shooter pop out from an opening in the rocks. He was hiding in Cleopatra's cave, the cave I'd been searching for.

It was a very thin Dr. Marcus Pearson in the flesh. Behind him, huge flames and torrents of smoke were streaming out of the cave.

DIDIER, 2

While in Sochi, Russia, I am alerted by colleagues in The Business that Tripp Regan has been shot in Hawaii and is in critical condition. If the man is in grave danger, no doubt Cleopatra will want to go there from Dubai. I need to let my daughter know, even if I am not sure she ever forgave him for lying to her. I do not believe he is her daughter, Zelli's, father.

Sergei Kominitz and I are in Sochi, keeping an eye on Anatoly Rustikoff, an oligarch doing strange things at Lake Balakai, where Sergei is from. For reasons yet to be determined, this unimaginably wealthy guy is bringing in a steady stream of large cargo airplanes. We have been unable to find out what he's bringing in in those planes.

Born in Siberia at Lake Baikal, Sergei Kominitz is Russian to the core. He is also extremely handsome and wealthy. An oligarch for sure yet he is also one of my most trusted friends. And my instincts for people are superb. We ski together here and in St. Moritz. We never discuss politics, but both know what the other does, and that is a reason we need one another. He allows me to be in Sochi, I allow him to meet everyone he wants in Paris and St. Moritz. By allowed, I mean protected.

DIDIER, 2

And we are now joining forces against Anatoly Rustikoff, who has no moral core. No one is reining him in, and his power is growing every day.

Last night when Sergei and I had dinner in Sochi, Rustikoff stopped by our table.

He glanced over at me and said to Sergei in a loud whisper, "Why are you dining with the spies' spy?" Without awaiting an answer, he turned on his heel and left.

Not good, as I have always flown under the radar. It was quite an interesting warning.

CLEO, 5

I'm drinking my morning iced cappuccino in the Dubai desert when the phone rings. I am enjoying this quiet time and don't even glance down at the caller ID as it goes to voicemail. I love this time of day and hate to disturb it. Right away the phone rings again.

It's my father. He never calls me twice in a row unless something is wrong.

"Hi, Daddy. Everything okay? It's very early in Paris."

"Actually, I'm in Sochi."

That's strange. "Sochi, why?"

He easily avoids my question. "Are you sitting in the library glancing out the window at my beautiful granddaughter while she plays?"

I look out at Zelli who is growing so fast. She is sixteen months and she and Nannie are frolicking in the sand. In Dubai, Zelli has access to what must be the world's largest sandbox. Her very own desert.

"Good guess. She and Nannie seem to be enjoying some sort of game which consists of throwing sand up in the air and laughing. And Delia came by for a few hours as well. They are so happy."

"Well, I hate to interrupt your lovely morning, but you need to hear this." He exhales his cigarette.

I wait. My heart starts pounding.

"I'm so sorry to be the bearer of sad news, Cleopatra, but your friend Tripp Regan has been shot, and it's not certain that he will make it. He's in a hospital in Honolulu called Queens Medical."

I was stunned. "What? Shot by whom?"

"I'm not sure. I've yet to get the details."

My mind is spinning. "What was he doing in Honolulu, Daddy? Do you think it has to do with Jimbo?"

"I couldn't say, Cleopatra, but it is certainly well within the realm of possibility."

As much as I can, I try not to think about that dreadful day on the cliff. Had I not thrown Jimbo to his death, who knows what would have happened to the Island.

After asking my father to call me back as soon as he learns anything further, I hang up. Trying to act like nothing has happened, I sip my cappuccino. After a few minutes, I stand up and force myself to smile as I walk outside to Zelli.

By some lucky genetic quirk, Zelli inherited her great-grandmother's Algerian skin so the sun never bothers her. She is crawling and toddling, still a bit unsteadily, with the ever-attentive Nannie nearby. Delia is watching her carefully as well. Delia adores her Zel as she calls her and Zel adores her back.

I glance out across the peaceful golden desert sand dunes with its thousands of migratory birds and graceful gazelles. Then, returning my gaze to Zelli, my heart breaks for her. She may never get to meet her father.

I was so sure Tripp would come to us in this oasis of green, the place where Zelli arrived into the world. It was only three weeks ago that I sent the photo of Zelli to her father on Christmas. Every day since, I was expecting Tripp to turn up.

Now I expect he never will.

Tripp's name is on the Dubai entry list and if he were to mention the tall American woman and her father who live out in the desert, we would be alerted. After I smother Zelli with kisses, I go back inside to my computer where I find an article in the *Honolulu Star Advertiser*. The headline reads: "New York Lawyer Shot in Honolulu."

My eyes dart across my computer screen, ingesting the article as quickly as I can. The *Advertiser* reports that the shot was random, but I know better. Maybe Tripp was on an undercover CIA mission that went wrong. Still trembling, I seek out other newscasts on the KHON2 site.

Now I understand why Tripp didn't come to us. On-screen is a photo of him, smiling and laughing at some black-tie event. I print it out, but I can hardly focus on it as tears well up in my eyes.

Back outside, I pick up Zelli again and hug her tight until she finally starts squirming and wiggles to get down. She will never know him. Delia walks over and takes my hand.

I cannot imagine walking through life without my father. All my life, Didier has been my confidante, my protector, my therapist, my mentor, and friend. It is also true that he broke my heart when I was young. Again and again at the last minute, Daddy would break our plans. But, when I was finally with him, I was at the center of his universe. And that's what I must do for Zelli, somehow manage to be both parents rolled into one.

I will take her to Honolulu to see Tripp.

I put down squirming Zelli, smile at Delia as I go inside and pick up my phone to call my old friends from Honolulu, named for reasons you understand when you see them: Pudge and Pudding. As owners of a television station, they should know the insider scoop.

"WKOL," answers a friendly voice I didn't know.

"Hello, may I please speak with Pudge and Pudding—both of them—if they're available? It's Cleopatra Gallier."

"Just a moment, Ms. Gallier."

Moments later, Pudding screams into the phone. "Cleo! There you are!"

"Here I am!"

"Where the heck have you been, girl? The big guy and I have been trying to track you down. Are you still in Dubai? Pudge even sent you a Facebook message!"

"What?" I laugh. "I don't have Facebook!"

"Uh-oh, then another Cleopatra Gallier—though surely there cannot be another one—must have been very confused when she read Pudge's message."

Even through my devastation over Tripp, I laugh along with Pudding. God, I have missed her.

"It's so lonely without you here," she says. "Tell me you're calling to tell us you're coming back. WKOL misses the host of *Close Encounters!*"

I feel warm all over just hearing Pudding's voice. I picture her sitting in her shared office with Pudge, where they have matching huge chairs for their quite substantial bodies.

"Well, actually … yes, I'm coming back, but just for a visit."

"Really? Pudge, get in here!" she yells, and I can hear her chewing on something that no doubt has a lot of sugar.

The phone rattles around and then Pudge joins us on the line. "Cleo! How the hell are ya?"

"Hi, Pudge! I'm well, but I miss you both!"

"Well, what are ya waiting for? Book a flight," says Pudding.

"Yes, I know, I'm going to."

"We'll make a reservation at Fluffy's!" she exclaims.

"Ah, I miss Fluffy's too. Will be like old times!" I pause. I need to be delicate with my next question. "I'm so sorry, I hate to do this, but I don't know who else to ask ..."

"Sure. What is it, Cleo?"

"Yeah, just name it."

"Is it possible to find out how Tripp Regan is doing? As I'm sure you know, he's the lawyer that was shot. Remember you met his son Jake on the show?"

"Sure, I remember Jake well," says Pudding.

"Yeah, he was one of our ... less chatty guests," says Pudge. "Good-looking young man, though. Jeez, that's his dad—the guy who was shot?"

"Yes."

"We have Linda Kahale covering that story. She was a junior reporter when you were here, but she's one of our biggest stars now. Ring any bells?"

"No, her name doesn't sound familiar—"

"Well, I'm looking at Linda's coverage, and it looks like he's been in a coma ever since the incident. Her report says the police caught his shooter, but the authorities aren't releasing his name. The cops are being very tight-lipped. Won't even say where he was shot."

I don't know what to say but I'm positive this all connects back to my old friend, Jimbo.

"I'm so sorry to hear about your friend's dad," says Pudge. "But it's been so long. Can't we talk about something a touch cheerier?"

She's right. I owe them that. "Yes, of course."

"Where are you, Cleo, and what have you been doing these—? Darn, it's been nearly two years since you've been home. Honolulu just isn't the same without you."

"Oh, I'll tell you all about my ... rather interesting life changes as soon as I see your faces, which I have missed very much."

Pudge laughs. "I'd expect nothing short of *interesting* from you, Cleo."

"We'll have to get pedicures and go shoe shopping," Pudding adds.

"Yes, I can't wait!" I pause, and then say, "Pudge, if you can, will you please just see what more you can find out about Tripp Regan's condition? I met him with Jake, so as you can imagine, I'd like to be kept updated."

"Yup, I'll see what I can do. But just to manage expectations, as I said, the cops have been very hush-hush. You know what, I'll give my cuz on the force a call."

"Thank you so much, Pudge." I hear his phone hang up.

"Wait, so, where are you Cleo? Paris ? I know your father has a house there or are you still with him in Dubai?"

"Yes, I'm still at my father's in Dubai. But I need a break from the desert. I'm in desperate need of the ocean ..."

From Pudding's end of the phone, I can barely hear Pudge speaking to someone, presumably his cousin at the police station.

"Wow, Dubai! How exotic! I've been dying to get over there one day and ride the camels." The image of her on a camel makes me smile.

Pudge comes back on the line. "Apparently, the guy who shot Tripp has clammed up tight, won't say a word, but my cousin will let me know if he gets any news."

"Okay, thank you again."

"When do you arrive? We'll pick you up at the airport," Pudding says. She is so honed in on my coming.

"I'm making my flight arrangements now!"

"Woo-hoo! Is there anything we can do to help?"

"No, I don't think so. I just need to get Consuelo over there to open the house and buy groceries and let the men in with the crib and so on."

"A crib? Did you hear that, Pudge?" Pudding shouts. "Cleo's bought a crib!"

"Well, I had to tell you somehow," I laugh. Pudge and Pudding have always had a way of bringing out the playful side of me.

"I can't believe it, Cleo. Congrats!"

"How wonderful! I can't wait to shower the little one with mountains of presents." Pudding agrees. "Boy or girl?"

"A baby girl. Zelli. She's nearly seventeen months old and looks just like me. Okay, so now you know why I didn't come back."

After a few more minutes of regaling them with tidbits about Zelli, I hang up. They will love her and spoil her to pieces. My Honolulu family.

"MRS. CLEO?"

"Yes? Oh, Consuelo!"

"Yes! I get your message. I so glad you come back! It is very lonely when you not here!"

Consuelo, my wonderful housekeeper, is as devoted to me as I am to her. She is also a fabulous cook, her specialties include turkey with stuffing and gravy and cranberry sauce and homemade hot fudge sundaes. Sometimes she makes me quesadillas and enchiladas with sour cream. Consuelo ended up in Hawaii decades ago with her two children, though she never told me why she moved here from Mexico. I asked once if she missed her home and she said "no" so emphatically that I never pursued it. I always suspect abuse when someone changes their life so abruptly.

Consuelo worked at the Prince Waikiki Hotel but wasn't impressed with it so when a local couple gave her a full-time job that paid her well and a house for her and her children to live in she took it. But then, as Consuelo tells it, the couple began to throw things at each other and constantly fight. Their divorce meant that Consuelo was out of a job and a house, too, but that's when she walked into my life and made everything perfect. I got her a new place to live and a car to drive—which she is still terrified of so her son, Felix, drives her to work every day. I also got him a job at another TV studio as a guard.

"Aw, and I am so excited to be coming back! I can't wait to see you, Consuelo."

"Yes. When you get here?"

"Tomorrow or the day after. Not sure yet!"

"Oh, so soon!"

"I know. Which is partially why I called. Can you, by chance, go to the house today?"

"Yes, Mrs. Cleo. What you need?"

"Well, I'm having a large package delivered by 3:00 p.m. today, and I'm looking at the weather ..." I click on one of my saved weather.com tabs in my Bookmark bar in Google. It still says that it's going to rain in Honolulu today, but not tomorrow. I was hoping the skies would be blue upon my return to Honolulu, and thank goodness they will be ...

"It says it's going to rain today. So can you please ask the delivery men to bring it into the house? I don't want it to get ruined."

"Yes, no problem. I go now."

"As a matter of fact, please have them put it in the white bedroom with the lilies of the valley wallpaper. You might need to move the sofa out."

"Yes, Mrs. Cleo. What is the package?"

"Well ... actually, Consuelo, it's a baby's crib! For my daughter, Zelli."

"Oh, Mrs. Cleo!" She is screaming with joy. "I get toys and baby foods and diapers and all things the baby need." Consuelo giggles.

"Thank you so much, Consuelo. You're a godsend."

"I can't wait to meet her, Mrs. Cleo!" She pauses. "Who else is coming, Mrs. Cleo?" Subtle!

"Her Nannie whom you will have to fight with to get any time with the baby, Uelo." Already back to my nickname for her.

As we talk, I click on the *Honolulu Star Advertiser*, my chosen local news source from the Bookmark bar. That's when I fall silent, noticing that there's another story about Tripp's shooting on their home page.

This article is different from the others I've read. It not only details where the shooting took place, it includes a photo of the crime scene. The crime scene is on my property! The lead photo shows the entrance to my house with yellow police tape blocking off the driveway. *Police Line Do Not Cross*. The second photo is of Sweet Dreams with a handful of police cars, their blue-and-red lights illuminated, parked outside. The third photo is of Mohammed Abdul Rahman's old cottage, with just as many police cars parked outside. Oh God ... And the fourth photo is a shot of the rocky cliff hidden in the back of my property where my secret cave is. The cave that can only be found if you know what you're looking for. My head is spinning. This cannot be real.

"Mrs. Cleo? You there?"

"Uh, yes. Sorry, Consuelo, but can I call you back?"

"Yes, of course, Mrs. Cleo. I—"

As soon as I hang up on her, my phone rings again. Though I don't recognize the number, the 808 area code tells me that the caller is from Honolulu.

I let it ring once more before I answer.

"Cleo?" I hear Pudge before I even have the chance to say hello.

"Pudge, thank God! I just saw the news!"

"Yeah, I got a call from Linda. The cops had been keeping the crime scene sealed until one of them leaked its location to someone at the *Advertiser.* Linda is livid—"

"Okay, but what happened, Pudge?" I ask. "The shooting was at my house? I don't get it! Why?"

"It's a developing story. That's all we got so far. Linda's working on it. I'm trying to get hold of my cousin too."

I call my father in Sochi, and in just a few hours he has some of the answers I want. Tripp was climbing the cliff on my property when he was shot by someone in a cave. The police still won't give the name of the shooter. And who else knew about the cave? With all the lies that Jimbo told me, it's more than possible that he followed me there and perhaps even used it himself.

Maybe someone from Abdul Rahman's underground AQ cell evaded authorities after his death and was living in my cave. Tripp might have been tipped off and gone looking for him. Oh, Tripp, why did you have to be so brave?

IT'S CHAOS AS NANNIE and I frantically pack for a trip halfway around the world. Nannie packs Zelli's gear, and I fill my bags and put Endy in a carton for cats that will go underneath my seat. I order cars to the airport and plane rides to Honolulu.

But first I go down to the Abuse Center and take Delia with me. I need to say goodbye to the girls as I don't know how long I will be away. Delia holds my hand as I tell them I have to leave for I don't know how long but that I will be checking on them all the time from Honolulu. Delia asks if they can all come with me. And I have to say no, though it breaks my heart and hers, too, I can see.

Nannie is thrilled to be going with us to Hawaii. And when we land after a grueling trip of stops to change planes, of Zelli toddling up and down the aisles again and again and crying and not wanting to be buckled into her seat, she's finally placed into the welcoming arms of Pudge and Pudding. They load us with all our things, including Endy, into their huge black Escalade—all the while kissing and hugging and oohing and aahing over Zelli and me. Pudding is playing peekaboo with Zelli as Pudge drives us to Sweet Dreams.

But when we get to the driveway, the policeman guarding the property doesn't want to let us in.

JAKE, 5

Mom hasn't left Queen's Medical once since we arrived almost a week ago. Management should start charging her rent. She eats all of her meals in the gnarly cafeteria that smells like old people and Clorox. She showers in the bathroom off my dad's room and has either Matt, Ricky, or yours truly bring her a new change of clothes every day from the Aston Hotel—which, at only half a mile, is the closest hotel on island to the hospital.

The ironic thing is, even though we're all in this mess because of my dad, everyone but Dad is driving me nuts. Ricky Facetimes with Julia twenty-seven times an hour, Matt won't stop complaining about having to stay indoors all day, and Mom is such a nervous wreck that she's making Nurse Ratched seem laid back.

Sensing my restlessness, Mom suggests I get some fresh air. After being at the hospital for the past five days straight, I definitely needed a break. I sprinted out of there so fast I practically left a Jake-sized hole in my dad's hospital room.

Finally outside in the warm sun, I hop in the rental car and I'm just about to peel out of the parking lot when I hear Matt's high-pitched voice.

"Jake? Where are you going? Wait for me!"

I slam on the brakes and roll down the passenger window of the Tahoe. "Hey, bud. I'm actually headed out to do some work. Need a lift anywhere?"

"Oh." Matt frowns. "I thought you might be going to say hi to Cleo. You haven't seen her in so long, so I was thinking that you probably miss her a lot and I wanted to go with you to look at all of her beautiful plants."

I hate lying to my brother. "Nah. Unfortunately not, bro." How did he know I was heading there? I didn't even know.

Then Matt gets distracted by something in the shrubbery family around the perimeter of the parking lot. He goes up to the big green bush and starts gently caressing its leaves. Jeez, kid, buy her dinner first.

"Okay. Bye, Jake," says Matt absentmindedly.

As I had so many other times, I'd lost Matt's attention to the plants.

When I pull up to Cleo's house, as expected the driveway is still roped off with police tape. A rent-a-cop with a bad goatee is standing guard in his black-and-white cop car.

"Hey, man," I say as I pull up and flash my CIA badge.

Rent-A-Cop tears himself away from his phone and looks over at me, then at my badge, seemingly annoyed that I interrupted what is presumably a riveting game of brickbreaker.

"You're CIA?" he asks with a hint of surprise. As if someone this young and good looking couldn't possibly be with the agency.

I nod. "And the shooting victim is my father."

That gets his attention.

"Oh, wow. He doin' alright?"

"Day by day. Thanks for asking." I smile. "Mind if I enter? I'm only going to the main house."

He grabs a clipboard from the passenger seat and searches for my name. "Jake Regan, right?"

I nod again.

"Tell your dad we're all pulling for him." He steps outside the car and lifts up the police tape. "Go ahead."

"Thanks, man." I give a wave before driving off.

I park in front of Cleo's house. It looks just as I remember. This has been quite the popular setting of many a fantasy of mine over the last two years, let me tell you. I'll never forget that first time with Cleo ... She looked like a goddess when she stepped out of her yellow convertible in that dress. I'd never seen someone so beautiful. Once we were inside the house, it took less than five minutes for us to shed all of our clothes. That's the fastest your boy has ever worked, but those were the longest five minutes of my life. All I wanted to do when she was rambling on about some insane topic like spelunking was to rip off her dress with my teeth, one tiny white button at a time.

She must have been nervous too. No normal human being willingly blabs on about spelunking unless they're nervous. At least let's hope not. I don't know what I would've done if she'd turned me down. It didn't even matter that Julia was arriving in just a few short hours. Cleo was who I wanted. I remember, like a total loser, asking if I could have a tour of her—

"Mister?"

The sound of a woman's voice with a Spanish accent jolts me out of my fantasy. Holy hell, that scared me. I take a second to gravitate back down to earth and put on a big, goofy smile as I step out of the car.

"Hi there." I flash my badge. "I'm Jake Regan."

"Oh. Sorry. Your car, I don't know." She smiles back meekly.

She's a small, dark-haired woman with flecks of gray streaks in hair that's pulled back into a low bun. Her tan skin has wrinkles that are probably deeper than they would be had she lived somewhere else with considerably less sunshine.

"Are you Consuelo?" I ask her.

Her thick eyebrows crinkle. "Me? Yes, Consuelo. How you know?"

"Cleo told me about you. I'm an old friend of hers."

Consuelo smiles as she glances at her tiny watch. "Oh … Mrs. Cleo coming here any minute now."

Wait. "Coming back here? But I thought she lived in Dubai. I was just coming to—"

"Yes. Here. Should be home soon."

Cleopatra Gallier in the flesh, after two years. Holy shit. "Oh. Okay. Wow. Well, I don't want to bother you. Do you mind if I just wait in my car?"

"Sure." She shrugs. And like that, Consuelo heads back inside with a big smile.

Sweat is pouring down my forehead by the time I get back into the driver's seat. In my own car, I always keep an emergency stick of Old Spice stashed in the glove compartment and boy, do I wish I'd had the wherewithal to have pulled the same move with this rental. There's no way I can stink when I see Cleo for the first time in two years.

Should I leave? Should I stay? Just then, my cell phone buzzes, and it answers my question for me. It's a text from Ricky.

"Yo. Dad's awake. Come back."

Halle-freaking-lujah! I knew the old man would pull through. I start the car and pull out of the driveway.

Well, I guess that's that. I'm dying to see Cleo, but maybe it's better this way. We can reunite when I'm on top of my game. My family needs me now. After six days, my father, the hero, has opened his eyes. I put the pedal to the metal and the palm trees that dot Cleo's driveway whiz past me like one big green blur.

I smile to myself, thinking about my mom probably doing cartwheels in the hallways of Queen's Medical Center right about now. Dad's never given her a scare like this, and she'd absolutely crumble having to go through life without him by her side. For Mom, the sun rises and sets with my father. It's kind of strange how obsessed she is with him, but they're old school I guess. Most chicks today will hardly even let you hold the door for them without jumping down your throat about wage equality. Actually, I've always liked women who make you chase them. That shit still works like a charm. Who knows? Maybe Mom made Dad put in work back in the day. I can't wait to see how happy she is now that Dad's finally awake again. But I get a pit in my stomach thinking about how he will react to his new reality.

And how she'll react to it too. Part of me is even thankful that I wasn't there when he woke up. It would've broken my big black heart. But I should've been there. Once again, I have abandoned my family in their time of need in favor of reliving some stupid little fantasy. I wouldn't blame them if they're pissed.

New plan. After I've seen my dad and changed into a clean shirt, I'll shoot Cleo a text. I'll say something devastatingly witty like *Hey, stranger. I hear you're back in town.* No, that's dumb. Maybe something more direct. Chicks dig it when you don't beat around the bush. I could just text her something really simple about how much I want to see her and see how she reacts.

As I pull around the final bend of Cleo's long driveway, I notice a black Escalade stopped at the entrance. And none other than one Ms. Cleopatra Gallier is stepping out of the Escalade and chatting up Rent-a-cop.

I'm in such a state of absolute shock that I almost forget to put on the brakes.

Errrrrr! The tires squeal against the pavement. Both Cleo and Rent-a-Cop's heads whip around, and their jaws drop as my Tahoe slams to a stop just a few feet in front of them.

"Oh. My. God." I say to myself through gritted teeth. The whole reason why Cleo even walked into my life in the first place was because of a car accident. That one was her fault. And now we were about to be reunited with yet another accident. Number two would've been on me.

Cleo squints at me in the driver's seat. I sit there, frozen like a total moron for a few seconds, until a big smile eventually widens across her face. Seeing her in the flesh and not in my fantasies, I can hardly speak. She realizes that no, I'm not a mirage, and it really is me. I think she looks happy to see me?

Welp. Guess there's nothing left to do other than get the hell outta the goddamn car and say hello.

"Cleo!"

"Jake! Oh my god, what on earth are you doing ?"

I haven't even gotten as far as a cover story. I can't exactly say to her: *Oh yeah. Surprise! I'm in the CIA now and I'm just checking on your property seeing as my old man was shot here. You know Mohammed Abdul Rahman, right? Remember, you pushed him off a cliff? Yeah, cool. Oh, and spoiler alert: my dad's in the CIA too! But maybe you already knew that! Fun times!*

"I didn't think you'd be here!" I say as we both approach each other as if we're both in slow motion.

"Oh?" Cleo makes a face.

And then she's in my arms and I'm in hers. Unlike me, Cleo smells fantastic. Like a fresh meadow or a garden at springtime. Did I mention that Cleo has the tendency to bring out the poetic side of me? Yes, Jake Regan has a poetic side.

We hold on to each other too long. I never want to let go of her, and I hope she never wants to let go of me either. But all good things must come to an end.

"I mean, I'd obviously *hoped* you'd be here," I say. "But I heard through the grapevine that you were living in Dubai?"

"You heard right! So, did you just want to see the place for old time's sake?" She smiles.

God, that smile."Um. Well ... kind of," I blush. "We had some good times here."

Our eyes lock. It's two years ago all over again. Except this time, a car accident was narrowly avoided.

"Is that the famous Jake?"

I turn toward the Escalade and find a friendly face in the passenger seat that I recognize but can't place.

"It's Pudding! We met when you came to the studio to film our show."

"And Pudge!" A large dude waves from the driver's side.

And I realize there's someone else in the back seat whom I can't see.

"Oh, wow. Hi, guys!" I wave back. "So nice to see you." I turn back to Cleo, blushing all over again. "Oh man, that show ... definitely not my finest hour."

We both laugh.

"I was so sorry to hear about your father. How is he doing?"

My father. "Better. He actually just woke up from the coma."

Cleo's entire face brightens. "Oh, Jake, that's fantastic!"

"Yeah, it's great news." I glance down at my watch. "I'm so sorry, I'd love to stay and catch up, but I actually have to get to the hospital."

"Of course. I'm just glad you ran—and didn't crash—into us!" she smiles again.

Rent-A-Cop clears his throat. He wants something. I glance at him, then back at Cleo.

"Is everything alright here?" I ask her.

"Well, this gentleman is understandably being cautious given everything that just happened here," says Cleo. "I was told, however, that we were cleared to return along with Consuelo and a truck delivery." She turns back to the guard. "And you see, they got in and it is my house, and I just traveled all the way from Dubai …"

This is my time to shine. "Ms. Gallier is cleared to return to her property," I tell Rent-A-Cop in my sternest, most professional voice.

He hesitates a moment but nods his head obediently. It wouldn't be a good look if his supervisor found out that he disobeyed a CIA officer, especially seeing as this is our crime scene and not Honolulu PD.

"Very well. Go on up, Ms. Gallier."

Cleo looks at me, surprised. If she knows my father is in the CIA, then she might put two and two together. I'm not worried. Regardless, Cleo can keep a secret … but still, I need to at least try to maintain my cover.

"Let's just say it helps to have friends in high places."

"Yes, it does." She winks.

2014

TRIPP, 6

"Tripp? Tripp, are you awake?" It's Miranda's voice, but she sounds like she's ten feet underwater. Or maybe it's me who's underwater. Then I feel her squeeze my left hand. Or at least someone is squeezing my hand.

I try to open my eyes, but all I can see is darkness. Goddammit, why can't I see anything?

"Ricky, go get the doctor. Matt, go with him," Miranda says. She sounds upset. "Quick, your father is awake. Go on, go!"

Doctor? Where am I? Ricky and Matt are here too? There's an urgency in Miranda's voice. She's trying to be calm, but I know better. I know that tone. That's where over thirty years of marriage lands you. I try to open my eyes again, but still can't see a damn thing. I bring my hands up and I feel my eyeball.

My eyes are open, but I can't see. Something's wrong. Jesus Christ, something is definitely wrong. Is this a dream? Please God, tell me this is a dream.

"Miranda?" I manage to say. My voice is hoarse and my throat has never been this dry.

"Oh, Tripp! You are awake!"

"Awake? What's happening? Tell me, what's happening?"
I try to sit up, but my entire body is in awful pain. It hurts
to move. It feels as if I have been put through a meat grinder.
I paw at my chest and arms. I'm covered in bandages, and
there's something sticking out of my right arm.

"It's—the doctors will explain." Miranda squeezes my
hand again. "You're at the hospital, but it's going to be alright."

"What? Why?" It feels like I haven't spoken in months.
"How long have I been here? Where am I?"

Miranda tries to sound calm as she explains, "We're at
Queens Medical Center in Honolulu. I'm here with you. And
so are Ricky, Matt, and Jake. We're all here with you. You've
been in a coma for a while."

This can't be happening. "A coma? What the hell are you
talking about? What the hell happened to me, Miranda? Tell
me!"

"Dad, everything will be okay," I hear Ricky. "Just take
a breath." He must've come back into the room, but I have
no idea where he is.

"Oh, easy for you to say! You're not the one lying here
without a clue what's going on! I can't see. Why can't I see?"

"I KNOW TRIPP. The doctors will explain everything," Miranda
says again with fear in her voice.

"Jesus, how many more times do I have to say it? I don't
want to wait for a doctor! Just tell me what the hell's going
on!" I explode.

I hardly ever yell, least of all at Miranda. My arms must
have been windmilling, gesturing wildly, because I feel them
crash into someone's chest. "Shit, I'm sorry—Miranda, is that
you? I didn't mean to hit you."

"It's your nurse," says my wife. "Your nurse, Ignacio."

"It's okay. It happens," says a meek male voice I've never heard before.

"Jesus, I'm sorry. I didn't … see you there." I want to laugh. I can't believe this is my new reality.

Then I hear another voice I've never heard before. "Good morning, Mr. Regan. I'm Dr. Akana. How are you feeling?"

"How the fuck do you think I'm feeling? Terrified, awful, scared, I can't see. What the hell is going on?" I scream at them.

"Mrs. Regan, do you and your sons mind giving us a minute? As we discussed, when a patient first emerges from a coma, we like to go over everything with them one on one."

"Of course, Dr. Akana. I'll be back, Tripp. I'm so happy you're awake. It will all be alright." She squeezes my hand once again.

I'd really like her to stop saying everything will be alright 'cause it sure doesn't goddamn feel that way.

After my family leaves, Dr. Akana starts right in. "Mr. Regan, my colleague and I, Dr. Copperman—"

"Good morning, Mr. Regan," chirps a female voice and I jump.

I had no idea that a third person was even in the room, but I do feel bustling all around me.

"Dr. Copperman and I have been informed about your line of work and so we intend to take the necessary precautions to keep all of that under wraps as best we can." Dr. Akana pauses.

He must be waiting for me to acknowledge that. "Right."

"That said, two of your colleagues are waiting outside and will fill you in on all of the—uh, nonmedical details—once we're done here."

I cut to the chase. "So, am I blind now? Just tell me for God's sake. Right now, that's all I care about."

Silence. I picture the doctors trading sidelong glances across the room, neither wanting to take on the responsibility of breaking the terrible news.

Until then, Dr. Copperman has been fairly quiet. Now she says, "There's a chance you might regain your sight, Mr. Regan, but no promises, I'm afraid. Blood in the eye, known as hyphema, has started to go away on its own. That's the first step—having the blood naturally drain from your eye. The hyphema came as a result of the fall you took, the trauma which landed you with such force. You did fall onto a layer of soft vegetation on a slope which was very lucky. I was most concerned about retinal hemorrhages which can lead to blindness but the blood is leaving. That will reduce the inflammation response when you are operated on for the injury to your eyes."

"Ok, so what you are saying is this hyphema is just a by-product of the fall? The trauma of my fall caused me to go blind? So now what? We just have to ... wait? For what?"

"An operation. I've been consulting with an eye surgeon in Florida, a specialist, and he agrees that it's best if the blood dissipates on its own. He's examined your X-rays. It's too early for him to give a prognosis, but he's monitoring it. We're keeping him apprised."

"Right, not too bright a picture. Okay, so what's the plan in the meantime? Is there some sort of rehab that can expedite the draining?"

"Unfortunately not," says Akana. "As difficult as it may sound for an active man such as yourself, rest is the biggest favor you can do for your body right now, Mr. Regan. It takes two to three weeks for the hyphema to disperse, but we'll be overseeing your progress every step of the way. And the good news is, your back is healing."

"What happened to my back? You still haven't told me a goddamn thing about what happened to me. I ache all over. My lower back is very painful. And my elbows on both arms."

"Do you remember anything about the night of January 16?" asks the male doctor.

The night of January 16. That was the first night I got to Honolulu. "Um …"

"You went over to Cleopatra Gallier's property," Dr. Copperman prompts me.

Cleo's house? I did?… It's starting to come back to me. "Oh, that's right."

"Yes," Copperman goes on. "You suffered injuries to your lower back where some discs have been impacted and a great deal of bruising after you fell about fifteen feet from off a cliff that you were scaling."

I don't remember that at all. "I did?"

"You were shot once on the right side of your chest."

Jesus. "Are my colleagues outside? I'd like to speak to them now please, unless you want to add anything or maybe give me some more terrible news."

"No, that should do for the moment," says Dr. Akana. "It is *good* news you woke from your coma," he adds before both doctors say their goodbyes.

I'd been operating as I always have, relying on a combination of external cues and gut instincts. The same instincts that I have thankfully passed onto my oldest son. Only this time, my instincts failed me in monumental fashion.

"Hey, boss," I hear Castillo say. "Durita is here too."

Durita and Castillo were at that first briefing after I landed.

How many days ago was that? I have no clue. In case you've never had the pleasure of being in a coma, it majorly screws your concept of time.

I've never heard Castillo in such a state. The poor guy sounded like he was going to burst into a puddle of tears, and something tells me he looks even worse. But Durita is all business, a real pro, briefing me on the events that occurred at Cleo's seven nights and six days prior.

It's still a blur. I remember pulling into Cleo's long, winding driveway and parking in front of her house for a few minutes but then … nothing.

"You don't remember driving down to the rocks?" Durita asks.

Huh? Does he mean the cave? "The rocks?"

Castillo must have read the confusion on my face. "You drove down a dirt road to a rock embankment on the edge of Ms. Gallier's property," he tells me in a softer than usual tone—like everyone else's tone I've heard since being roused to this waking nightmare. The tone of sympathy. I hate pity, but something tells me I better get used to it.

"Oh…." I mutter, implying something that I remember. But I don't. I recall having the hunch to drive down to the rocks in search of Cleo's secret cave, but I don't have any memory after that.

"Marcus Pearson is now in custody." Durita pauses, "Are you ready to hear this, sir?"

I nod.

"After Pearson left Inouye airport, he got in a taxi and headed straight to Miss Gallier's. The two agents we had on his tail were under strict instructions not to engage with Pearson under any circumstances. Whatever he was up to, we needed to catch him red-handed. When he arrived at Abdul Rahman's old cottage, he stayed there for exactly twelve hours, eighteen minutes. The cottage had long been cleared out by our agents, myself included. We'd removed all of Abdul Rahman's belongings and entered them into evidence over two years ago. But Pearson must've been looking for something else. He left Abdul Rahman's house and headed directly to a cave on Ms. Gallier's property. See, before he died, we now think it is possible Abdul Rahman hid something in the cave for Pearson. We couldn't very well search a cave that we didn't even know existed in the first place. Why Pearson waited so long at Rahman's house before going to find it, we don't know yet. Best guess, he was building a firebomb with items from his backpack. Based on his behavior, we don't believe that Pearson had any idea he was being tailed, though a call came into him when he disembarked from his plane as you might remember us discussing before you were shot. Untraceable, and therefore questionable."

This is a lot to take in. What Pearson didn't take into account is that I also knew about the cave. The surveillance team followed him, but I had never previously told the CIA about the cave's existence. At the time, I didn't think it was necessary. I'd only been there once, and Abdul Rahman was already dead by then. There wasn't anything in there that directly linked us to him anyway. How wrong I'd been. Because the two agents were following orders with a loose tail, Pearson had disappeared by the time they got down to the rock face. I have no memory of this, but according to Castillo and Durita, that's when the agents approached and told me they'd lost eyes on Pearson. That's when I was fifteen feet off the ground, moments before I was shot by Pearson.

The fall knocked me out. It's a miracle I'm not paralyzed from the neck down—if I was, I probably would've just told the doctors to end it right here and now. Pearson didn't want me to get inside that cave. But why? Of all the gin joints on all the islands on all of Honolulu, Pearson had to hole up in mine ...

"Pearson was interrogated days ago," says Castillo and Durita adds, "He lawyered up and is keeping his mouth shut." Was he on a suicide mission?

"Asshole refuses to give up anything about his brother. But we figure Abdul Rahman tipped him off about something in the cave that needed to be destroyed," Castillo says. It sounds like he's moved to another part of the room. "How did you know about the cave, boss?"

Hmm. I can't answer that so I don't. But Durita comes to my rescue. "I am guessing you saw Pearson go up and followed him." I say nothing but nod and ask "How did Pearson know about the cave?"

Two years ago, when Cleo and I spent our night together there, she told me that no one else knew about it. Either Cleo was lying or she didn't realize that her good pal Jimbo had found out about her secret hideaway. And then he used it for his *own* secret hideaway. That seems more likely.

"What do Miranda and the boys know?" I ask.

"Larry Forbes went to the townhouse. Told her they changed your trip at the last minute from Dubai to Honolulu while you were still at JFK," Castillo tells me.

Larry Forbes is the managing partner at Weinstein, Forbes, Regan, and Lowe.

"Jesus."

"Yeah, he told your wife that you had to assist in a high-profile bankruptcy case at a pineapple plantation, and that's where you were when you were shot by a disgruntled employee who thought you were his boss," Durita says.

The agency sure has gotten creative lately. "You're kidding."

"Sometimes the truth's stranger than fiction, boss." Then he adds, "Jake has been fully debriefed."

Under different circumstances, I bet Jake would've been over the moon to get on a plane to Honolulu. It would give him the chance to see Cleo. Little does he know, she ain't here but in Dubai with my daughter.

"Miranda's been a real trooper," Castillo adds. "After the firm told her what happened, she had them arrange a plane for your family to get everyone over here ASAP."

"Yeah, that sounds like her." Poor Miranda. That conversation with Larry must've been one of the low points in her life—but knowing her, she walked calmly upstairs and packed her bags without so much as a word. I have forever admired my wife's quiet strength, especially in a crisis.

"Cas, do you mind? I need some water and I can't seem to"

"Oh! Yeah, sure, boss." I hear Castillo hustle closer toward me. He gently places the cup in my left hand. It's true what they say, when you lose one of your senses, the remaining four are heightened. Each of the small, smooth ridges of the cup—I count five on the top half and another five on the bottom—register against the tips of my fingers.

I know I'm drinking out of a clear plastic Sysco cup. The same type of Sysco cup I've drunk out of a million times, only this time I can't see it. I can only feel the brim kiss my bottom lip as the room temperature liquid glides down my esophagus.

Pearson is in custody. I'm blind and terrified and I ache all over.

CLEO, 6

Driving to meet Walter for our first Krav Maga workout in a long time, I can't stop worrying about Tripp. I heard from Pudge that he's been blinded. I can't stop picturing how he awoke from a coma to find he could no longer see. Oh, it would be terrifying to be in pitch black and somehow, I also can't keep my thoughts from Jake. When he put his arms around me, we both held that hug far too long. He was as gorgeous as I remembered and just a little bit older—though not much. When we met, he was far too young for me, but neither of us let that stop us. Nothing stopped us. It was a cyclone of lovemaking, and we barely talked.

I don't believe I have thought about sex once since I found out I was having a baby. Zelli took over my life until Jake put his arms around me, and now I want him to do that again.

I really want him to do that again.

In the gym, it felt great to see my old friend.

"Walter! Oh, how I have missed our sessions! The trainer in Dubai was good but you are great."

Walter hugs me. "Yes, I am," he laughs.

"Are you teaching many new clients?" I smile. "I bet you are."

"Yeah, a few. Business has been good."

"My trainer in Dubai, Alfie, is teaching at the abuse center while I am away, though I so worry about the girls there. He promised to keep me up to date every week. There is a little girl named Delia whom I wish I had brought with me but she has a new family and I knew it was better to leave her in Dubai."

He smirks at me. "Cleo, this isn't like you."

"What?"

"Putting off the workout with banter." He slides on his defensive pads. "Let's get started."

"Walter, just as a reminder, I had a baby about a year and a half ago." I laugh, knowing full well he won't go gently on me.

"Yeah, you mentioned that when you didn't come back," he laughs as he passes me my defensive pads. I really am nervous, but after some warm-up calisthenics of jumping jacks, pushups, and sit-ups, I feel ready to put on my protective gear. We practice inside chops, then move onto kicks to the groin. By the time we call it quits, I am soaked and thrilled to be back in my physical fitness addiction with the best trainer.

"Walter," I say breathlessly in between sips from my water bottle, "do you, by chance, know any reiki healers? A friend of mine is in the hospital having just woken from a coma."

Walter looks at me in a funny way and lets down his guard, changing the subject. "I know you took him down, Cleo," Walter says. "I saw you and Jimbo biking together the day he died."

Goodness. "He was my best friend. We went on bike rides all the time."

"I know, but c'mon. He was an Ironman."

"So?"

"He just skidded off the road?"

I say nothing.

"We all owe you, you know," says Walter. "I just wanted to express my gratitude."

By my silence, Walter knows I'm not about to respond. He thankfully changes the subject again and takes out his cell phone.

"Call Magda. She's a pretty remarkable healer. I just texted you her number."

"Do you think there's any way that Magda could come over today? I'd love her to start helping my friend right away."

A FEW HOURS LATER, Magda pulls into my driveway at Sweet Dreams in her little green Subaru.

"Over here!" I call out from the terrace where I am still in my sweaty gym clothes, playing dolls with Zelli.

Magda steps onto the patio, wearing a black tank top tucked into a pair of coral gaucho pants. Her hair is gray, her eyes are green, and her skin is pale. She greets me with a warm smile, and I sense right away I can trust her.

As we shake hands the rainbow of colored bangles on Magda's wrists jingle and jangle as her hand meets mine. She looks down at Zelli who is sucking on her thumb with one hand and clutching my left leg with the other.

"And who is this gorgeous girl?"

"Zelli, can you say hello to Mommy's new friend Magda?"

All Zelli offers Magda is the sweetest smile. She is quite shy around new people. I call for Nannie and she comes outside and retrieves Zelli. Even though she wouldn't understand it, I don't feel right about having her here when Magda and I have this conversation about her father.

"You have a beautiful home," says Magda as she looks around my property.

"Thanks, I'm glad you like it. Let's sit. Would you like some iced tea or lemonade?"

Endy wanders out and jumps directly into Magda's lap. Just as she did with Beebe in Dubai. It looks like they've known one another for years. Endy recognizes the good people.

Magda shakes her head no to the drinks as we take seats across from each other on the white wicker chairs with puffy white pillows that flatten the minute we sit in them. Must look into that.

Magda smiles. "Why don't you tell me what you're looking for, Cleo? I assume Walter told you about my practice."

"Yes. And he said that you're the very best ... You see, a good friend of mine was recently shot."

"Oh, no." The many bracelets on Magda's wrists jangle as she brings a hand up to her chest. "I'm so sorry to hear that."

Endy bolts up and then resits in Magda's lap.

"Yes. The doctors at Queens Medical aren't sure if he's ever going to get his sight back, so I want to do anything that I can to help."

"I understand. If it gives you any comfort, I've worked with another client who was blind. I can't make any promises about his sight, but overall, my treatments—along with the doctors' work—have offered some degree of success."

"Well, that's good to hear." I pause for a moment. "Is there any way that we can keep this a secret between you and me? I want to help, but I would also prefer that his friends and family don't know that your services are a gift from me."

"Oh," she says with a touch of surprise in her voice. This must be a new one for Magda. "Okay, sure. I suppose you just need to call the hospital and arrange everything. I have worked with patients at Queens Medical before."

"Yes, I will do that. And thanks for understanding."

CLEO, 6

"I do. Privacy is very important to my practice. My sessions are always behind closed doors. It's just my client and me."

"Ah, good to know." I would like to see Tripp and certainly don't want Miranda to be upset so perhaps Magda's schedule would be a good time to see him.

TRIPP, 7

It's been four days since I woke up, and I still can't see a goddamn thing. I only leave my room for tests on my eyes and X-rays for my back. I didn't break my back but some discs have been squashed. Miranda has fresh flowers delivered every day, which I can at least smell. The doctors tell me that my back will heal just fine which, given the extent of my fall, is surprising ... so I'm going to take that with a giant grain of salt.

Without my vision, I'm useless. I can no longer do my job, not just at the CIA or the law firm, but at home too. The thought of Miranda having to feed me breakfast, lunch, and dinner, or escort me to the bathroom makes my stomach turn. I know the blind eventually learn how to manage many activities on their own, but never watching another football game or throwing another ball around with Jake and Ricky presents me with a depressing picture of the future. The days of searching dense woods for exotic plants with Matt are over. And missing out on seeing Ricky kiss Julia up on the altar breaks my heart.

Something else within has changed as the days pass in this godforsaken hospital bed. I try to be positive and upbeat for my family, but I can tell by the forced cheeriness in their voices that my prognosis is not good.

Only one other time have I felt this miserable. It was when Cindy, my first wife, died in a boating accident. Back then, I drank for months and months. This time is different and strange. Something is being answered in me, but I have no clue what it is. I can't rush it, so for once I have to just pretend to everyone that I am fine, the same as ever, even without my sight.

The hospital offers me a treatment I've never even heard of called Reiki. The name alone implies some holistic, Eastern medicine voodoo. Dr. Copperman, who uses the practice herself, suggests it might help alleviate my anxiety. I want to ask, what about my debilitating depression? Will it help that too? But I keep that to myself. They must know I'm miserable, even as we continue to dance this dance where we pretend all is well.

"I'll try anything if it might increase the chances of getting my sight back." I told her.

"Great, I'll set it up. Magda's the best."

When Dr. Copperman elaborated on Reiki, it started to sound more and more like something that would attract the dearly departed Danny Mortimer—my former undercover identity as a pony-tailed hippie. Reiki is a Japanese form of alternative medicine that emerged in the late 1800s, based on the principle that the therapist—in my case, a woman named Magda—can channel energy into me by means of hand apposition. In a nutshell, it's the transfer of universal energy from the therapist's palms to their patient. It's all a bit nutty to me but since I don't have many other options, I'll pretend to smile and go along with the Reiki plan like a good little patient. Magda is supposed to activate the natural healing processes and restore my physical and emotional well-being. I'm dubious, but I have nothing to lose.

A day later, Magda enters my room and introduces herself as a Master Reiki therapist. Her voice imbues a sense of serenity and healing. I picture Magda as having long, beautiful gray hair and wearing a flowing Bohemian dress with several beaded necklaces around her neck.

There's something entertaining about imagining what every new person I meet looks like based only on their voice. It reminds me of listening to an audiobook where the only clues of a character's physicality are their vocabulary, tone, and inflection. My version of Holden Caulfield—tall, skinny, and blond with sunken cheeks—probably looks nothing like Miranda's Holden.

I force a smile as she shakes my outstretched hand. "Tripp Regan, not yet a Master blind person."

"Nice to meet you, Tripp." She laughs politely at my lame joke. I hear a chair gently dragging across the floor before Magda takes a seat at my bedside. "Do you know anything about Reiki or what I do?"

"Dr. Copperman gave me very broad strokes."

"In my view, what's most important is the question: Do you really want to be healed? And can you open your heart and soul to whatever may come to you by the means of a universal energy?"

I guess? "Yes, to all of the above."

"Very good. Now the way Reiki actually works is directly on the body's seven main chakras—"

"Sorry to cut you off, but remind me what a chakra is?"

"Yes, of course. The seven chakras are the various focal points that we use in a variety of meditation processes. There's the crown, which is the top of your head. Your third eye, located on your forehead. And then, the throat, the heart, the solar plexus otherwise known as your abdomen, your sacral, which is two inches below your belly button and last but certainly not least, your root. The root is at the base of our spine, close to the tailbone. It acts as our center of emotional and spiritual balance. And the one that balances all the others is the Cardiac. "

"Glad I asked."

"Yes, please feel comfortable asking me anything. That's what I'm here for."

I like Magda. Already I feel a hair less anxious.

"And here's one more thing: When we apply Reiki, we don't actually touch the person in need. I just have to feel where the unbalanced energy is," she pauses. "Ready to get started?"

"Let's do it."

Magda doesn't touch me, but when she puts her hands above my eyes, a tingling sensation starts to radiate around both eyelids. The feeling grows stronger and stronger until I have goosebumps emanating all over my face. It's hard to describe the feeling. You know that pins and needles sensation you get when your foot falls asleep? It's like that, but in my eyes and much more pleasant.

Let's hope that this is, indeed, a Higher energy hard at work.

2014

TRIPP, 8

"Are you crazy?" says a flabber-gasted Castillo after I request that the CIA bring Marcus Pearson to the hospital for a chat with me.

"I need to know what he was hiding in that cave. He set fire to the cave, so what was in there? We need to know."

"Alright, well then, let's set up a call. You can talk to him in prison." Castillo pauses. "It's not like you can see him anyway."

No shit, Sherlock. "Oh, really. I'd forgotten…"

"C'mon. There's no way we can bring a known terrorist in here. The place is filled with sick, weak civilians."

"Pearson wouldn't even be in custody if it wasn't for me."

"I know, but—"

"Goddammit, it's his fault I can't see anymore. I was blinded in the line of duty, Castillo. "

"Right, I get that. But I'm just looking out for—"

"Look, Castillo, I worked with the guy for years. I know him or I thought I did. I will have a reading on him no one else will. I read his damn book which I got published for him when I thought he had died and I figured out who he dedicated it to. I used Dr. Marcus Pearson as my cover in Manila for a long time. He turned on me and I damn well want him here, understand?" That felt good, really good.

A FEW DAYS LATER, Pearson walks into my hospital room along with Castillo, Durita, and several cops. His leg cuffs jingle and jangle as he gets closer to my bed.

The higher-ups at the CIA granted my request after I agreed that the meeting would last no more than fifteen minutes, it would take place at 11:00 p.m. when visiting hours were over and most other patients would be asleep in their rooms. Pearson would be escorted by three plainclothes cops, along with Castillo and Durita—all of whom would be armed.

"Stand here," I hear Durita instruct Pearson. His voice is curt and borders on annoyed.

"Okay, boss," Castillo tells me from somewhere on the left side of the room. "Dr. Pearson is here. Ask him anything you want."

I take a breath. Ever since Castillo told me that my request had been approved, I'd been rehearsing what I was going to say. But now that the moment is here, I'm clamming up.

Pearson makes the first move.

"Hey, big guy," he says. In happier days, "big guy" was a nickname the professor used to call me. Something tells me he's smiling. The nerve of this guy.

"Marcus," is all I manage to get out at first.

Interesting: Marcus Pearson and Marcus Brutus. I wonder if he intentionally chose the name of an infamous traitor.

"Et tu, Brute?" I say.

There's a momentary silence before the professor starts to laugh. Not the reaction I was going for.

I cut him off. "So, why'd you do it?"

"Which part?"

"All of it."

"You can't see me anymore but—"

"Yeah, thanks to you."

"Right. Sorry about that. Anyway—"

He sure doesn't sound like he's sorry. "Apology not accepted."

"Okay. Well, do you want me to answer your question or not?"

"Hey. Watch it, Pearson," Durita chimes in. "Or whatever the hell your name is."

I take another breath. "Yes. Go ahead. Why did you do it?"

"Very well. I no longer sit at my desk all day writing about Shakespeare's plays. Now I'm living in one. The thrill of my betrayal—it's *Julius Caesar!* And then, though it was completely accidental, *King Lear* was added to the mix after I blinded you. Isn't it poetic? And like *Macbeth*, I betrayed Duncan to fulfill the witches' prophecy. I sought revenge, so even if I failed, my heart remains pure. For seeking revenge, there's only glory for me to be executed. I am blissfully living in extremes, like the mythic and literary heroes I taught and wrote about for decades. Truly, I am Iago. So if you are desirous today of my motive, I'm afraid you will have no satisfaction. No reason will be given from me to you."

What in God's name is this guy talking about?

"Just to make sure I'm understanding you correctly," I say, "are you actually saying that you became a traitor to your country in order to live out a Shakespearean fantasy?"

Pearson laughs again. "People have done crazier things for less."

Have they? I don't know what I was expecting as an explanation but certainly not this. "Why'd you come to Honolulu?"

"Oh, foolish you. You didn't know what my brother hid in that woman's secret cave. I idolized my brother and hadn't seen him since he disappeared in the Philippines over thirty years ago. Yes, and now he's dead. Our family was ostracized by our entire community when they found out my brother, whom you knew as Jimbo, blew up that nightclub in Bali. And then when people found out that my parents were close with Fernando and Imelda Marcos, well, we had to go into witness protection. The government renamed us Pearson."

Is that why Pearson squeaked through our background checks? Sort of odd he didn't turn up in the Witness Protection Program as that is part of background checks. Someone in our organization had to be helping him or it would have come up.

"He never got back in touch with us," said Pearson. "But somehow—you must wonder how—he knew when I was interviewed by the CIA. I received a message from him. After that, each time you left for Manila, using my name as cover, my brother and I stayed in touch." The prisoner chuckled. "Through Othello, my brother arranged to fake my death."

"What are you talking about? Who the hell's Othello?"

"Only one of Shakespeare's most tragic characters."

"Yes, I know that. And I also know you can tell me who he is."

"That's the question of the hour, isn't it?" Pearson pauses. "With Othello's help, I hid out for two years and patiently waited until the day I could come here to retrieve my brother's belongings—which included names and hideouts of the highest AQ members throughout the world. And his plans to use Anatoly Rustikoff for his jihad. It would be a huge coup to have seen those names for the CIA—yes, Tripp Regan? Othello also warned me my cover was blown when I arrived in Honolulu."

"Are you going to tell us who Othello is or not?"

"I will only tell you that he's alive. As is Desdemona, but not for long, I shouldn't think. As in the play Othello will kill her," he says, making a noise like he shot a gun.

"Desdemona will die by Othello's hand? When? Where? Who is she?" I ask knowing I won't get an answer. But in a state of near panic as my blindness seems to make this a swamp I can't escape from. And the panic increases as I am pretty sure I know who Desdemona is in this insane drama.

Pearson clears his throat, readying himself for his dramatic climax. "As Iago said, 'Demand me nothing: what you know, you know: From this time forth, I never will speak word."

And that was that. Dr. Marcus Pearson didn't speak another word.

They took him away. Among other charges, he will stand trial for treason and the attempted murder of a high-ranking CIA agent.

After his departure, Durita, Castillo, and I sit in stunned silence. We know less than before he came in.

"The lunatic seems to believe that shooting you has somehow given his life meaning," Castillo says. "And what the hell was all that Shakespeare mumbo jumbo?" he adds.

"Pearson was a Shakespeare professor all his life." I answer weakly.

"Anybody understand what all of that was about with Desdemona and Othello?" asks Durita. "Any ideas? It was like he was speaking another language."

"No idea," says Castillo, "but Pearson said Desdemona would die soon, so we better figure it out."

"Right. Hey, I'm no Shakespeare buff. So, anybody know what happens in the play?" queries Durita.

"Othello kills Desdemona," I tell Durita and Castillo.

"And," I add, "Pearson said Othello helped him fake his death and helped him hide out and warned him we knew his cover was blown. It would be wishful thinking on our part that he's AQ. Nope. Othello is CIA. One of our own." The three of us just sit there. We have been taken down an Alice in Wonderland hole.

Durita agrees with me that Othello is CIA. He walks toward the door after handing me a glass of water as he always does. He knows how thirsty I get so it is his good night to me every night.

Castillo follows him, but I call out after them, "Let's get started on who was working on getting a Shakespeare professor for me."

"I already started that, boss, and boy, it's covered up real good, but I will work on it more," Durita says, and then I hear them leave with an exhausted, "Good Night, boss." And they're gone.

I know I have a guard outside my door, but the silence is oppressive. I also know I won't sleep since we certainly have a traitor in our midst. And I am sure Desdemona is Cleo. She killed Abdul Rahman and somehow Othello, whoever he is, knows this.

2014

JAKE, 6

Don Durita has been spending a lot of time with Dad. He visits him almost daily, always with a large cup of coffee, as the old man has mentioned on more than one occasion that the hospital coffee is shit. He's not wrong.

At first, Durita's timing seemed coincidental, if not comical. He'd waltz into my dad's room, two cups of Kiki's Coffee in tow, just as I was on my way out. Or he'd be right about to make his exit as soon as I arrived. We'd joke about it.

"As always, my timing is impeccable ..." Durita laughs. In *Fight Club*, one of the most badass movies ever, Brad Pitt and Ed Norton are never in the same room together when another character is present. It's the type of small detail you don't notice until you watch the movie again, after you're in on the big twist.

"Tyler. We meet again," I say to Durita whenever he shows up.

My father is Durita's superior and Durita is mine. Before arriving in Honolulu over two weeks ago, I'd heard Durita's name and we'd been copied on some of the same confidential emails, but I never had the pleasure of meeting him in person.

I like him. He has a pretty good sense of humor, he knows his shit, and he seems to be a big fan of my dad's.

The CIA gets off on its hierarchy and complicated levels of security clearance, all of which are designated by The Department of State's Bureau of Human Resources—not exactly a group of guys who you want to grab a beer with. Dad has Top Secret clearance, the highest level. After pulling in almost thirty years with the agency, the old man has earned it. I can't even imagine what types of crazy shit he's found out about over the years. My plan is to fire off as many questions as possible when he's on his deathbed—which better be in the very distant future. This whole episode came way too close for comfort.

Durita has security clearance a rung below Dad's. A young gun like me only has confidential clearance, which means that I'm privy to information in which the unauthorized disclosure of said info could reasonably be expected to cause damage to the national security. Eventually, I realize that the timing of Durita's visits is deliberate. He and my father have higher clearances than me, so from a legal standpoint there are certain parts of the investigation that they cannot discuss in my presence. On my way in or way out of Dad's room, I've heard tidbits of their conversations about the usual suspects: Pearson, Othello, Abdul Rahman, Desdemona.

But today as I entered Dad's room with Mom, I overheard a word that I haven't heard in a while: "cave." At first, I didn't think much of it. I know that Judas traitor shot at my father while he was perched inside a cave on Cleo's property. But after a thorough investigation, the cave didn't yield any promising leads in terms of helping us figure out the identity of Othello, the person who we're pretty sure was working with Abdul Rahman and Pearson.

JAKE, 6

This is the cover story that the CIA came up with for my mom and the newspapers: my dad was called in at the last minute to assist with a high profile bankruptcy case at Paina Pineapple Plantation. Paina Pineapple Plantation, say that three times fast. Hawaii used to be the world's biggest pineapple exporter, but the Philippines and Costa Rica moved in and now the two of them make up for 95 percent of the market share, leaving Paina out in the cold. Weinstein, Forbes, Regan, and Lowe really are representing Paina in their bankruptcy case against their creditor, the Federal Land Bank Association of Hawaii. It's a whole shitshow that I won't get into. The salient facts are this: my dad was shot at the plantation after a disgruntled former employee came to seek revenge on the owner after he was unceremoniously fired. We'd pull something else out of our ass if they didn't, but it's a pretty lucky break that Forbes actually has an Hawaiian client.

Mom and my brothers seem to have bought it and that's all that matters. My mother has been so consumed with the future and making sure Dad just gets better that she's less concerned with what's already in the past. Ricky asked Dad and his doctors all of the usual questions, but their answers were prepped thoroughly beforehand. As for Matt, he asked all of the unusual questions. Having anticipated so much, I made sure that the higher-ups were as thorough with the cover story as possible.

After the four of us all said our hellos, Durita catches my eye and motions that he'd like a word with me in the hall.

"You've never been inside the cave on Cleopatra Gallier's property, have you?" Durita asks quietly.

I shake my head. "No, why?"

"You doing anything right now? I know you're on Rustikoff, but a fresh set of eyes could maybe help us out."

I agreed and off we went. We took my car. At first, there's an awkward silence. Durita and I haven't had much one-on-one time yet. "So, how's he seem to you?"

Durita turns to me in the driver's seat. "Your father?"

I nod. I can't stand referring to Tripp as "my father" or "my dad" or anything that reeks of paternity whatsoever. No need to broadcast nepotism. It makes me feel like a little boy or the teacher's pet, but as long as my father works for the agency, it's unavoidable, unfortunately.

"Not bad. I mean, a helluva lot better than I'd be doing if it was me in his shoes."

I nod again. "You think?"

"Sure. All things considered, your father seems to be taking it relatively well. The doctors and nurses would have to strap me down to keep me from sprinting out of that hospital and going to kill Pearson with my own two hands," Durita laughs.

"I think the blindness is the only thing holding him back ..." I force a smile.

"Well, and your mother hardly leaves his side. He'd have to get through her first!"

I'd really rather Durita cool it with all of the "your father" and "your mother's." But I bite my tongue. After all, he's several rungs above me and has been around at the agency a lot longer than I have. So, I just smile and nod.

"Anyway, besides that, are you enjoying our little island? Must be kind of nice escaping the cold?"

I put the blinker on and turn into Cleo's long, tree-lined driveway. "Oh yeah, January in the city is bleak."

"You New Yorkers ..." Durita smiles. "Referring to 'the city' as if there are no other cities in the whole wide world."

"There aren't," I smile back.

Durita turns and looks out the window. "So, how're things going with Rustikoff?"

"Eh, slow going. You know how it is."

"Sure do. My first case out of training almost killed me. Out of boredom, that is."

I laugh. "No kidding."

"We're worried Rustikoff's in cahoots with Putin?"

"Something like that. We're just making sure that they're not secretly building enough nuclear warheads to start World War III."

Durita sighs and looks out the window. "God. At this rate, we're all gonna blow each other up and there'll be no world left to protect."

He ain't wrong. If our worst fears are realized, along with one of the most ruthless and powerful men in the world, Rustikoff is harvesting enough missiles to blow us all to smithereens. I try not to dwell on the hypotheticals too much, it's enough to drive you crazy. We sit in heavy silence for a few moments, winding along Cleo's curved driveway. If only Durita knew how well I knew this drive. "Mind if we stop at the main house first and give Miss Gallier a heads up?" This is protocol, but I can't say that I've ever gotten butterflies about notifying any other property owner.

"No, of course not," Durita smiles at me again.

I get to Cleo's door first. Cleo doesn't answer. Instead, it's her housekeeper, Consuelo.

"Hey, Consuelo. Cleo home?"

Consuelo shakes her head. "Sorry. Mrs. Cleo at Sweet Pea for lunch."

Durita and I will go there after we see the cave. It's our favorite place to eat. Real Hawaiian vibe. "Got it. Could you please just tell her that Agent Durita and I were here to have another look at the property?"

Consuelo smiles, nods, and closes the door.

FOR ME, "CAVE" conjures up hieroglyphics on walls, a small burning fire, and gnarly, and dirty, hairy men eating meat off the bone. What I've just stepped inside is vastly different, and that's even after it was ravaged by an explosion.

The ceiling and stone walls have been painted a cheery shade of white, though the explosion left behind streaks of black soot, nothing a new paint job can't take care of. There are a few framed photos of other caves from around the world hung on the walls, and I suspect there were even more pre-explosion. Orange and white remnants of fabric are littered here and there, and in the corner of the room is a silver tray.

Cleo really went all out. I'm surprised she never brought me up here. We could have had some wild times …

The smell of smoke still permeates, but the place seems to have been wiped clean by the previous agents who inspected it after Dad got shot. After walking around the cave and looking for anything out of the ordinary, I turn to Durita. "What am I looking for?"

"That's what I'm trying to figure out, Regan. Pearson left nothing behind, not even microscopic fibers or hair. This asshole knew what he was doing."

"That worries me …" I say. "Maybe he's got more up his sleeve."

"I know. The only prints we found were from two years ago, when your father and Ms. Gallier were up here the night Rahman died."

What the fuck. "Excuse me?"

Durita looks surprised at my surprise. "Oh, I thought you knew."

"Knew what?"

"That your dad and Ms. Gallier came up here after she showed us where Abdul Rahman went over the cliff."

He sure didn't. "Uh…"

"We were able to pull prints from a few bottles of Veuve Clicquot. Cleo was in pretty bad shape when they left the cliff."

A few bottles of Veuve?

"Yeah, I'm sure he mentioned it at some point," I lie. I don't want to sound like I'm out of the loop or insanely jealous. "I'll bring it up again. What'd he say to you about it?" I ask, trying to sound casual.

"Just that Cleo was a wreck after Abdul Rahman died. She must've been in shock. Your father said that this was where she felt the safest and so that's where he took her."

But why did she need to feel safe with him?

"Well, she's at Sweet Pea," I remind Durita. "Let's go pay her a visit."

I head toward the cave's exit.

MY HEAD IS SPINNING. So this is where Dad actually was when he was supposedly "working" on the infamous China deal. There's a pit in my stomach as I picture the scene. Cleo and my dad are drinking two bottles of champagne here, in a place she never brought me.

So many questions. Did Cleo know he was in the CIA? How close were/are they? It's beyond fishy that he'd never mention it. I'll wait and see if he does. And why did Cleo return to Honolulu right after he was shot? Is it more than coincidence? Has to be. The CIA doesn't believe in coincidence and neither do I. And here's one more. WHY did Durita bring me here? He knew there was nothing to see.

JULIA, 3

When we first heard the terrifying news about Tripp, I offered to hop on a flight with Ricky like a good little fiancé, but he thought it was better that I stick around New York. Ricky would already have the whole family by his side, and anyway, there were several key wedding decisions that had to be made in person, by at least one of us.

Ricky was probably only looking out for me. The Regans can be a handful. He told me that Miranda was a wreck, Jake had shut down, and poor Matt didn't know what hit him. It was a situation already fraught with panic, anxiety, and stress. I'd only make things worse.

Ricky needed to focus on his dad, and I could just picture myself being a total nuisance, trying to walk that fine line between being as helpful as humanly possible and somehow managing to just stay out of the way. *How are you feeling, babe? Do you need anything? Ricky, you really should eat. You look tired, why don't I grab us coffees? What do you think of these centerpieces for the reception?*

While of course I would've loved to have been there for Ricky in his time of need, it was better that he had some alone time with his family first. But now that Tripp has woken out of his coma and the blood is leaving his eyes, everyone seems to be feeling a bit more relieved. It's been almost three weeks since Tripp's accident and boy, do I miss my fiancé.

Ricky doesn't know that I'm coming. The only person I trusted with my little secret about my surprise visit to Honolulu was Miranda. I didn't want to totally crash. Even though I'll be a Regan in just a few short months, I'm still technically an outsider. It'd be tragic if I wore out my welcome before I even became part of the family.

But I was surprised at how ecstatic and truly over-the-moon Miranda sounded on the phone a few days ago when I pitched her the idea. From the tone of her voice, I got the sense that perhaps the family was getting a little more sick of each other than Ricky had let on ...

Palm tree after palm tree passes by our black Honda Accord as it careens down the scenic Kalakaua Avenue. I can't believe I'm back in Hawaii, I think to myself as I open the mirror app on my iPhone and check my makeup one last time. It feels like I was just here five minutes ago but, at the same time, it seems like I've lived a whole other life since I was last in Honolulu. And in some ways, I guess I have. Even though they're brothers, life with Ricky doesn't remotely resemble my old life with Jake. I smile to myself, grateful for the change, as my Uber pulls into the Aston Hotel where the Regans are all staying.

Miranda has been giving me constant updates in regard to my fiance's whereabouts. I think she's really been enjoying this little top secret mission of ours. Right after the New Year, she clued me in about her love of Nancy Drew mysteries, so I think this has brought out that sly, sneaky side of Miranda. God bless her. The poor woman deserves this. Ricky tells me that she's hardly left Tripp's side the past three weeks. And no matter what anyone says, no one—and I mean, no one—enjoys spending their time inside of a hospital room.

As long as Ricky has his laptop and a Wi-Fi connection, his job at Slate allows him to work from anywhere. And present circumstances aside, what better place is there to be remote from than a gorgeous hotel with an ocean view. No doubt that beats the Lexington Avenue scene from his office in Midtown.

"Thank you," I say to the friendly Uber driver as he removes my T. Anthony roller bag from his trunk and hands it to me.

"Have a great trip," he smiles.

I turn and enter through the Aston's sliding glass doors. The hotel isn't as luxurious or grand as The Halekulani, but it's much closer to the hospital. I can't tell you how relieved I was when Ricky informed me that they weren't staying at The Halekulani. That place should come with a trigger warning.

I spot the elevators across the lobby and make a beeline for them. There's an extra spring in my step and I smile to myself as the elevator doors open, taking me closer and closer to the man I love.

I knock three times on room number 815.

"One second," I hear Ricky call out from inside. The sound of his voice brings a big smile to my face. My heart starts to race and the butterflies in my stomach flutter. Until this very moment, I didn't realize just how excited I was to see my fiancé again. I know that three weeks isn't *that* long, but still. Not that there's much of a comparison, but I can't imagine how those poor women who send their husbands off to war don't lose their minds. I don't think I'd be able to stand it. Every day without them must be pure torture—and at least I've had the luxury of knowing where Ricky was this whole time.

Moments later, the door swings open and Ricky is standing in front of me, looking sexy as hell wearing jeans and no shirt.

"Housekeeping," I smirk.

"Jules!" Ricky screams as he takes me into his buff arms. "What are you doing here?!"

"Surprise!" My legs wrap around his rock-hard torso and my arms hug his tanned neck tightly. I take his perfect face in my hands and look into those baby blue eyes that I've so desperately missed.

"Man, I forgot how much you weigh!"

I laugh. "Ricky!"

"Just kidding." He smiles again and kisses me. "Now get your ass in here." Ricky puts me back down on the floor, grabs my roller bag and holds the door open for me.

The room is nice. Maybe not Halekelani nice, but I sure wouldn't mind being holed up here for almost a month. There's a king-size bed in the middle with a beige carpet, a workspace in the corner where Ricky's computer is set up, and a balcony overlooking the azure sea.

"So, what do you think?"

"I like it," I smile as I walk out onto the balcony. After an unusually cold winter in New York, the warm sun feels fantastic on my extraordinarily pale skin. "Great view ..."

Ricky comes up from behind me. He grabs my waist and starts kissing my neck. "I'll say."

I laugh as he sticks his hand down the front of my jeans. "God, I missed you," I manage to say, although I'm quite certain that I could orgasm. Three weeks is a while if you're used to sex on the regular.

"I missed you, too, Jules."

I turn around to face him. "Yeah, you better ..."

"And I don't know if it's the time away or what, damn. You look amazing."

Why, thank you, Danielle from Drybar and Irene from Rescue Spa. "Who, *moi?*"

"Yeah, you." Ricky leans in and gives me the deep, romantic kiss I need. He picks me up in his arms again and throws me onto the king-sized hotel bed. Bliss.

2014

MIRANDA, 3

At breakfast in the hospital cafeteria, Matt looks downright melancholy. I'm on the verge of tears myself as this whole ordeal has started to wear on us all, but Matt just stares off down the hall. He is so easy and peaceful compared to his noisy brothers. I'd never say this out loud, but it's quite a relief when Jake and Ricky are not constantly around. It's so much more peaceful when they're off doing their work. They take up so much space and air and I need quiet to process what our life might be like if Tripp never regains his sight, which is certainly possible, though there is hope from a doctor in Florida who will fly out here to operate if the blood leaves his eyes completely.

AFTER OUR MEDIOCRE MEAL, I observe my middle son as he aimlessly wanders down the long, white, clinical hallway teeming with doctors, nurses, and sick patients. "Matt, what is it? Everything alright?"

He shrugs and keeps walking.

"This whole thing has been a lot for all of us, but you've been such a great sport. And I'm so glad you're here with me. I don't know what I'd do if you weren't here to keep me company." But when I look over at him, half expecting a smile, he's still lost in thought. "Matt, seriously. What's wrong?"

He takes a seat on one of the chairs that line the hall. "I don't know, but I think there's a secret."

Oh, boy. "A secret?" I sit in the chair next to him.

"Yeah, something doesn't feel right with what happened to Dad."

I can't imagine what Matt could possibly mean. Dr. Copperman, Dr. Akana, and all of the nurses have been so kind, so professional, and so transparent with Tripp. But then again, Matt was born with a sixth sense. He feels things that the rest of us are oblivious to. That's why he loves plants and wildlife so much, I think. Matt is one with nature. "Okay ... Well, tell me more. What do you think is a secret?"

"What really happened to Dad. I asked the nice men outside his door—who seem to be guarding him—if I could go to see the pineapple plantation where he was shot because I was interested in the fibers they can extract from the leaves to make shirts."

"And what did they say?"

"Well, they said 'fine' but never did anything about it and I asked them a few more times too. They were nice but it just seemed like they weren't telling me the truth. They smiled and took down notes about what I wanted to do but when I asked again, they smiled again and said they would see what they could do but next time, it was the same story."

"Well, Matt honey, just remember that they're very busy. Maybe—"

"Jake knows the secret too. He's in Dad's room with him alone every day."

"I know. But those two have always been close."

"Mom, c'mon. What could they possibly be talking about?"

I'd like to think that Matt is only letting his imagination run wild but in these moments, it's better to placate him. He has thin skin. "You really think something's going on? Could they be discussing what will happen if Tripp doesn't get his sight back?"

Matt looks at me and shakes his head no.

On one hand, I'm afraid we've all spent way too much time in this hospital over the past few weeks, and Matt's patience and sense of reality might be starting to wear on him. It's starting to wear on us all. But on the other hand, this whiff of intrigue ignites my Nancy Drew soul. If there really is a mystery to be solved, and Matt is usually right about things like this, my trusty sidekick and I need to find out what it is.

Detectives Matt and Miranda at your service.

"Why don't we see if Jake will take us out to that plantation?" Before Matt answers, I have my phone out—which, I don't believe is allowed in the hallways of the hospital—and dial Jake. It goes straight to voicemail, so I leave him a message. "Jake, Matt and I would love to go have a look at the pineapple plantation, and I wanted to see if you'd join us? Give me a call when you get a chance and let me know."

"Really, Mom?" Matt whispers, the beginnings of a smile starting to tug at the corners of his mouth.

"Yes, really. Let's start investigating, shall we?"

Less than a minute later, my phone vibrates and lo and behold, it's Jake. I'm shaking with the excitement of it all. Nancy Drew has been off duty for quite a while now.

"Hey, Mom. Just got your message. Why do you want to go out there?"

I glance over at Matt. "Oh, I don't know. Matt and I were just thinking that something quite major happened to your father there and so it might be good for us to see it. The scene of the crime if you will."

"Um. Okay, sure. I'll pick you and Matt up tomorrow morning around ten, and we'll head out. Sound good?"

I look over at Matt and smile broadly. "Yes, Jake. See you at ten. Thank you."

THE NEXT MORNING Jake pulls up at our hotel in his black SUV. He has a man with him in the front seat.

"Mom and Matt, meet Kai, our interpreter. For the most part, the men who work the plantation only speak Hawaiian."

"Nice to meet you," Kai smiles back at us from the front seat.

Jake tells us: "Only about 5 percent of people on the island speak Hawaiian, but Kai is fluent and he'll also be our tour guide around Oahu. GPS is not great on some of these trails and roads."

I'm quite thrilled to be out of the hospital for the day, seeing green forests and not Tripp's dismal gray room.

Kai smiles. "Nice to meet you, Mrs. Regan and Matt. My name means 'Of The Sea,' which I only mention as it also means Hawaii's gorgeous coastline that we are now passing."

Matt questions him nonstop about the local fauna and loss of pineapple plantations.

"Most of Hawaii's pineapples, called *hala kahiki* in Hawaiian, came here on boats from Brazil," Kai tells us. "They prevented scurvy. Hawaii used to export 80 percent of the world's pineapples, but now Costa Rica and the Philippines mostly dominate the market. That's why your father was here, correct? Something to do with a bankruptcy case?"

"You know, Kai, the lawyer who heads Tripp's firm, Larry Forbes, came to our house to tell me about the shooting but I was obviously not taking it in," I said. "I was undone by the news, and all I wanted was to get out here to my husband. I remember nothing of the next few days. Larry, Tripp's law partner, also came out here to Honolulu to be with us, and he explained Tripp was at a pineapple plantation when a furious worker who was just fired, shot Tripp, thinking he was the owner. I keep picturing it in my mind so I need to see where it happened."

"Got it," Kai pauses. "Anyone want to hear a fun fact about pineapples?" A somewhat clumsy change of subject, but I can't blame him.

Matt raises his hand.

Kai smiles at him. "The bromelain enzyme in pineapple stems eats the worker's fingerprints. At least that's the theory why they don't have fingerprints."

Matt interrupts, "Oh no, I have to tell Cleo. She's growing pineapples in her kitchen garden. She has to be careful of the stems."

"Well, it takes years of handling the pineapple day in and day out so I wouldn't worry for your friend, Matt."

I'm surprised to learn she is on the island. I watch Jake, who says nothing. Matt would say he was going to look at plants but he never shared where. Well, he never shares anything ever.

As we continue on the drive to the plantation, Kai tells us all about Hawaiian legends. He has quite a gift for gab.

"Oh, yes. My friend Cleo told us all about Pele and her sister, Polihauna." Matt is talking nonstop. A welcome change. He must feel safe.

"I didn't know Cleo was here." I can't help myself asking Matt. He nods, "Yes, I visited her trees and plants once. Jake dropped me off there and then picked me up after his work." Hmm.

Finally, after almost two hours of vistas and jungle, we all pile out of the black SUV. Kai points to the vast land and announces, "We are at three hundred meters, the perfect altitude, and this red soil is the best soil to grow pineapples." Then he sees a few workers and waves them over.

Jake tells us: "I asked Dad how to get in touch with the plantation, and then I called ahead to see if the men who were here when he was shot could be available. Do you just want to see where it happened?"

"Yes, it'd be great if they could show us where it happened. I'd like to thank them for getting Tripp to the hospital as well."

Kai starts speaking to three workers. The workers look down and seem shy. Kai tells us what they say when he asks them about the shooting. "Apparently, your father was well dressed and of a similar height to the owner who recently fired one of his men," Kai points to the worker in the middle. "This is Kapono, and the worker who was fired is his cousin. Kapono says his cousin Matamo has always been trouble. Now he's in jail and admitted trying to kill the owner. Kapono says they are sorry your father was shot. He will show you where it happened."

Matt and I both nod as we trudge behind Jake, Kai, Kapono, and the two other men. When we get to the plantation's main house, there's a patio and a long staircase to the upper level, which we're told is a restaurant. This patio is where Matamo was standing when Tripp came out of the restaurant onto the balcony. Now I can imagine exactly how it happened. Gosh, it upsets me to think of him landing on this patio.

"Matt, do you have any questions for these nice men?" I ask.

Matt smiles, shakes his head no, says goodbye, and heads to the car. I catch up to him and he seems soothed by this. He asks Jake to drop him at Cleo's so he can tell her about the enzyme in pineapples.

Now it's me, not Matt, who is unconvinced. I wonder why the plantation owner has never been in touch, and I'm suspicious how Jake jumped right in and organized things so fast. It seems too convenient that the men were all here and that they spoke a language only Kai understood. It felt like a play that was rehearsed. Ok let's say there is a secret. I don't think I want to know what it is. Tripp says he loves that I am not suspicious and that an apple is just an apple. Well maybe a pineapple is just a pineapple or maybe—no, I'm not going there. I have too much else to worry about right now.

2014

TRIPP, 9

"I'll see you tomorrow, Tripp," Magda whispers.

Her voice woke me up. I had fallen asleep during our session, which had been happening with greater and greater frequency. At first I was embarrassed, but Magda assured me that it occurs with most of her patients.

She ends each of our sessions by putting her hands above my head and imagining a green light. Without touching me, she moves her hands over my body all the way down to my root, the seventh chakra. This is supposed to leave me with a calming feeling, which, like today, it usually does. I never want her to leave. She gives me such peace, but I know she has a life of her own to go home to. She's very private, but she's mentioned her partner, Liz, a few times.

"Alright. See you tomorrow, Magda. Thanks again."

Her bracelets rattle as she rises out of her chair and makes her way toward the door. Magda has a light walk, so thank goodness for the bracelets or I'd never know she was coming or going. There she goes, clinking down the hall like a wind chime.

TRIPP, 9

I am thinking about our session when the aroma hits me like a ton of bricks. It's Endgame, a perfume whose scent I know well. Only one woman I know wears it.

"Cleo?" I stammer.

CLEO, 7

I tiptoe into Tripp's room. He looks so peaceful lying in bed with his eyes closed. I'm thinking about whether or not I should wake him when the decision is made for me.

His eyes open. "Cleo?"

"Tripp, oh, thank God. You can see!"

"Nope. Still blind."

"Then how did you—"

He smiles. "Your perfume gave you away."

That deflates me as I bend over to kiss his forehead. "When I heard what happened, I flew from Dubai. I was so afraid you might die and I wanted to see you one more time to tell you what a wonderful man you are—well, as Danny, I thought you were wonderful."

"I wish I could see you one more time too."

"I have on your favorite color, or at least back on Mt. Kilimanjaro, Danny told me it was his favorite color." I laugh as I say, "But then, you told me many things that weren't true."

"Pink," Tripp says, then adds, "I see you in my mind all the time."

I let this go. I thought I was being funny, but I see I wasn't.

"Tripp, I want you to meet Zelli. She has your blue eyes and my dimples."

"She's here with you?"

I shake my head. Then I remember he can't see me. "No."

"Oh. Why did you never tell me about her, Cleo?"

"Because you are married with sons and a whole life in New York, and I wasn't going to interfere with that. A baby was what I wanted and was pretty sure you didn't. I am sorry, Tripp, as I made all the choices, but you weren't going to throw over your life to move into mine."

He doesn't say anything. He knows I'm right.

"Also, I loved Danny, not you. We had one wonderful night together that resulted in a beautiful child ... but not a life together."

"As you can imagine, I've had a lot of idle time to think about this. And I agree."

"I didn't bring Zelli, Tripp, but she's at my house. Magda let me know when you would be alone. I didn't want to intrude on family time. And maybe you don't want to meet her? "

When Tripp doesn't say anything, I start rattling off questions.

"Why were you shot on my property at my cave?" I blush, remembering what we did in that cave. "And why was Jimbo's brother there? I mean, how did he even know about it? I never told anyone but you about that place."

"I don't know. Pearson hasn't said anything yet, except that he's living a Shakespeare play and not just teaching one, and that has made him fulfilled."

"Fulfilled, really?."

"Hey, maybe if you pay his cell a visit, he'll tell you. Just be honest and let him know that he tried to kill the wrong person." Tripp is stone-faced but I know this is his humor. "Then he can shoot you too."

Finally, a smile. Tripp starts laughing as do I, out of total relief.

"Obviously, I'm not supposed to tell you any of this but we think Pearson was sent to destroy something his brother had left there," says Tripp. "But Special Agent Durita, who was with you and me the night we looked for Mohammed's body, searched the cave with several other agents and they found nothing." He pauses. "Well, nothing except the two champagne bottles we drank. Our prints are still all over the place, so I told our guys that we went there because you were so devastated after Jimbo's death. The cave, I said, was your safe place. We had a few bottles of champagne to calm you down and to celebrate the terrorist was dead. And celebrate we did."

"Yes, Tripp Regan, we did."

In the silence that follows, I think of how devastating it must be for Tripp to have his sight snatched away. I see tears start to well in his useless blue eyes. I go to him, my heart breaking, and put my arms gently around him, frightened of hurting him more.

"Oh Tripp, I am so sorry."

After a moment, he says, "First time I've cried. I've had to be so brave for Miranda, the boys, my colleagues, and for myself. But not for you, I guess." He smiles a bit.

"You never need to be brave around me, Tripp. Remember how you helped me climb Kilimanjaro when I was so afraid. You made me brave then, so I'm only returning the favor."

Another pause. Then finally, he asks, "Did you ever see the play, *Our Town*?"

I nod. Goodness, I've done it again. "Of course," I say. "My mother took us, my sisters and me, when we were teenagers. I have never forgotten it."

"Being blind reminds me a bit of *Our Town*."

"You mean when the young girl—Emily, I think her name was—dies and comes back for one day? She's so overcome with clocks ticking and the sight of her mother making breakfast. It's so painful she can't stay."

"Exactly. Things she never really saw when she was alive."

Neither of us says anything for a few moments. I sit in the chair next to him and take his hand. He looks gaunt and old. And frightened.

"Want a story?" I ask.

He nods.

"You know who Art Garfunkel is, right?"

"I lost my sight, Cleo, not my memory." He smirks.

"Right. Well then, you remember the song, 'The Sound of Silence?'

Tripp nods again.

Art Garfunkel wrote it for a friend of his who suddenly went blind. Remember how it starts out: 'Hello darkness, my old friend?'

"Yeah ..."

"You will like this story, I promise. And when I'm done I will leave, as Miranda may be coming back soon. The last thing I want is to upset her. But I'll come back with Zelli another day if you'd like, and you can smell her too."

Aha, another smile from him.

"Okay, the back story is that Garfunkel's roommate and best friend, Sandy, suddenly went blind from glaucoma while they were in college. And because of that, Garfunkel calls himself 'Darkness.' He would say to Sandy, 'Darkness is going to read to you now.' Garfunkel would take him to class, to get food, to visit friends, prepare for exams, write his graduate school applications. He did everything for Sandy, who went on to graduate school and married his high school sweetheart. Years later, Garfunkel called Sandy for a four-hundred-dollar loan to finance his first album. All Sandy and his wife had was four hundred and four dollars in their bank account, but without hesitation, Sandy gave it to him and with that money, Simon and Garfunkel recorded the now legendary song, 'The Sound of Silence.'"

I turn on the iPod I brought so he can listen to the song whenever he'd like and take his hand to show him where I put it next to his bed and which buttons to push.

I get up to go and see that Tripp is smiling again. It's a genuine smile.

As I start to walk out, I say to Tripp over my shoulder: "Hopefully Pearson won't be so close-lipped with me."

"You are the most exquisite and seductive woman in the world, Cleo, but even you won't get Pearson to talk. He quoted Iago to me when he was here and then clammed up."

I walk back to Tripp and ask if I can take the glass he was drinking out of.

"I'm sure Zelli is your child, Tripp, but I am taking the glass you drank out of to have a DNA test. As you well know I slept with Jake many times. He used protection always and you didn't but still I should do the test. Do you agree?"

He nods and I take the glass and bend over him and kiss him on each eye. "Goodbye Darkness, my old friend. You are being so brave, Tripp. The sound of silence must be terrifying when you are alone here and I can only imagine what thoughts are going through your head all night and the effort it takes all day to pretend all is well. I can see that all is not well. I don't like Kafka, but he said something I have never forgotten: 'A book must be the ax for the frozen sea inside us.' I think your blindness is like the ax for the frozen sea inside you, Tripp. We all live in a bit of a trance to get through life. So perhaps your blindness is the ax that will strengthen your spirit. And with that, I leave you for now." He nods at me as he always did when I got too philosophical. And then he laughs.

After departing, I head to the office of my physician, Dr. Harry Lodge, on the floor below.

HE IS WAITING FOR ME in his office, chatting with a patient who looks to be at least ninety-nine years old. As the gentleman gets up to leave, I see the pain he is in and feel so embarrassed that I am healthy and young. He looks my way before he leaves and elegantly bows. I bow without thinking and he is once again, for a moment, young and painless.

I hand my doctor the glass from Tripp and some of Zelli's curls.

"DNA test results will be back soon," Dr. Lodge assures me as I leave. I head to the hospital's chapel to pray for Tripp and for that lovely old man, whoever he is. And to cry for them both.

SPENCER, 4

Walking toward Sweet Pea from my car, I immediately spot Cleo, chatting with a man at an outdoor table. In my business, I'm constantly surrounded by gorgeous women but, God, she takes my breath away. Turns out she isn't in Dubai after all, but right here in Honolulu. I wonder if Pudge and Pudding know she is here. They didn't call me but maybe they told her I was looking for her and she said not to tell me. Certainly possible. Since Q has been looking into Mohammed Abdul Rahman's death it is either a cover-up that is handled brilliantly or else he did slip off the road. I go with the cover-up. But doing spy movies has made me suspicious of everyone. Including Cleo.

I recognize the man Cleo is dining with as Walter, the ex-Navy Seal and physical trainer. I know him from surfing the Banzai Pipeline, though I suspect that he doesn't love the sport as much as I do. It's only on calmer days that I've seen him around. Contrary to the bristly reputation of most film directors, I'm actually a pretty friendly guy. The first time I saw Walter in the water, I noticed that he was having trouble getting up on his board. He has a Seal's ultratoned physique, but also a Seal's pride. He didn't want to ask for my help even

251

after he saw me, wave after wave, easily getting up on my board and riding the waves to shore.

Finally, I paddled over to him again and told him to lean back a bit more. If your body is too far forward, you'll just keep falling over the front of the board, which, by then, Walter had done about twenty times. Ever since, Walter's been a pro.

I keep walking toward their table on the restaurant patio, studying Cleo's face. Indeed, her expression changes drastically when she sees me. Her smile drops and there's that same look she gave me years ago in the studio parking lot. It's as if she's trapped, or maybe like I'm going to whip out a pistol and shoot her in broad daylight. What have I done to this woman that incites such terror in her eyes every time she sees me? I have to believe the answer has something to do with what my father did before he killed himself.

Walter also notes the change in Cleopatra's demeanor. When he turns to see who she's afraid of, I stop. He's an ex-Seal, after all.

I offer them both a friendly wave.

Then, Jake Regan—who Pudge and Pudding told me Cleo was crazy about and who way back when, was on Cleo's show with me—gets out of a dark sedan in the parking lot with another dude. The other guy is dressed in a black suit and looks like an overweight Agent Smith from *The Matrix*. Since Jake's father was shot here, I imagine he came right over. Is he CIA and is his father? My instincts are yes they both are and that Cleo knows it and so does Walter. Is that how Cleo disappeared so completely—with help from the CIA? But why did she need to disappear?

When Jake sees Cleo, sunlit under a perfect blue sky, it's like a movie shot in slow motion. It brings to mind that famous scene in *10* when the bodacious Bo Derek runs in slow motion into the arms of dorky Dudley Moore—though Jake is certainly no goofy Dudley Moore. If memory serves, Jake seems to have bulked up since we were both on the show together.

He and the *Matrix* dude stop in their tracks just beside Cleo's table when she looks up from her salad bowl and spots him. In sharp contrast to her expression upon seeing me, she smiles at Jake, a smile that lights up the pavement for me and anyone passing by. The chubby guy in the black suit nods at her—he seems to know her too. A party with no words being spoken. And then there's me, the party-crasher. Now seems like as good a time as any to jump in. I approach Jake and stick out my hand.

"Wow, small world! Weren't we on Cleo's show together a few years ago?"

Jake smiles affably, but he can hardly tear his eyes away from Cleo. "Oh, shit! Yeah, that's right! You direct movies or something, right?"

I try not to take offense at the understatement. Last year my film grossed $22 million. "Yes, good memory."

"Good to see you, man," says Jake. "And this is Don Durita."

I shake Don's hand. "Hey, Spencer Stone."

He gives me a curt nod. "Nice to meet you."

Jake pulls up a chair and then he and Durita join Cleo and Walter at their table. Cleo asks, "Which of you smells a bit like Chanel No. 5?" They both look stunned and laugh. Probably one of them has a girlfriend who wears it.

I turn to Cleo and Walter. "Hey, Cleo, I'm not sure if you remember me but—"

"Of course. Spencer. So nice to see you." She forces a smile. "You know my friend Walter, right?" Walter and I say our hellos.

"How's your father this morning, Jake?" Cleo asks.

"He's okay," he says. "Someone gave Dad an iPod, and he won't stop playing with the thing."

Cleo nods, biting her lip, then glances at Durita. She whispers, "Did they learn anything more about why Tripp was shot, Don?"

He says nothing as he glances at me then shakes his head no.

If I was shooting this scene, I'd use jerky cuts, focusing on me: left out of the action and, therefore, very crucial. Obviously Durita and Jake are CIA; their black SUV and sunglasses and dark clothes and even their walks herald CIA. My film's center around the CIA or FBI so I know what they look like and how they hold themselves, but I am not sure how Cleo fits in—or Walter, but they are all somehow involved in this shooting incident, I'm guessing.

"Mind if I join you?" I ask. This feels sort of tricky but it's worth a shot. Cleo may say no, but she is most likely too polite to do that. Walter eyes Cleo, and she blinks her approval back at him. We are all in close quarters at this little outdoor round table, so I have to squeeze in.

"Cleo, I saw Pudge and Pudding a week or so ago," I say, after the server leaves to get me a cup of coffee and Jake an iced tea. "They mentioned to me that you'd moved to Dubai."

She glances down at her salad. "Yes, I was living there for a few years. But now I'm back in Honolulu and couldn't be happier." She turns to Jake. "And I'm so glad you dropped Matt off so he can look at my garden and other foliage he loves on the property." She laughs. "I am so glad you stayed."

Jake's arm is next to mine, and I feel him shudder. He leans closer to Cleo and whispers, "Durita said you went to the cave with my dad after—"

Cleo's look clearly warns him to stop. For God's sake, I can hear what Jake is saying—we are at the same table.

I interrupt, "I read about your father, Jake. I'm so sorry."

"Yeah, some crazy guy," Jake replies, shaking his head. What the hell is going on here? These people clearly know more than is being said about Tripp Regan's shooting—and what is the cave Jake just mentioned to Cleo? Better if I just change the subject.

I look at Walter. "You thinking of heading to the Banzai today, Walter? I think the wind has stirred the waves up."

Jake gives Cleo a big smile. "Man, I love the Banzai Pipeline. Great memories."

I note that Cleo blushes. Really blushes. Wonder what those two did there on the beach. No, actually, I don't wonder. I'm pretty sure I can guess.

Well, I'll try Agent Durita. "You must be wondering why the shooting of Jake's father is near Abdul Rahman's house, or I guess he is called Jimbo?"

Durita looks up from his plate where he has grabbed a roll from the bread basket and starts buttering it big time, and I know I have stumbled onto something.

Cleo, Jake, and Walter pretend they didn't hear what I said. So I am guessing Jake's father was involved in Abdul Rahman/ Jimbo's death. And it's for sure that Durita is CIA since I can see his badge under his jacket peeking out. Since Cleo came back right away from Dubai, I have to believe she is somehow part of this. I mean, she's suddenly back after all this time? All these puzzle-piece characters need to fit into place.

"So you work in the film industry, Spencer?" Durita asks.

"I do," I nod.

"No kidding. Doing what?"

"I'm a director."

"Like Spielberg?"

I wish. "Kind of." I smile. "Thrillers, mostly. Some spy stuff. I just finished one in London so I came back home here to surf for a while and be with my wife and kids."

Durita seems to relax. He's relieved, or am I dreaming all this?

"As a matter of fact," I add, "Cleo interviewed me after my last spy film a few years back on her show and Jake was on the same day."

Jake laughs. "God, I was so terrible."

Cleo is flirting with him as she laughs. "You were great—well, maybe a tad quiet."

"I don't think I said a word. Did I, Spencer?" He is flirting back.

She takes the iced tea Jake is nearly finished drinking and takes a final sip.

"Well, you didn't say much, Jake, I agree, so I jumped in," I offer diplomatically. "I did need to promote my film and I wanted to meet Cleo." I look around the table and explain, "My parents were friends with Cleo's father."

Cleo looks at me like I'm an ignorant or misbehaving child, and she puts her hand out. "Come with me, Spencer."

Cleo leads me to her tiny yellow convertible and tells me to get in. I do. She's still got the iced tea glass in her hand, which she puts it in the cup holder before turning on the ignition.

CLEO DRIVES US TO her house, where at the front door a beautiful toddler wiggles out of her nanny's arms and runs up to Cleo. After hugging and kissing, Cleo takes a seat in the grass with the child and indicates for me to do the same. Then she looks up at me. "Why are you doing this, Spencer?"

I take a deep breath. "My mother has a letter from my father, which he wrote just before he killed himself. I saw it for the first time when I was in London visiting my mother on the anniversary of his death. I had asked her if she had any idea why my father committed suicide and she retrieved his suicide note and showed it to me. He wrote that he had committed a dishonorable deed and had to take his own life as payment. He didn't say what the dishonorable deed was." I paused. "When my mother and I were discussing it, I kept seeing your face when I said my parent's names.

She nods and says quite simply, "Yes."

"It would be really nice to live my life without this hanging over me, Cleo. Suicide is an awful legacy to be left by one's father, especially if it is unexplained."

She is fiddling with the grass we are sitting on. "I am not sure if I tell you it will provide you with the peace you seek. It might even be worse for you."

"Cleo, as the Bible says, 'The truth shall set you free.' I know it might be horrible but the stories I've made up my entire life are pretty bad. I was planning to do a movie about it."

"No, Spencer, don't do that. Promise me." She won't take her eyes off me.

I offer a reluctant nod, suddenly more apprehensive about where this is going but I promise her. The beautiful child is sitting absolutely still, sensing the deep emotions her mother and I are both feeling. The little imp breaks the intensity of the moment by jumping into my lap. Cleo and I laugh.

But Cleo also looks like she wants to cry, as do I. Her daughter moves back to her mother's lap. This is a scene for the movie I'm now not making anymore. And now I know why Cleo Gallier stayed in Dubai: she was pregnant with this glorious child. Has Jake not seen this baby with his big blue eyes? I look again at the sweet child. Yes, indeed, definitely Jake's eyes. And of course that is why she confiscated his iced tea glass: a DNA test.

I wonder if Jake has any idea he's a daddy.

"I will tell you what your father did, but not just yet," says Cleo, jolting me back to the moment I fear. "I will tell you," she cautions, "but don't pressure me."

I nod back at her.

"I am changing the conversation now, Spencer. Since you make spy and thriller movies, how would you portray the motive of Tripp Regan's shooter? This is top secret stuff, but here goes. Tripp Regan's shooter offered one convoluted clue about why he did what he did: he is Iago and must protect Othello." Cleo shakes her head. "Before becoming a criminal, this man was apparently a Shakespeare professor. "

The little toddler, now bored, pulls her mother to get up, which Cleo does before offering me a half-smile and saying, "Can you call an Uber?"

"Can I see where the shooter was? I'm pretty good at solving riddles, so let me in on what you know. I have no presupposed ideas so I'll be able to look at it with fresh eyes."

Cleo gets to her feet, and I follow her across the lawn. She hands over her child to a cozy-looking nanny who has a terrific British accent.

Cleo gazes at me for a long while and then, like my mother, decides to let me in on the secret. But a different secret—where the shooting of Tripp Regan happened.

I still want to ask about my father but I can tell she isn't ready to tell me so I'll become indispensable to her and eventually she'll tell me. You can't direct films for years without realizing how to motivate people to do what you want.

Once back in her car, she drives us down a narrow lane to a rocky area, explaining that the cave from which the shooter emerged was above us. I'm determined to determine the motive of the shooter for her. Feel like a knight in olden times slaying a dragon for the fair lady.

But I don't desire the fair lady. I crave the reason behind my father's suicide. I will continue plotting out the movie that will never be. I promised and I keep my promises.

I jump out of her car and tell her I'm going to use my camera to work out the answer to her question. I want a new perspective. I climb up the rock face to the cave's entrance, then look down at the angle where the shooter took aim at Tripp Regan. The shooter who said he was Iago protecting Othello. Interesting concept.

I call an Uber to go back to my car. Eleven minutes later, I arrive back at Sweet Pea in a hunter green Honda Accord driven by Jade, a friendly twenty-something who probably enjoys the occasional marijuana cigarette in his spare time. From the window in the back seat, I see Jake and Durita have finished eating, but they're still at the table, talking with Sweet Pea's owner, Duncan.

"Do you actually mind pulling up to that black Wrangler?" I ask Jade, pointing at my Jeep Wrangler a few cars away. It isn't the nicest car I've ever owned, but it sure as hell is the most fun to drive.

"No problem," Jade smiles as he pulls up to my Jeep.

"Thanks, man. Have a good one," I say to Jade as I duck out of the Honda. Five stars.

I fish out my keys and hop into my Jeep. I don't want Jake and Durita to see that I'm back. Not yet at least. I reach into the back seat and grab my camera. My windows are already cracked, and I'm hoping that the camera will pick up audio that my ears cannot.

At the patio table, all three men—Jake, Durita, Duncan—are smiling. It looks like they're just shooting the breeze. The odds of this footage breaking the case wide open are doubtful, but you never know. Uh-oh. Restaurant owner Duncan shields his eyes from the sun and strains his neck. Is he looking at me? Admittedly, I don't know him well, but certainly well enough to warrant a hello.

Certainly not well enough to be secretly taping him.

Duncan is waving. He's waving at me.

I stash my camera on the passenger seat before hopping out of my Jeep to say hello.

"Only one famous film director comes into Sweet Pea ..." says Duncan as I approach Jake and Durita's table. "So when I saw a guy playing with his video camera in the parking lot, I knew it had to be you."

Jake and Durita bristle. Their eyes meet across the table.

"What were you filming, Hollywood?" Durita asks.

"Not filming, just rewatching footage I need to send to my editor before I head to the Pipeline." I know they'll go back to their office and look me up and find I am just who I said I was.

I turn to Duncan and change the subject. "How are you? Sweet Pea seems to be thriving."

"Yeah, thanks to loyal customers like Don here—" he nods at Durita "—business is good."

"Best kale salad I've ever had," Jake chimes in. I can see why Cleo is so taken with the guy. I could easily see that mug in front of the camera. Maybe I should give him the card for my casting director, Anita.

"Ah, you're very kind." Duncan beams down at Jake. "You know, you and Cleo make a cute couple."

Jake laughs and shakes his head. "Yeah, why don't you tell her that?"

"Oh, I didn't realize you two were even together," I say. "Did you meet when you were on the show?"

"Nah, it's a really long story that I won't bore you with." Jake stands. "Anyway, back to the salt mines." He looks up and our eyes meet—those blue eyes the same as Cleo's baby. "We're actually not a couple," he says. "Duncan's messing around. But feel free to put in a good word ..." He laughs.

I smile at Jake and put my investigative director hat back on. I lower my voice. "So, that terrorist. She wasn't actually ... his friend, was she?"

The mood changes. The smile disappears from Jake's face. Don Durita stands up, and Duncan looks like he might be sick. "You sure ask a lot of questions, don't you, Hollywood?"

"Sorry, I didn't mean—"

"Don't worry about it," says Jake. "Dorito always gets a little grumpy after a meal. Gets pissed at himself for eating all those carbs. He's put on about thirty pounds in the last few years, or so he tells me."

Durita laughs. "Ahem, young man. You shouldn't speak about your superior like that."

Jake ignores that. "And to answer your question. They were *good friends*, so she was devastated at what he was planning to do to Pearl Harbor."

Durita looks at his watch. Looks like a watch that tracks all your exercise, and I must say Durita doesn't look like he ever uses it. Bet he bought it with intentions to get back in shape.

"We should ..." He tells Jake as he grabs a cookie.

Jake nods. He waves at Duncan, then at me. "Thanks, Duncan. Until next time! Nice to see you again, Spencer."

They hop into the black sedan, and they're off.

Duncan starts clearing the plates off Jake and Don's table. "They were here together all the time, you know." He means Cleo and Jimbo.

I try buttering Duncan up. "Well, who can blame them? You serve Honolulu's finest!"

"They had their favorite table by the window." Duncan points across the restaurant. "In case they came in, I hated to ever let anyone else sit there."

"I hear they were inseparable," I pry.

"I know everyone always says this after some villain is unmasked as a maniac, but I still don't believe it. Jimbo really was the nicest man." Duncan catches himself. "Well, nice to me at least." He gets up from the table to head back inside, carrying plates, cups, and silverware.

I need more info. "You need a hand?"

Duncan shakes his head.

"I'm gonna use your restroom real quick before I head out." As I hustle to the back of the restaurant, I try to work out in my head just how I'm going to play this. Since I don't even know what I'm looking for, this is tricky.

Okay, think Spencer. Everyone knows that Duncan had quite the crush on Jimbo. Jimbo and Cleo came here often. Cleo knows what happened to my dad. And she definitely knows more about Jimbo's death than she's letting on. In the loo, I zip my jeans, wash my hands, and give myself a once-over in the mirror. As I walk back out the double doors, I still have no idea what I'm going to say to Duncan that will help me get to the bottom of whatever the hell it is that I'm trying to figure out here.

Think, Spencer.

I got nothing. "Thanks, Duncan! Have a good one."

He looks up at me but doesn't say a thing. There's something wrong. Is he waiting for me to speak? This is my in.

I lower my voice. "Hey, is everything alright?"

Duncan's lips purse. He takes a breath. Removes his reading glasses. "You're sweet." Another deep breath.

"Everything's fine. It's just—" He catches himself and breaks into a smile. "Jesus, look at me. You're a busy man. Places to go! People to see!"

I return his smile. "No, no. Tell me what's on your mind. I really want to know."

He studies me. "You know, you kind of look like him."

I know he means Jimbo. I have seen photos of him on the news, but I play dumb. The blond hair, the blue eyes. "Who?"

"Jimbo, or whatever the heck his other name was. Abdul Mohammed who-sy whatsit ... or something rather. But he bleached his hair. It was actually dark. I read all about it and everything else in all the papers and magazines."

"You're kidding." But I know he isn't.

Duncan nods. "You didn't know him, did you?"

"I'd heard his name because I casually followed the Ironman, but no. I didn't know him personally."

He nods again. I imagine that I sort of understand the disillusionment that Duncan is feeling. I'd always assumed my father was a good guy. From what my mother and all of his friends have told me about him, I had no reason to think otherwise. And maybe he was. But even if the most acclaimed Broadway actor gets ninety-nine rave reviews, he tends to only remember that one rotten tomato. Am I supposed to magically change my opinion of my father based on one horrid thing that he did? Well, I guess that depends.

As for Jimbo, wanting to needlessly murder hundreds of innocent people in the name of Allah or whomever those religious freaks are in service to seems a touch beyond the realm of forgiveness or redemption, but maybe that's just me.

"You know, I'm going through something similar with my father," I say.

Duncan bites his bottom lip, then says, "How so?"

"Well, I'm not totally sure yet. But it turns out he probably wasn't the perfect gentleman, knight in shining armor that I'd always pictured him to be." I have Duncan's attention. "He killed himself when I was a kid."

"Oh, Spencer. I'm so sorry to hear that."

"It was a long time ago. My point is that I know what it's like to be disappointed by someone close to you."

"I knew you were sweet." Duncan smiles. "Yeah, I mean, it's crazy. It's not like Jimbo was my best friend or anything like that but I don't know, it really makes you think, doesn't it? Do you really ever know anyone?"

"I wish I could answer that. Bet Cleo would give an emphatic no."

"Or that red-haired woman."

Who? "Oh, Jimbo had a special friend?"

Duncan scoffs. "Well, he and she sure as heck weren't workout buddies."

We laugh.

"No, I don't know if they were friends." Duncan clarifies. "I saw them together a few times, that's all."

I can't press any further or my intentions will go from pretty obvious to achingly transparent. I put Duncan's information in my back pocket and made a note to circle back to it—another day, soon.

CLEO, 8

I have just learned Tripp's DNA is not an exact match for Zelli's, though it did establish a genetic relationship to her. It can only mean one thing.

I bring Jake's glass from Sweet Pea into Dr. Henry Lodge's medical office, where I invariably barge in, and he always seems happy that I do. Long ago when I first moved to Hawaii and had my first appointment with Henry, his secretary whispered very low to me: "The doctor is still at lunch." I kept looking around to see why she was whispering when no one else was there. Every time I came for an appointment, she whispered. "He will be ready in a few minutes ..." "He is ready to see you ..." "He's running late. I am sorry ..."

Finally, I asked Henry why it always seemed that his assistant was telling me a secret. It seemed sort of silly to me.

"She had esophageal cancer long ago and it affected her vocal cords."

"Oh, I feel awful, Henry. Poor woman."

"If my door is open, come right in and I will tell Emma that it's alright."

I always wave to Emma and go right in, as I do today since Dr. Lodge's office door is wide open.

Yet again, the ninety-nine-year-old man is there, sitting in a chair in front of Henry's desk. The ancient man once again bows from his seat. I am so aware how older people feel they are never really seen. My Tati told me when she was very old that even at her own birthday parties, people ignored her. She said that was the hardest part of growing old: you disappear from sight.

I pass Jake's glass to Henry, then smile at his aged patient while asking him a question that had been rattling around my brain lately: "What did you do in your life that you loved most, or are you still doing it?" I smile as I await his answer.

He shrugs gently as though it was unimportant and as I glance at Dr. Lodge, I see him smiling.

I sit beside his patient and take his veined, arthritic hand in mine and say nothing. I just sit there with him for a long time. I feel something pass between us. He's dying and I'm alive, but for a moment we connect and touch one another.

There are moments in our lives that are truly important, and for me that was one of them.

"Hi, Henry," I say into the phone the next morning, reading the caller ID. "Gosh, you're quick getting back to me."

"But of course, Cleo. I won't take up your time. Jake Regan's DNA is a match to Zelli's."

"Thanks, Harry. And thanks for letting me know so fast. But of course I knew yesterday when it wasn't Tripp. I processed it then. Tell me: is that wonderful elderly gentleman in your office again?"

"No, my father was already in to get his daily shot." *His father! Why didn't he tell me that?* "Though I must say what you did for him yesterday was the shot he really needed. After you left, he went on and on about your beauty and sensitivity.

He told me, 'If that gracious woman ever needs anything, I will see to it.' And believe me, my father can work miracles."

"Tell him thank you and if he needs company I am happy to visit him."

"That's kind of you and I look forward to meeting your daughter as well. Does she have your purple eyes?"

"No, they are bright blue like Jake's. But she has my dimples. And I am not sure I will tell Jake for the moment about his paternity," I say as I hang up.

Jake is Zelli's father. I had the romantic idea that my baby's father was Tripp—or really, Danny.

On the other hand, I'm relieved not to have a secret with Tripp that he would have to keep from Miranda and his children. For the time being, I am not planning to tell Jake he is Zelli's father. I am not ready and he is so very young he might feel obliged to be part of my life and Zelli's life even if he didn't want to be a father. I want to do this slowly.

TWO DAYS LATER, all the complicated arrangements have been made by Tripp and I am to see Dr. Pearson in jail.

During another visit to his hospital room, Tripp had said, "Cleo, since I can't be there, I offer this suggestion. Before meeting with Dr. Pearson, read his book and use Shakespeare quotes. That's his real weakness, and it triggers him to talk. He says he's Iago, so who is Othello and who is Desdemona? That's what you need to find out."

"Thanks, and Tripp, I was wondering if I could get permission for the director Spencer Rensellear to film my talk with Pearson. Then I could bring the footage for you to hear."

"Yes, I know his films, Cleo. Interesting he wants to film this interview."

"Well he wants a favor from me so he is being very helpful."

"I won't ask." Tripp laughs.

The warden who called me yesterday had warned me to wear no jewelry and loose clothes. So I'm dressed in a loose-fitting pair of black slacks and, even though it's seventy-six degrees outside, I decided on a black shirt that's buttoned all the way up to the top with long sleeves.

Soon after Spencer and I sign in with the authorities, we walk through the jail's interior steel doors. I want to turn and get out of there. Oh, it smells awful. The bedlam starts as we pass the first cell. They warned me we would pass a few cells on the way to the interrogation room.

"Look at this babe!" I hear but my eyes stay adamantly forward. There are more hoots and catcalls as I pass the other two cells.

All I want to do is roll up the sleeves and undo the top three buttons so that I can breathe, but I don't dare. Surrounded by three guards, my hands are shaking as I take a seat in an interrogation room across from Dr. Marcus Pearson.

I glance over at Spencer, who is setting up his camera: a friendly face in a mostly unfriendly crowd. I smile at Durita and Castillo, who are also in the interrogation room. More friendly faces.

Pearson looks absolutely nothing like the man I'd seen on the news. The photos splashed across the pages of the news-papers showed a large man who indulged in way too many pizzas, a man who weighed at least two hundred and fifty pounds. But this thin man sitting before me in a jumpsuit the color of a tangerine, looks to be not much more than half of that. He's still wearing the same round glasses, but his gray streaked-brown hair is longer than the close-cropped haircut I'd seen in pictures on the local news. Pearson doesn't acknowledge my presence.

Wanting this to be over as quickly as possible, I cut right to the chase.

I clear my throat, but my voice is shaky when I ask, "Dr. Pearson, Tripp Regan did not kill your brother. Did you think he did? Is that why you shot him?"

Pearson says nothing. He doesn't even look up.

"Was it revenge? What I want to ask is who Othello is and what he plans to do to this island."

Nothing, so, I take a breath and continue. "Perhaps we could make an exchange?"

That suggestion makes him smirk. I wait for the professor to say something, *anything*, but he stays mum.

I glance at Spencer, and he gives me a much-needed nod of encouragement.

I move my chair closer to Pearson to show him that I am not intimidated by him. My voice is firmer this time. "If I tell you who killed your brother, will you tell me Othello's identity? Such an exchange is downright Shakespearean, don't you agree, Professor?" I pause, hoping he'll take the bait. He doesn't. "Think about it. You'll be Hamlet, finding out who killed his father."

Pearson gives a small little smile. Tripp was right. Shakespeare is the way to this man's heart.

"I read your book, you know. You're Iago, aren't you?"

The smile disappears.

"Yes, let's agree you are Iago. And as Iago, you wanted Othello to become the warrior he once was. But Othello isn't a warrior in this scenario. Or, is he? If he is a warrior, he must either be a warrior for Al Qaeda or a double agent in the CIA. He must believe in Islam—do you, Dr. Pearson? If you do, then I see you must protect your Othello, but if you believe in the great tragedies of Shakespeare, you will want to know who really killed your brother. And I must wonder, too, about Desdemona? Am I missing something, or has Othello already killed her? Who is Desdemona?

He looks up and says in a voice rife with cruelty: "I'm looking at her."

The words jolted me like a lightning strike. I tried to hide my terror as I looked at Spencer and the CIA men. They, too, were stunned. The guards came right over and took Pearson away.

I had killed Pearson's brother and he knows it. Othello would want to take revenge on me. But I have no idea who Othello is.

I can't breathe. And I can't die since I must be there for Zelli. When I first saw her she was so heartbreakingly lovely I couldn't breathe and every day since she has been my reason to smile. I need to live to see her go to first grade and be a cheerleader and learn to read and to ski and sing and fall in love. I need to live. And all those women in Dubai at the Abuse Center and Delia, I need to stay alive.

Who is Othello? How will I find out? I realize I need protection for Zelli and for me.

2014

TRIPP, 10

I can smell her before I hear her. "Welcome back, Cleo. Is Zelli with you today?"

"No, I'm sorry, just me and my Endgame perfume."

"Don't apologize. That's enough for me."

"So, how are you progressing with the Reiki, Tripp?"

I flinch when I feel Cleo's weight on the bed. All my senses are heightened, I tell you.

"Sorry, Tripp. I'm just smoothing your covers. They're a mess. Is that okay?"

I nod as she sets to straightening out my quilt and fluffing up my pillows. Miranda has bought me soft pillows, nice sheets and a comforter, which has made all the difference from the two hundred count sheets the hospital initially hooked me up with.

"I heard about Ricky and Julia," Cleo says. I can hear the smile in her voice.

I return the gesture. "Matt tell you?"

"He did. I think I should get some credit for that match, don't you?"

I laugh and turn on my iPod so "The Sound of Silence" fills the room. We listen together. I tell Cleo that Miranda and Matt are shopping today, so we let down our guard and relax a little.

"So ... how'd it go?"

"What?"

She's playing coy and I can't say that it bothers me. "C'mon ... out with it. How was Pearson?"

I hear Cleo take a deep breath, "Well, like Iago, Pearson 'spoke nothing' as you expected—until I asked him about Desdemona, that is. He looked up from the table he wouldn't stop staring at and gazed at me maliciously, uttering with menace: 'I'm looking at her.' I have the tape Spencer made but really there is nothing to hear for you except the hatred in his voice."

"Jesus. Really?"

"Yes, and the threat was so clear that the guards scooped him up and took him away."

"What about Durita and Castillo? Were they there?"

"Yes. I stayed behind and asked them what they thought but they were as stunned as I was. I really don't know what will happen next ..."

We're both quiet for a few seconds.

"Can you help me find out who Othello is, Tripp? Clearly, I am his intended victim and he knows I killed Jimbo."

She sits close to me and takes my hand. "Tripp, one more thing to tell you ..."

My turn to take a breath.

"Zelli is Jake's daughter."

"So, I'm not a hot young stud after all, just an old grand-father," I laugh.

"At least your sense of humor is improving ..." she smiles. "Just for now, let's keep this between us."

She's standing to my left, so I turn to my right as if I'm looking away from her forlornly. "You and I both know it would've killed Miranda—and Jake—if they found out that I was the father. The grandfather route, though I'm not sure I'll ever get used to the 'g' word, is probably the way to go."

I wait for Cleo to say something, but she says nothing.

"And even though it may be 'wrong,' to tell you the truth, I would've loved to have had a child with you. I did love you. And yes, I lied to you, but I wanted a bond to tie us together. And now we have one. Though we have to get through Jake to get to that bond ..." I laugh an awkward laugh. Jesus.

Cleo squeezes my hand.

I can hear the sadness in my own voice as I say, "With this latest Othello wrinkle, I'm very concerned about your security. I'll get guards to watch your house and protect you and my ... granddaughter."

"Thank you. I want protection for her especially. I am able to defend myself with my Krav Maga, but I have no idea who I will be fighting. Who can Othello be? We know he wants to kill me so I have to believe he knows I killed Jimbo. But who knows that except us and Jake? Then again, my trainer, Walter, guessed as well so maybe others have come to the same conclusion. I look behind me a lot for a knife, as that's how the real Desdemona was killed. I wonder if I should leave Hawaii? I came here to see you, and I am so happy here, as is Zelli, but maybe I need to go?"

I squeeze her hand. "You can stay, Cleo. We'll be sure you are safe."

Cleo nervously fixes my bedspread again. "Anyway, enough about me. Has the Reiki been helping?"

"Reiki has been a great help. Both emotionally and physically, actually ..."

"And have you gotten any more info on the eye operation?"

I nod. "Yes, I've been having some conversations with a specialist. Dr. Maharani."

"And?"

"And, well, my hyphema is thankfully all gone. All the blood has drained from my eyes."

"What does that mean?"

"That the inflammation response will be reduced when I am operated on. It took these last four weeks for it to leave my eyes."

"Oh, Tripp. Will he operate soon?"

I nod. "I'll have the IOL implantation for my traumatic cataract with corneal injury in a few days. Lots of new words in my vocabulary! Dr. Maharani seems reasonably sure it'll work. He's flying here tomorrow for some preop stuff."

"Tripp, this is wonderful news. I am thrilled for you!"

She throws her arms around me.

"You're the only person I'm telling, Cleo. I can't bear disappointing my family in case something goes wrong. But I had to tell someone. What can I say, another moment of weakness with you ..."

She laughs.

"I guess I'm trading the disappointment about Zelli for sheer joy at the possible return of my sight."

That's her cue to leave I guess. I hear her stand.

"Okay, Darkness, my old friend, I'll see you soon. I will be storming the heavens that this Dr. Maharani makes your Darkness leave."

"Thank you, Cleo. And I'll get that security for you."

"Thank you, Tripp. I am going to head to the chapel. I have so much to pray for. Your sight, an elderly new friend, and safety for Zelli and me and a prayer for a very young friend of mine in Dubai named Delia. I went into the chapel for a minute on my way to see you just now and heard someone behind me and I was so fidgety I turned fast to use my Krav Maga and it was a young girl in braids with her father both in tears. Oh dear. How sad this world can be." And with that I hear her close the door.

JULIA, 4

It's funny how much your perception about a certain place can change when you're there with the right person. I have only just fallen in love with Hawaii.

Before my surprise visit, if you'd have asked whether I'd like to go on an all-expenses-paid trip to Honolulu, it would've been a hard pass. Fast-forward a week later, I feel like I'm living in paradise. For an island that used to conjure up feelings of confusion, betrayal, and heartbreak, after seven days with Ricky those painful emotions have been replaced with joy, appreciation, and the best vacation sex ever.

"Ready, babe?" I turn to Ricky before we embark on our new daily ritual of walking the beach at sunset.

"Yeah, I was just trying to find that other cup for the wine," Ricky tells me as he closes the minibar.

"That's alright, we can share."

The sunset is especially delicious tonight. With a confection of pinks, oranges, yellows, blues, and purples, she looks good enough to eat.

"Left or right?"

I survey the stretch of land to our left, then our right. "Mmm, left," I suggest to my fiancé, wanting to avoid a group of rowdy teenagers to the right.

Ricky nods in agreement and puts an arm around me. "Peach and pit?"

About six months ago, Ricky and I rented a house in Nantucket with three other couples. On the last night of the trip, our friends Nick and Gabbi looked around the dinner table at Lola 41 and asked the rest of us what our peach and pit of the trip had been. I'd heard of the game before—the peach meaning something positive, and the pit something not so positive—but I've never actually played it. Must be more of an American thing. Anyway, ever since we were in Nantucket last summer, Ricky and I try to remember it when we can. It keeps the two of us engaged (no pun intended), and it gives us insights into how each of us view ourselves and even our lives—especially after there's a distance between us or we've just had a fight, which is rare but not unheard of. "My pit would probably be ... sleeping through my alarm this morning and missing that yoga class."

"Hey, at least it can only go up from there," Ricky smiles.

"Good point," I say. "And my peach is probably ... this. Walking on the beach with the love of my life."

Ricky looks up at the candy-colored sky. "Yeah, she sure is putting on a show for us tonight."

"Okay, your turn."

"Would have to say that my pit was getting back pretty brutal notes from my boss on that cryo story."

"Yup, don't blame you."

"And then, my peach ... yeah, I can't argue with you. This right here is pretty hard to beat." Ricky leans in and sweetly kisses my cheek. "Shall we?" He motions toward the sand.

I nod. "I don't know how I'm ever gonna go back to New York. We've gotten so spoiled here."

Ricky unscrews the twist-off bottle of Oyster Bay sauvignon blanc, pours it into the plastic cup, and hands it to me with ceremony, muttering, "Madam."

"Thank you, sir." I take the cup and then a sip.

Ricky stares out at the ocean as the sun disappears beneath the horizon. "What if we just got married here?"

I almost choke on the wine. "What?"

"Yeah, I mean, why not? We're here, this is where we fell in love, neither of us have any doubts. Why wait?"

I—maybe he has a point. I mean, why should we wait? "You're serious."

"Sure am." He puts his hand on my thigh. "What do you think? I know we've—well, *you've*—invested a lot of time and money into everything in New York." He pauses. "Screw it, why not do both? Have an intimate, oceanfront ceremony with my family here and then go all out as planned back home?"

Just the thought of it makes me smile. I have been counting down the days until I get to walk down the aisle and we proclaim our everlasting love. Ricky's right. Why the hell should we wait?

"Let's do it."

2014

SPENCER, 5

If I come often enough to Sweet Pea, I'm hoping Duncan will give me my own table like he gave to Jimbo and Cleo. My very own corner table by the window where I can watch all of the cars and bikes and people in the gravelly parking lot. My daughters would love it. They have a fondness for anything that makes them feel "VIP"—their words, not mine—and their own corner table at one of the island's hotspots would make them feel like the Hadid sisters.

When I enter the restaurant, the rush of the lunch crowd has dwindled to only two tables of lingerers. I planned it like this, hoping that Duncan would be less busy and less preoccupied with the hustle and bustle of his precious customers. And more important, that he might feel more comfortable speaking to me about something so clandestine in his place of business.

Duncan is posted in his usual spot by the host stand, reviewing the reservation book. He looks up when I enter and gives me a crooked smile. He must know I don't just keep coming back for the tuna melts and great customer service ...

"You're back," Duncan smiles as he approaches the two-top where I've taken the liberty of seating myself.

"What can I say, I had a craving." I smile back.

He thinks for a moment. "Tuna melt on rye, right?"

"Good memory. And a Coke, please."

After Duncan leaves, I look around at this place he's created over the twenty years. Sweet Pea has all the right ingredients. I especially appreciate the awning outside made entirely of leaves, which makes you think you're in a forest. It's the over-thirty set who often gather out there with their kids so they can run around unimpeded. But inside is where it's happening. It probably didn't hurt Duncan's business to have the famous Ironman Jimbo stop in all the time with Cleo, the famous Honolulu TV show host, on his arm. They were a pretty gorgeous pair. The name Sweet Pea is on all the tourist lists. They are usually all seated on the right, with views of the beautiful palm trees. The "in crowd" is seated on the left, looking out at the road and the ocean beyond. Sweet Pea's floor is bare wood scrubbed clean, and the seats are comfy but not so comfy that you'd want to overstay your welcome. Part of Duncan's genius is knowing who to seat where, and that adds to Sweet Pea's legendary charm and appeal. And not for nothing, the menu shows a great understanding of the dichotomy of his clientele, mixing healthy food with burgers and fries. Everybody's happy—and with this booming restaurant, so is Duncan.

Less than five minutes later, Duncan is back with my tuna melt. The ice inside the water pitcher he carries clatters as he refills my water glass. Duncan sets down my Coke as well.

"Big lunch crowd today?" I ask. I've got to warm Duncan up a bit before launching directly into my game of Twenty Questions. This part is foreplay. Let's hope Duncan's in the mood.

"Yeah, and some tourist flipped out because there were anchovies in his Caesar salad. It was a whole big thing."

"Uh-oh."

"Yeah, I don't know who this guy thinks he is. It says on our menu clear as day that we serve anchovies with our Caesar. A Caesar salad just isn't authentic without them."

"You don't like anchovies in your Caesar, order something else!" I declare.

"Exactly! The guy was from New York. He thought the louder he yelled, the more willing we'd be to accommodate him."

"*Ah,* one of those ..."

"But alas, Sweet Pea is old fashioned. We're one of the few places that still believes the customer is always right. So, the big man from The Big Apple got his way and we brought a new salad which we comped. I must say he left a nice tip."

"You're a good man, Duncan. Not sure I would have reacted so solicitously."

Duncan smiles down at me. "Enjoy your lunch, Spencer. I'm here if you need anything," he says, before starting to leave.

This is my moment. "Actually, Duncan?"

He stops and swivels his head back toward me. He looks at me in anticipation.

"Hey, I don't mean to pry but you definitely piqued my curiosity the other day."

"Oh?" He turns to face me.

"About Jimbo and the red-haired woman?"

At first, Duncan doesn't say anything. "I see. So maybe you found the plot for your next big movie. Is that it, Mr. Movie Man?" He smiles.

That's the angle at least. "Maybe. Can you tell me where you saw them together?"

"Just as long as you name a character after me," he says with a poker face.

"Deal."

Duncan takes a seat across from me and sets the pitcher between the two of us. "It was on this pebbly trail off Kilhea Road, right near St. Luke's. You know where that is?"

I nod, picturing the pretty brick church.

"I was passing it on my motor scooter when I noticed Jimbo turn and bike down the trail. I'd never even noticed that trail before and, well, I guess you could say I'm a curious man." Duncan pauses. "Especially when it came to Jimbo."

"I don't blame you."

"Anyway, about a hundred yards or so down the trail, Jimbo's at this big, huge gate. In order to enter, he had to punch in a code on a keypad. I wondered, what was this secret road off the beaten path that needs such security? The whole thing just seemed so bizarre. I was going to keep on following him, but then I noticed a 'Private, Keep Out' sign posted, and so like a good citizen, I obeyed. The last thing the restaurant needs is a mugshot of me in the local papers detailing some embarrassing trespassing charges."

"Not a great look." I laugh.

"As I said, I'm a curious man so I waited around for a while for Jimbo. Twenty minutes later, however, a woman with red hair drove in." He stopped to recall the moment. "Anyway, I kept waiting for Jimbo, but when he never came out, I finally just left." Duncan looks out at the parking lot. One of the remaining two lunch tables has just left. "Anyway, I added the trail to my path for Monday, when Sweet Pea is closed, and lo and behold a couple of weeks later, I'm on my scooter when I see the same red-haired woman turn into the pebbly path. Now I'm really curious—I told you, I had a thing for Jimbo—and so now I'm thinking this has got to be like a special meeting spot for him and this mystery woman. So, I pulled my scooter into the St. Luke's lot, and waited to see if Jimbo was going to show up too. About thirty minutes later, he does!"

"Okay ..." I nod. I'm not sure where Duncan is going with this.

"I ducked out of sight and watched as Jimbo turned into the trail." Duncan pauses. "Then, the third time was the same routine, but then I actually saw them together. Jimbo came to the gate and there was the red-haired woman right behind his bike in her car. He waved to her and said something before he went off on his merry way. I saw her wave and say something back."

"But they didn't see you?"

Duncan shakes his head. "No, I wised up and bought a pair of binoculars. I was pretty far away, in my hiding spot at St. Luke's."

"Smart."

"And if it hadn't happened again, I'd probably write it off ... One day, only about two days before he died, Jimbo comes in here. Everything is totally normal, he's being his same friendly self, orders the usual. And then, while he's midway through his salad, the red-haired woman walks through that door," Duncan points to the entrance. "I saw her first and figured that she was here to meet Jimbo. But it was the strangest thing. I watched them like a hawk and the two of them didn't even acknowledge each other. It was totally weird. The only reason two people who know each other don't acknowledge the other in public is because they're up to no good."

"Or they're in a fight."

"That wasn't the vibe I got."

"Okay, so what do you think this means?" I ask, because I don't have a clue.

Duncan sips his water. "Whatever it is, it can't be good. A mystery woman and an alleged terrorist?"

"What did she look like?"

"Striking. Her red hair was striking. I remember she had on a nice dress with low heels. She had a salad but didn't eat much of it, though all her chocolate soda was gone when she left."

I love how Duncan described her in terms of what she did and didn't eat.

AFTER I PAY FOR MY sandwich and tip more than generously, I head out to my car in the lot and dial Cleo's number from the driver's seat. It only rings twice.

"Hello, Spencer."

"Cleo, hey. Sorry to disturb you, but I was just at Sweet Pea and had a pretty interesting convo with Duncan ..."

"Oh?"

"Yeah, I'm wondering if you want to come check it out with me. It could be nothing, but figure it's probably worth a shot."

"Well, what is 'it'?" Cleo is understandably hesitant.

"I'll explain in the car. I'm leaving Sweet Pea now and happy to pick you up."

FIONA, 4

Jimbo was a gentleman. He would stand when I got up from our bench. He constantly thanked me for letting him into my magical world. One day as we watched a hummingbird, Jimbo marveled at it. When I told him the hummingbird's heart beats five hundred times and breathes two hundred and fifty times a minute, he said, "You know, you're kind of like a hummingbird, Fiona."

I never quite figured out what he meant by that, but I smiled. "I imagine it wouldn't take a huge storm to kill that poor little bird."

And then a huge storm nearly did kill me. The huge storm was the death of Jimbo, a.k.a. Mohammed Abdul Rahman. I was bereft and could tell no one why, so I was left to grieve alone. When I unwittingly discovered that his death was, in fact, not an accident and I learned who was responsible, my life path changed.

The woman whom I once thought was amazing killed him and left Honolulu the day after the "accident."

But now she's back.

I didn't see the end coming until it was upon me.

FIONA, 4

Jimbo's impending departure had been occupying my every thought for months and months, as I'd known that he'd eventually return to Manila after the Pearl Harbor mission. I helped him secure passports and tickets. Even though his wife and child were in Manila, Jimbo asked me to join him there, and I was seriously considering it. We worked so well together conspiring and deceiving everyone else and were quite close friends in our treacherous way. We reveled in the world of undercover lives.

But the decision was one I never had to make. And because of that, Cleopatra Gallier will die.

2014

SPENCER, 6

When I walk toward the front courtyard of Cleo's sprawling Tuscan house, I hear happy voices coming from inside. And then I spot Pudge and Pudding on their way out.

"Spencer, you handsome man, you!" Pudding shouts when she sees me.

"Aw, you flatter me," I say, kissing Pudding's cheeks Euro-style and shaking Pudge's massive hand.

"Hello, Spencer," Pudge nods.

Pudge has a great face and reminds me of that large and in charge character actor whose name I'm blanking on. I vow to give him a cameo in my next film.

Pudding looks like she might explode into a million pieces. "Guess who just became godparents?"

I venture a guess. "You two?"

"Yeah, Cleo just popped the big question!"

"Clearly, we're thinking it over," jokes Pudge.

We all laugh, they suggest dinner sometime next week, then wobble over to their black Ford SUV.

I enter the courtyard of Sweet Dreams, noticing a few undercover cops. They were at the foot of the driveway too.

Cleo is sitting on a blanket in the grass next to her adorable daughter, Zelli, with a black cat on her lap. They're both holding colored pencils and scribbling on pieces of white parchment paper. The nanny is there again too. She has dark hair, looks to be in her early fifties, and is sporting a chunky sweater that seems way too goddamn hot for the seventy-five degree weather. As a group, they look like a Norman Rockwell painting. Or maybe an Edward Hopper.

"Hey there," I wave over to them.

Three sets of human eyes and one cat look up at me. Cleo smiles and helps Zelli up so that she can toddle over to me and say hello. Zelli hugs my left leg tightly and holds on for dear life. She won't let me go, which is a fresh breath of air compared to my two teenage daughters who haven't shown me anything close to this affection in years.

"Well, Zelli seems happy to see you," Cleo laughs.

"Hello, Zelli!" I smile down at her.

"And have you met Nannie? She is Zelli's wonderful nanny. I don't know what we'd do around here without her."

"Nice to meet you, Nannie. I'm Spencer." I reach my hand out to shake hers, but I can't move my legs to get any closer because Zelli is still holding on for dear life.

Nannie shakes my hand and warmly smiles at me.

"Nannie, will you put Zelli down, please? I should be back in, what?" Cleo turns to me. "About an hour, Spencer?"

I nod.

"And will you take Endy inside with you?" Cleo passes Nannie the black cat.

"Come on, little Miss Zelli," Nannie gently pries the child's arms off my legs and leads her into the house. "Time for your favorite book!"

"Bye, Zelli," I wave, missing the days when my girls were toddlers. Back then they didn't roll their eyes at everything their dear old dad had to say.

Before we set out, we settle on chaise lounges to again view the film footage on my iPad that I took in the interrogation room with Dr. Pearson. We viewed it before and saw nothing more this time. So we got up to go.

"Are you going to tell me where we're going?" Cleo asks as we exit the courtyard.

I turn to her. "Okay, so as I said, this could be nothing, but Duncan said he saw a mystery woman with Jimbo several times, including just a few days before he died."

"Who?"

"A woman with red hair..."

Speaking of redheads, I almost jump out of my skin when a redheaded young man pops out from a palm tree several feet to our left.

"Matt, come say hello to a friend of mine." Cleo laughs.

Cleo whispers to me as this Matt fellow trudges over to us: "Matt is Jake's younger brother, and he is my favorite Regan."

He sure as hell doesn't look like Jake.

Cleo introduces us, but when I put my hand out to shake Matt's, he moves away. *Rain Man* is one of my favorite films and so, right away I get that Matt has autism or Asperger's—though a much milder version than Dustin Hoffman's character.

"Matt lives and breathes for plant life and so he has an open invitation to come over here and check out mine whenever he'd like."

Matt smiles shyly at us both.

"That's so funny. Cleo and I are just on our way to a botanical garden."

Cleo turns to me. "We are?"

"I'll tell you more about it in the car." I nod.

"Well, should we ...?" Cleo gestures to Matt, indicating that maybe we should bring him along.

It's not that I'd mind, I have always prided myself on being a "more the merrier" kinda guy, but we really have no freakin' clue what the hell's actually in this botanical garden. It could be nuclear missiles or escaped prisoners from Alcatraz for all I know. "Tell you what. How 'bout another time, Matt? I gotta talk to Cleo about something really boring today."

Cleo and I trade looks. She understands.

"Okay," Matt says softly.

"Cleo?" Nannie calls out from inside the courtyard.

"Yes, Nannie?" she calls back.

"Can you please come inside for a second? Zelli says she needs to tell you something."

"I'll be right back," Cleo tells Matt and me.

We nod, and off she goes. Matt and I stand there for a few painfully awkward moments before he speaks up. "Want to see a palm tree that sheds its bark for no reason?"

"Sure," I say, and wander in the bushes with him.

"You know, The Tree of Knowledge that Adam and Eve took their apple from became the cross that Jesus died on. Or at least that's what it says in the book that I have about barkless palms."

"No way. I actually did not know that!"

"Where's the garden you're going to?"

Matt seems to feel more comfortable talking about trees and plants. I tell him the garden is by St. Luke's, and he nods, then seems to lose interest in the conversation as he saunters away from me, then down the driveway and away without a goodbye or parting word.

"Sorry about that. Zelli wanted me to read her part of the book. Ready?" says Cleo as she exits out from the courtyard again.

Once we're in the car, I tell Cleo all about Duncan's sightings of Jimbo and the red-headed woman.

"How do you know it's a garden?" she asks.

"I had my tech girl Q look into it. She was able to figure out from some aerial shots online what was inside."

A few moments pass as Cleo takes all of this in. "Maybe they were just friends? And like me, she had no idea who Jimbo really was."

"Maybe, but don't you think it's strange that they pretended not to know each other at Sweet Pea?"

Cleo looks out the window at the passing scenery. I can see all the wheels turning inside her head from here. "Could she have been helping with his plotting?"

"The thought crossed my mind," I tell her as I make a left turn. "It makes sense, right?"

"Or maybe they were lovers?" Cleo is trying to give this woman the benefit of the doubt.

"Maybe both?" I venture.

"Or maybe it's just this great, secret restaurant behind the gate," Cleo tries to lighten the mood.

"Yeah, Jimbo wouldn't want Duncan to know he was eating anywhere else." I laugh, then switch gears back to reality. "Q pulled up some drone images and found a massive property, full of trees and odd-shaped bushes."

"I am certainly not dressed for a garden party." Cleo glances at her face in the mirror. And she isn't. She's wearing yellow shorts with a top that has tiny straps and sandals. I don't argue with her nor do I flatter her with what she must hear *ad nauseum* about how lovely she is.

Her dimples, which her daughter inherited, appear as she laughs. "Really, a Garden of Eden on this Island of Paradise?"

We're passing St. Luke's and nearing the pebbly road, unsure what will happen or what we'll discover. The adrenaline junkie in me is secretly hoping for a dangerous adventure that won't cause us good guys any harm. I pull up to a beautiful, huge wrought-iron gate that's tall, ornate, and black. And there's the keypad Duncan mentioned. It's all just how he described it. I put the car in park and glance over at Cleo, "Duncan didn't know the code."

"Should we at least get out and take a look?"

I nod and we both climb out of my Jeep. "Pretty sure we're being watched," I say, nodding toward a small camera atop the right gate.

"Let's smile and wave." Cleo smiles through clenched teeth. She knows how to work it for the camera.

We do.

"Look at those," Cleo points to the giant, seven-foot-long topiary on either side of the gate. They're shaped like a peacock, with green leaves and with a red flower for the head. There are a few others behind it. "I know squat about flowers, or plants, or greenery in general," I say, "but these things are pretty cool."

Cleo nods, "But who would Jimbo be meeting here? I doubt it was for a picnic ..."

"That's what we're here to find out," I say, as I make my way over to the keypad.

When a voice booms over the intercom speaker, Cleo and I both jump.

"Name?" the voice says.

Cleo and I look at each other with wide eyes. I'm about to take the lead, but she beats me to the punch.

"Cleopatra Gallier and Spencer Stone," she says with a friendly lilt in her voice into the intercom.

There's no acknowledgment from the voice over the intercom. I feel as if we're Dorothy and the Scarecrow and we're waiting to be granted an audience with The Great and Powerful Oz at the gates of Emerald City.

"We're totally mad to come here, aren't we?" Cleo says to me without looking in my direction.

"Yup, totally."

"Do you think we should leave?" she asks as the minutes go by.

Then the decision is made for us. There's a loud buzzing and the gates slowly start to open sesame. Cleo and I share a small smile, then hop back into my car.

"Here goes nothing," I say as we drive through the gates.

"Here goes nothing, indeed."

The gates close behind us, quicker than when they opened and suddenly Cleo and I are ensconced in a real-life Garden of Eden. There are giant green sculptures and surrounding us seem to be every possible species of exotic plant and flower and tree. Cleo's eyes and mine are glued to the car windows.

"You said at the gate you don't know much about horticulture, Spencer?" Cleo asks as we wind down a curvy road. I can tell that she's as uneasy as me, but she's trying to quiet her mind with pleasant conversation.

"Eh, don't know much," I respond, "and I can say with 100 percent certainty that I've never seen sculptures like these." We drive by a massive sculpture of a flamingo made entirely out of pink flowers. "My wife and daughters would love that one." God, why did I mention my wife and kids? I think, probably so that Cleo won't think I'm hitting on her.

I'm really not. I've been in love with my wife since we met in high school.

"I sort of feel like Alice in Wonderland first with the peacocks and now these strange trees," says Cleo.

"Funny you should say that. I was feeling a Wizard of Oz vibe."

Cleo laughs. "Is it just me or does it look like the bark has been stripped off some of these trees?"

I take a closer look as we drive by a grouping of trees that I can actually identify as lollipop palms that come from Cuba where I shot a film a few years back. "I think you're right. Weird."

Cleo points ahead of us. "Look at those colors on the grasses ahead."

I stop the car, reach back for my camera and start filming the colors on the grasses. Miraculously, they start to rise up in front of us as we approach. Thousands of colorful birds move upward in a ballet for us.

"Wow," I gasp. It's quite a sight. "I gotta use this location for a movie someday."

"This is quite magical, isn't it? I think I'm starting to understand why Jimbo wanted to spend so much time here." In awe, Cleo watches the rainbow flock of birds lift into the air.

I squint. "Do those birds look native to you?"

"Not really," she says. "I certainly have never seen anything like them before."

"Let me call Q." I pass the camera to Cleo and start dialing.

Q picks up on the second ring. "Hey, boss."

"Hey, so I'm at that garden. Do you know if it's a bird refuge too?"

"A bird refuge?" Q repeats.

"Yeah, I'll text you some pictures once we hang up. It's pretty wild."

I can hear her fingers flying across her computer keyboard. Q moves fast and I love her for it.

"Copy that. Send me the pics. Talk soon."

I snap pictures of the birds, then fire them off to Q. Cleo is holding my camera somewhat unsteadily as she takes out her cell phone, and so I take it back from her. My camera is my most prized possession. I start driving again through this incredible world.

Cleo smiles at me, then dials her phone. "Didier, I'm driving through a gorgeous botanical garden off Kilhae Road. You should see it. There are thousands of magnificent, colorful birds. I don't think I have ever seen anything so lovely! Anyway, I'm wondering if you can find out who owns it. It's a long story that I'll explain once you call me back. Talk soon. I love you."

After Cleo hangs up, I stop the car again as we are totally enveloped in the magic of color and life.

Cleo says, "Let's get out and walk toward that bench. I want to be closer to those birds, don't you?"

I nod. We get out of the Jeep, leaving it on the side of the road as we start strolling toward a bench.

Cleo looks down. "I think that it's time I tell you what you want to know about your father."

Well, I was not expecting this.

She is smiling at me as she says, "I have been rehearsing it for you, Spencer." She takes a big breath as we reach the bench, and something tells me I better take one too. We sit.

"I was nine years old, and I loved your dad," Cleo begins. "Of all my father's friends who came to the house in Algeria, he was the one I adored and who played with me the most."

She is still smiling. If she doesn't smile, it seems like she might burst into tears. "During one of those evenings, I came in to say good night to all six of the men who were dining with my father. Then I went to my room and as usual, I brushed my teeth and washed my face with my favorite pink washcloth and got in bed. I was sound asleep when suddenly, I woke up with a hand over my mouth." Cleo seems unable to breathe after she says this, and I start to stand up. "Spencer?"

I'm terrified. I think I know what I'm about to hear but still can't believe it. I don't want to believe it. "Yes. Just tell me, please," I whisper.

She nods. "At first I didn't know what was happening. But then I felt a terrible weight on top of me as I was smothered by that hand over my mouth and my eyes. I tried to bite that hand, but I couldn't. It was just so strong. And the other hand …" I can see she is feeling the hand all over again as her terror rises and takes away her breath. I can almost feel the pounding of her heart from here. She can't speak.

I whisper to her: "The worst moment of your life is now the worst moment of my life."

2014

JAKE, 7

My cell rings. It's Matt. I want to ignore it, but my younger brother is unrelenting—six calls, one after the other. Even for Matt, that's overkill. A mounting sense of guilt becomes hard to ignore. The CIA has been pulling me in a zillion different directions ever since I've been in Hawaii and every day Matt has practically begged me to venture outside Dad's hospital room and go on another adventure with him. What can I say? Little bro loves hangin' with cool big bro.

But between Rustikoff and figuring out just what the hell happened to my father, I haven't had a minute to catch my breath. Making matters worse, I can't make Matt understand that I'm really not blowing him off by clarifying the type of pressing, critical work I am tasked with.

Anyway, I have a brief lull in my afternoon today so I promised that I'd take him to see the Banzai Pipeline. He's never been and I think he'd really dig all of the naturey shit at the beach there. It's in Matt's nature to be anxious, so I suspect the reason he's calling is because he thinks I forgot about our afternoon hang.

I take a breath, bracing for impact, then pick up. "Hey, Bud. I'm just leaving the office now."

There's an urgency to Matt's voice that I was not expecting. "Jake, come to Cleo's right now and get me."

"Yeah, that's the plan. I'll be there in about fifteen minutes or so. Just sit tight—"

"Hurry! Cleo's going to some botanical garden with a friend."

"Okay—"

"We have to follow them!"

I can tell Matt is pacing. He paces when anxious, a trait Ricky shares.

"Uh. Why do we have to follow them? Don't you want to go to the Pipeli—"

"No! Jake, this is very important!"

"Why, Bud? What's going on?"

"It's important for what you're working on." Now he's really lost me. How the hell does he know what I'm working on? Matt whispers into the phone, "You know that I know things, and I know this." This is true. Being on the spectrum, Matt's brain works differently than most people. He manages to observe things and connect the dots most of us miss. Though blowing things out of proportion usually comes with the territory as well.

"Alright, I'm getting in the car now. I'll drive as quickly as I can without getting a ticket."

"Okay, I'll meet you at the bottom of the driveway."

"Sounds good." I'm about to hang up when I ask Matt what I need to know. "What friend is Cleo with?"

"A British man named Spencer. He has very blond hair and is six foot two inches tall. They're trying to figure out something to do with Dad."

Jesus. *That guy?* Selfishly, I'm annoyed—and yes, jealous—that Spencer is again hanging out with Cleo. But back to Dad. Even for Matt, this sounds like a stretch. "How do you know it has to do with Dad?"

"Because Spencer went to jail with her and took a video of the man who shot Dad."

"What?" Now it sounds like he's making things up. "Run that by me again."

"I saw it! Jake, I saw it. Spencer showed the video to Cleo a few minutes ago. I was in her courtyard when he showed her the video on his iPad."

"Are you sure, Matt? Maybe—"

"I know what I saw, Jake! And they didn't want me to go with them to the garden even though Cleo knows how much I love flowers. I just know that they're going to the garden to find something out, so get over here!"

Matt is unrelenting. I take a deep breath. "Alright, bud, hang tight. I'll be there in a few."

"Hurry!" Matt tells me before hanging up.

I toss my phone onto the passenger seat and put the pedal to the metal. Driving to Cleo's might just be my favorite journey in the world. Sadly, she won't be waiting there for me naked in her bedroom with a white flower between her teeth. Instead, lucky me, I'm greeted by my younger brother, waiting for me in a tree—yes, a tree, ladies and gentleman, at the bottom of her driveway. When I think about it a bit more, I realize it's actually a clever, if not totally ridiculous hiding spot.

As I pull over to the side hidden from the road, I almost burst into laughter at the sight of Matt crouched up there on a branch. Then I hear a vehicle approaching and duck down in my seat. Spencer's Jeep careens down Cleo's hill and passes Matt's tree. Homeboy turns his whole head the other direction, as if he can't see them then they can't see him either. Spencer has dark tinted windows, which makes it impossible for me to see anything inside the car.

Keep your hands to yourself, Spencer. Cleo's mine. His Jeep turns right onto the road where Cleo and I met.

Matt hops to the ground, clumsy AF, landing with a big thud. He isn't the most graceful of creatures as he comically sprints over to my car and hops in. Out of breath and in true Hollywood fashion, he tells me to: "Follow that car!"

"Aye, aye." I nod. Matt loves it when I follow his orders.

"Okay, so let's go over this again. What exactly did you see on the iPad?" I have a sneaking suspicion that he's over-dramatizing this whole thing, just to lure me to the garden.

Matt catches his breath. "Spencer was showing Cleo the video with them and the guy who shot Dad in prison. They didn't know I was there, but I was behind them looking at this palm tree with no bark. It's pretty ugly ... it looks kind of like an intestine and I—"

"Dude. Focus. What did you see on the video?"

"I saw this guy in orange jail clothes. Cleo sat across the table from him and she was dressed in these big frumpy clothes like Mom wears when she's cleaning. I have never seen Cleo look like that!"

"Matt! Focus here."

"There were cops and Dad's friends who visit him a lot in the video. Durita and Castillo."

Matt doesn't know I work with them. It's strange that Durita didn't at least fill me in about this afterward, but I am the low guy on the rung of information so maybe my clearance didn't allow it.

"Spencer must've been filming from the other side, because he was mostly focused on the man in the jail clothes. But now and then Spencer took in the whole scene, and that's when I saw it!"

"Saw what, Matt?"

He's quiet.

"Saw what, Matt?" I say more urgently.

"Durita's feet."

I'm speeding to keep Spencer's Jeep in sight. I slow the car with my foot on the brake, pull over, and glance at Matt. He can see the fury in my eyes. And he can hear the frustration in my voice, I make sure of it.

Finally Matt opens his trap and starts talking. "The man in the orange was looking down. The whole time, he never even looked at Cleo. Not even once. She kept asking him questions, but the man in the orange never moved or acknowledged her. Instead he just looked at the table. Never anywhere else."

I realize I sound like my mother here, but Goddammit, I want to turn this car around right this minute and teach Matt a lesson. "Matt, what is it you are trying to say?!"

"Okay, remember how I studied body language at school? So I could better understand emotions?"

"Yeah." I nod. I had to go through similar training at the CIA. Every agent needs to learn how to read body language, especially when having to deal with foreigners.

"You know, like, if someone rubs his hands together, it means he's confident. No way I'd know that unless I learned body language. But Durita's feet were pointing at someone way on the right and tapping. I know he is not good."

I deeply inhale, needing all the patience in the world to get me through the rest of this drive. But Durita did make me wonder why he brought me to the cave. And if Matt feels something is wrong then. I mean someone has been feeding Pearson and someone set up Pearson as uh oh—my eyes are glued to Spencer's Jeep about two hundred yards ahead of us as he suddenly takes a sharp left just after the church.

"Did you see that, Jake? Spencer just—"

"Yes, Matt. I saw it." My voice is laced with a touch more malice than I intend. Now that we know where they're headed, I slow the car to fifteen miles per hour until we're passing the church on our right. My blinker goes on, and I calmly make the same left that Spencer did a few minutes earlier. I pull over on the side of the road for what seems like an eternity but is probably not more than five minutes. I certainly don't want to pull in behind them.

"Jake, look!" Matt points ahead.

About a hundred yards in front of us, Spencer's car enters through a wrought iron gate. Careful not to be seen yet, I pull over to the side of the trail behind a tree and wait. For the record, yes, I feel silly as fuck following Cleo to some strange garden that may or may not be a suicide mission.

"I hope you're right about this, buddy," I tell Matt.

"Don't worry. I am."

I put the car in drive and slowly accelerate toward the big gate that Spencer's car entered several minutes ago. The two huge peacocks on either side of the gates made entirely of leaves and flowers catch Matt's attention, and he jumps out to take a look.

"Wait, Matt—"

I want to stop Matt and have him stay safely within the confines of the car, but the pull of flora and fauna are impossible for him to resist. I'm probably overreacting anyway. There's only a small chance that this garden or wherever the hell we are will yield the CIA any valuable intelligence. But we were trained to chase down every lead, so here I am. I notice a small security camera to the right. I wave at it, but nothing happens.

I holster my gun out of sight and get out of the car and pretend to be mesmerized by the flower peacocks just like Matt. Like we do this shit all the time.

Matt is mumbling, "No, no, no," and pulling orchids out of the body of the seven-foot-tall peacock. I'm about to tell my brother to cut it out when a red-haired woman drives up to the gate without even a glance in our direction. Apparently she's in much too big of a hurry for manners. She punches a code onto the keypad, the gates open, and she drives through.

Matt looks over at her. "Jake, that's her."

"Her?"

"The red-haired woman that Spencer was telling Cleo about. She was always with Jimbo in this garden. I didn't get to that part yet, but the red-haired woman was always with Jimbo."

I have to call Cleo and warn her. I call her cell phone.

When she answers, she sounds upset and like she's been crying. "Jake, hi."

"Cleo, I'll explain everything later but heads up. A woman with red hair who used to come here with Jimbo just went through the garden gates in a fury. Do you have the code so that I can follow her in?"

"No, we just gave our names and the gates eventually opened. I take it Matt steered you here," she says, sounding slightly better.

"Good guess. He—"

"Jake ... a car is heading straight toward us. It's coming at us really fast. Oh God, it's going to crash into Spencer's Jeep!"

I hear a collision as I grab Matt and pull him into the car and start waving madly at the camera to open the gates, showing my ID as I call for backup.

FIONA, 5

My heart leapt when I got the call from Anatoly's guardhouse that Cleopatra Gallier and a man named Spencer Stone were outside the gates and that they wanted to come into my garden. I was shopping for sandals in a tiny store with a white picket fence behind the church when I got the call. I was out of that tiny store in a flash.

I tremble with rage whenever I happen to get a glimpse of her parading around town and shaking hands like she's some kind of celebrity. She was a local talk show host for Christ's sake, not Barbra Streisand. That she knows me, but doesn't really have any idea who I really am is my greatest weapon.

And it will be her downfall.

This is the moment. The garden is the perfect place to kill her. Poetic justice, after all. Here is where I met Jimbo, and here is where his killer will die. Anger is said by some to be the creative urge gone wrong. My fury leads me right where I need to go. It's almost karmic that I will kill her where I met my love.

She dares to venture into my lair, and as if climbing into a spider's web, she will be taken here.

2014

CLEO, 9

I just finished telling Spencer what his father had done when Jake called to warn us that we might be in danger. I would feel so much better if Jake could get past those iron gates and be in here with us if trouble arrives. Somehow I feel safer in Jake's presence. But even with his badge, the mysterious unseen guards watching the gate are not letting him through.

While still on the phone with Jake, I turn to Spencer. "Someone's entering the garden gates. Jake thinks we might be in danger."

"Who?" he asks.

"It's the woman with red hair."

Just as I say that, Spencer and I turn to the building sound of an accelerating car engine. A black Ford Focus suddenly appears through the clearing, tearing through gardens, trees, and statues, heading straight for Spencer's Jeep.

"Jake! A car is heading straight toward us. It's coming at us really fast. Oh God, it's going to crash into Spencer's Jeep!"

Spencer grabs my wrist, and we hurry over to a large sculpture of a beautiful peacock. I hang up on Jake, and we crouch behind extravagant plumage, fully fanned out to capture the bird's unique courtship ritual. The bird's torso is composed of bright blue hydrangeas, its feathers a combination of cobalt delphiniums, green baby's breath, and yellow craspedia billy buttons.

Spencer turns to me. "What the hell's going on?"

I shake my head. I have no idea.

Both of our heads poke out ever so slightly from behind the peacock statue so that we can keep an eye on the crazy red-haired driver. The tires screech as the Ford stops abruptly next to the driver's side of Spencer's Jeep.

"She thinks we're inside your car ..." I whisper.

The windows of Spencer's Jeep are tinted so heavily that it's nearly impossible for anyone to see anything from the outside. Slowly, the front windows on the Focus lower on both sides.

Spencer and I recoil behind the giant peacock, even though it's highly unlikely that she can see us from her vantage point. The peacock's lavish display is a good distraction. Funny how art can imitate life.

Spencer tries to sound calm, but his ragged breathing betrays him when he says, "Maybe she just wants to talk. We might get a read on what she knows and what she doesn't—"

One, two, three, four, five bullets ring out. Glass shatters Spencer's car windows.

"Shit!" Spencer pokes his head out from behind the statue.

It appears that his proposed diplomatic solution is a no-go.

Thousands of birds are shocked into flight. The ear-splitting sounds of gunshots and the glass smashing are replaced by loud squawks, chirps, and ca-caws. In an instant, the blue sky becomes one big swirl of bright greens, yellows, reds, purples, and blues too.

Spencer and I look overhead, petrified by the growing tornado of feathered creatures above.

He says, "God, I feel claustrophobic."

I nod in agreement. I have a terrifying sensation of being covered by thousands of birds, the flapping and the noise. How long will they stay flying and swooping above us?

"We would be dead if we hadn't gotten out of the car! She was shooting at us." I scream above the shrieking of the birds. I tuck myself in a ball between my knees, as does Spencer, with our hands over our heads.

Peeking up at what seems like thousands of different species, I'm hypnotized by their grace and elegance as they fly and swoop through the air. Oh, how envious I am. If only Spencer and I could flap our wings and lift off to escape from the dangers here on land.

All the excitement up in the air has nearly distracted me from the peril down here on the ground. Spencer is equally spellbound by the birds. I hesitate to shout above them again, terrified that the woman will hear me and discover our hiding place.

I poke my head out from behind the peacock's gigantic feet.

There's no sign of Red. Before, the advantage was that she had a gun, but ours was that we knew where she was. Now the only thing Spencer and I have going for us is that there are two of us—not really much of an asset when a gun is in the picture.

Spencer follows my lead and sticks his head out behind his side of the statue.

I freeze. All of my krav maga training jogs through my mind as I anticipate a violent showdown between us and whoever this insane woman is. I manage to take out my phone and text Jake as quickly as my shaking fingers will allow.

"911 she has a gun," I type.

CLEO, 9

Three gray dots immediately appear, telling me Jake is typing a response. And then my phone falls from my shaking hands into a puddle of water at the peacock's feet.

"Dammit!"

The birds flying above are starting to scatter. My eyes dart around the garden, hoping and praying that I will see something that'll give me an idea. Ah, there in the distance, is that a gardener's shed or are my eyes playing tricks on me after staring for too long at the psychedelic kaleidoscope above?

The shed probably has a lock. Not that a lock is any match for a gun, but it might buy us some time before Jake and the police come and save the day. I scoot closer to Spencer and point.

He follows my eyeline. "The shed?"

At least that confirms the shed is real, and it could be our saving grace.

"We need to move, Spencer! She's gonna find us if we stay here."

Another gunshot rings out. *Oh God.*

The birds shriek and screech and flap all over again but this time, it seems they have the good sense to get the hell out of Dodge. In mere seconds the sky is clear blue again, and an eerie silence hangs in the air.

Six shots, I tell myself. Six shots. My father has a Glock 19, and those hold fifteen rounds. *Damn.* Whoever she is, she probably has at least nine more bullets, plenty of opportunity to shoot and kill us.

"Cleo?" a voice calls out somewhere to our right.

Oh no. My heart races, and my head feels dizzy. Spencer grabs my hand. He's scared too.

"Cleo's friend?" the voice is getting closer.

It's now or never. We have to move. I point to the shed and count down with my fingers. Three ... two ... one ...

"Come out, come out wherever you are ..." Her voice is high and mocking.

Spencer and I hop up from our crouches and run as fast as our legs will carry us toward the green shed about one hundred and fifty yards in the distance. Open gardens and half a dozen other bird sculptures separate us from the shed. There's a blue jay, a cardinal, a goldfinch, a parrot, and a macaw.

Another shot rings out, though it's unclear if she's spotted us or just gone totally crackers and is spouting out more bullets.

Eight shots. Then nine. *Six bullets left.* We're not going to make it all the way to the shed in one fell swoop.

"Here!" Spencer grabs my arm to pull me behind another enormous toucan. We huddle behind its torso which is covered in a beautiful swath of "Black Delight" violas.

"You okay?" Spencer asks. We only ran about thirty yards, but he's completely out of breath, as am I.

I nod. "We should split up. I'll go this way and you go that way."

"Are you sure?" he asks me, incredulous.

I nod again. "It'll give us the best chance. We'll meet in the middle at the shed."

Spencer thinks for a half-second before nodding. "Ready?"

I count down again with my fingers. Three ... two ... one ... and off we go in opposite directions.

Adrenaline kicks in, carrying me to the finish line and making me feel like I'm at the Olympics running the one-hundred-yard dash. A tenth shot rings out, and my heart stops when I hear Spencer cry out in pain.

I shouldn't stop, I have to keep going, and I make it to the green shed. My body is in control now, and it stops me in my tracks. I turn, frantically looking around, desperately searching for Spencer.

I don't see him, but I do see the Avenging Angel in a pale green dress. It looks tight on her.

She's about twenty yards behind me. With her gun pointed directly at my head, I see she's wearing a big smile.

"Well, there you are. If I wasn't mistaken, I'd say you were running away from me, Miss Gallier. Have I done something to offend you?" she mocks in a high falsetto voice.

I can't speak. Instead I turn around and sprint toward the shed.

Another shot whizzes by my ear, missing me by inches. Then another, and another. My heart races, my adrenaline is pumping, and my head turns to find that the red-haired woman has gained on me significantly. The woman raises her right arm and aims her gun at me. I'm just about to turn my head around again, when I hear a loud howl that I know isn't Spencer's. Suddenly, the woman's body contorts violently as bullets rip through her. Even as she continues to get shot, she's looking right at me and keeps chasing me down. It's only when a bullet hits her in the kneecap, does she finally stop chasing me. Her body wobbles back and forth, she's fighting to stay on her feet, valiantly refusing to concede this losing battle. Birds, smelling the blood, swoop down and swirl all around her. All of them are screeching and screaming so loudly and so uncontrollably that I have to cover my ears. But I cannot cover my eyes, it's too shocking a sight. And then I see an image that I'm sure I'll never quite be able to get out of my head.

As the red-haired woman's knees finally start to give out, a big rainbow-colored bird pounces on her. She tries to fight off the bird, but her energy and strength are quickly dwindling as the life is rapidly leaving her body. Its wings flap, its beak opens and for a second, I think the bird is going to gobble her head up whole. Instead, it takes the woman's hair in its beak and lifts it off her head. Goodness, it was a wig. The red-haired woman is not a woman at all. And he doesn't have red hair. I know that man. I know him.

I stand there frozen, staring as he lands with a thud on the perfectly manicured lawn. The birds swirl around him like a vicious tornado and peck at his lifeless body. If the bullets didn't kill him first, the birds certainly finished him off. I scream in horror as two red birds peck at his eyes. Finally, I look away from the horrifying sight and see a most wonderful one.

Several feet beyond, Jake stands halfway out of his car with his gun still cocked.

Oh, Jake.

Neither of us can speak. The silence lasting a moment or an eternity is like a communion. I imagine men in battle, hearing guns or planes or bombs all day for months on end, gradually becoming inured to it, but I don't think I will ever forget the noise or the smell or the frantic flapping of those birds above us.

Lying on the ground, Spencer is white as a sheet when he looks over at me. His leg is covered in blood.

"You okay?" he asks me weakly.

"I've been better. You?"

He tries to get to his feet. "I was once caught at the Pipeline in a terribly ferocious wave," he says, "but that was nothing compared to how I felt with those crazy birds above us, blocking out the sun."

I walk over to the dead body. Even without his eyes, I can still recognize that it's Don Durita. My God. Don. Don. Don Durita is Othello. He still has on gold hoop earrings. He was right there with us all the time, and he wanted to kill me every minute. I can't believe it. I truly can't believe it. The sight of Don Durita without his eyes and wearing a dress will haunt me forever.

Around his neck, peeking out from his dress is the Ironman Medal. Jimbo must have given it to him. But why?

Durita was Jake's boss and his father's friend. We had lunch with him and all knew him. He was in the CIA, betraying us every day. But why? Why was he Othello?

JAKE, 8

My first kill.

I didn't expect it to feel like this. I thought I'd feel nothing. No remorse, no guilt, no emotions at all.

But seeing my superior's dead body—wearing a dress and a crumpled red wig next to him no less—I'm overcome with pangs of anguish and shame. Yellow crime-scene tape surrounds Durita's body and all around me are blue and red police sirens, CIA agents, cops, and dogs on leashes.

"You okay, Regan?" asks a familiar voice. I turn to find Agent Chris Castillo.

I pull myself together. "Um, yeah, I'm fine."

"Hey, you did the right thing." He pats me on the back. "If you didn't take Durita out, Miss Gallier and Mr. Stone would be dead."

Cleo. "Where is—Miss Gallier?"

Castillo flicks his head toward the ambulance.

"I'm gonna go see if she's alright," I say. "I imagine she's pretty shaken up."

He nods. "Just don't wander off too far. SBI will be here soon, and they'll want to ask you a bunch of questions."

I nod confidently, though I've never had to deal with The State Bureau of Investigation before.

Castillo can see the worry on my face. "It's just protocol. You did everything by the book."

"I know, but—"

"Look, there will be more red tape, more questions and investigations, but again, Regan, you did nothing wrong, even if it feels like it. Trust me, the only thing the agency hates more than an agent killing another agent is a traitor. I can't believe it was Don betraying us."

"Yeah, I'm still wrapping my head around that one."

As I make my way over to the ambulance, I notice all of the flashing sirens on the black-and-whites. I count six in total.

In the blurry aftermath of shooting Durita, they had all faded away. It was just Durita, Cleo, and me. With her life flashing before my eyes, I didn't hesitate. I whipped my gun out of my holster and pulled the trigger. I didn't think.

But now I had to quiet the growing chorus of questions growing increasingly louder inside my head ever since Matt dragged me here on what I thought was a cockamamie outing.

I stop and turn back to Castillo. "Do you know where my brother is?"

"One of the uni's drove him back to the hotel."

"Great, thanks."

Bless Matt. If my younger bro wasn't such a ginormous pain in the ass, all signs point to Cleo and Spencer being taken away in body bags. God, I don't even want to think about it. From now on, I'm all ears anytime Matt has a hunch—no matter how preposterous it sounds.

After Durita in his red wig stormed the gate, I waited with Matt until back-up arrived. I couldn't get inside anyway, and the last thing I needed was to have my little brother running around when there was a terrorist's accomplice on the loose. Matt put up a small fight at first—he truly couldn't get over the giant, jumbo peacocks—but finally acquiesced and sat in the car until the cavalry arrived. Less than four minutes later, they got there, and I could then be damn sure that Matt wasn't even going to get so much as his pinky toe inside those gates.

What went down in here would've scarred him for life. I'm going to have to concoct one helluva good story so that he still doesn't have a clue as to what his big bro actually does for a living. That'll be interesting. Not much gets past Matt.

I find Spencer sitting on the back of an ambulance. "How's the patient?" I ask as an EMT bandages his right calf.

"Fine. Not much more than a nick."

"No bullet fragments," the EMT adds. "Might give him a pair of crutches just in case."

"Woulda been a whole lot worse if you didn't show up, man," Spencer says.

"Just doin' my job. Can't tell you how relieved we all are that you and Miss Gallier over here are alright." My eyes wander above Spencer's head and land on Cleo in the back of the ambulance. She sits on a gurney with a dark gray blanket covering her shoulders as she speaks with a female EMT.

"'Scuse me," I say to Spencer as I slowly walk back toward her.

I gently put a hand on one of her shoulders.

The last thing you want to do, we're taught in training, is startle someone just after a brush with death. All their senses are heightened, and they're prone to agitation. On top of that, the effects of adrenaline can stay in the system for up to an hour after a big rush, meaning Cleo is probably starting to come down right about now.

So I simply say, "Hey."

She looks up at me, her eyes big and alert, and I think she might burst into tears.

"Jake," she answers so quietly that I have to strain to hear.

I sit next to her on the gurney. "Yeah, it's me. I'm here. Are you okay?"

"I can't thank you enough. I don't know what would've happened if you didn't come when you did. I think we would have died."

"Sure a gal like you would've figured something out. You managed to keep yourself alive far longer than most people in your situation, I bet."

Cleo leans her body into mine, then wraps her arms around my neck.

I'm instantly intoxicated by her scent.

"Take me home, Jake. Please, I want to go home."

I look over at the female EMT, whose name I haven't caught.

She nods her approval. I tell Castillo I'll be back to talk to the authorities after I take Cleo and Spencer home. He tells me to come back right away.

CLEO IS SITTING NEXT TO me in the driver's seat. I wish it was just the two of us, but seeing as Spencer's Jeep isn't driv-able and counts as evidence, I offered to take him back to his place too. It isn't too far from Cleo's, and technically it makes more sense for me to drop her off first but for obvious reasons, that's not gonna happen.

From the back seat, Spencer asks, "You guys ever see that old Hitchcock movie *The Birds*?"

Cleo nods her head. "I think so."

"Tippi Hedren plays a socialite who follows this guy to some little town on the coast in Norcal where she ends up getting terrorized by a homicidal flock of birds. Tippi makes it out alive, but she's about the only one. Scared the shit outta me when I watched it at USC. It was like an update of *Dante's Inferno.*"

"Sounds freaky," I say.

I glance at Cleo as she stares out the window. She seems fine. Cleo is anything if not tough, but who could blame her for being shaken up?

"Very," says Spencer. He seems chatty, and I wonder if he's still a little freaked out too. "Like those birds in the garden just now. Granted, they were prettier and more colorful than Tippi's crows—but I dunno, I couldn't help thinking about them. It's this next left," Spencer leans over the center console and points to a road with a wooden white marker on the corner. In black block letters, the sign reads *Honu Way.*

I take the turn, and we're taken up a long, spindly path leading us eventually to a large glass house. It's cool. I pegged Spencer as a modern architecture guy, so seeing the minimalist white structure and glass is no surprise.

"Oh, God," says Spencer.

His pretty, petite blond wife is already waiting for him out front. She stands up and hurries over to my car before I put on the brakes.

"Oh, she's probably just so glad that you're alright, Spencer." Cleo smiles. "Don't be hard on her."

"I know, I know. Melinda can just be a bit of a worrier, so this little episode is probably going to send her over the edge," Spencer tells us before he hops gingerly out of the car to meet his wife. I notice him trying to cover up his limp.

Cleo and I watch the Stones' emotional driveway reunion. Their hug goes on for at least thirty seconds. Spencer rubs Melinda's back as she cries into his shoulders.

JAKE, 8

I glance over at Cleo, hoping she'll look my way, but her eyes stay fixed on the Stones.

Spencer eventually turns to the car and says, "Thanks for the ride, man. And Cleo ... wow. No one I'd rather be down in the proverbial foxhole with!"

"Thanks for bringing him home to me," a teary-eyed Melinda says to both of us.

I put the car into drive and at long last, Cleo and I are alone.

She takes me by surprise when she puts her hand in mine, asking, "Why did Durita want to kill me? He was Othello we know now, but what was his motive? And why was he dressed like a woman? It's just so awful, all of it."

2014

CLEO, 10

I got up during the night and brought Zelli to my bed to sleep with me. I often let her sleep with me after a long day of exploring the outdoors—all those sticks and flowers and yucky worms to touch. Even when she's fast asleep, Zelli loves being close to me. But tonight it's me who needs her to feel safe. As I look at her she is just so heart-stoppingly lovely and the greatest gift of my life. To think I could have lost my life and left her crushes me. She is my world and I finally start to sob at what just happened.

I can still hear the birds' awful cawing and the frightening sounds of their wings flapping while Durita shot at us. I stroke Zelli's hair while she's curled up next to me, blissfully ignorant to the evils of this world. Back in the garden with Spencer, I kept thinking I have to live for Zelli. I can't leave her alone. I have to get through this.

When I wake up and look out the French doors upon another perfect day, it's already eight thirty. Nannie is always at my door at seven thirty, which is the time Zelli gets up and toddles out of my room. The first thing I do is walk to the back of the house and take down the bird feeder. What were once graceful, beautiful creatures are now terrifying to me.

Tragedy or not, the play has no ending. Now that Durita is gone, I feel compelled to go back to the jail to find out from Dr. Pearson why Don Durita a.k.a. Othello had been helping Pearson. I am sure it has to do with Jimbo. Durita had on Jimbo's Ironman medal under his dress. He must have known I killed Jimbo and was seeking revenge but why?? Why??

After spending a few hours outdoors with Zelli reading her favorite book, *The Princess and The Pig,* twelve times—I decide to pass on *Flora and the Flamingo* today—I wave goodbye to her as she goes to Pudge and Pudding's for a playdate. The timing is purposeful as I just scheduled an emergency krav maga session with Walter.

"Thanks for coming on such short notice, Walter," I say to my trainer as he walks through the door to my studio.

"Yeah, no problem. Everything okay?"

"Not exactly...."

"What happened?" Walter looks at me with questioning eyes.

"I'm still trying to process it, I suppose."

"Okay ..." He shoots me a suspicious look.

I guess I have to tell him now. "Long story short, my friend Spencer and I almost got killed."

"Killed?" Walter's brow crinkles. "By whom?"

"This crazy CIA agent who turned out to be a traitor! Don Durita. You met him at lunch at Sweet Pea. He was with Jake. It's just so bizarre that I can hardly believe it."

"Is Spencer okay?"

"Yes, thank God. We were at this exquisite garden that I never knew existed. It was huge, filled with trees and plants and thousands of exotic birds and they attacked us. It was horrible, Walter."

Walter is so calm. He smiles at me. "Too bad you couldn't use krav maga on them. What matters Cleo is that you're here and this is where you should be. In the present moment." With that, he throws me my defensive pads and asks, "How did you protect yourself?"

"I got into a crouch and put one hand over my eyes and the other on my neck and put my head between my legs. It was pure instinct. I imagine all of mankind would do that."

He smiles. He dons his defensive pads, and we go at it for a good hour until I was so exhausted that I had to stop. I think it helped my fears dissipate a bit.

I SHOWER AND PUT ON a pretty, green sundress with white scallops on the hem and add white pearl earrings to go see Dr. Lodge at his office. As usual, Henry's receptionist knows me and I pass through his open door.

"Henry, I hate to bother you, but do you mind putting me in touch with your father? I told him I'd come for a visit."

Henry pulls himself away from his computer and looks up at me. "My father is quite taken with you, you know." He laughs.

"Oh, yes? Well the feeling is mutual."

Henry jots something down on his prescription pad. "Here's his address. He's ninety-nine, so the best way to communicate with him is to show up on his doorstep."

I take the paper. "Are you sure?"

Henry nods. "He mentioned he'd like to see you again. Just don't give the old man a heart attack." He winks.

When I arrive at the address for Mr. Lodge, I'm greeted by an extraordinary cherry blossom tree in the front yard, with a wooden swing hanging from one of its branches. Something fun for the grandchildren, no doubt. Or maybe he swings in it himself. The image of that makes me smile. I am sure Mr. Lodge was a fantastic father and now a grandfather—probably even a great-grandfather. I knock on the front door, which is painted a lovely shade of royal blue.

It's as if Mr. Lodge knew I was coming. But of course he did. His son would've called to warn him. He smiles as he opens the door mere seconds after I knock.

"Welcome, Ms. Gallier."

"It's so nice to see you, Mr. Lodge," I say as I enter his charming, very Hawaiian home. I glance around looking for any signs of Mrs. Lodge—a pair of shoes by the door, a straw hat to garden in, a tube of lipstick—but I don't see any. And of course I am not surprised. By the looks of it, Mr. Lodge must have lived in this fascinating house for quite some time. He has on a suit and tie, which is the only way he seems to dress.

"Would you like something to drink? I have my water with me all the time."

"No, I'm quite alright. Thank you though."

"Shall we sit on the porch? I love it out there this time of day, before the heat gets too unbearable." He taps his cane toward the porch.

Mr. Lodge and I sit in a pair of beautiful white wrought iron chairs on his wraparound porch with the thatched roof above us. Once upon a time, perhaps the chair I'm sitting in belonged to Mrs. Lodge.

"So, my dear. Tell me what is happening in your lovely life."

And so I tell Mr. Lodge the story of Dr. Marcus Pearson, a Shakespeare professor who seems to be living out his own Shakespeare tragedy and from whom we need a confession. I am not sure why I went to Mr. Lodge. Perhaps because I need to hear myself talk. "I'm struggling to figure out why Durita wanted to kill me though I have a suspicion, and I also want to understand Pearson's duplicity and both answers are known by Pearson. Most terrifying of all, Mr. Lodge, were millions of kamikaze birds in the garden yesterday. It's so raw, I can't seem to stop thinking about them."

After I finish the diatribe, Mr. Lodge says, "I'd like to accompany you to the interrogation you've arranged with Dr. Pearson tomorrow—if you will let me—to meet the infamous Shakespeare professor."

He smiles at me when I offer to pick him up, saying, "That's alright, dear. I have a girl whom I pay for that sort of thing."

Driving Mr. Lodge. I imagine it would be a great job for her.

TRIPP, 11

I haven't told anyone that the operation will be performed early this morning. It sounds suspect, I know, but I just don't want my family worrying about me any more than they already are. Miranda wouldn't sleep, Jake would insist on speaking with Dr. Maharani himself even though he doesn't have the first clue about ophthalmology, and Matt would ply me with a thousand questions. Hell, even Castillo would toss in his two cents. It's just easier this way.

As a man of routine, I've grown to appreciate my morning rituals at the hospital. Breakfast at eight, followed by Ignacio's daily sponge bath, then my vitals are checked. My operation is scheduled for eight in the morning so when Miranda arrives at 10:00 a.m. on the dot, nurse Malia will inform her of the operation, which will already be well underway, and escort her to the operating theater on the first floor. At best, Malia was dubious when I clued her in about my plan last night.

"You want me to do what now?" she asked, her hands probably on her hips.

They came to get me at seven thirty and naturally not a bite of breakfast or even water was allowed after midnight last night. I was already wide awake when the orderlies entered my room.

"Morning, Mr. Regan," said a husky voice I didn't recognize. "Are you ready to go down to the OR?"

I nod and spout out a cliché. "Ready as I'll ever be."

"That's what we like to hear," said the same husky voice as he and another set of hands helped me out of bed and into the gurney. And now more voices I don't recognize have me sitting up while I'm asked my date of birth.

"Left eye, right?" I hear one nurse ask.

Well, that's pretty unnerving. She doesn't know both eyes are being operated on? Then something occurs to me. I realized that perhaps this was all part of the plan. They were asking me these basic questions for my own benefit instead of theirs. Making sure that I'm in the right headspace before they put me under. Then, after I'm out like a light, I'll be wheeled into Dr. Maharani who will be waiting for me in the operating room. Dr. Maharani will make space for the implants that should, God willing, give me the gift of sight once again. An intraocular lens (IOL) implant is an acrylic replacement for your eye's natural lens and takes over the image-focusing function in your eye. Inserting the implant won't take long—probably just a half an hour for each eye. Yikes, that sounds quick.

No need to rush, Dr. Maharani. Take your time!

"Mr. Regan! Big day for you, isn't it? My name is Miranda." She puts her cold hand on mine.

"No kidding. That's my wife's name. Do you have curly hair like she does?"

She laughs. "I wish. Mine is steel gray and straight as a stick."

I met nurse Miranda hours ago—or at least it feels that way when finally, the anesthesiologist introduces herself.

"Morning, Mr. Regan. I'm your anesthesiologist, Dr. Holmes," she shakes my hand. "We're ready for you to go under. Is that alright?"

I nod. "Let's do it."

"Great. Unless there are any complications, which we don't anticipate, the operation will be quite short. Perhaps an hour. Would you like the IV in the right or left arm?"

"Uh, left, please."

These past four weeks the blood has drained completely from my eyes, which is what my doctor wanted, so at least I have that to feel good about. Dr. Maharani came to my room when he arrived yesterday from Florida and expressed rather flatly that he was glad not to detect any more hyphema—blood in the anterior chamber of my eyes. This is the space in between the cornea and the iris, Dr. Maharani explained.

He seems entirely competent, though not exactly soft and cozy. No chit chat. I felt him examining my eyes even more thoroughly than Dr. Copperman. When at long last he finished the exam, he made an attempt at small talk by telling me he was meeting an old medical school classmate for dinner.

I kept wanting to say, "Well, don't stay out too late, doc …" But I didn't and here I am in a chair that feels like the ones I sit in when I'm at the dentist as Dr. Holmes inserts the IV into my left arm.

"What do you do, Mr. Regan?"

I'm one of the most senior intelligence agents with the CIA, I want to say. But I don't. "I'm a lawyer."

"Good for you. My parents wanted me to be a lawyer."

"Too bad you had to go and disappoint them by becoming a doctor."

Dr. Holmes laughs. "If I was going to be a doctor, they think I should have been a brain surgeon. What kind of lawyer are you?"

And that's the last thing I remember. I don't recall getting woozy or falling asleep or even waking up. I just hear voices and have no idea where I am, though I sense a lot of bustling around me. My eyes blink several times as I try to get my bearings. I feel as if I'm halfway between waking up and still being in a dream.

Wait. Is that ... light?

I blink my eyes a few more times to confirm that I'm not actually still stuck in a dream. My head turns to the left, and I see more light. Then even more light floods in as I hear the sound of curtains opening. So much light.

The curtain is blue. I can see that the curtain is blue. Oh, blue, how I've missed you. This better not be another dream.

I see movement by the curtains. The silhouette of someone moves closer to me.

"How are you feeling, Mr. Tripp?" It's a voice I recognize.

"Malia?" I ask as a big smile comes into focus. "Is that you?"

"It's me, alright," she says as she takes my pulse. Not only can I feel her taking my pulse, but also I can *see* her taking my pulse. It's a goddamn miracle.

Miranda walks in, and she's crying. Seeing her red hair and green eyes for the first time in a month makes me cry too. What a sap I've become.

"Tripp!" she says as she leans down and cradles my face in her hands. The early afternoon light bounces off her engagement ring, and it's a glorious sight to see.

"You can see?"

I close one eye and I can see, and then I close the other eye and I can see with that eye too. "Yep." I smile through tears.

"I can't believe you didn't say a word about your operation!"

I'm grateful to see that she's smiling.

"Oh, I could just kill you, Tripp Regan—"

I'm saved by the arrival of Dr. Maharani. "Good news, Mr. Regan. The IOL implant worked, and the corneal injury is nearly healed. How do you feel?"

"I can't even find the words, Dr. Maharani. I don't think I've ever been this emotional."

"EVERYTHING LOOKS GOOD, but I'd like you to stay here for another few days while you recover. You need to get used to all of the eye drops I'm prescribing—some temporary, some not. Your wife can help you with this. And you'll need to wear sunglasses for a long while too. Your eyes will be very sensitive to light for quite some time."

"Anything you say, doc." I laugh. "You say jump, I ask how high."

Apart from his height of over six-foot-six—which I was certainly not expecting—Dr. Maharani is almost exactly as I pictured. Thin, tan, and very good looking. No wonder his deep voice oozes confidence and self-assuredness. I'm not shocked to find a gold wedding band when I glance down at his ring finger.

It's amazing the things you can learn about someone in an instant, even a total stranger. I'd missed that very much when I couldn't see. Soon I'd learn that most of the other voices I'd been hearing during my stay at Queen's Medical did not match the visions I'd concocted in my head.

"Dr. Maharani, I can't thank you enough. I owe you my happiness."

TRIPP, 11

He smiles and leaves. For him, this is just another Thursday. But for me, it's the gift of a brand new life and I promise myself that I will do wonderful things with this new life.

2014

CLEO, 11

The next day I arrived at the jail early, a good ten minutes before Mr. Lodge. I hate to be late, and I invariably recall my father's words. "If you're not five minutes early, you are late, Cleopatra. It's an insult to be late for someone."

Mr. Lodge arrives in a wheelchair, pushed by a woman in her midforties. Yesterday, he could walk pretty well, but our talk might have tired him out. He cradles a parcel in his arms.

I say hello and don't ask what it is, though I am curious.

Mr. Lodge introduces me to his "girl, Florence."

She's not on the list and, therefore, not allowed to go any further than the waiting area, so the warden wheels Mr. Lodge's chair toward the interrogation room. The warden seems to know Mr. Lodge well. The prisoners are quieter this time, not as enthusiastic about catcalling a woman when she's accompanied by an elderly man and the prison warden. I am dressed in baggy clothes with no skin showing, like the first time I came here.

Dr. Pearson awaits us in the interrogation room, along with Chris Castillo. And as before, two prison guards stand on either side of Pearson. I recognize the short one, but the taller guard with the nice tan is unfamiliar. Both of them nod hello but don't speak.

"Did you know about the bird sanctuary?" "What was Don Durita really up to?" "Why did he want to kill me?" "When did you reconnect with your brother?" "Why did you betray your country? "Why did you want to kill Tripp Regan?" These are all the questions that I want to barrage Pearson with.

But before I say a thing, Mr. Lodge wheels over to him, opens his mysterious parcel and whispers to Pearson. With shock, I recognize what's in that parcel. It is a Fourth Folio of William Shakespeare. Several years ago, when I was hosting *Close Encounters*, I had an erudite, rather stuffy man who worked at the Folger Library in Washington on as a guest. He stole the whole show when he told the audience about the First Folio of William Shakespeare. Never has the show had so many viewers write and call in as they did after that episode. So as a curious person, that night I went online and educated myself all about the folios.

The First Folio is the first collected edition of William Shakespeare's plays, collated and published in 1623, seven years after his death. In the 1600s, Folio editions were large and expensive books that were treated as prestige items. Shakespeare wrote around thirty-seven plays, thirty-six of which are amazingly contained in the First Folio. Out of the original seven hundred editions that were printed hundreds of years ago, there are about two hundred fifty First Folios remaining today. As you can imagine, they're worth a bloody fortune.

But what Mr. Lodge has with him is not the First or the Second Folio or even the Third. I recognize it as the Fourth Folio. Funny how he didn't mention having possession of this yesterday.

Dr. Pearson listens to Mr. Lodge as he continues to speak softly to him. Whatever he's saying, I wish he would speak up!

Pearson looks at the parcel and then at Mr. Lodge in disbelief. Then, finally, the doctor opens his mouth to speak. And when he begins to talk it comes out in a torrent. "You're offering me the Fourth Folio?"

Mr. Lodge just nods.

"It contains the additional seven plays that first appeared in the 1663 edition, including the authentic *Pericles, Prince of Tyre,* mind you, as well as a good deal of correction and modernization of the text designed to make it easier to read and understand." Dr. Pearson eyes Mr. Lodge again and with great reverence says, "And I know this one—it came from the Shuckburgh Collection."

Mr. Lodge nods again.

"You're telling me this is all mine if I answer her questions?" Pearson barely glances my way.

Mr. Lodge benevolently nods, then asks Pearson: "What is your favorite quote of the Immortal Bard?"

Pearson answers as though he's never met Iago and his famous quote: "Demand me nothing: what you know, you know. From this time forth, I never will speak a word." Instead, Pearson answers the perfect thing for a man in jail for attempted murder ... "The quality of mercy is not strained."

"Of course, *The Merchant of Venice.*" Mr. Lodge smiles. "'It blesses him that gives and him that takes.' So give the answers to Ms. Gallier and take this from me."

Dr. Pearson looks at me and cracks a smile. Then, as if something has just occurred to him, he looks up at Chris Castillo. "Where's Don Durita? He normally sits in on all of my meetings."

My eyes meet Castillo's.

Pearson senses that something's wrong. "What is it?"

"Mr. Durita … is no longer with us," says Chris Castillo.

"As in, he quit the CIA or he is no longer with us, with us?"

"The latter," Castillo answers.

From Dr. Pearson's face, it's difficult to understand exactly what's going through his mind. Again, he looks at Chris for confirmation, but the CIA agent stays mum.

"How?"

Castillo waits a few moments. It seems intentional. "Doesn't really matter, does it, doc? You don't have to lie for him or protect him anymore. Your Othello."

"I beg your pardon?"

"Durita dead is much better for you," says Castillo.

Pearson knows better than to respond to that.

"Just another loose end that you need not worry about anymore, right? And so you can tell the story as he no longer needs to be protected."

Chris Castillo sure has a flair for the dramatic. I am glad that he and Tripp are great friends. Chris turns to me and makes a gesture with his hands. Carry on.

Mr. Lodge interrupts, "Let's get back to the Folio, Dr. Pearson. I presume that's a small piece of history that you'd be interested in keeping for yourself. Some of the world's most exquisite plays are now at your fingertips. Could make all the years behind bars far more bearable," adds Mr. Lodge, a twinkle in his eyes.

Taking a page out of Castillo's book, Pearson makes us wait a while until he responds, building upon the room's already mounting tension. At last, he says, "Very well."

Oh, my goodness. *Very well?* Even I wasn't anticipating Pearson would agree to this. My heart is pounding, and I struggle to not react. If Pearson gets any inkling about how excited I am, he might change his mind.

How ingenious of Mr. Lodge to have brought the Folio as a bargaining chip. Dr Pearson is so overcome with the Folio he can hardly speak. Oh, how invaluable Mr. Lodge is.

Pearson motions for me to speak.

I say, "the iPhone is on, Dr. Pearson."

Begrudgingly, Dr. Pearson looks at me. "Alright. Where should I start?"

"The beginning."

Dr. Pearson is like a faucet who has been turned on after a long drought. A little leaky at first, but before you know it the sink is full of water.

His eyes linger on mine. "As you know, Jimbo was a local celebrity. And red-haired Fiona, a.k.a. Don Durita, was flattered by the famous Ironman's friendship. My brother's mind was always in motion, he was always anticipating his next move. When he realized what Fiona/Durita was up to in the garden and her relationship with Russian oligarch Anatoly Rustikoff, it was irresistible to him. Jimbo saw dollar signs to fund future missions. Al Qaeda was funding his Pearl Harbor mission, but Jimbo had other ideas for jihad here in Hawaii and all over the world. To use as leverage, he took photos of Rustikoff's planes loading and unloading crazy things: birds and trees. These were highly illegal and so Jimbo knew he could get the garden shut down as a way to blackmail Rustikoff to fund his jihad. And, Ms. Gallier, do you know where he hid those photos to blackmail and manipulate Rustikoff?"

"In my cave," I answer without betraying any emotion. But I also know a Russian oligarch would laugh at a blackmail attempt by anyone. The fact that Jimbo was an AQ leader might have tempted him to hand over some money but it would be his choice not because he was afraid.

"Yes, indeed."

My cave, my tribute to Africa where I'd slept in caves while climbing Tanzania's Mt. Kilimanjaro with the love of my life, Danny Mortimer. My cave, which I thought was mine alone, was used by a traitor. Jimbo knew all about it and he used it, just as he used me.

"Jimbo hid everything behind one of your wall hangings. He fashioned a fake stone in the wall of your cave and put in it a great deal of money, two guns, passports, photos of Rustikoff's planes, trees, and birds, lists of AQ terrorists world wide—his eyes blurred as he appeared to recall the scene in his head. "After he died, I received a letter at my house in Austin. In this letter, Jimbo gave me strict instructions. After two years—and only then—I should return to Honolulu and retrieve everything from the cave, then bring it into AQ Headquarters in Manila and to Jimbo's wife." Another surprise. Jimbo had a wife. At least he was faithful to her.

Pearson glances over at Chris Castillo. "Durita warned me that my cover was blown after this asshole saw me at the airport." He shakes his head. "When I got to Jimbo's cabin and saw no one around, I waited till dark to head to the cave. And while I waited, I went over all of Durita's instructions again and again. At the cave, I retrieved the hidden booty and the gun from behind the wall hanging. Then I heard someone outside. I panicked. When I peered over the edge and saw my old pal, Tripp Regan, climbing up, I had a choice: betray my brother or protect him. There was a list of the AQ members I was to contact. If I didn't destroy this information, Jimbo's operations would be ruined, so I set off the explosive and blew up everything." Dr. Pearson pauses, looking me in the eyes. "I didn't mean to shoot Tripp. Well, I mean, I wasn't trying to kill him. I just wanted him out of the way so I could escape. I shot him on the right side of his chest. I knew he'd survive that." Dr. Pearson's eyes remain on mine as he asks, "You and Tripp Regan are close?"

"Yes, we are friends."

"I'm only assuming that's partly why—" Pearson inhales deeply and yells at me "—*you killed my brother.*"

My world goes momentarily black as I think I will pass out.

But I don't. I feel Mr. Lodge and Chris Castillo's eyes boring into me. Even the two guards are staring. *Oh God.* I open my mouth to speak, but no words come out.

"Did you forget about the video cameras that line the beautiful palm trees up your driveway?" asks Pearson. "They caught you biking with my brother on the last ride of his life, and they recorded you coming home, shaking and crying. Durita had all the footage. Oh, and even some of Tripp Regan driving you home that night after you showed him and Durita where my brother had *skidded* off the road. And they caught him leaving the next morning ..."

I don't dare look at either Mr. Lodge or Chris Castillo. I still can't breathe.

"Don Durita knew you killed my brother," Pearson continues. "DNA was found under Jimbo's fingernails. Durita ran the test himself, and guess who it belonged to? He had gotten a hair from your house to match it. And it matched. But he told no one. He didn't want to make you a hero for killing one of the top Al Qaeda terrorists. They'd say some bullshit about you saving the world from terrorism. You would probably go to the White House and be given all sorts of honors and medals for killing Mohammed Abdul Rahman. Durita hated the idea of the attention you'd have gotten. He loved Jimbo, and so he hated you. He wanted you dead.

"When you first came here and offered to tell me who killed Jimbo in exchange for my confession, I was laughing inside. Silly girl, I already knew it was you, sitting right in front of me. I've spent a lot of my time here wondering just how in the hell you were able to kill the Ironman."

"That's enough, Pearson!" yells Chris Castillo.

Mr. Lodge wheels over to me, taking my hand as the guards move to grab Pearson and pull him up. Chris Castillo motions the guards to remove the prisoner.

Pearson looks at Mr. Lodge. "I did as you asked. I told her everything."

Mr Lodge nods. "The Folio is yours. How strange we all have different ideologies to unite us. The common bond of mountain climbers, dying to reach the peak. And in this case, your brother's cause caught you up into what you believed to be a higher calling but, in truth, was murder and betrayal of your country."

After they take him away, there is silence. Mr. Lodge is still holding my hand.

"Thank you, my dear. You are like a fantasy hovering between magic and reality. You dip in and out as your heightened intuition keeps you busy."

BEFORE I LEAVE THE ROOM, I bend over to Mr. Lodge. "What you did was so brilliant. Thank you for realizing the Folio was the only way to open Pearson up."

At the door, Castillo comes over and takes my hand. "I will talk to the guards who overheard this."

2014

TRIPP, 12

Hours later, Malia and Miranda—wife Miranda, not nurse Miranda—escort me back to my hospital room. It's not exactly as I pictured it, but pretty close.

"Home, sweet home," I joke as I slowly climb into the fresh sheets on my bed.

"Just as you imagined?" Malia asks.

"Not quite. In my head, the wallpaper was white, not blue."

"We love pops of color here at Queen's Medical," Malia laughs. "You need anything before my shift ends?"

Miranda cuts in. "Thank you so much, Malia. I can take it from here."

Malia smiles, nods, and leaves Miranda and me.

"You must be starving. Why don't I pick you up something from the cafeteria?"

My eyelids feel heavy as soon as my head hits the pillow. "No, I'm alright."

"Are you sure?"

"Yeah, even though I was only out for little over an hour, I'm really quite tired."

"Well, I'll leave you to it then," Miranda kisses my forehead. "I'm having a cookie craving, so if I see anything that would strike your fancy at the cafeteria, I'll grab it for you."

It's only when I look at Miranda now, do I realize how much I missed her face. With the way the sunlight is hitting her, she looks like an angel. A red-haired, cherubic angel. "Have I told you lately that you're the best?" I smile.

She smiles back. "Not lately," she says as she kisses my forehead again, and leaves.

I look around at the room. It's the very first time I have been completely alone since regaining my vision. I can practically hear a pin drop. A peaceful smile washes over my face as my eyelids start to droop again. I'm about to drift off when my phone beeps from my bedside table. With all the chaos over the past month, I'd practically forgotten about that thing.

My eyes blink and I roll over toward the bedside table on my left. I pick up my phone, fully charged thanks to Miranda I'm sure.

"Hello, old friend," I mutter under my breath as I enter the passcode. Yikes, there are hundreds of emails, texts, and missed calls. I don't even know where to start. I have 722 unread text messages, an overwhelming number, and so I decide to put that off for later. It says I have 46 voicemails that I'm really not in the mood to listen to. There are 345 unread emails. I guess I'll start there, emails it is.

I notice it immediately. An email from Don Durita. There's no text in the body of the email, just a video attachment. That's strange. I click the video and Don Durita's large face takes over the entirety of my phone screen.

He takes a deep breath. "Hey, Tripp. Don Durita here, in case you can't see me. Last I spoke to your doctors, they seemed pretty optimistic that they'd be able to fix your vision and so I hope for your sake and the sake of your family, that they were right." Don takes another breath. "Anyway, I wanted to explain ... well, a lot of things ..."

Huh? My brow crinkles. What the hell's he talking about?

"First off, you should know why I had to kill Cleopatra."

My heart sinks. "What?! No, no, no, no, no." I'm about to be sick. Because of my operation earlier, my stomach is completely empty, but still, it feels like my insides are about to be on the outside. I continue watching Durita's fat face on my phone screen, unable to look away.

"After all the time we've spent together—especially these last few weeks in the hospital—I think you deserve to hear the truth. The truth, from me."

I'm shaking now. My face feels hot, my whole body is trembling and sweat starts to pour down my brow.

"You see, she took Jimbo from me. But you already knew that, didn't you? What you don't know is how well I knew Jimbo. We spent a great deal of time together these past few years—ever since we met in 2010. Until she so callously murdered him."

Durita knows Cleo killed Jimbo. But I was so careful. We were so careful. I thought Cleo and I were so convincing with our story that his death was an accident. People tend to ask a helluva lot less questions when it comes to the murder of an international terrorist.

Durita takes another breath and steps further away from the camera. He's wearing a white undershirt. "I know this might sound pretty jarring, but I loved Jimbo. No one knew, including him ..."

That, I was not expecting.

Durita clears his throat. "You see, Jimbo was my light, and when that light was extinguished, I had to grieve alone. My pain turned to anger. And it festered. And from then on, I lived for revenge," he pauses. "I'm sure you feel unspeakably betrayed by me and I can't blame you for that. But please, hear me out...."

"Get to the fucking point, man," I say through gritted teeth.

"See, I knew the noose was tightening when you realized someone had added the dedication to my Jimbo in Pearson's book. It tightened more as the Agency started searching for who helped Marcus Pearson fake his own death and when we were ordered to get to the bottom of who suggested Pearson be your cover in Manila, the bullseye was on me. I'm sure this is difficult for you to hear and trust me, it's difficult for me to say ... but I was the one who warned Pearson about his blown cover after Castillo spotted him at the airport. I know you won't understand, but I had to tell him."

"You're goddamn right, I don't," I say aloud as if Durita can hear me.

"Unbeknownst to little ol' Cleo, Jimbo had been using the cave for years," Durita laughs tauntingly before he turns serious again. "Anyway, you know the rest. You were there. And I'm sorry for that, Tripp. I hope you will believe me when I say that I never meant for you to get hurt. You weren't supposed to be there that night," he says to the camera. It's as if he's pleading with me to believe him.

"Oh, so it's my fault now?"

Durita takes a few steps back from the camera. He's only wearing the white undershirt and boxer briefs. "I disguised myself as a woman to work at Anatoly Rustikoff's garden. To you, maybe this is even the craziest part."

Now I've heard everything. But compared to the news about Cleo, it hardly phases me. I'm frozen into silence and I need Durita to get back to the part about Cleo. She can't really be dead. No. I refuse to believe it.

Durita reaches to his right for something off camera. It's a modest, short-sleeved, navy blue dress with polka dots. "My job was to oversee the arrival of Rustikoff's biweekly shipments. The drop-offs were always at night," Durita tells me as he pulls the navy dress over his head. "You see, I bribed TSA officials. Amazing what a little money can do ... Really makes you question our national security, doesn't it?" Durita smirks as he buttons up his dress.

I want to punch that smirk off his stupid face.

"Rustikoff, as I'm sure you know, owns half the planes in Russia, which made things easier. And the gardeners were easy. We paid them triple the rate of any local landscaper and had them sign NDAs in exchange for transforming the land into a home for Rustikoff's trees and birds."

Durita reaches off camera again and this time, his hands are holding a red wig. "I was always dressed as a woman when I was working at Rustikoff's, where I met Jimbo." Durita sets the wig on top of his head, "Even after I fell in love with him, I remained Fiona, because Jimbo seemed to be very fond of her." He smiles, "Anyway, I couldn't very well switch back to Don after he'd already met Fiona ... though one time, on my way back from the CIA office, I was filling my car with gas when Jimbo rode by on his bike. He stopped at the gas station's convenience store for something," Durita smiles at the memory as he secures the wig. "I was in my suit and tie. My heart never pounded so hard. But Jimbo just nodded and waltzed right past me. No double takes. He had no idea I was Fiona, though, trust me, I have often wondered if he had any inkling that I was actually a man."

Durita grabs a mirror from a table behind him. With one hand he holds it up, and with the other he starts applying foundation to his face. "Jimbo often said how much he appreciated Fiona's modesty. He hated all the vulgar women on the island in their skimpy sundresses and bikinis. It offended his Muslim beliefs...."

I wanted to scream into the phone. Who gives a shit about his Muslim beliefs?! Get to the part about Cleo!

Durita sets the foundation down and begins applying mascara to his brown eyes. "I began going out of the garden into town dressed as her. I know this sounds crazy, but by now, you've probably guessed that I was a gay man. That's why I never married or brought a date to any of the CIA functions. As a woman, I could embrace my true identity. And as a woman, I lived for the dissembling. Taking on another identity, even though it was a real me, was such a thrill." Durita rubs blush onto his cheeks.

He takes a moment to rub on pink lipstick and then looks directly at the camera. "After all, I'm much better looking as a woman, don't you think?" Durita smiles.

Again, I feel sick. It's not because Durita is gay or enjoyed crossdressing. I can't get past all the layers of betrayal that the CIA and I so totally missed.

"But Tripp, I hope you know that I truly did think of you as my friend and I regret using you to feed my addiction for revenge. I liked and respected you."

I gag. This traitor is not my friend.

"I know the last thing I should do is ask anything of you...."

You got that right.

"But if you can find it in your heart to please put my ashes next to Jimbo's Ironman medal in the garden, I'd be forever grateful from the grave. You see I plan to take my own life when I kill Cleo so I am preparing this for you before I do that. She has arrived back on the island and revenge will be soon. I am as you now know Othello. I put one of the two Ironman medals he gave me along with Jimbo's ashes, by the dracaena draco tree. Matt will be able to find it. The garden only has one," Durita pauses. "When we're all dead and gone, that tree will still be here, giving deeper continuity to my life and Jimbo's life. I'm sure this final request leaves you appalled," Durita pauses again. "But we both know what you, too, once did in the name of love on Christmas Eve in a cave. You see, all of us have betrayed for love."

Jesus.

"Before I go, I should tell you that Jake should be warned. Anatoly Rustikoff knows who Jake is, and that he's looking into his dealings. What Rustikoff does elsewhere in the world is evil. But in the garden, it is not," Durita reaches up to the camera. "See you on the other side."

And the screen goes black. I reach for the pillow behind me and scream into it. I'm screaming for Cleo and I'm screaming at Durita, but really, I'm screaming at myself. How the hell could I have missed this? I scream for as long as my lungs will allow and don't even notice that Chris Castillo has walked through my door. His happiness for me regaining my sight quickly evaporates.

"Jesus, boss. What is it? Your eyes? Do they hurt?"

I turn to Castillo, who's looking at me as if I've just escaped the asylum. "Is she dead?"

"Who?"

Looking back on this moment later on, I realized that Castillo thought I meant Durita. Durita as Fiona. I choke back tears, "Cleo."

Castillo, mercifully, does not impose one of his famous dramatic pauses. He shakes his head, "No. Jake saved her."

Oh, thank God. I feel a weight lift off my shoulders and I can breathe again. "From ... from Durita?"

Castillo nods. "Jake killed him."

"He did?"

Castillo nods again since he knows I can see the nod. And I have never been so proud.

2014

MIRANDA, 4

Tripp's a bit unsteady after his operation, so Dr. Maharani's suggestion of a few extra days rest in the hospital is a good idea. I am always at his side.

I will always be at his side.

After all the paperwork and check-ups, we finally leave the hospital three days later. As we enter the parking lot, Tripp has on his "shades," as he calls them, and thinks he looks like a Formula One driver. Maybe he does, a little.

Tripp and I have decided to stay in the warmth for a few more days while he sees Dr. Lee, a top ophthalmologist in Honolulu. His eyedrop routine takes hours each day, or so it seems to me, as he takes some when he gets up and others two hours later and then at lunch, midafternoon, bedtime. Slowly, they won't all be necessary. I can't wait.

No hospital can replace the privacy, luxury, and convenience of a fancy hotel. We loved our stay at The Halekulani a few years ago, but thought we'd be adventurous and try somewhere new. When I called The Kahala Resort and Spa yesterday on a recommendation from Malia, I was pleased that they had a last-minute cancellation and could accommodate us. The research I did online got me even more excited. In

351

the early 1960s, the famous Conrad Hilton set out to create a hotel that would replicate that of the Royal Hawaiian. This was before Waikiki exploded around it, crowding the area with way too many tourists. Hilton wanted a hotel where the guests could enjoy the serenity of an uncrowded beach, gorgeous rooms, and outstanding gourmet food. Well, old Conrad, mission accomplished. A secluded sandy beach, private golf club, breathtaking views, and even dolphins. Really, there are six bottlenose dolphins in one of the pools! It's heaven.

Once we get into our room, Tripp phones Magda. I have already told the kids to come over tomorrow for breakfast. The dears have visited Tripp in the hospital every single day and deserve a meal with a more scenic backdrop. I wasn't sure we would ever be able to make plans again. I can't believe how happy and grateful I am.

Tripp keeps looking around and smiling. "The colors are so vibrant, Miranda! Look at this." He pulls me over to observe an ant marching along the ground. As we enter the hotel, he looks at every flower and every tree. It's as though he's morphed into Matt. After we enter our room, Tripp stares at himself in the mirror for a long time. He's pale and thin, and the past month has aged him, though he will always be the handsomest man in the world to me.

His eyes meet mine. He walks over and just stares at me as though I'm so precious to him. I'm a little worried, I have put on a few pounds of stress-eating donuts and bagels all day in the hospital, but then he kisses me as he did when we first met. He motions to the bed and says, "Let's take a nap, Miranda."

Nap. Oh, I know what that means, as does everyone who's been married for decades.

We close the blinds and I start to undress when he grabs me and undresses me himself, all the while staring and kissing my arms and legs and neck and breasts. I can hardly believe it. We are like teenagers as we touch one another gently, then harder. We kiss passionately, and it feels like we're on our honeymoon. I can't have enough of him, and he obviously feels the same as I do. When I get up to shower, he joins me in there and soaps me with such tenderness.

IN THE MORNING, Matt, Jake, Ricky, and Julia join us for breakfast—walking and strutting respectively—into the Plumeria Beach House, an outdoor waterfront restaurant that, like everything at The Kahala Hotel, boasts incredible views. I proudly admit to myself that Tripp and I have had a repeat performance of yesterday's glorious nap this morning.

Tripp is so delighted to see their faces and remarks on their fitness levels. He hugs each of them for so long. Even Matt, who hates to be touched, allows this briefly.

Ricky is as happy and friendly as ever. "Hey, guys! Thanks for having us over!"

"This hotel is much nicer than ours …" Matt tells us.

"Mom, you look great," Jake tells me after our hug.

I look back at him and try not to be offended at the tone of surprise in his voice.

"You do, Miranda," Julia smiles. Hardly, compared to a beauty like her …

I feel myself blush, and Jake looks at his father who is also beaming, smiling, as he looks down at the menu. Then I think I see Jake put two and two together, realizing exactly why I look so great. It's sort of fun to see him embarrassed by this.

"Anyway, what's good here?" Jake sits, trying to hide his embarrassment as a fabulous-looking waitress comes over to our table, carrying a big glass bottle of Aqua Panna.

As she smiles at us and fills my sons' water glasses, I realize that, *goodness,* she looks just like Julia if she had a deep tan. I glance around at the table to gauge my boys' reactions, to see if any of my less observant family members notice the resemblance. Apparently not.

"Good morning. Have you had a chance to look at the menu or do you need a few minutes?" She sets the bottle down in the middle of the table.

"Coffee, please," Jake says.

"Sure. Anyone else?" the waitress asks us.

Tripp raises his hand. "Please."

Matt doesn't say anything.

Ricky orders a coffee as well and Julia, her iced cappuccino.

"I'm okay with my water," I smile.

"Great, I'll be back in just a few minutes with those."

"Thanks!" says Tripp as the waitress goes. He is patting my shoulder and smiling at everyone.

"Jeez, Dad. Did you take happy pills this morning?" Ricky laughs.

Julia playfully love taps him on the arm.

"What? I've just never seen him so ... cheerful," Ricky laughs.

"I'm just glad to see all of your beautiful faces again. Sue me."

Jake reaches for the glass bottle of Aqua Panna and refills his glass. He's about to set it back down.

"Mind sharing with the rest of us?" Tripp motions to the water bottle.

Jake obliges and fills my glass first, then everyone else's. As he goes to set the bottle back down on the table, it nearly slips out of his hands. "Whoa!" Jake laughs as he recovers it.

"Nice save," Matt says flatly.

"Thing's slippery in this heat...."

Tripp hands Jake a napkin. "Here you go."

"Thanks." Jake starts drying the bottle with the paper napkin. "Don't want to drop it and ruin everyone's breakfast!" Jake glances at his father and says under his breath, "Much easier to pull fingerprints off dry bottles too."

Huh? Fingerprints? Sometimes my boys say things that thoroughly confuse me. Jake glances at his father, who looks just as confused as I am.

"Especially fingerprints on champagne bottles," says Jake.

Okay, now I'm really lost.

Ricky sips his water. "Huh?"

"Fingerprints? What are you talking about, Jake?" Julia half laughs.

But when I look across the table at Tripp, something in my husband's face has changed. His confusion has given way to upset when he realizes what Jake is referring to.

"Oh, I just mean now that you can see again, we need to get some bottles of Veuve, Dad." Then Jake looks at me and says, "We need to celebrate the old man with a few bottles of champagne, don't you think?"

I nod and Tripp smiles vaguely.

After breakfast, we decide to visit the now infamous botanical garden, the "Garden of Paradise." Jake drives Tripp, Matt, and me to one of the most miraculous places I've ever seen. Jake says he saw an article in the paper that the garden was seized from someone who owned it illegally.

Sadly, Ricky and Julia declined coming along as they have some organizing to do at the beach for their impromptu wedding. On a recommendation from the hotel, they're meeting with a potential officiant. I'm so glad that they decided to get married here. It will give us all a happy ending to an otherwise nightmare of a trip.

"Wow," Tripp looks around in pure disbelief. Spotting the rainbow-colored birds on a hill across the garden almost makes his jaw drop onto the ground. Surely a sight for his sore eyes. As we drive through this miraculous place, we're all stunned. The colors of the birds, the abundance of such strange, gorgeous trees. "For a second there, I thought my new eyes were playing tricks on me." He laughs.

We drive through the vast panorama. Matt could certainly live here for the rest of his life. He's especially taken with the gigantic bird sculptures that are made of flowers. At over fifteen feet tall, the sculptures look like giant art installations.

"Look, Toucan Sam!" Matt points through the car window to an enormous toucan that I'm able to identify by its rainbow-colored beak.

"... Who?"

"You know, the bird on the Fruit Loops box, Mom."

"It was only his favorite cereal growing up," Jake teases me.

"Oh, of course. How could I have forgotten?" I smile.

Matt points to an odd, mushroom-shaped bush that I can't quite identify. It looks like it belongs somewhere even more exotic than Hawaii. Like in Fantasia or Never Never Land.

"Dad, that's the tree you asked me about," Matt points.

Jake glances at his father, and they share a look. Yet again! Matt was so right about secrets, but I'm too happy to care. Julia and Ricky are getting married here in Honolulu on the beach and Tripp can see! What more could a gal ask for?

"Thanks, Matt." Jake parks on the grass and we all climb out of the car and it feels wonderful to stretch and walk toward this strange looking, thirty-foot-tall tree.

"Any idea what it's called, Matt?" I ask as we all stroll toward it. The trunk is splintered and the branches are mostly vertical instead of horizontal.

"It's a dragon tree. *Dracaena draco*," says Matt, clearly in awe. "One of the rarest trees in the world. It's subtropical, native to the Canary Islands and some are in Morocco and Portugal."

Then I almost trip over a large round stone with a medal sealed into the base. Tripp bends down for a closer look.

"What is it?" Matt asks.

"It's a medal. For finishing the Ironman," Jake answers for his father.

"You're kidding," I say. "Does it belong to that friend of Cleo's?" Funny how I am not the least bit worried about mentioning her or her damn perfume anymore. I have won the chess match by saying nothing. I have him for sure.

"Jimbo," Jake nods. "The terrorist who planned to blow up Pearl Harbor."

I had tried to block all of that out. I am instantly infuriated.

I look at Tripp who says nothing. "Well, what's it doing here? Surely, there shouldn't be any sort of shrine for an anti-American terrorist on our soil, right?" I say outraged.

"I'm sure it's only a matter of time before this whole thing gets ripped up and thrown in the trash," says Jake.

Tripp, still looking down at that awful Jimbo's medal, just nods.

Finally Tripp speaks. "When I was blind, Magda read me a line from a book of quotations. 'It is in pardoning that we are pardoned.' I pondered that for weeks but it makes sense to me now."

Tripp sits on the bench and asks us to leave him alone for a bit. As we approach the car, I look back and see him take a plastic bag and a spoon from his pocket. I turn away quickly as I don't want him to think I'm spying. But when he returns to the car a while later, he looks calm and happy and sad all at once.

JULIA, 5

Our wedding isn't when or where and certainly is not *what* I thought it would be. But who cares?

At long last, the day has arrived, and I can't wait a minute longer to be Mrs. Richard Regan. There will be no bridesmaids in blue dresses or groomsmen in navy blazers, no adorable little flower girls or charming little ring bearers. I won't be wearing the perfect, strapless Monique Lhuillier tulle gown that my father generously paid for. In fact, even my father isn't here. It will just be the Regans and me on the beach at The Halekulani Hotel, where Ricky and I fell in love, and that's enough for us.

After all, it's not like the blue bridesmaid dresses or blue groomsmen's blazers or my Monique Lhuilier gown will go to waste. No way! Ricky and I will still hold our wedding back in New York at The Colony Club this spring as planned. Boy, did I never think the day would come where I'd be one of those women with the audacity to have two weddings—and I'm not, not *really* at least—but in my defense, there were extenuating circumstances.

The white sand beach at the Halekulani is just too perfect and too meaningful and too breathtaking for Ricky and me to leave Honolulu without getting married on it. At first, Miranda was a bit skeptical of the idea—she's not the spontaneous type—but she warmed up to it as soon as Tripp enthused over the idea.

Poor, sweet Tripp. He's been cooped up in a hospital room for over a month. I've never seen the man more excited. He told us rather tearily that one of his biggest fears in never regaining his sight was missing out on seeing Ricky and I say our 'I Dos' up on the altar. When he said that over breakfast one day, we all started crying. It was a whole big thing.

Tripp is our witness, Matt is Ricky's Best Man, and Miranda is my honorary Maid of Honor. It's really kind of cute; she's an only child and I get the sense that she probably didn't have many close girlfriends at my age who asked her to be their bridesmaid, let alone the Maid of Honor.

"Would you like a glass of champagne?" Miranda asks me from across the hotel room.

Halekelani was kind enough to rent us two rooms—one for the boys and a separate room for Miranda and me—at a discounted price in exchange for promoting our wedding ceremony at the hotel in *Slate* magazine and on their Instagram account. Oh yes, the power of social media.

"I thought you'd never ask," I smile and take the flute from Miranda. "And I hope you'll join me...."

I've never seen her look so pretty. Miranda is absolutely radiant in her navy blue cap-sleeved dress that we picked out together two days ago from a little boutique off Kapiolani Boulevard.

"Of course. I mean, how many times does your middle son get married?" She laughs as she fills another flute with champagne. Honestly, it's touching how joyous Miranda is over Ricky and me.

For about the hundredth time, I turn to the mirror and check myself out. I chose a brand I knew well because there was no time for alterations. I needed this particular dress to fit like a glove, and I just knew that the white, floor-length Reformation number I overnighted to the Halekulani would do the trick. It's a simple dress: spaghetti straps with a sweetheart neckline and a scoop back. All of that bridal, blinged-out, poofy, princess shit is so not me. My dress is quite the opposite; it reminds me of something that Kate Moss would wear in the 90s. She's kind of a fashion idol of mine. The queen of minimalist chic, eternally classic, and above following current trends. Kate was my inspiration today, and I think I'm doing her proud.

"It's your day," Miranda says calmly as she takes a baby sip of champagne. "So we're all working off of your schedule, Julia. But just so you know, it's a quarter to five."

Oh, fuck. The wedding starts at five. "Goodness!" I set my glass down. "Thank you, Miranda, I completely lost track of time!"

"That's what I'm here for." She smiles.

I can't tell if it's because this is the happiest day of my life or if it's the butterflies or the champagne but right now, in this moment, I feel such genuine love for Miranda in a way I've never experienced before. In spirit, I know that my own mother is here with me today, like she is every day, but it almost seems as if she's channeling herself through Miranda.

"Would you like me to help you put on your flower crown?" she asks.

"That'd be wonderful."

You'll never guess who's walking me down the aisle.

Actually, it's quite poetic. At least Ricky and I think so. Funny to think that just two years ago I fantasized about walking down the aisle *toward* Jake, and now I'm getting escorted down the aisle *by* Jake into the loving arms of his brother.

"Ready?" Jake asks, extending his left arm as I hear the ukulele start playing *Over The Rainbow*. I'm overcome with emotion, but I push the butterflies down and the tears back into their ducts. I don't want to be one of those blubbering brides, and I refuse to ruin my make-up.

As the sun starts to sneak away, she leaves behind a sky that's painted a glassy swirl of pinks, oranges, and blues. The colors remind me of the sherbet my mother used to buy me from our local ice cream store as a girl. Now I truly know my mother is here with me today.

I take a deep breath and turn to Jake. "Ready," I say tightly.

We start walking from the edge of the infinity pool toward the beach where Ricky and the rest of my life awaits.

"Somewhere over the rainbow, way up high, there's a land that I heard of once in a lullaby ..." sings the ukulele player.

Keep it together, Jules. Keep it together.

"Breathe, Jules. You're doing great," Jake whispers to me.

This eases my tension a bit, and I let out all the air in my lungs that I've been holding in. "Thanks for doing this, Jake."

"I wouldn't have it any other way." He winks.

Ricky is looking at me with such love in his eyes. I'm still too far away, but I think they might just be filled with tears.

To his left, Matt looks as if this is just another day at the beach. *Oh, Matt.* To Ricky's right, Miranda's smile is as wide and vast as the ocean behind her. And last but certainly not least, in front of Ricky stands Tripp. He's able to see Ricky and I say our 'I Dos' after all, and you can practically see the weight that's been lifted off his shoulders.

"Somewhere over the rainbow, Bluebirds fly," the ukulele player serenades us as Jake walks me closer and closer to the man of my dreams. And yes, those are tears in Ricky's blue eyes.

"I love you," Ricky mouths to me as I'm mere steps away from him now.

Keep it together, Jules. Keep it together.

I'm so overcome with joy, excitement, and honestly, shock that this day has finally arrived. They say your whole life flashes before you on the day you die, but that very same sensation is happening to me right now. It's like a highlight reel of all the romantic heartbreak I've suffered in the past. But those days are long gone! From this day forward, I will be Mrs. Richard Regan and life will never taste so sweet.

The ukulele player belts out the end of the song, *"If happy little bluebirds fly beyond the rainbow, why oh why, can't I?"*

His timing is perfect. At long last, I'm standing in front of Ricky. I'm so close that I can touch him.

"Welcome to the family." Jake smiles as he unhooks his arm from mine, and I walk up to the man I'm going to marry.

2014

TRIPP, 13

Julia and Ricky's wedding yesterday still feels like a dream. I know it wasn't the wedding they'd planned when they first got engaged, but I wouldn't change a thing. And if I could bestow any words of wisdom onto them, it'd be just that. Plans change. Expect the unexpected. Life throws you curveballs, kids. It's Murphy's Law: whatever can go wrong, will. The sooner you figure that out, the better off you'll be.

After the lovebirds said their "I Dos" the officiant, who hilariously doubled as the photographer, snapped what felt like thousands of family photos of the six of us at sunset. Each of us gave sappy toasts, many laughs and happy tears were shed, and a few cracks about Jake and Julia's former fling, and a good time was had by all.

Early this morning, Julia and Ricky set off on a little boat to the nearby island of Kuai for their minimoon. As you can imagine, the whole trip was planned extremely last minute but I'm told that they're staying at a mountain hotel that takes half an hour to get to up a steep mountain road. Like I said, anything can happen.

Miranda and I thought inviting the doctors, nurses, and other hospital staff to a thank you party would be a nice gesture before we get on a plane back to The Big Apple. They all worked tirelessly and helped me and my whole family get through the past harrowing month. I wouldn't be surprised if Miranda took down each of their names and added them to her Christmas list.

She'd never tell me, but I have no doubt there were plenty of incredibly dark moments for Miranda over the past few months, moments when she thought the life we'd built for the past three-plus decades together was crumbling beneath her feet. We owe so much to Queen's Medical.

Duncan from Sweet Pea also provides catering, and he convinced us to entrust him with every little detail.

"Sit back, relax, and let Sweet Pea show you a good time!" he quipped.

Hosting the party at his place was also a big thank you to Duncan from all of us at the CIA. Unbeknown to Miranda, he passed on a vital clue to Spencer that ended up unraveling the whole Othello Desdemona mystery once and for all.

I'm still in such shock about Don Durita. How was I so easily fooled by him and Pearson? I detected no red flags. Sadly, the time has definitely come for me to pass on the baton and retire from ops to a desk job.

I'm a bit unsteady as I get out of our rental car in the Sweet Pea parking lot and adjust my dark glasses. As always, Miranda is by my side. We enter through the glass doors to be greeted by a steel drum band that's dazzling us with Jimmy Cliff's *I Can See Clearly Now*.

Har-dee-har-har. Miranda and I turn to each other and laugh. Nice touch, Duncan. What a welcome! I squeeze Miranda's hand, flattered by how many smiling faces have shown up at Sweet Pea to celebrate. There's Dr. Akana and Dr. Copperman and Magda who is next to a woman who must be her partner, Liz, as well as nurse Malia who brought me three hot meals five days a week, and nurse Ignacio who changed my sheets, and so many others. As the only attendee in his tenth decade, I recognize Mr. Lodge off to the side with Cleo and a middle-aged man. And of course, Chris Castillo, Agents Wu, Keough, Ventura, and several other buddies from the CIA are here too. I told Miranda they were orderlies from the hospital when they were really guards brought in by Castillo, on shifts when she wasn't allowed to visit.

As all of those gathered turn to me, they smile and applaud.

Pangs of sadness remind me that soon my family and I will be leaving Hawaii and saying goodbye to all these smiling faces.

Speaking of films, Spencer is here with his lovely wife Melinda and their teenage daughters, Alden and Catherine. They look like surfer girls, one with long blond hair and one with long red hair but both with shells tied around their necks and wrists. Spencer kindly came to see me this past week in the hospital as I wanted to hear his recollections and insights on what happened at the garden.

"Girls, say hi to the man of the hour," their mother tells them as they approach. She gives me a look that says, *teenagers ...*

They do as they are told. "Hello, Mr. Regan," they say, smiling with big white teeth.

"Thanks for coming, girls! I'm sure you must've had much cooler things to do than come to some old man's party."

"Not on a Monday," the older one, Alden, quips.

"Yeah, Mondays are pretty dead," the younger one agrees.

Melinda gasps. "Girls! Mr. Regan is a big deal!"

"Huge!" Spencer agrees with his wife. "Without saying too much, he's basically like Harrison Ford in *Patriot Games*."

The girls exchange looks. "Who?" They say in unison.

Spencer looks like he might have a stroke, but it gets a laugh out of the rest of the adults.

"Why don't you two go get something to drink?"

"Cool, I heard they're serving vodka," the younger one cracks.

"Haha, very funny," Spencer calls out as the girls make their way toward the bar.

"Sorry about that ... " Melinda smiles and shakes her head.

"Nah, we remember that age well. Don't we, Mir?"

"Yes, before you know it, they'll be heading off to college!"

A server in a black shirt and trousers offers us a plate of pigs in a blanket. My favorite. Spencer, Miranda, Melinda, and I all grab one.

"Wow, delicious," says Miranda. "Melinda, let's go to the bar. I could use something to wash these down."

As the two women cross the restaurant, I see Cleo.... I am so happy Cleo is still in this world. That was so terrifying when Durita announced he had killed her on his video. Must say, Cleo looks stunning in a long white dress with her long wavy dark hair and that exquisite face and those dimples. To think Zelli could have lost her mother by the insanity of Durita. And to think Cleo could be gone. One of the worst moments I have had.

"HEY, THANKS AGAIN for everything," I say to Spencer once we're alone.

"It was my pleasure. Really. And the good news is, I've had a brilliant inspiration for a film after my next film!" Spencer peppers me with questions about the CIA until we're interrupted by Ignacio, who has to head back to the hospital for the night shift.

"Look us up if you're ever in New York," I tell him before he goes.

For the next hour, Miranda and I circulate around the room, speaking with everyone from the hospital. I was bummed when Dr. Maharani left the night of my operation to rush back to his practice at Bascomb Palmer in Palm Beach Gardens. At least my main docs, Akana and Copperman, are here. They were with me from day one.

Reaching for my fifth pig in a blanket and chatting with the two doctors about winter in New York, I feel a hand on my back. I turn to find Cleo standing there beside Mr. Lodge, seated in his wheelchair.

"So sorry to interrupt, but someone would love to meet you," says Cleo, her amazing eyes twinkling beneath those dark, thick lashes.

I excuse myself from the doctors.

"Mr. Lodge! How nice to meet you."

"Congratulations on regaining your sight. The world is too beautiful not to see it," he smiles.

"And this is his son, Dr. Henry Lodge," Cleo tells me, indicating another man behind the wheelchair. He's a handsome guy with salt-and-pepper hair and a nice smile.

Indicating all the medical professionals at the party, I say, "Dr. Lodge, you must fit right in here." I shake his hand.

"I do, actually." He laughs. "I run my practice out of Queen's Medical too."

"What a small world. What's your field?"

"I'm a GP."

How interesting. I wonder to myself if Dr. Lodge was the one who had the lab run the DNA tests regarding Zelli's father.

"Do you need anything to drink?" Cleo asks the elder Mr. Lodge.

How Cleo dotes on him. The old guy looks younger by the minute as she gazes at him with those big, beautiful purple eyes. I know that gaze, and oh, it's a powerful drug. She bends over his wheelchair, and I can hear her ask him: "Mr. Lodge, did you have the Folio that you gave Pearson for a long time?"

I know this is my cue to thank him so I bend over him and whisper, "Mr. Lodge, that folio was such an instrumental contribution to solving the Othello case. I can't thank you enough."

His answer is charming. "The folio was a present on my eighty-fifth birthday from my family. But at ninety-nine, it was time to pass it on, and I was happy to find the compassion to give it to a man who had manifestations of pure evil. In a way, it allowed me to offer hope that he might change his heart someday." He turns to Cleo. "And now, my dear, as much as I hate to do this, it's time for me to bid you adieu. It's almost eight o'clock, which means that soon I'll turn into a pumpkin."

"I don't want you to leave, but I certainly don't want you to turn into a pumpkin, so I will walk you out." She smiles. When she leaves with the Lodges, I notice Jake following them. At first, I thought maybe Cleo had something going with the young Dr. Lodge but watching her now, I can tell that she doesn't. I know her too well for her to put anything over on me.

I also know in my gut that she's no longer in love with me—well, Danny really. Funny how easily you can tell when someone just doesn't care anymore. The urgency to talk, to share thoughts on the novel you just read or the walk you just took. All those things that Cleo and I once had on Kilimanjaro.

And yet again, Cleo found herself intertwined in a dangerous plot and managed to get to the bottom of it. Call it whatever you want, woman's intuition or a superior gut instinct, she saved my ass.

SOMETIMES I FIND that parties celebrating major events can be a bit anticlimactic. The major event is over so the one that follows can feel like an afterthought. But just as I'm settling into the magnificent lull and ebb of the anticlimax, thrilled that things are at long last slowing and calming down, the Sweet Pea doors swing open with such force that they crash into the wall with a loud bang.

Some guests gasp, others jump, and everyone turns toward the commotion as five men who can't be described as anything other than thugs trudge into the restaurant. They're wearing shiny suits with dress shirts unbuttoned down to their navel and each of them wears more jewelry than Miranda owns. And if I thought they were bad, five more men who are wider than they are tall waltz in after them, their arms crossed and guns on their hips. They look like bodyguards, but for whom?

Out of the corner of my eye, I see Miranda instinctively turn her body so she's shielding as much of Matt as she can. I'm the closest to the door. To comfort my wife, I put my hand on her thigh and shift my body so that I'm protecting her should push come to shove. I curse myself for leaving my gun in the hotel safe. The drama, I'm learning, really does never end.

As he struts in, I recognize Russian oligarch and white-collar criminal, Anatoly Rustikoff. His dark hair is slicked back, and out of all the menacing party crashers, he's the only one wearing a suit that isn't tacky. He's shorter than I imagined, but no less intimidating.

Last I heard from Jake and Castillo, Rustikoff was promptly informed that because his sanctuary was on U.S. soil, the government was seizing control and converting it into a park filled with his trees and exotic birds for all the public to enjoy. I imagine that's why Mr. Rustikoff is gracing us with his presence tonight. He's determined to not let that happen.

And just like that, it's no longer an anticlimactic party.

Rustikoff scans the room, looking for someone in particular. My eye catches Castillo's across the table, and we both know what the other is thinking. It's either him, Jake, or me that Rustikoff is looking for. The Russian spots me in the crowd, and his search is over. It's me.

A smile dances across Rustikoff's face as he makes his way across the room with one of the men in the ugly shiny suits obediently trailing closely behind.

"It's okay, it's okay," I whisper as quietly as I can to Miranda.

"Dobryy vecher, Tripp Regan," begins Rustikoff in Russian. He continues, though I have absolutely no clue what the hell he's saying.

"Good evening, Tripp Regan," the translator says in a heavy Russki accent. "Glad to see you. And so nice that you can see again. But I can assure you, you do *not* want to see me again." Rustikoff smirks. "You understand, right?"

Rustikoff doesn't wait around for my response. He just turns on his heel and exits Sweet Pea as swiftly as he marched in.

2014

JAKE, 9

I saw Cleo in the parking lot return from walking her friend Mr. Lodge out of Sweet Pea. At long last, here's my opening.

I grab her by the arm. "Miss, you're gonna have to come with me, please," I say in a stern tone, as if I was a police officer who just pulled her over for speeding.

Cleo jumps into a Krav Maga posture, but quickly recovers. "Jake. What are you doing?"

"What does it look like I'm doing?" I press my body into hers.

She smiles. "I just said goodbye to your ninety-nine-year-old competition, Mr. Lodge."

I lean into Cleo and whisper, "This is a competition I think I can win ..."

"Oh? Is that so?"

"Yes," I nod. "I want to make love to you right here and now."

She pretends to mull it over. "Hmm. Well, you did save my life, Jake Regan...."

"And don't you forget it," I wink.

"So, I guess the least I can do is grant you one wish."

I bring her body into mine. I'm already hard. "I remember that white dress from when we first met. You wore it to the Outrigger Canoe Club and all I wanted was to take it off you." I kiss her, and part of me—every part of me—wants to rip it off her right here in the parking lot.

She's breathless as she looks around and points to a shaded area with lots of palm trees that's about a half a football field away from the parking lot.

"Over there."

Hell yeah. Before we go, I kiss Cleo again. Harder this time. Then, as the day ends and the sun sets, I take her hand and lead her away from the restaurant to the cover of trees. There, I grab her waist with both my hands and guide her so that she's up against one of the palm trees.

"Are you hoping someone sees us?" she whispers as I lean in to give her another kiss.

"Let 'em watch," I smile. Then I kiss her lips, her cheeks, her neck, her chest, her everywhere. I can't help myself. Kissing Cleo is like eating steak after going for years on bread and water. She grabs my back, and I can feel her delicate bare hands underneath my shirt.

"God, I want you so bad," I pant, looking into those purple stunners.

"Jake ..." Cleo starts to undo my belt.

When I reach under that white dress of hers, she digs her nails into my back.

"Oh my god," she moans into my ear. Her nails dig even deeper into my back. Her legs are shaking. "Yes," she moans again. "Jake, don't stop."

There aren't enough diamonds in the world to get me to stop. Looking back at this moment later, Cleo and I were so totally absorbed in one another that we didn't even notice the five expensive cars pulling into the parking lot. We didn't register the gravel under the tires, the doors slamming or the Russian accents.

We stand there against the tree entangled in one another and breathing in unison for a few moments. My sweaty forehead is resting against Cleo's and both my hands are intertwined with hers. I never want to let go. I don't think I will.

Then Cleo notices something behind my shoulder. "I don't think those cars were here when we walked over here, were they?" She points toward the parking lot.

A black Bugatti, silver Maybach, and three black Maseratis stand out like sore thumbs amid a sea of beat-up Jeeps, Toyotas, and Priuses.

"Jesus. No way, I definitely would've noticed those."

"Your father must have friends in high places." Cleo laughs.

I take her hand. "C'mon, let's see who they are."

Cleo nods in agreement as we both start pulling ourselves back together.

As we get closer to the restaurant, I look inside the windows and make out a group of men in tacky-ass suits with their backs to us. "What in the...?" I squeeze Cleo's hand tighter as I swing open the door. As I do, the Russians are letting their leader go out the door first. I am pretty sure the woman with him is his wife. She goes everywhere with him.

He waves Cleo aside.

She smiles, and says, "Tyvy Gladish' opasnim."

What the fuck? Since when has Cleo been able to speak Russian?

His men, I count ten of them, just stand there stock still until he laughs.

"Ya opasen," he says, and they're out the door but not before he points at me. We watch as they get in their million-dollar rides. His wife turns and stares at Cleo as she gets in their car. For some reason she has sunglasses on.

I look inside the restaurant and scan the crowd for my father. I spot him speaking to Mom and Matt. I grab Cleo's arm and pull her away from the door.

"Do you know who that was?" I'm seething with anger. "Why did you talk to him?" She looks at me, shocked. Cleo's never seen me angry before—well, except the first time we met three years ago. It doesn't bring me much joy to admit that I still have a temper.

"I'm serious, Cleo. Do you know him?"

Cleo pulls her arm away from me. "What's wrong with you, Jake?"

"You said something to him in Russian but I didn't hear what you said. What was it?!"

"Don't yell at me! All I said to him was that he 'looked dangerous.'"

"Yeah, well, that's the understatement of the decade. What was his response?"

She pauses. "He just laughed and said, 'I am dangerous.'"

Christ. "You really have no idea who that was?"

Cleo shakes her head. "No, I told you I don't." Now she is angry.

I take a breath. "His name's Anatoly Rustikoff, the Russian oligarch who owns half the fucking world, including that sketchy garden where Durita almost killed you."

"*That* was Anatoly Rustikoff?"

"So you have heard of him?"

"Yes, my father has mentioned him and Pearson mentioned the garden, trees, birds, and topiaries were his. She thinks for a moment, then shakes her head. "If I knew it was him, obviously I wouldn't have—or maybe I would have. I did make him laugh." She's smiling at me.

God, that smile. "Hey, I'm sorry, I didn't mean to yell."

I take her in my arms and pull her closer. Oh, I'm definitely still livid, but I don't want to freak her out any more than I need to. Then again, now and then I forget that this is a woman who threw an Al Qaeda leader over a cliff. Cleo doesn't scare easily.

"I didn't know you could speak Russian...." I plaster on a grin, feeling kind of foolish.

"There's a lot about me you don't know, Jake." She smiles, then leans in and kisses me. Nothing quite like Cleo's sweet lips on mine to get me to calm the hell down.

I take Cleo's hand and lead her into a corner of the room. "Seeing Rustikoff reminds me ... I, uh, was just informed that I have to leave Hawaii ... just when I've found you again. Now that Dad's headed home, I'm expected back at work in New York."

"How long do we have, Jake?"

"Three days."

"OK! Let's spend it at the Halekulani for old time's sake. And for new times too. We'll make the most of it." Cleo switches to Russian and says, "Medoviy mesyats."

"Yes, a honeymoon." Jake laughs.

She looks astounded. "So you, too, speak Russian?"

"You're not the only one with hidden depths, Cleo."

2014

CLEO, 12

My father phones while Nanny, Zelli, and I are in the kitchen having our breakfast. I'm eating my usual raspberries with cottage cheese, and as usual Zelli is trying to steal my fruit. She loves to sneak raspberries from me while watching to see if I notice. Of course I pretend I don't.

"Is that my granddaughter babbling?" asks Didier from thousands of miles away.

I bring the phone to Zelli's high chair and tell her that DiDi wants to speak to her. Her little face lights up as it always does when she hears her grandfather's voice.

My father and daughter have a brilliant one-sided conversation. Didier coos, declaring to Zelli just how much he loves and misses her and wants to give her a great big hug. Zelli giggles and keeps saying, "DiDi," looking around as if he is going to walk through the door at any moment.

Nannie and I share a smile as Zelli tells my father all about her new favorite book, *Dora The Explorer*. Didier asks Zelli a few questions about Dora, tells her he loves her for the umpteenth time, and then asks to speak to me again.

I take Daddy off speaker phone and wander into the hallway off the kitchen.

"So, when are you two coming home?" he asks.

"We are home," I laugh.

"I mean, to Paris. You love the winter here with the opera and the ballet. One day, Zelli will love all those cultural things as well...."

"Yes, but I love it here too." I tell my father as I look out my window toward the cliffs and the vast ocean beyond.

"*Ah.*" Didier hates being apart from me for too long and now that Zelli is in the picture, he feels this even more intensely.

"And what does that 'ah' mean?"

"Nothing. It's just that I saw this beautiful house near mine that made me think of you."

"Oh?"

"Yes, it's on Rue de Verneuil—isn't that your favorite street? Well, anyway, it's for sale and it reminded me of you. I'll send you a photo."

I smile. "You never change, do you, Daddy?"

"I should hope not." He pauses. "How are you feeling after that ordeal in the garden? Better, I hope?"

"Yes, much better. Thank you."

"Good. And how are the Regans? Are they still on the island?"

I take a breath. "Well, Jake is."

"*Ah.*"

There's that 'ah' again. "Actually, Jake and I are going to spend a few days together at The Halekulani." Gosh, I don't know why I felt the need to tell him that. Too much information, Cleo.

"I see."

"He is Zelli's father, after all," I blurt. I have been meaning to tell Didier since I found out.

There is no surprise or shock in Didier's voice. I suppose he knew all along and was just waiting for me to be ready to tell him. "Does Jake know?" he asks.

"No. He has no idea Zelli even exists."

"Well, it's up to you, Cleopatra. But you might consider telling him."

I really don't have the energy for this conversation. I should never have brought it up. "Daddy, I have to go."

"Fine, I'm off to meet with Sergei. I'll see you and my little Zelli soon, Cleopatra."

I don't recognize the name. "Who's Sergei, Daddy?"

"Oh, I've told you about him before. Sergei is a Russian friend from Lake Baikal. You'd like him."

"I met Anatoly Rustikoff last night at Sweet Pea at the Regan's farewell party.

"Did he know who you were, Cleopatra?"

"No, he just found me amusing. I spoke to him in Russian."

"Well, be careful. I'll wager he found out who you were five minutes after he met you. Nothing escapes him. And he fears me."

While I pack for my three days with Jake, Zelli sits on my bed and takes out of my suitcase each piece I put in, then laughs as I put them back in again. Bathing suits, running clothes, tennis clothes. We can repeat this for hours and I have such joy just seeing her so happy.

After the horror of the garden, I am happy, too, that Jake and I can celebrate the miracle of being alive, of our resilience. I take Zelli off the bed and we go to find Nannie. When I tell Nannie that I'll be "away," I offer few details and she doesn't ask.

Zelli listens as I say I am going away and pouts, but Nannie knows just how to placate her. She gets out a book and some cookies and puts her on her lap and reads to her.

"Pudge and I will come over and kidnap our goddaughter," Pudding suggests when I call to inform her of my plans.

"Oh, you don't have to do that. Nannie and Consuelo will be here."

"Nonsense, me and the Mister will come to yours and keep an eye on the little one. Give Nannie a helping hand."

And of course, I agree. What Pudding wants, Pudding gets.

"Have fun, Cleo. You lucky girl, you."

After a tearful goodbye with Zelli, I head out to meet Jake, feeling my excitement rise as with each mile I get closer to our rendezvous.

HE ARRIVES AT THE Halekulani a few seconds before me. As my little yellow convertible pulls into a shaded spot in the parking lot, I see Jake getting out of an Uber with his suitcase. He looks devastatingly handsome in his white button-down rolled up at the sleeves and blue jeans that fit him perfectly. He's about fifty yards away and even though his trademark Ray-Bans cover his blue eyes, I can tell that he hasn't seen me.

His back is to me as I enter the large marble lobby. Slowly, I walk up to him, my heels click-clacking across the floor, and tap him on the shoulder.

"Pardon, monsieur," I whisper into his ear with a French accent. "Can you please tell me where I can get a drink?"

Jake nods, his eyes slowly moving from my head all the way down to my toes. "Let me show you," he smiles. Jake's smile. Its power over me is even stronger today than it was when we first met those three long years ago. "I take it you've come from far away?" He leads me out of the lobby and toward the bar that we never had time to go to when we were last here three years ago. Our luggage is forgotten near the front desk.

"Oh, *mais oui*, I am so happy to be here. I come from Paris where it is cold and wintry and where I work as a dancer."

"A dancer. Really?" Jake perks up as he escorts me over to a pair of seats at the far end of the bar.

"Yes, at a famous nightclub."

"What kind of a nightclub?"

"The kind of nightclub where I dance every night. And every night, while I dance I take off my clothes ... very, very slowly."

The bartender tries to get Jake's attention, but he just ignores him. "Do you *like* taking off your clothes?"

Realizing what he's just walked into, the bartender makes a face and turns to take another customer's order. This can't be the first time the bartender has witnessed a scene such as this, but I want to giggle.

"Oh yes, I love it but it's so much work. I'm so glad I have three whole days where I get to keep all my clothes on."

"You know, I've never been to this kind of nightclub," he says. "Maybe you could give me a private show."

"Oh no, monsieur. I could never."

"No?" Jake tugs on the hem of my cream-colored sundress.

"No," I smile and slowly lick my lips. "But maybe ... I could give you a tiny peek."

Jake just nods.

And then, in the bar, I uncross my legs very slowly, looking at Jake seductively all the while. Jake can't take it any longer. He pulls me off the stool and marches us over to one of the nearby meeting rooms. He looks inside. Full. He pulls the next door open.

Empty, thank goodness. Pulling me inside, Jake puts me on the table and is instantly inside me, and with such passion.... We are so excited, and this is just the start of our honeymoon.

CLEO, 12

OVER THE NEXT THREE DAYS, we play all sorts of characters. We leave the bedroom, go to the lobby and start a different story. After I am a dancer in Paris, I'm a princess, then a flight attendant, then a masseuse.

Jake and I love these role-playing fantasies and I am not sure if I've ever had so much fun. Jake was a bodyguard, a pilot, a cowboy, and on and on. We also spend time swimming and playing tennis, and even croquet which I love. Everything we did was just easy and fun and we both so needed this. I challenged him at dinner on trivia and asked him questions which led to some pretty fascinating insights into each other.

I am so much older than he is but right now, it really doesn't seem to matter. And he has changed so much these past two-plus years.

One evening, we're sitting on the edge of the hot tub, having emerged from our room for a late swim. I am wearing the necklace Jake gave me on the beach three years ago, and he's quite touched I still wear it.

Jake leaves for a moment, then returns and says, "May I join you, miss?" He offers me his hand to shake and introduces himself.

"Why, of course," I smile as I run my fingers over my necklace.

"What brings you to Hawaii? A shoot for the swimsuit edition of *Sports Illustrated*?"

"Why, yes. How did you know?"

"Lucky guess."

"What about you? What brings you to the island?"

"I just needed some quiet time away from my kids."

Now this is an interesting game. I didn't see this turn of events. "Oh. You're married?"

"Not anymore. Just me and my two daughters."

This I was really not expecting. "I'm surprised. You don't look old enough to have children."

"Yeah, I get that a lot," Jake tells me as he slips into the hot tub next to me. "What can I say? They're the apples of my eyes."

I can't speak. Is it possible that Jake knows about Zelli? Is this his strange way of telling me that he wants to be part of her life?

"That's sweet. But everyone needs some alone time." I scoot closer to Jake, steering the conversation away from children. Thankfully, Jake takes my cue.

We are so in lust with one another and having such a good time playing sports and having long talks over intimate dinners that our three days are over in an instant. We don't talk about the future because I won't let him, but Jake nevertheless tells me again and again that he loves me. I think he does, and I certainly love being with him this way. He saved my life. And he is Zelli's father, after all. But I know I am not in love with him.

I was tempted to tell him last night in the hot tub about Zelli but I wasn't quite ready to step out of the fantasy world that Jake and I worked so tirelessly to create. There is only room for the two of us here, and I didn't want to ruin it. And then, there's the CIA part of it all. Just like Tripp, Jake is so definitely CIA and I'm not sure that's who I want for Zelli's father. And yet.

On our last day, we took a long run on the beach at dawn. Then back in our room, we get ready to go. Jake is on the afternoon flight to New York, the last plane he can take that allows him to make it back in time for his work. We're just about to go downstairs to the lobby and check out when there's a knock on our door.

"It's probably housekeeping, telling us it's time for us to go," I laugh, zipping up my luggage.

Jake opens the door to find a bellboy standing there holding a rather large package.

"Mr. Jake Regan and Ms. Cleopatra Gallier?"

We both nod.

"Special delivery." The bellboy hands a package to Jake.

"Oh. Uh, thanks, man." Jake gives the bellboy a tip and quickly shuts the door behind him. He is as confused as I am.

What could this be? Jake and I look at each other.

"Does anyone know you're here?" he asks.

"Just Pudge and Pudding." I leave out the part that I also told my father.

He raises an eyebrow and tears open the red wrapping to find a seedling of a tree and a yellow bird in a lovely cage. I cringe when I see the bird.

"What the …?" Jake says.

I just stare at this totally bizarre gift until I notice the small card at the bottom of the gilded cage. I lean closer and read. I nudge Jake and point at the words: *Ya opasen! Anatoly Rustikoff.*

"Oh my God," I stammer. "What do you think it means?"

Jake stops to think. "No fucking clue. But let's get the hell out of here," he says, putting down the cage and grabbing my suitcase.

"Are you just going to leave—?"

"It'll be fine. Housekeeping will deal with it."

And we're off. "Let me drive you to the airport," I say to Jake when we're in the elevator.

"Are you sure? I can easily call an Uber if—"

"I'm sure."

And I am. My single most prized possession is half his and in this moment, I feel closer to him than I ever have before. Jake is the father of my daughter and he has a right to know. As we exit the elevator and cross the marble lobby toward the parking lot, I text Nannie and ask her to meet me at the American Airlines terminal with Zelli as soon as possible.

I PULL UP TO THE CURB in my little yellow convertible. As usual, Daniel K. Inouye Airport is a madhouse.

"Why don't you go inside and get in line to check your luggage? I'll find a parking spot and then meet you."

He turns to me and smiles. I'll miss that smile. So much more than he even realizes. "Are you sure? You don't have—"

"I'm sure, Jake. Just give me a minute."

He nods. He kisses me. He smiles again. And then he gets out of my car.

It takes longer than I anticipated to find a parking spot. Instead of five minutes, it nearly takes me fifteen. I drive up, up, up each level closer to the sky and farther and farther away from Jake and Zelli. My tires squeal as, at long last, I finally pull into an empty parking spot.

My phone rings as I hurry out of the car toward the elevator. It's Nannie.

"Hi, Nannie. Are you outside?"

"Yes, we're here. But where are you?"

"I'll be right there. Sorry, parking took much longer— Anyway, don't leave. I'll be there in a minute."

I hang up with Nannie as the elevator doors open and I rush inside. My phone makes another sound. A text from Jake: *Hey, are you coming back? Just asking because I have to get in the security line.*

CLEO, 12

Damn. My fingers fly across the keyboard of my phone as the elevator brings me back down to earth, closer to Jake and closer to Zelli.

I text him back: *Sorry! I'll be right there. Don't go without saying goodbye.*

The doors open on the bottom floor, and I run as fast as my legs will carry me. Thankfully, Nannie and Zelli are already at the curb, just where they said they'd be.

"Mommy!" Zelli smiles as I take her into my arms.

"Hi, my precious. Come with me. We're going to say goodbye to a good friend of Mommy's," I tell her and turn to Nannie. "Thank you so much for getting her here, Nannie. Please take the rest of the day off. You must need it. See you tomorrow morning."

Nannie smiles, nods, and turns back to the parking lot as Zelli and I turn in the opposite direction. We race through the American Airlines terminal, dodging suitcases and frantic travelers. Finally, we make it to security.

I scan the crowd for Jake. He's nowhere to be found. Where is he? Oh, where is he?

"Cleo!"

Finally, I spot him in the crowd. "Jake!"

"I'm sorry! I had to get in line. My flight is boarding and I can't miss this flight." And then he sees her.

Jake looks down at Zelli and a look of recognition comes over his blue eyes. The same blue eyes that he has thankfully passed on to his daughter. He doesn't say a word. He doesn't even have to ask. He knows. He looks up at me and back down at her.

She's snuggling close to me but looking up at him, flirting.

I smile down at our beautiful child, "Say goodbye to Daddy, Zelli."

EPILOGUE

He calls me the moment he arrived in DC. "Why didn't you tell me, Cleo?" he asked me. The pain and shock in his gravelly voice nearly destroyed me. "Jake, after I killed Jimbo, or Mohammed Abdul Rahman, I flew to Dubai to be with my father for Christmas. Three months later he insisted I go to a doctor as I was exhausted all the time and after some tests the doctor told me I was going to have a baby. I was stunned, Jake."

"Okay, but Cleo—" He interrupted me. I didn't blame him for being upset.

"I know. I should have called you right away. But I was thrown, Jake. I thought I was too old to have a baby. I wasn't even sure if I could carry it to full term and I didn't want to burden you with all this when you were just beginning your career. We all need a reason to keep going."

"What does that mean?"

"It means if you are honest as to what your reason is to keep going, I think it will be your work."

"Yes, my work, but I love you. You know that. And after all, she looks like me."

"That is perfect for you to say, she looks like you." I am laughing. "Jake, I'm fifteen years older than you and you know I adore you," I pause, not wanting to hurt him.

EPILOGUE

"But you don't love me back, is that what you're trying to say?" He blurted it out just like that. And we both knew it was the truth.

"Jake, I am sending you my private phone which only my father has and you can call me anytime you want to come to see her or I will bring her to you whenever you want. That is my promise. I also am sending you by email a photo of her and if you want more, just tell me."

"Good bye, Cleo." He hung up the phone. I held it in my hand and then sent him the photo of her with his big blue eyes. But I never heard back from him. Never.

Made in the USA
Middletown, DE
06 December 2022

17329101R00221